WHAT REVIEWERS ON YOUWRITEON.COM
HAVE SAID ABOUT THE LAST STITCH IN 2009:

The writing is first rate... the storyline is supple, but tough. The characters are strongly depicted. It's a testament to good writing.

It's inventive, playful and beautifully written... enthralling. The idea of a story woven into a robe is great and (the) metafictional tricks were lovely.

A masterpiece of imagination and ingenuity. The concept is fresh...

Also by Prue Batten

THE EIRIE CHRONICLES:
THE STUMPWORK ROBE

THE LAST STITCH

THE SEQUEL TO
The Stumpwork Robe

Published in 2009 by YouWriteOn.com

Copyright © Text Prue Batten

First Edition

The author asserts the moral right under the Copyright, Designs and Patents Act 1988 to be identified as the author of this work.

All rights reserved. No part of this publication may be reproduced, stored in a retrieval system, or transmitted, in any form or by any means without prior written consent of the author, nor be otherwise circulated in any form of binding or cover other than that which it is published and without a similar condition being imposed on the subsequent purchaser.

Published by YouWriteOn.com

For my parents
Claire and Brian

ACKNOWLEDGEMENTS

To Jane Nicholas for her support and consummate embroidery skill. Adelina's hands would never have been guided so masterfully, right up to the last stitch.

To tellers of fable and folklore throughout the centuries, the literature of the world would have been the poorer without them.

To all those at YouWriteOn.com who wrote such kind words about the first book and have reviewed this second one with such positive words. A publishing exercise like the one YWO has initiated gives hope in what is a stringent industry.

To Helen Corner and the staff at Cornerstones Literary Consultancy UK. They have assessed, educated, pushed and pulled and their patience has known no bounds, leading me on a journey that is like no other.

Finally I would like to commend my family. Clare for her superlative cover and content designs, Angus for taking up the slack during pressured times and Rob because he has made it all possible.

GLOSSARY:

Stumpwork	A form of raised embroidery. Motifs include birds, beasts, flowers, fruits, flies and fish. Gold thread, silk and chenille threads, metal purl and beads are used in thick embroidery with a three dimensional aspect
Frisson	A sensation that indicates the proximity of a Færan
Muirnin	Beloved, darling
Cabyll Ushtey	Celtic folklore. A shape-changing waterhorse that eats mortals, leaving only the entrails
Bitseach	Bitch
Bain As	Piss off
Aine	Irish folklore. A Færan princess. In this novel, the Goddess Creator
Mesmer	A form of enchantment
Swan Maid	Northern European folklore. Beauties who shift shape from swan to woman
Glamarye	Enchantment
Wight	An enchanted person, an Other
Ceasg	Scottish folklore. A Maiden of the Wave or mermaid
Ganconer	Irish folklore. Seducer of women
Far Dorocha	Irish folklore. The Dark Haired Man, silent abductor of women, spiriting them back to Færan
Washi paper	Cobweb-fine Oriental paper, made in Japan
Trow	Orkney folkore. Melancholy Other who could be malicious
Siofra	Irish folklore. Small faeries who can equally be cruel or benevolent toward mortals
Seelie	Benevolent, as opposed to unseelie which means malicious

Ymp Trees	Irish folklore. Rows of trees that have been grafted and pruned to form long unbroken lines. Thought to hide one of the Gates to Færan
Eldritch	Magic
Oscailt Amach!	Open wide
Bean Sidhe	Celtic folklore. Also known as a banshee
Buckthorn	Legendary source of immortality, recounted in the story of Gilgamesh. Variously one could prick one's finger on the thorns or eat the leaves, thereby securing immortality
Ná	No
Welkin wind	A breeze from an Other source inspiring fear

THE STORY SO FAR:

The Traveller Adelina, a master embroiderer, is a prisoner and has begun to create a robe that she is covering in stumpwork stitchery. Underneath the sculptural pieces, she has sequestred many tiny books revealing her tragic adventures – meeting and journeying with Ana, her own growing love for Kholi Khatoun who accompanies them and Ana's blighted passion for Liam, the Færan who it could be argued brought them all together in the first place.

Her story relates that after a series of misadventures, they arrive at Star on the Stair, a tiny town twinkling in the snowy stratosphere of the Celestine Stairway. It is here they meet the dire Severine Di Accia, bane of Adelina's early life. No one is aware that Severine has studied and become steeped in occult law in her desperate attempt to become immortal. To secure such immortality she must possess two Færan souls and so she kills the Færan Lara and then Liam, also murdering Kholi Khatoun and entrapping Adelina.

It is said if the souls are cut in half and sewn onto a garment, then the wearer shall achieve immortality as it seeps through the fabric fibres and skin-cells, to *'become'* a part of the wearer. Severine presents the imprisoned stitcher with the souls to be sewn onto the gown, unaware that one of her servants, the one she gives to Adelina, is a Færan hell-bent on retrieving the souls and returning them to their bodies in Færan for burial. Adelina and this Other become friends and a promise is exacted from the stitcher that she will avenge the murderered loved ones on pain of her own death.

Part One finishes with Adelina's words...

'At this point my hatred consumes me.

It fills me with a smouldering blackness and each time Severine comes near me, she fans the coals a little bit more. Here a spark, there a flame. I swear on Liam's and Ana's souls and on the soul of my beloved Kholi Khatoun that vengeance will be sought.

It merely remains to be seen whether you would journey onward with me. For this story shall end, mark my words, and it will all be the better when it does. For do they not say in Eirie that revenge is sweet?

So repair to the right front of the robe and let us read on...

PROLOGUE

I lurch between sanity and lunacy as the walls of this place press on me and with each stitch I embroider, in my mind I sew Severine into a shroud, having dispatched her in the most brutal way. Sometimes though, like the flame of a lamp in the blackest space, the thought I may have a reader for my secret words gives me comfort in my lonliness – as though they sit beside me. An imagined friend is the only barrier I have between myself and madness. Some days I teeter, even crumble, but Aine willing I will survive.

I spend a lot of time wondering what you are like, you who reads so assiduously. Are you a man or a woman? Are you one of the Museo conservitors? Or are you one of the Museo night-guards?

But then perhaps you're a thief creeping into the darkened halls, the only noises the slap slap of the wavelets on the canals outside the windows and your own tense, irregular breathing. Were you unable to stop your fingers reaching out to stroke my embroidery? And in so doing, did you discover its secrets? It thrills me that you might be a thief for *I* am an accessory to theft. My friend Lhiannon of the Færan stole something of inestimable value and is even now running away. And I helped her.

But I must be careful, secretive. My only family is close by. Ajax – he of the back broad enough to be that of the Cabyll Ushtey is being held to ransom. I've lost so much and he's all that remains. His life is in my *obedient* hands.

And thus as you begin again to read, having found three tiny books under the stitching of the shepherd and his sheep, remember that I am threatened... it is my only defence for all that has happened to those I loved. Say the words '*grow bigger and be, pages to see*' and read on.

CHAPTER ONE

'Yain, tain, tethera.' Phelim counted the last of the ewes from the scrub as they emerged through the creeping fingers of mist like wraiths. He pulled his oilskin tighter. At the house he knew hands would be reaching for talismans because when a mist threatened, folk became superstitious, aware of the omniscience of Others in the lives of Eirie. As if out of the miasma, a dark and dangerous foe should come riding to create murder and mayhem.

The wooly mob circled like a swirl of water running down a sinkhole, round and round as he sent his dog after the animals. 'Go over, over, good boy.' The black and white dog flew clockwise around the mob, drawing them in like string atop a jute bag. 'Go back, back.' Back the dog shot the other way, always keeping the mob tight, the ewes rumbling in their throats. Phelim stood at the gate squinting through the opacity as the cloven hooves rattled on the scrubby hillside. 'Yain, tain, tethera, methera,' he counted in the language of the Travellers. 'Tethera-bumfitt, methera-bumfitt, giggott! Twenty!' With his dog at his heels like a piebald shadow, he headed across the bottom of the yard searching for the Squire, unaware of the maids who watched him surreptitiously. If he knew they desired him, beguiled by his face and his fine form, he kept silent. Those who had bed him would wed him but he never returned twice to the same woman, declining wanton invitation.

Invariably these young maids would succumb to a form love-sickness and the carlin would be called and by administering judicious herbs and some words of carlin-tongue, the situation would be remedied and the women would glance at Phelim and whilst sighing as he passed them by, would cast more lingering glances at other, plainer men.

Ebba could hear some of the wiser maids as they whispered amongst themselves. 'It's like he's the Ganconer himself, so charming and winsome is he.'

'To be sure. And the way girls are left love-sick!'

'Oh don't be ninnies! Look you, he doesn't smoke a pipe as the Ganconer is rumoured to do and besides Ebba would as like never repair them as is lovelorn if Phelim were the real Love Talker.'

Ebba heard them and her mouth twisted as if she tasted lemons but her boy had to be a man just like any other on the estate and like any mother she wanted only the best for her child. She had found him by the shore as a tiny infant as she fossicked for weeds and seeds for her herbals. He lay in amongst feathers and grasses on a rocky shelf under a cliff overhang. He hadn't been crying – he just gazed through earnest wide eyes at his surrounds, playing with star-like fingers. When Ebba investigated the grassy crib she fell in love, her own yearnings sparked by the soft down of his hair, the delicate smell of baby.

She bent over and touched him, his tiny hands curling around her finger and a shock fizzed up her arm, across her chest to her heart. 'Oh, my babe,' she sighed, as her sight blurred. A vision of a dark-headed man walking away into a familiar distance wafted in front of her like a gossamer cloud. Ebba ran her hand over the infant's head. 'Aye it's jet, as black as an unseelie night. Is it you in my vision, *muirnin*?'

She eased him out of the nest into her arms where he cuddled unconcerned, eyes locking onto the carlin and she felt bonds looping like a Traveller's knot, over, under and through. In her wise way, she saw a linking destiny and headed back to the estate to apprise the Squire of her new family member.

She rigged a story – the babe was her sister's child and sadly the mother had died giving birth, for tough times had led to a fraught labour. Had not many mothers and infants died in the Archipelago this last year? The Squire, Merrick by name, saw no reason to doubt the words of the carlin, by all means adopt him, rear him and good luck. He chucked the baby under the chin and nodded vaguely. 'It's your life, your family blood, Ebba. You must do what you believe is right.' He would never have disputed the woman's decisions anyway. Not a carlin, never, this she knew.

So Phelim and Ebba coexisted quietly, fondly – Ebba aware of the incipient difference in her child. As he grew older, she heard him sing in the Travellers' language when she had taught him none and chanting rhymes that weren't childish and in an altogether different language she could fear. In his turn Phelim loved Ebba fiercely. He had been made aware early on that Ebba was his step-mother and he minded little as he had seen foundling lambs mothered up with ewes whose own lambs had died and he thought there was a similarity in his own story. In addition Ebba's unique nature, that of an exceptional mortal wise-woman and healer, thrilled him and he felt comfortable in her presence, watching with studious care when she talked to the elements or mixed potions.

Ebba's skill was linked with the earth and the air, with fire and water. She talked to the wind and received answers from the sea. Squire Merrick considered Ebba's domicile a blessing on the fecundity of his estate. She kept he and his workers happy and safe, but none in the demesnes, neither worker nor Squire, were aware that for all of Phelim's life, the carlin had never revealed his true identity to him or anyone else, a secret that forever weighed heavily on the conscience of the woman.

The evenings were long with light on Maria Island. It gave the inhabitants pleasure to eat a meal after a hard day's work and then watch the sun set, leaning back on a settle against a west-facing wall warm with the day's heat. Ebba would sit in the arbor at the front of her house, Grimalkin the white cat at her side. She would light her pipe, filling it with a sweet weed and puffing away, a glass of the best of her wines within fingertip's reach. She often had a vision at this most relaxed of times. Good or bad, it never worried her deeply. Later she would note it down and if necessary impart a precaution to whomever it concerned.

Phelim would spend such evenings lying on a tussocky headland overlooking his favorite cove, head propped on folded arms, staring out to the Passage. This evening a strong seabreeze herded waves from the windward side of the island. Grey and blue shadows chased each other across the water and gannets and gulls skimmed the surface, the cries of larger seabirds filling the air as they jostled for position on the rocky coast.

Sandbanks rose up and skirted the shore of the cove, shielding it from the onslaught of coastal grasses and clear water lapped at the edges of the bay, reminding Phelim of a delicately coloured glass pitcher the Squire had ordered from the artisans of Veniche, the city of canals. He heard tell of these farflung places when journeymen took advantage of Ebba's hospitality. Sometimes the need to travel, to find the end of the cord that pulled at his soul was so strong his feet could almost begin walking before his mind could catch up. But he would look at Ebba grinding her herbs to a paste, delivering a child, seeing some message in the drift of a leaf or a cloud in the sky and his heart would tug his soul and thence his feet and he would settle again.

He sighed with relative content and focused on a swell of dark blue wafting past the headland and his attention sharpened as he discerned a shape forcing through the wave towards his cove rather than being pushed away to the far distant shore. He put a hand to his forehead to shield his eyes from the glare of the setting sun.

A kayak approached on a zig-zag path. The ends of the paddle hit the water on either side of the craft with a thump as though the boatsman was exhausted, weak beyond belief. Rather than jumping up, Phelim lay very still and watched as the kayak floundered around the headland. The rower, a girl Phelim thought, slumped for a second and he could see a small back heaving. And then the paddle dipped again and the vessel made for the shallows whereupon she clambered out, fell to her knees, staggered up and pulled the craft onto the wet sand by the side of a cluster of rocks. Grabbing a small bag from inside the kayak, she passed a hand over the boat and it dissolved into a pile of dust on the sand.

Unsurprised, Phelim knew this action was the right thing to do and that it was as strangely familiar to him as the action of breathing. What did distress him was the subsequent action of the slim young woman. She clutched the stuffed pack to her chest and began to cry as she leaned on one arm, the hand and fingers spread out over the rocks.

The seashore was one of the places most feared by mortals, with its conglomeration of unseelie water-wights who could shape-change in order to devour a luckless soul as quickly as a thief pockets a coin. On this evening a normal creature, neither malicious nor Other, sensed the fingertips trailing in the shallow rock pool and with blue spangles flashing, it wrapped six of its eight tentacles around the fingers and wrist of the woman, to grip and bite hard.

She gave a sharp cry, rubbed at the hand and then lurched up the beach. Within seconds she had fallen to her knees, groaning and sucking in vast lung-fulls of air. Then she collapsed to lie very, very still.

CHAPTER TWO

Phelim ran down over the rocks, through the sandy sags and swathes of samphyr, aware of the dangers of the rockpools. Before him the fragile chest heaved, the liquid black eyes sightless, registering nothing of his presence. The slim hands clutching at the bag had long fingers that were chafed and red with blisters and the lips through which each agonized breath was sucked were split and dry. As Phelim's glance searched the victim's wrist, he saw it – the telltale carmine sucker marks from a tiny poisonous octopus. Within seconds the creeping paralysis had started, within minutes rictus would occur and no air would be able to enter, the heart stopping dead.

'Get Ebba, Spot! Go!' The dog sprinted away in a skirl of sand and Phelim hefted the slight woman into his arms just as the final breath stopped, the eyes vacant and wide. Holding her close, her matted hair hanging in ropey skeins over his arm, he puffed air into the rigid lips as he had done for struggling newborn lambs, as he had seen Ebba do with human babes. Then he began to run awkwardly, stopping to puff, squeezing the chest against his own but gaining ground nevertheless. Her fingers had stiffened around the small shabby bag she had clutched moments earlier before her life had been so dramatically altered and Phelim despaired of saving her – so quick and powerful was the poison from the sea-creature that it could kill twenty men in three minutes but he puffed and squeezed and ran anyway.

Above him the heavens darkened to evening. The breeze dropped and from the sea came the haunting song of the roanes who graced the further rocks. Phelim could see them in his mind's eye as he jumped over tussocks – beauteous as such wights always were, their graceful tails undulating in the tidal wash, phosphorescence caught in the moonlight gleam, their shoulders and breasts creamy white and covered in a shawl of trailing silver hair. Their song echoed and murmured, murmured and echoed – an eery melody to entrap the unwary, as evil and full of intent as the octopus that had given the kiss of death to Phelim's burden.

The bay glittered under the light of a full moon. Its reflection traced a path almost to Phelim's feet so that he could walk on it if he chose – a moon bridge, a path to the Others or so the folks in the village would say and he wished now that he could walk this woman away from her doom along the bridge to safety.

His path along the cliff-top was dogged by spriggans who chanted quaint rhymes and teased the shepherd.

Shepherd carries bag of wool
Silly man, silly fool
Færan gives 'ee much despair
Leaves 'ee lost wi'out a care.

They repeated the same verse but in Other language and whilst the word *'Færan'* set up a tingle, Phelim endeavoured to ignore them, hearing a bark close by. As he rounded a corner in the track, Ebba and Spot met him.

'She was lucky you were there.' Ebba reached for the delicate arm as Phelim laid the girl on a bed of bracken.

'You knew?'

'Aye,' she said in her matter-of-fact manner. 'I met Spot halfway. Aine Phelim, I hope we're not too late.' She prised the girl's fingers away from the bag and tossed it to her stepson and bent and placed her ear against the girl's slight chest. 'It beats faintly.' She pushed a breath between the girl's lips. 'Phelim, she's very cold, light a fire while I work.'

Phelim piled bark and twigs and stroked a deft spark off his knife. In the flaring flame as Ebba pumped the girl's chest and then stopped to breathe into the girl's mouth, he could see the rigidity of the body, the wide eyes, the faint lilac of the lips.

'Ebba.' He touched her thin shoulders thinking she wasted her time.

'Phelim, I shall tell you something,' she puffed again and then compressed the chest. 'This girl is Færan, I can feel the *frisson* that is Other. I may yet be able to save her.' Puff. Compress. 'If I can breathe for her for a little while, she may survive the poison more so than a mortal.' Puff. Compress. 'Other than that,' puff, compress, 'there is nothing – no medic, no carlin's charm to stop a poison strong enough to kill twenty mortals.' Puff, compress.

They took turns as the night dragged the moon across the sky and as the first bird called in the Squire's avenue of oaks, a gasp echoed around the clearing.

'That's better! Come on *muirnin,* again.'

Another throaty breath followed and the eyes, so fixed and dilated before, moved to focus. Black eyelashes feathered down over pallid cheeks and then wafted open again, the reduced pupils gazing vaguely at Ebba.

'Cannot.' The Færan's voice rasped, her chest rising as each agonizing, greedy gasp was sucked. 'Bane.'

'Rubbish child!' Ebba scoffed. 'Just breathe slowly.'

'Soul flies.' A tear trickled from the dark eyes and over the sculpted face of the girl. 'Name Lhiannon. Help me!' Her delicate fingers sought for something.

'Phelim, the bag!' Ebba grabbed the dirty chamois bag from her stepson and laid it in the clutching fingers as the hopeless eyes scrutinised the carlin.

'Must help. Carlin. Almost Other.' Breaths sucked in and out. 'Bag to Jasper. Veniche.' More breaths and fingers grasping Ebba's own with bone-white strength. 'Must help Others!' The vague eyes sharpened momentarily and Ebba felt herself sucked into the vortex of their depths.

'Jasper, the bag, I understand, *muirnin*. Rest you now.' Ebba's hand gently stroked the girl's forehead as the breathing softened, becoming distanced and shallow. The eyes had closed and the boyish chest suddenly ceased its irregular rise and fall and Ebba, having placed a finger on the fragile neck, ran a soft and gentle hand round the girl's face, blessing her in carlin-tongue.

She stood up, her stepson helping her. 'She's gone.' The carlin whose daily life familiarized her with death, spoke with empathetic calm. 'She did well to battle as long as she did. The octopus kills swiftly.' She looked down at the girl. 'What a mystery!'

She and Phelim laid the girl on a shawl in their dory in the creek by the side of Ebba's house. Birds twittered lightly, welcoming the warmth of morning, and an welkin wind laced through the trees with whispers and sighs that came from some Other source. But they were kind whispers, sad sighs, as if whoever watched was bereaved and grieved.

'If she was Other, Ebba, why didn't she survive the bite? Is there not glamarye she could have used? And if she is on a quest, why did she not return to Færan through one of the Gates. Why even venture into the mortal world?' Phelim folded the girl's hands gently.

'Indeed. But you must remember that Færan are not infallible. They are as prone to bad judgment, Fate and timing as the rest of us. Patently the sea-creature was her bane and that proving so, she would never have survived. To be immortal was not Fate's choice for her, poor wee thing, although I confess I'm surprised, she seems terribly young to have died, it's not normal. Færan usually go lifetimes beyond our own before they meet their bane. Why so young for this one?' She tucked the fringes of the shawl away from the water with thoughtful fingers. 'As to the Gate, the closest is a long way from here and I suspect she was under some sort of duress, being hunted perhaps. Who knows? And her glamarye? That I don't know, perhaps she was exhausted beyond belief, Aine knows she looked it. Like I said Phelim my love, it's a mystery. But all that aside, here is a shade that must be sent on its way with all the respect it is due.' A longer sigh whispered from under the veil of a willow and Ebba looked up and even though she saw nothing, her skin tingled and she felt the touch of something odd and a knowledge that she didn't want and wouldn't countenance.

Phelim pushed the dory away from the bank and watched the current grasp it as the bag swung by its cords in Ebba's hands and as the craft floated to the centre of the creek he touched Ebba's shoulder.

A dawn mist curled over the water. Birds called and the lacy vapour wrapped around the boat so that it vanished from their sight, although had Phelim been asked he may have said he saw a throng of beautiful people sighing and crying as the dory entered their midst on the other bank but he wasn't asked and much preferred to think it was his imagination at work.

Later Ebba watched as Phelim strode off shadowed by Spot. Every day she watched her stepson walk away filled her heart with pain because she knew it was one day closer to the moment of her vision. The calm that habitually flavoured her life disappeared as she gazed, so she shook her head and turned to the sink to wash and stow her utensils. Then picking up her ashwood staff, she walked to a plain settle at the window and seated herself amongst cushions, Grimalkin leaping onto her lap, and she and the cat sat together staring at the chamois bag lying on the seat. She took it gently in her hands, mouthing a protective charm and turning to the window to get a better look.

The soft grey chamois had a layer of dirt and dried salt crystals in its folds and its neck was gathered tightly in a cord. Ebba's bent and swollen fingers worked at the fibres, easing the knot apart until it slipped free. An opaque white mist drifted out intimating winter, frost, ice.

And something else.

She couldn't bear to leave the bag open, grabbed the ends of the dark cord and jerked it shut and sat with it closed in her fingers, her chest rising and falling. *They're souls! Færan souls! Aine protect them!* Aghast, she quickly placed the bag back on the seat and shrank against the window embrasure. Grimalkin had arched his back, hissing as the hair stood rigidly down his spine.

The frigid puzzle in front of her was something of which she only had the most basic knowledge. Færan souls could be stolen with the legendary soul-syphon she remembered. Was it about then? Against all belief had it reared its terrifying head?

And what about Jasper? The girl had mentioned him as if he were the solution to all the mysteries that curled in frightening fashion around Ebba's shoulders. She had hoped never to hear *his* name again and suddenly his existence was as noticeable as the headache that threatened to crush her skull. She sat back and lit a pipe with the fragrant weed she so liked tamped into the bowl and sucked away with anxious puffs.

I could imagine Ebba's disquiet as she handled the souls. I had felt the same when they were in my own hands. Their black texture was indescribable, it made every part of me shiver and tremble and I felt guilty of an assault as I handled them weeks before – such intimate things, the very life-source of a being. I could imagine it would be like someone touching my own naked body without invitation! And to see them so vulnerable and treated with such disrespect by

Severine made me not only viciously angry but in the same breath unbelievably sad. Even then everything seemed so black, so hopeless, and it just seemed to get worse, like sinking into quicksand. But at least I knew the provenance of the souls and I had the advantage of Lhiannon as knowledgable helpmeet and companion. Poor Ebba knew nothing, neither whether the souls represented friend or foe to she and Phelim or from whence they came and why.

You must follow the bees again until you come to the stumpwork piece of blue and yellow heartsease with the smiling kitten-like faces. The whole is arched over by a sprig of honesty with its mother of pearl casings holding precious seeds and a sprig of mauve honesty flower. I hoped the astute observer would mark the bud, the flower and the mother of pearl seedpods and imagine a season passing from the end of spring, through the heat of summer to the beginning of golden autumn – a reflection of time passing in this accursed place and it gives me some sort of perverse pleasure to mark this passage.

I want you to lift each of the leaves and you will find two books. Then carefully peel back the three lower ochre petals of the heartsease flowers. Underneath you will find another three books filled with more of my story.

CHAPTER THREE

'Adelina, this is hopeless! Where is the progress I demanded? At this rate you shall be in your dotage before you finish half of it. What in Hell's name have you been doing?'

'Stitching, what do you think? That I play games with myself in your absence?' Adelina turned an insolent eye on Severine, daring her to strike again. Like the times she had hit her when Lhiannon escaped, but Severine folded her angry hands into a knot, refusing to be drawn. Instead she spoke in quicksilver tones.

'Have you looked through the gate into the field lately, at your beloved Ajax.'

'If you think to scare me with your threats Severine, don't bother! I am doing the best I can. But then this you know, don't you – I *am* the best or you wouldn't have imprisoned me to do your wretched embroidery for you. Aine knows you could never have stitched it yourself because you never were an embroiderer, were you? Never inherited your mother's skill. *There* was a stitcher.' She looked at her captor, every word, every action designed to cause loss of control for there was masochistic pleasure in punishment, each little word aimed to strike with the sharpness of a stiletto point. 'Besides, have you got the souls back? The need is hardly great when you have still to find them. Oh but of course!' Her laugh rang hard as she stared at her adversary. 'You *do* have that loathsome ring, you could find some more Færan, syphon more souls... couldn't you?'

Palpable anger rippled across Severine's face. Adelina's convoluted spirit soared to triumphant heights as the woman hastened to the embroiderer's side and pinched her shoulder in a painful grip. 'You push too hard, *bitseach*! Keep pushing and I shall kill that nag of yours.'

'Kill that nag of mine and I shall never finish the robe. You kill him, you kill me, end of embroiderer, and oh dear, end of robe. Go away, Severine! Leave me solitary. The more you are in my ambit, the less I feel like working.'

Severine sucked in a frenzied breath, the nostrils dilating and the storm grey eyes freezing further. Her hair fluttered about her face as she turned, black strands slick with a silky sheen. Her gown flowed like liquid around her body.

'Work, Adelina! Your life will be worse if you don't!' Severine stormed from the room, her henchman Luther pulling the door shut behind the two of them. Adelina thought back to a Færan phrase Liam had taught her. *Bain as*, oh, *bain as*! Piss off, she thought with disgust and then sighed as she wondered how many months she had been imprisoned and counted on her fingers. One, two, three – three since Liam and Kholi had been murdered – three months during which time she had been intimately privy to the evil Severine and Luther manifested.

One day in the acres of garden, waterfowl had exploded into the air with a cacophany of bird cries as gunshot after gunshot peppered the air. Ducks, geese and heron had fled in a feathered stampede as one after another of the flock was hit by gunshot and plummeted to the ground in a horrifying eruption of down. Adelina froze to the spot, her hands over her mouth, eyes wide.

A swan-cry echoed across the sky as she saw the elegant bird banking to flee the massacre. She heard Severine scream orders to Luther and then the bark of the harquebus, saw the ebony shape tumble and flutter and found herself running to the killing-field.

Surrounded by the bloodied and shattered bodies of birds, a swan-maid lay in a huddled black heap gasping, her shoulder shot to pieces. Severine rolled her over with a disdainful toe, grinning at Adelina as the brutalized maid uttered a faint cry. Adelina threw herself down by the Other's side, wadding a kerchief and trying to staunch the blood from the gaping hole.

'Oh please stitcher, control yourself!' Severine gazed down, her voice stripping away the last of Adelina's sensiblities. 'She's a damned shape-changer, no doubt sister to the one who took my souls. What does it matter? One less methinks and glorious retribution for me.'

'*Bitseach! BITSEACH!*' Adelina screamed but the woman laughed – a single ugly sound. Adelina went to leap at her but the swan-maid grabbed her hand and pulled her down close by the beautiful mouth. She whispered a faint plea.

'Tell Maeve Swan Maid. Revenge!' Her eyes closed and her hand fell away, leaving her just another lifeless shell amongst the feathered debris of the killing spree.

Back in her room, Adelina had shivered as the black morass of hate bubbled away. She needed the comfort of companionship and care. She missed Ajax... even as she sat and sewed she could smell that wonderful equine fragrance. She could feel his muzzle brushing over the top of her hand, tickling with his chin whiskers and she could hear the quaint 'lollop' sound he made as his lips mouthed her palm, licking off the saltiness of human sweat. And then she imagined another altogether more lusty mouth licking her palm and other parts but she pricked her finger with the needle in agitation and resolved not to dwell on Kholi for if she did she would cry a stream, a river, perhaps even an ocean.

She missed her kindred spirit Ana, missed the sisterhood. She missed Liam, the love of Ana's life. Adelina had watched him, this Færan who was supposedly immune to pain and grief, watched him curl in upon himself and suffer the same gut-wrenching pangs any mortal endured. Adelina had held strong views about the avaricious egoism of all Færan and he was some of that – a little bit – maybe. Ah, he had been such an enigma! He had wanted to learn about mortal life, to feel the pain, experience the dross as well as the gold. He had forgone his immortality, desiring to be as close to Ana in death as life, never imagining death would be waiting only seconds away for both of them. How Adelina had delighted in telling Severine that Liam had taken potions to remove his immortality. But the insane woman still maintained it was an immortal Færan soul she had syphoned through her grim little ring that fateful day. Adelina gave a wry, watery smirk. A Færan soul to be sure... but a soul as afflicted with mortality as Luther's or her own.

'Don't fret, milady of the thread.'

Adelina's head jerked up at the voice that spoke from behind her and she spun around.

Standing leaning against the wall was a thin young man with wispy gold hair urchin cut around his face. His clothes seemed covered in shadows, patterning him as if broken light dropped through leaves and buds. Boots laced up his skinny legs and his grin alighted on her in a friendly way. The angular face exhibited a chin dusted in golden down, as though by growing a fledgling whisker he was learning to be a man.

'A time spent in melancholy is time wasted. Better to enjoy the moments you are given and let sadness drift away,' he spoke melodically and picked up a piece of silk thread to toss it in the air, 'like a piece of silk on the breeze.' The cerise thread hovered for a moment and then drifted on a current towards the open window and out, up into the sky. The lad pointed with a lazy finger. 'Like so.'

'Indeed.' Adelina's crisp voice replied. 'And as you are Other for how else would you manifest in my room, that would be easy to do. Enjoy the time rather than dwell on sadness, no matter how profound.'

'Sadness is an emotion that has little place in my life because I *choose* not to let it, Needlewoman. If that be Other then so be it. But I tell you this, I *know* sadness, I *could* be sad.' He walked to the window and squinted into the light, perhaps to discern the thread he had consigned to the air. 'But I *choose* not to.' He spun round quickly and walked to her side to lean back against the table and look down at her. He grinned, two dimples marking the lower edges of his cheeks, and she noticed his green-flecked eyes. 'Do what I do, Adelina. You have work to finish and plans to be made. Such introspection wastes your time.'

'I shall do what I like and when, thank you sir. Who are you anyway?' Adelina picked up her sewing and feigned interest in a loop of rather boring stem-stitch.

'Oh what a conundrum! Do I tell you my real name and be under your thrall or do I give you another name?' The lad placed a fey finger on his chin.

Adelina put her birchwood hoop on the table and pushed back her chair to move to the window, the afore-mentioned thread long gone from her view. She turned to the young man and raised an eyebrow before tossing her tawny hair over her shoulder. 'Well you know *my* name but if you don't mind my saying, I think your opinion of yourself is altogether too big to even warrant me wanting you in my thrall. Truly sir, I would rather know *what* you are than who you are?'

'I am a Goodfellow, a shape-shifter, a hob. I can be anything. A urisk.' He spun around on the spot and became that most unusual faun and stood hands fanned out, one ankle crossed languidly over the other. 'The Bodachan Sabhaill.' Again he spun around, re-appearing as a man with a threshing tool, wrinkles and a drooping cap and liripipe failing to camouflage the glinting young eyes. 'I can even be a silky, if you like.' As he spun, the room filled with the scent of lily of the valley and his form became a beauteous woman garbed in honeyed silk that rustled as she moved.

Adelina had never seen such Others in her life and was in secret awe. Fascinated with the unique flow of the silky's dress fabric, she watched it undulating and shifting in the welkin wind and longed to run it through her fingers. But she had heard of the Silky of Denton Hall who had uncharmingly become a feared poltergeist and the Silky of Gilsland who was so protective of its household family, it strangled an unwanted intruder.

'I don't care for silkies thank you, somewhat frightening. And as the Bodachan Sabhaill you would be useless. As you can see, I don't live in a barn. I liked the urisk best but should you be seen, you will drag attention to me and no doubt I will be punished more than I am already, for mingling with Others. So if you must be anything, be a *good* fellow.'

'Goodfellow,' he returned a trifle sourly. 'Have you not heard of Robin Goodfellow? Of Puck?'

'I have and know mischief figures as strong as make good.'

'But I'm not here to make mischief.' He seemed aggrieved, having failed to make any impression with the crisp, dry woman standing before him.

'Indeed. Then why *are* you here?'

'Under orders lady. Did Lhiannon not say?'

'Lhiannon? What do you mean?' Adelina's heart jumped two beats.

'She told me to mind you, keep company, help sometimes? But,' he began to turn away. 'If you are happy as you are then I shall be on my way.' He walked towards the blank wall in front of him as if it were an open door.

Adelina hurried over to him, the thought of an empty room too much to bear. 'No! No, don't go! I'm sorry. I'm always ill humoured these days.

Please. If you are the sprite Lhiannon said would come, then stay.'

'Not today I think, Lady Stitcher. I need time to consider whether I want to be with such a melancholic crotchet. Adieu.'

And with that he was gone. Vanished. As if he had never manifested in the first place.

Her room, echoing faintly with the low shush of the wave-sucked shingle from way below, was filled with the silence of one person – a prisoner whose only contact was with an assassin and a lunatic. She sat back at the table and picked up the birchwood hoop and looked at it. The thought of any of the hob's forms for company was suddenly what she craved even more than her freedom.

She threw the hoop as hard as she could against the wall so that it cracked and splintered and fell apart, leaving the embroidered fabric to slide miserably down the wall.

CHAPTER FOUR

Ebba sat thinking of the Færan and her morbid quest to deliver the souls to Veniche and into the waiting hands of Jasper. Why, why? *Oh Aine, Mother Mine, please help me, tell me what this is about.* She had hoped *never* to have dealings with the Færan, not whilst Phelim...

She thought of her stepson in the shearing shed, sweat dripping off his brow, the sheep gripped between his legs. She could imagine the dusty light filtering down through the high windows, the bleating and moaning of the sheep, the smell of lanolin and ovine droppings. The roar of a shearer as he reached for another ewe. Her Phelim would be enjoying every sweaty, aching, exhausting moment despite...

Jasper! His name came back again and again and she shuddered at the memory. Damn, the pipe had gone out! She thrust it on the settle and walked to the door, determined a walk would heal her troubled mind.

The fragrance of ocean wafted amongst the trees and the wind shifted once again more southerly. Ebba stopped on the track to dig between the roots of a wild hazelnut tree and presently a dark mound of rotted fungus lay in her hands. The smell wafted deliciously as she stowed the truffles, later to be shaved into the creamy potage that simmered in her kitchen. Further on she found some honeysuckle crawling up the tumbled remains of an old mill and which would aid in the understanding of mysteries. She shook out a calico bag to place the leaves gently inside, being careful not to bruise or damage the surfaces, and hung the bag from her belt along with the fungus. As she walked on she seemed like some strange chatelaine whose belted keys were strange bags of herbage and flower and which neither rattled or clanged.

'Lady, I can smell the truffles from the other side of the glade.'

A figure materialised at her side and stepped along in unison and Ebba betrayed no surprise at her companion's sudden appearance. Indeed the arrival was welcome because she could feel herself beginning to dwell on her stepson and unpleasant matters. 'Mr. No Name, it's a while since we spoke.' She was wary of thanking him directly for speaking to her. To show such gratitude would send her Other companion on his way, far from her side.

'It's a pleasure, I'm sure.' The figure put his hands behind his back under the tails of a fine brown coat.

'It's unusual to spy you in daylight. Are you not afraid that a mortal will see you, saving myself of course, and be startled out of their wits?'

'Why mistress, are you sure it is not you who are addled? For I am far more like to scare a mortal at night should they see me, than during the sunlit hours. Have you forgotten it is good fortune to sight a urisk in the day?'

Ebba stopped and turned, her frosted hair lifting in the breeze winding amongst the trees. She frowned at her companion, noting the fawn hirsute legs and the cloven hooves. She marked the way he ran a slim hand over his head, smoothing back the flowing taupe locks. In amongst the abundance on his head, two small cream horns curled shyly skywards. A crewel embroidered vest and lawn shirt underneath the attractive brown tailcoat indicated a degree of fastidiousness at which she smiled. 'Of course! Forgive me. I am confused of mind today.' She tapped him on the arm, clearing her head. 'You *do* look smart. Where did you find such apparel for I know if the manor people had laid it out for you, you would have departed.'

'Yes, it's true. But I *found* these shall we say, on the clothesline behind the dairy. A bit of alteration and they fit well.'

Ebba laughed. 'Then I'll not tell a soul. You look well, my friend. They're looking after you at the manor.'

'They leave milk out each night but I'd rather quaff a wine and so I feed the milk to the cat who is becoming rather rotund and I help myself to the squire's grog and vittles while I wave a finger at the house brownies as they slave away – as all house brownies should.' He tossed his coat tails upward with his hands.

'Mr. No Name, you have no shame and you make me laugh which helps me through my current dilemmas.' Ebba touched his arm.

'Shall we sit?' Mr. No-Name took her hand and led her to a mossy covered log by the side of a wide pond. Above them a pale blue sky was streaked with the wisps of mares' tail clouds and a black swan flew over the trees, casting low for a place to land. Ebba and the urisk watched the bird as it settled and swam towards them, both realizing it could be, probably was a swan-maid. As they talked, it drifted gracefully back and forth. The urisk spoke. 'I think you have had an interesting night, have you not?'

Ebba looked at him with slitted eyes but realised he knew more than she of the past, maybe even the future and everything in between. He continued.

'To hold a bag inside which lie Færan souls must surely un-nerve you.'

She nodded.

'There is a story behind them and because I am a urisk and wise and all-seeing, I could tell you if you want.'

She opened her eyes wide, her heart beating fast. She had always respected the urisk, he treated her well and she had no misgivings about the trust she placed on their relationship. As to his knowledge and how he came upon such, he was Other, she was mortal. It would be rude and insensitive to cross-question him. She nodded and said quietly, 'But of course, I'm all ears.'

Thus the tale of Adelina, Liam and Ana was revealed and the role of the Færan Lhiannon and of the outrageous Severine and her henchman, Luther. Of the urisk's anger and disgust towards the latter two there was absolutely no doubt as his voice crispened like an autumn leaf and the expression on his face chilled like a breeze from Oighear Dubh. Ebba sat overawed with the scope of the telling, aware the urisk was coming around to something she knew would shift her own life profoundly sideways for had not her skin prickled earlier in the day?

'And you have a problem Lady, for it is you who holds the bag of souls and you who must continue them on their journey. But the Fates have intervened and I'll tell you this, and as I am Other and as old as the universe and wiser than the wise, you should hearken to me.'

Ebba nodded again, her eyes searching the brown orbs of her quaint friend.

'It is for another to *deliver* the souls. And you know, Lady, who it must be.

For his journey begins now and if he is ever to find his true place in Eirie then it must begin by carrying the souls of those to whom he is connected.'

Ebba's heart missed two, even three beats, as close a feeling to putting her life on hold as she could imagine.

'The wind blows southerly,' the fellow continued. 'There are boats handy and Veniche lies to the north.' The urisk rubbed contemplatively at his pointed, smooth face. 'Your harder problem is your secret, isn't it? It is time, mistress, to reveal all. You know in your way and I know in mine, the time has finally come. Eight and twenty years is a long time to conceal the truth and the Fates have finally decreed the moment.'

Ebba looked down at her hands and found to her horror they swam before her, tears filling her eyes. *But no, you don't understand! He is happy with the life he has, as am I. Why change what is to what must be? I am not ready.* 'Yes,' she whispered. 'The moment has arrived. The time for fact and the time for farewell.'

The urisk tucked her hand in under his elbow. 'Mistress, you have always been kind and courteous to me and shared much with me. I shall share my name with you.'

Had Ebba given it a thought, she would have realised quaint Mr. No-Name was moved by her tears as they ran down her face to her chin and wanted to help somehow, but it wasn't the sensitive motivation of his action which surprised her. She looked up sharply. Name-giving! 'Then *muirnin,* if that's the case you shall call me Ebba.'

'Alright and you shall call me Balthazar.'

She took his other hand in her spare one and shook it as if meeting him for the first time.

They sat in shared silence, listening to the rattling of the beech discs above them and feeling the moistness of the southerly on their cheeks.

'I like your waistcoast.' Ebba touched the stitching.

"Thank you, it was embroidered by a Traveller. Adelina by name, quite famous, as you now know."

CHAPTER FIVE

The smell of truffles laced upwards through the small spirals of steam as Ebba and Phelim sat at the table and tore up chunks of bread with which to sop up the potage. Ebba tapped her crust a couple of times on the table as if prompting herself to speak and finally she began. 'Phelim, we need to talk. We need to talk about the girl and her bag for I have some knowledge which I must impart.'

Wisps of frosted hair curled on the edge of her lined face and she had twisted a cable of lavender wool to frame the hair and decorate herself, as if the trimmings would armour her and ease the task ahead. The heather colour drew out the intense blue of her eyes as she stared at her son.

She told him the story... the saga so lately relayed to herself. The soup grew cold and congealed and the breadcrumbs dried a little on the table as the story stretched itself into the hours of night. Finally, Ebba picked up the bag and laid it in front of Phelim. 'In there are the souls.'

Phelim touched the bag with a finger and then looked at Ebba. 'But,' he said.

'But indeed,' Ebba sighed and shook her head.

'Where did you hear all this, Ebba? Not from your leaves and feathers or from the breeze, I'll wager.' He continued to run a finger softly over the chamois, as if he stroked a fragile kitten. The bag was cool to the touch, unusually so and one almost felt the need to remove one's fingers from the unfriendly lack of warmth.

'I have a friend of a lifetime's standing. A urisk. He is erudite and wise and I trust him. That is the most important thing to remember.'

She told her stepson that it had become his duty to return the souls to Jasper. She touched on Fate and Destiny as if such things would swing the balance of his thoughts but it was that more than anything that was her undoing. Her stepson leaned back in his chair, a faint air about him. Not rebellion, she thought, no, not that but he had raised an eyebrow and his eyes darkened.

'Ebba, Fate and Destiny uttered out of the mouth of an Other are hardly like to convince me I should give up all I hold dear to travel on some vague quest. And for the betterment of those I don't know and have never heard of, let alone trust! To do something for Others! Aine help us, why should I? What do they ever do for us, especially the Færan! Except cause fear and concern! Let the urisk do it if he is so wise and honourable.'

Ebba cringed at his sore words. 'Phelim, it has been written differently.'

He swung forward on his chair, the legs hitting the flagstones with a crack. '*What* has been written differently? And what on earth does it have to do with me? I begin to think you speak in riddles!'

Ebba stood and carried the bowls to the sink, scraping the remnants into a bucket for the fowl. She could see her reflection in the window but when she sought her stepson's it wasn't there and it frightened her, even though she was aware it was because he sat in shadow. 'Oh *my love,* she turned back, her shoulders bent as if all the world's troubles weighed her down. Aine she felt old. 'How can I say this? I may have wronged you and I want to know before I begin to tell you, that you will forgive me.'

'Ebba, you're beginning to worry me. When did you ever do anything for which you needed to be forgiven. As like to be congratulated I think!'

'Huh,' she muttered with a face as sour as bad milk. 'You ask when?' She sat back in front of him. 'I would say it was twenty-eight years ago.'

At Mevagavinney, before the day had begun to turn to night, Adelina stared out the open window. A breeze blew in carrying the smell of the cold wastes of Oighear Dubh. The cold reminded her of snow which reminded her of Star on the Stair and snow angels and fire festivals and a tear crept down her cheek as she realised she had curled her fingers at her side as if slipping them into Kholi Khatoun's hand. Her throat tightened and she sniffed, shivering as she pulled the window shut.

She turned away, spying the broken hoop by the wall and the robe swinging in the inanimate air. Silence smothered her and suddenly the urge to escape from the four walls surrounding her became an imperative and she hammered on the door. 'Luther, Luther! Where are you, I want to go out! Take me out! I want to walk! Luther!'

As she hammered her fist on the wood, the swarthy gaoler threw the door open. 'Shut your mouth, *bitseach,* shut the hell up! You've been for a walk this morning! Once a day only.' He began to pull the door shut, his face flushed.

'No! Luther, I have such an ache in my head – just some fresh air before dark. Please.' Adelina aimed the full force of her tawny smile at him and noticed the loathsome apple in his throat bob up and down as he swallowed.

'If you must, damn you. Come quickly.'

His hand glided across her rump as she sidled past and she ripped on her coat and buttoned it, hurrying down the stairwell, trying to keep ahead of him, arriving breathless at the garden and having to wait whilst he squeezed in front of her, pressing against her to open the gate, aware he watched her as she stepped to the pond and the willows. She heard him lock the gate and guessed he was licking his lips and making some lewd gesture as he turned away. The fear of his lust for her had grown bigger each day, trying to crowd out the vengeful thoughts that most often ran round her head.

She sat on the bench used by she and Lhiannon, trembling at what Luther might do and she had never felt as alone in her life. She knew Luther waited like some obscene flycatcher to carry off his prey and demolish it and she knew her life hung by a thread only as long as the last thread it took to finish the robe. She was under no illusions. Severine would no doubt kill she and Ajax just as she had killed the others, after tossing her to Luther like a bone to a dog. She sighed, her shoulders rising high and dropping with a rush as the air fled her lips.

'Needlewoman is sad. Thy sighs make willows dance.'

Adelina turned quickly at the voice behind her. Maeve Swan Maid stood in her elongated black beauty, a stark column of loveliness with an expression Adelina could not read.

'You've come back! Is Lhian...'

Maeve broke in. 'Thy Færan friend is faraway. Fret not, Threadlady.'

'Thank Aine.' A weight lifted from the pile of cares and woes Adelina carried.

'Thy thanks are misplaced, mortal maid. Thou would do better to thank I and my sister maid who so kindly loaned a cloak to thy friend. Thou should speak in realities not hypotheticals. If Aine gave a care, She would help thee escape this prison and bring foul Other-killer to her death, she who murdered one of my sisters!' Maeve moved from behind the seat to sit by Adelina, making sure none of her midnight blackness touched the mortal.

'I know, I'm so sorry for your loss. But she spoke to me Maeve, as she died.' She repeated the dying swan's words and Maeve's eyes darkened to the endless colour of death. She said nothing and Adelina squirmed, plucking at the strings of courage to ask a question. 'Maeve, can you tell me where Lhiannon is?'

The woman shook herself from her shadowed revery. 'No but be assured Færan is forever safe.'

Adelina watched Maeve's swan-like neck turn as the dangerous eyes fixed her with a gaze that in the past may have produced shivers. But in her desperate state, all she wanted was for the swan-maid to feel some sadness for her, just as she felt wrenching sadness for the swan-maid's loss. But it was not to be.

'Souls begin journey across western seas to Færan healer in Veniche, where he shall wait. Fate decrees.'

Around Maeve and Adelina the birds had set up a loud chorus as the sky softened to dusk, the embroiderer marveling at the way her life was turning on its head. All those who would help her were Other. Her would-be, could-be friends were unbelievably Other!

'Thread-needle Lady, thou wouldst do well to begin to plan thy escape. Ugly manservant will have thee as soon as thy gaoler's back is turned and sooner rather than later for she comes and goes with great frequency. As to the woman, thou must surely have a plan for retribution?'

'Not precisely...'

Maeve Swan Maid hissed as she stood, a column of fury. 'Thy heartbreak is not as consuming as thou would have us believe. Thy lover was killed! Does that mean *nothing* to thee? And the witch-mortal killed Others who were your friends. It matters to us even if it does not matter to thee?'

'Of *course* it matters!' Adelina brought a fist down hard on the arm of the bench. 'I would kill her here and now if I could.'

Maeve's head flew back and she gave a harsh laugh like a swan's cry. 'Thou says! Thou says much but does little, Stitcher. Why dost thou not plan this retribution, woman? Do it, rather than think it! Dost thou still repudiate our offer to help thee avenge thyself on the woman?'

Adelina thought for a moment. She had many vengeful ideas. 'Maeve, your offer is generous,' she prevaricated, 'but I must do this myself, I swear. It is necessary for *my* soul.'

The swan-maid shrugged her shoulders. 'Remember this, Threadlady. Thou hast sworn to me. Thou hast given thy word to an Other. Thou must carry out thy pledge on pain of equal punishment. Dost thou understand?' Her eyes burned into Adelina's. 'And thou would do well to take help if it is offered. Thou will never get away from here otherwise. Evil Other-killer has many ugly tools at her disposal, more eldtrich than one such as a stitcher could ever dream – she has soul-syphon! Keeping prisoner is easy pickings. Thou must hearken or thou will end up in pieces like Maeve's sister maid!' As she uttered the last words, Maeve walked to the water without looking back, shapeshifting and becoming a graceful black bird that glided majestically away to the other side of the lake before launching itself into the darkening sky where it was hardly to be noticed.

Luther hovered close when he took Adelina back to her room. Inebriated, he brushed her with lingering fingers. Sick at the thought of her blatant vulnerability with Luther possessing the key to her room, she pulled a chair to the door and jammed it under the handle, knowing it would do nothing to stop the bull of a man.

Maeve's dark grey words had her almost like a jelly – dark grey because in truth nothing would ever be as black as the words that had told her Kholi and Liam were dead. But worse now, she had pledged to an Other and forfeited her own life should the pledge fail. She was threatened on all sides and as she trembled staring out at the dark sky, she thought of Lhiannon and how she had not demurred once as she began her dangerous journey. She had not let *anything* stop her.

And what hast thou done? Sat and embroidered for thy gaoler. Allowed thyself to be hit, bullied and provoked. She could hear Maeve as surely as if she sat by her shoulder.

I am pathetic, she railed, but as the souls make their way to the northern waters, this will be my turning point. She faced the wall near the door. 'Hola, Mr. Goodfellow, hola!' There was a hint of begging in her voice. 'I need you.'

And so I pleaded. For suddenly I could no longer continue alone. I needed a friend, I knew it the minute Maeve spoke to me, my heart had lifted with hope at the ridiculous thought she might be my helpmeet.

Someone familiar to whom I thought I could vent my angst.

And whilst Maeve's cool remove was a disappointment, I remembered the friendly gleam in the hob's eye. It had potential...

CHAPTER SIX

'Remember twenty-eight years ago, I found you by the sea?' Ebba dared not even look at Phelim's face, if she did she knew her courage would fail her and thus she ploughed on. 'Well I knew immediately why you were there and what you were, but for my own selfish reasons I told no one and now I must. Phelim, you are of the Færan.'

Phelim snorted like a horse, a grin beginning to creep across his face. But on observing Ebba's expression, he stood up, flinging the chair back to move out of her ambit. She raised a quieting finger and shook her head slightly, aware the one step back was a whole gulf between he and herself. Desperate to ignore her fears, she continued. 'Days before I found you, there was a Færan progress through the island. Things happened – children were taken and changelings left in their places, girls suffered the pining sickness, cows milk curdled, crops had patterns scattered through as if an Other dance had taken place. I was frantic ameliorating all the trouble! And when I went to gather herbs and grasses from the shore, there you were. Some absent-minded mother had left you – they often do this type of thing, it is well documented in our histories – so busy enjoying themselves they forget about the babe.' She took a breath. 'But at all costs I decided no one must know you were Færan because I had found you and I loved you instantly, so I spread a story, you know it well. I would not have you discriminated against for being Other nor returned to those who would not care for you. Thus it was a case of putting as much about you as I could to deter the most ardent hunter. And there was one, believe me. Every year for five years, Jasper the Færan Healer – he would come and search the isles and I would lay carlins' charms about your person and about the house. I would wash you and your clothes in herbs. You would have the amber around your neck – it was the gentlest charm to your Færan sensibilities, and I would use carlin-tongue. I longed to surround your crib with silver but it would have wounded you to the core. And when Jasper came, I would put you in a group of other infants and children to confound his senses. I was sure he would discover you such was his skill. I would plead with Aine to keep you safe for you were my little son.' A tear escaped, slipping across the top of Ebba's skin like water across velvet. Glancing at Phelim's eyes, she saw confusion, disbelief, and something else she couldn't bear to think about. 'It worked because after five years he never came back. Then it was a question of guiding you away from your Færan birthright to a mortal life. As I hoped, our life rubbed off. Occasionally you spoke Traveller when I had taught you not one word, and Færan as well. But to all whom you met you were indeed Ebba's stepson, child of my dead sister.' She stopped for a breath and looked at her audience. 'Forgive me?'

'Aine! Forgive you!' He raked fingers through the wavy hair. 'Why Ebba? Why did you do it? Why not give me back?' His voice hardened. 'Why wait so long to tell me something of such colossal import!'

A fearsome emptiness curled around the carlin. She had thought her beloved stepson would accept the reasons for her actions with the equanimity that had dominated his life. Her hopes had blown away in the fierceness of his response and all she saw fluttering in the air about her was disbelief and anger.

'Why not tell me when I was young?' He stamped away across the room and back again. 'I don't *want* to be Other. I want to be me, Phelim the shepherd, the man everyone knows! I have no greater aspiration beyond being the best I can be. People out there,' he waved an arm,' they respect me and like me. What do you think they would do if they found out I was Other? You obviously thought it enough of a problem when I was young to shield my real identity. They'd fear me, wouldn't they? Never call me by name, they'd exclude me.' He stopped and tapped the table with a taut finger. 'But there's a thing, how in all these years, if I am an Other, have I not left the minute someone spoke my name uninvited or thanked me for something?'

'Perhaps Phelim is not your real name.' She cringed as her stepson choked, even his name suspect, and the pain that grabbed her heart almost crushed it – *I can't do this, I can't*, she railed at the cruelty of truth. *But you must, you must*, she could hear the urisk say. 'And as I said I made sure you were inculcated with mortal ways and mores from the minute I held you in my arms. That and the charms I laid about you. And as happens when one spends a long time with someone, one absorbs their ways, their life. You were an infant, Phelim. You had no time to be Færan. You were like a piece of clay waiting to be moulded on the wheel and I chose to mould you as a mortal.'

'You must have powers verging on the unbelievable then, Ebba. To fool the Færan for this long.' His tone was bitter and it was such a shock. 'And now, you have ripped the rug of my mortal life from underneath my feet and given me a new persona. How dare you!'

'Dare, dare!' A flinty light burst into flame inside the carlin. 'I dared because if I had left you there as a babe you may have died.'

'Why,' he asked emptily. 'Was it my bane to die as a babe? If so, patently I owe you. I must be the first Færan to escape their bane.'

'Sarcasm doesn't become you, Phelim.'

'Then what does exactly, because I'm damned if I have a clue!'

A sparking silence hung between them, so much said, so much still to say.

'Surely in all this time, something of Færan would have shown itself.'

She could detect the faintest plea in his words as if she should say, *no, you're right, there wasn't* and they could forget about it all. 'Think Phelim,' Ebba's voice flattened as the weight of the night's revelations grew heavier. 'You spoke Traveller and Other when I had taught you not one word and you have mesmered unconsciously.'

'No, never!'

'Are you sure? Some animal, a person even?'

There was silence and then Phelim's eyes widened a little.

'And there have been other things.'

'What? Worse than a mesmer?'

Ebba nodded her head. 'Your relationship with women. I had always to remedy them. There was something of the Ganconer in it all.'

'No!' Phelim sat with a thump. 'They would have died.'

'Indeed. Thus my help and like the Ganconer, you never returned to the same woman twice.'

'The Ganconer! His victims die! I am a murderer!'

Ebba rushed around the table and folded him in a fierce grasp, laying her papery cheek on his head. 'No my son, no! You never hurt a soul knowingly. I refuse to believe you would *ever* do so! Listen to me! You may be Other but nothing changes. You can control this and be in charge. And perhaps the urisk is right, perhaps it *is* your destiny to courier these souls to Jasper, if only to prove to yourself that it can be done your way and not the Other way.'

Phelim's sadness hung in the air like a torn bannerol as he pushed her away. 'Perhaps,' he whispered. 'Leastways I have no choice. Besides, whether I do it or not, life will never ever be the same.'

'Oh Phelim.'

'No don't. I don't wish to talk about it anymore and I shall leave tonight. The sooner I leave, the less chance I shall hurt anyone.' He stood and walked to the door. 'I'll get a boat Ebba, and you set about collecting supplies.'

'Phelim, please!'

But he shook his head and left and Ebba was surrounded by the silence of recrimination. She grabbed her staff and banged hard on the floor but all that came from the top was the sound of wind and the crisp crackling of ice... the southerly still blew.

CHAPTER SEVEN

Phelim hunkered down, his arm over the tiller, the port sheets in his hand. He had let the mainsail out as far as he dared and had added a jib and the two canvases lifted the little craft atop the wave. It skimmed, the only sound being the whine of the wind in the stays, the odd flap as a sail ruckled and the swish of the bow wave. A fine spray blew in his face as he crossed the ocean almost abeam to the wind.

Færan! He cringed, all the skin that he had grown over his lifetime stripped off and an ugly, bloody sight to be seen by all. His self-belief had cracked and splintered and he wondered if Ebba truly had any idea of the mountaineous shock she had delivered to him. His world had tilted utterly. All he could think of was the suspicion and the fear rampant in mortals' views of Others. He wouldn't have countenanced any of it by choice. He couldn't believe that in twenty-eight years he never had reason to believe that he was anything other than the mortal stepson of the carlin. Never! He burned with disgust at his own naïvety and with anger at Ebba for her untimely, hurtful revelation. Pulling hard on the main sheet so the movement rocked the dory off its steady tack, he turned to survey the pale moon heading rapidly to the west. The southerly breeze chilled and he turned up the collar of his jacket and tried to burrow deeper into the warmth of his gear as if he were trying to hide from Ebba's confessions. Gauging the time was right to tack he pulled hard on the tiller.

The canvas cracked and smacked and the shackles rattled fiercely as they rolled in the rigging and took the strain of the swinging dory, Phelim dragging in the starboard sheets so the craft could head northerly through the waters.

He looked at the black water speeding past, thinking on the men who fished the waters and then remembered the story Ebba had told him as a babe, of Mathey Trevalla of Zennor and he could hear her voice as if it were yesterday, lulling him into a child's warm cocoon of sleep.

'It is a well-known fact the oceans around us are filled with the most beauteous of all the water-wights, the Ceasg. They were often seen by tired sailors, driving milk white cattle from under the sea to feed on the shore among the dunes. Such a sight foretold of great sea-storms and thus sailors knew to seek safe moorings. Mortals returned this faith by freeing trapped Ceasg from their nets and casting food and wine amongst the blood-red dulse and rocks of the shore so these half-mortal, half fish-folk could taste the beauty of the ordinary world.'

'One such Ceasg was known along the coast of Trevallyn, her beauty being legend in the inns and taverns clinging to the rocky walls of the fishing hamlets. She had eyes of blue and hair as pale as the nacreous lustre of pearl and indeed it was these gems that forever laced through her divine locks as they waved in the wind or undulated in the wave.'

'Along the pleated shoreline, close to the tiny fishing village of Zennor, the Ceasg would swim to a rock and sit, the pearly mists hiding her from view as the fishermen mended their nets, singing shanties and ballads.'

'Mathey Trevalla was the son of a fishing family and he often sat, needle plying as he mended holes in the nets, his tenor voice singing across the bay, inviting the Ceasg into the waters close by to listen.'

'It came to pass that selfsame Ceasg could no longer contain her own voice and with clear, bell-like tones she joined Mathey in a distant descant from her rock in the bay – a melody that brought tears to the eyes of the old fisherfolk.'

'She swam to the shore and when she reached the shallows she stood, her tail gone and two graceful legs conveying her over the sands. Clothed in lithe, pearlescent silks, she reached Mathey's side and sang a duet, casting a spell over the folk of Zennor so that when she left, they mused dreamily over their ales by the fires.'

'Did ee hear her voice? By the Southern Lights, it were like a bell it were, like a bell that rings on yon frosty eve, clear and crystal-like. Like the wavelets on the shore, running across them pebbles, like ripples of sound it were.' A leather seadog spoke to no one in particular as his stained yellow hand stuffed tobacco in his pipe and tamped it down.'

'A crone picked up her knitting and scratched her scalp with needles, through the grey strands of her bun. 'Did ee see her hair? By the blessings of the Zephyrs, it were like silver moonbeams. Like moonstrike on an autumn fern it were. Like the shallows when the sand glistens. Silver like a precious chaperon the Færan might wear!'

'And Mathey sighed longingly. 'Did ee see her walk? She were like a sea of harvest grass on Zennor Moor when the breeze do come. Like the ripple of wavelets when the Harmonies blow.'

'But one ancient grandmother who was stone deaf and had not been magicked by the singing of the Ceasg, spied Mathey's longing and poked him with her stick. 'Mathey Trevalla, keep your fingers off that mermaid! No good'll come of it, I'm telling ee. Thems that dally with a sea maid are not long fer this world!'

'But Mathey could barely wait for the morrow as his heart was trapped by the woman's charms. At dawn he sat at his nets and began sewing, allowing his tenor voice to fill the morning air with a ballad of boats and fair maids and honorable and lasting love.'

'She walked up the shore and joined him in a heavenly chorus. To those watching, the two were like charmed children of the Others, their beauty a sight to behold.'

'Mathey's eyes never left those of the sea maid and she held him by a thread of devotion the mortal folk feared could never be broken. She turned away, singing a song of her own people and walked to the sea, Mathey following blindly behind.'

'As the waves lapped at her toes, the fine legs transformed to become the infamous tail, covered in discs of incandescent green. Mathey, mesmered, waded into the ocean singing the chorus to her lilting tune and the folk of Zennor called feverishly to their son. But he waded, deaf to their entreaty, deeper and deeper.'

'Eventually the waters closed over his head and there was no sound except for the cruel water against the shore. The maid in her feckless way swam off, leaving the mesmered youth swimming far and deep, diving, searching, calling until weakness and waves conspired to drown the poor lad. The folk of Zennor found his body a day later on the rocks of Zennor Point and they buried him beneath a cairn on that same headland. And now on a foggy day and by the breath of a seawind, a silver bell tolls to remind the unwary of the melodic voice of the murderous Other who took away the life of Mathey Trevalla of Zennor.'

And Ebba would conclude, brushing Phelim's hair away from his forehead as his eyelids became heavy.

'A mermaid found a swimming lad,

Picked him for her own,
Pressed her body to his body,
Laughed; and plunging down
Forgot in cruel happiness
That even lovers drown.'

'It's an old Færan poem,' she would explain the lines away, 'feckless individuals!'

CHAPTER EIGHT

Adelina had spent the night on the chair she had jammed under the handle of her door, dozing intermittently, always waking with a start, eyes wide, heart thumping. But Luther left her alone.

She stretched the kinks from her back to walk to the window, the clear day affording a view across Mevagavinney Harbour. The water shone pale blue with silver discs of reflected light jostling in the early breeze. The fragrance of that tiny zephyr reminded Adelina of freedom and space and she felt her heart and soul curling tight and black again as she measured what she had lost.

Her reason strained at the cracked banks of her mind. She talked to herself constantly and became lost in dreams and fantasies of what might have been. In very bad moments she tried to invent a death for Severine and vomit would burn her gullet as she shook and fought for some form of self-control. That she trod the path to murder she had no doubt. Travellers would call it murder, so too the people of Trevallyn, the Archipelago and Veniche, especially Veniche, where the rule of law was deliberated and despatched. If she had sense she would escape and endeavour to bring Severine to swift justice from the judges.

If she had sense.

But her Traveller's sense had deserted her along with her morals the moment she heard Kholi had been murdered. She floundered in a bog filled with hate and revenge and had no one with whom to deliberate right or wrong. Her lonliness exacerbated her condition a hundredfold. Anxieties fed off her depression and a bleak future stretched before her which was why she had called desperately to the hob last night. And true to the Other fashion, reinforcing Adelina's long held view about the facile unreliability of Others, he had not come. As she went about her ablutions, one ear on her door should Luther approach, she cursed the hob and all Others for the importunate individuals they were, ranting, swearing, her voice a counterpoint to the emptiness of her situation.

She examined the robe hanging against the armoire. Three-quarters finished. She could finish it before the souls were retrieved as Severine had rightly guessed. It would be an easy, if uncomfortable task to sew the quarters of those unfortunate shades under the finished embroidery.

Despite her moments of madness or maybe even because of, it was the consummate need to finish the garment that kept her going. Like the artist who must finish the fresco despite strained eyes and blinding headaches, or the sculptor who despite bleeding hands and screaming muscles, must put the last chisel strokes to a muscular thigh or a mass of curls. Her masterpiece swallowed her whole. It obsessed her, dragged at her attention but she believed it diverted her from the pain of loss and her current predicament. If ever there was love-hate relationship, it was between Adelina and the robe.

A noise at the door had her hurrying to remove the chair and as the key turned in the lock she sat quickly at the table and picked up a hoop wired with a series of strappy fritillary leaves. Her needle flashed in and out as she overcast the wire in a fine blanket stitch. The door was pushed open and a seedy Luther entered, squinting at the bright sunlight filling the room from Adelina's open window. 'The Lady wants you to walk now. There will be a storm by this afternoon.'

Adelina closed her eyes. Outside she felt safe. Outside she could see Ajax, albeit far away. Outside she could breathe!

She had never been in the garden earlier than midday and it felt fresher, more pristine. The air tingled and she took a deep breath, thinking it sparkled like champagne. She liked the effervescent wine on the rare occasions she had been able to afford it. It seemed to demolish depression, as if each exploding bubble blasted apart the foundations of a black mood.

She walked quickly down the *allée* of weeping silver-pear trees to the willow and the pond, for if there was anywhere to alleviate her mood it was that almost eldritch stretch of water. And perhaps Maeve would come back, so she sat quietly on the grassy bank, stripping off her stockings and dangling her toes in the cool water in anticipation. Ducks watched the woman and dragonflies hovered and wove about her.

'If I didn't know you were in such strife, Needlewoman, I would say you present a relaxed and gracious picture.'

Adelina's head came up so fast she ricked her neck. 'Ouch! Mr.Goodfellow? Is it you?'

The youth to whom she spoke was leaning against another willow on the other side of the pond. Jacketless, his sleeves were rolled up and he appeared to have shaved. His chin shone like a baby's bottom as he grinned at her and called out. 'Hola!'

'Ssh! Luther will hear you!'

'Not if I don't want him to and they all think *you're* going mad anyway, you talk to yourself so often!'

She refused to rise to the bait. 'You can stop them seeing you or hearing you?'

'Indeed.'

'Then why didn't you say so before?'

'Threadlady, you were hardly in a mood to converse.'

Adelina was thrilled at his appearance, Other not withstanding. To talk to someone... she was *that* desperate. He leaned back again and crossed one languid ankle over the other. Had he not been so skinny it would have been an elegant stance. As it was... 'Why are we calling to each other, can you not come and sit by me?' Adelina smiled at him. Her tawny beauty beckoned and the hob uncrossed his ankles. He trotted around the side of the pool, amusing her with his energetic gait. Throwing himself down, pulling off his own boots and stockings, he thrust his toes in beside hers.

'So! Madame Embroiderer! You seem happier!'

'You think? And please, can you call me Adelina?'

'Yoho! You give me your name. Are you not afraid?'

'Of what? You know my name anyway! And besides I am a prisoner like to be killed when I have completed work to my gaoler's instructions. I have lost my love. If I am afraid of anything, I quiver and shake only when I think to be left alone in the manor with Luther. For he wants me and will no doubt try when his mistress leaves on business. To be afraid of you or any Other to be honest, pales into insignificance.'

'Then if *I* know your name, I shall tell you mine and then we can get down to the serious business of your future. I am... Gallivant.' He looked at her engagingly as if to say, *there, isn't that a wonderful name?*

Adelina laughed. 'Such an admirable, such a suitable name. Because you truly are a gallivanting sort of individual, aren't you? Gallivant ...' she spoke as if tasting the moniker. Rolling the 'l's' and stressing the 'v' and the 't', almost as if she had a lozenge in her mouth. She grinned. 'I like it.'

'ADELINA! ADELINA!' Luther's shouted tones sliced down the *allée* and split the willow branches apart.

'Quick, hide!' Adelina grabbed Gallivant by the arm.

'Worry not, dear lady. Don't forget, he can't see me if I don't wish it. Be yourself!' Gallivant ran a hand down Adelina's arm and she felt a honeyed warmth relaxing her as he pulled her to her feet. She hastily dragged on her stockings and boots and rushed out with a push from Gallivant, to meet Luther angrily striding toward her.

'You're to come back now. The Lady wants you at work immediately.'

'But I've only been here a short while. Why?'

'Ours is not to reason why!' Luther grabbed her and pushed her ahead of him. Glancing up, Adelina spotted Gallivant walking backwards in front of her, a finger held to his lips. Her eyes bulged. Then she remembered the barred window in the wall and its view of Ajax.

'My horse Luther, I haven't seen my horse.'

'Too bad. Come on!' He pushed her again and she staggered just as the air was filled with a shrieking blast from a horn. Everything shook and Adelina's ears reverberated, the hairs on her neck rising as surely as if an eldritch wand had orchestrated it. Ahead of her, Gallivant stopped dead and spun in the direction of the ugly sound. Birds arced into the sky and the previously quiet morning was filled with anxious calls as the horn echoed and re-echoed around every stone wall in Mevagavinney.

'What in Aine's name is that?' Adelina gasped as she put up shaking hands to her aching ears.

'Never you mind, just get on!' Luther pushed her through the open gate and she jumped as Gallivant appeared at her side.

'Don't worry! He can't see or hear me. Listen... you have just heard Huon's Horn. Your accursed gaoler has just called forth the minions of Hell! Go to your room quickly and I shall be with you anon.'

At that he melted into the shrubbery surrounding the manor walls and Adelina hurried indoors ahead of Luther. She ran from him to her room and went to push the door shut but his foot and then his shoulder slid into the opening. 'My mistress leaves for business today, woman. She will visit you before she goes but remember this – I am in charge and any move you make that displeases me, then I shall be about you so quickly you will beg for mercy. I am less understanding than my Lady.' He brushed a dirty finger down her cheek and let it linger on her pale lips. 'We could be friends...'

Adelina wanted to bite the finger, chomp down through the bone and sinew to sever it from the murderous hand but she heard Severine on the stair and Luther wisely withdrew. The echoes of the horn were fading as she made an entrance, flinging the whip-thin body into a leather-slung chair. 'I'm going away for a few days and I demand the robe be finished while I am gone. When I return I shall have the souls and then we are done, are we not?' She jumped up again and began to pace, her manner edgy and sharp.

Her voice had gloated as she mentioned the souls and Adelina's heart sank. *Has she found Lhiannon, is it that which fills the* bitseach *with brash confidence? I can't stand her! I can't stand the thought that she might win after all she has done!* 'So you think calling Huon will find the girl for you? On my honour Severine, you are pathetic! I fear she's more wily than to allow herself to be caught by some antlered hellhound.'

Severine bent her head over one of Adelina's hoops of embroidered insect wings that lay on the side-table, replying with sang-froid. 'Well well, you know the sound of Huon's horn, do you?' She swung round quickly, and sank her nails into Adelina's arm. 'Let me tell you, stitcher, my Ravens sniffed out the chit on the western seas. They flew across a little dory and the smell of Færan was tangible. The storm Huon will unleash will toss every being on every boat, mortal or Other, into the briny and the Færan chit will be left floating in the sea and he will find her. He and the Hunt will scour every shoreline and as each tide deposits body after body they will find her, alive or dead, and I shall have my souls. So don't worry about anything, just stitch. And don't forget your nag. His life depends on you, I will kill him if I have to.'

'Oh, I am sure you would, Severine.' Adelina pulled her shoulders back, her tone caustic. 'I am sure you would. Tell me, indulge me for a brief moment, how did you, a mundane mortal, get Huon's horn?'

Severine raised her eyebrows. 'Mundane, you think!' She laughed the crystal laugh. 'Adelina, all your life,' she leaned so close to her prisoner, the embroiderer was able smell cloves and wine on her breath, 'you have underestimated me. Be afraid woman, I am so much stronger than you could ever imagine!' She whispered this last as close to Adelina's ear as she could get and the embroiderer felt chills shiver all the way down her backbone as the woman's warm breath slid past her earlobe. But as quickly as she had invaded Adelina's space, Severine moved away. 'But... the Horn. I have an Other working for me and he stole it! As easy as that! Just sneaked into Huon's lair and pilfered it and now it's mine!' She stood before Adelina and reached forward and fondled a hank of the tawny hair. 'I am a changeling as you have told me so often and I have a destiny!' She tugged hard at the hair in her hands, bringing tears to Adelina's eyes. 'You know it.' She pulled again. 'Don't you?'

Adelina heard the first rattle of distant thunder from the Styx and thought of all those who were now under threat because of a bag containing two souls. She jerked her throbbing head away from the cruel hands and turned bitterly to the robe. 'I can finish the garment in a few days.' She stared at it as it swung in the atmosphere of the room. A last beam of sun alighted on the tiny figure of Aladdin and his face seemed to smile and say, *be heartened, all is not as it seems.* 'But I need one thing to complete my work. I need a charm, a little gold lamp to put in Aladdin's hand. Then it will all be as you want.'

'A charm you say? I have a box load of gold oddments my husband gave me with the idea I should have a bracelet made but I could not abide the jangle. I shall get Luther to bring them.' Severine turned an eye on the embroiderer. 'Are you sure you are well? No stinging rejoinder about my minions or my ambitions? I think your spark has gone.' She laughed unkindly as she walked to the door.

'No Severine, my spark still glows as red as ever. I am disgusted with all that you do and if I could stop you I would. As it is I can only protect my

Ajax by finishing the robe. That is all I shall say. I do this for Ajax, not for you.' Adelina turned her back deliberately on Severine, abhorrence in her rigid shoulders, and walked to the window.

Countess di Accia leaned against the door as Luther locked it.

'Go to my jewellry box, Luther. In it you will find a smaller box filled with gold charms. Bring them to Adelina immediately.' Her face twisted as she walked away. 'Oh another thing. Kill the horse.'

You must find more books with speed for I have so much more to detail. Come quickly! I find that the sense of urgency that seemed lacking in me earlier, that depressed lassitude and loss of purpose has disappeared to be replaced by a frenetic need. Severine, the bitch, has rubbed my back so powerfully up the wrong way that I see I must be strong and wily to survive. Somehow, somehow so help me, I must outwit her!

So seek the chequerboard-patterned frittilaria with its strappy green leaves and the bronze scarab beetle underneath. You will see a bud, a part opened flower and then a fully opened flowerhead with a most unnatural pattern like the squares on a shatranj board.

Find the fully opened flower and reach up inside the petals and you will discover a journal the colour of the stamens – not very thick for it would have distorted the flower and been obvious, but it is thick enough for my needs.

Then lift the elytra of the beetle as you have done before and there too will be another book.

Read on...

CHAPTER NINE

'Kill the horse!' Luther stalked along the passage with a small box in his hand. 'Kill the flaming horse. By the soul of Behir, the woman is mad!'

He unlocked Adelina's door and entered, dazzled by the woman's tawny glow as she bent her head over some hoop of damned silk embroidery. Hell she was a piece, he wanted her so badly. 'This is what milady wanted you to have.' He threw the small box at Adelina and left before the ache in his groin became uncontrollable. He ran down the stairs, stopping only to grab the harquebus and walked toward the paddock where Ajax shepherded the mares. They stood under the oak tree stamping their hooves and laying ears flat as the sound of the thunder reached them.

Ajax threw up his head, ears back, eyes wide, nostrils flared as he moved apart from the mares, snaking his head at the oncoming figure. Small half rears showed a fighting spirit – Luther liked that.

He stood for a moment and looked at the horse and thought what a pity Severine was so filled with the desire to hurt the stitcher that she couldn't realise the value of the beast. He lifted the harquebus and aimed to strike the horse on that exact spot above the eyes and in the centre of the forehead and took a steadying breath.

Ajax reared high, the air filled with a shrieking battle cry from horse to man. The sight of the massive body pawing the air was an epiphany for the thug who lost no sleep over a garotte slicing a throat. He could sell this horse in Veniche for so much gelt!

He lowered the harquebus.

The animal rolled his eyes and pranced a few steps, crest arched, the thick tail held high. Luther mused in admiration at the strong back, broad enough to be the unseelie Cabyll Ushtey, as Ajax stepped away giving fiery bucks and blowing wildly down his nose.

Luther rarely dithered. Now a sneaking lust for money warred with his loyalty to Madame. His fingers played with the harquebus trigger and he weighed the weapon as if it were the pros and cons of his dilemma. Checking over his shoulder to ascertain how much could be observed from the manor and realising he was concealed, he took a lanyard from his belt. Ajax stilled, his nervous ears cocked, his wither trembling. Murmuring gruff platitudes Luther walked closer and his hand slid around the thick neck to fasten the lanyard firmly enough to lead the beast. Ajax pulled back but a quick jerk of the tether and a hissing 'gid up' had him following unhappily after Luther.

They left the paddock by the far gate and traipsed through a copse to an old barn on the edge of the woods where Luther flung the bars across the gate. The thunder rumbled closer and the sky darkened, ragged sheets of lightning flashing in the distance. He thrust hay in the corner and thought he would organise one of the smuggler lads who owed him a favour to take the beast to one of the horse-markets. Madame would be none the wiser and he would be groats richer. He snorted and ran back the way he had come in order to beat the storm because beating the odds was always the best and better still, he had the house to himself and by Behir he would run it his own dark way.

Darkness appealed to him, a child bully who had tormented the weak, torturing cats and dogs and any less vulnerable than himself. As he grew older, brutality opened doors that to a rough, ill-made individual would have remained closed. Once one door opened, others followed. In time naturally, Severine opened her door to him and together they achieved much.

She made him wealthy when he'd been poor. By working within the Di Accia house he found status and in carrying out her crimes he secured a sexual gratification the like of which only existed in the truly debauched. It made him as content as he could be.

Until Adelina entered his life.

Now all his lusts centered on her. Willingly or no, by the time Madame returned he would have split the woman's thighs apart and taken the treasure he wanted.

Adelina was opening the small black suede box when Gallivant appeared by the wall. She looked up startled. 'Oh. It's you!'

'Yes, can you not be a little more excited?'

This was said to an accompaniment of thunder and lighting, the room brightly lit and just as quickly plunged into murk. She thrust the box on the table amongst a tangle of silk fabric and thread and hastily walked around the room lighting lamps and pulling the window shut. 'I hate thunderstorms! They make me edgy and give me a foul headache. Besides I can't shake the thought of all those who may lose their lives as Huon hunts. All for Severine! Gallivant, she says she's found Lhiannon! I HATE HER!'

'Tush! Never you worry. Many of we eldritch types detest Huon and will contrive to spoil his game. No one will be hurt, I swear. As to Lhiannon, she's Other, don't give up yet. Anyway, we've other things to plan. Your escape for one.'

She responded under her breath, a tiny snort, and continued to work sorting thread.

'You surprise me, Adelina.' Gallivant spoke with pointed irony as he watched her lose herself in a kaleidoscope of hot, angry colours. 'You seem to accept your situation with more equanimity than any other mortal I have known. You sit here daily – stitching, sorting your threads and taking walks in a pleasant garden.'

She said nothing but her hands had reached for a hank of threads and she began to unroll them, her fingers trying to tease apart fiery reds, acid yellows, bright oranges. She pulled and yanked and began to wind them jerkily onto a holder. As she came across knots, she would pick up her scissors, cut with one stroke and then throw the blades down on the table with a clatter until she came across a huge tangle. Unable to separate the silk yarn, she grabbed for the scissors, dropped them and then lobbed everything on the table. She threw back her chair and stood leaning over the table, hissing. 'Equanimity! EQUANIMITY! I have felt myself slipping down the slope to madness as I deal with grief, murder, assault and rape. And ANGER! ANGER THAT MAKES ME WANT TO JUMP OUT THAT WINDOW AND END IT ALL BECAUSE I DON'T KNOW WHAT TO MAKE OF IT!'

Gallivant rushed across to her. 'Hush, hush! I'm here now. I can help you. It's what we Goodfellows do. We can solve this, I swear.'

Adelina looked at him, tears beginning to trickle. He smiled and put his arm across her shoulder to pull her to him. And because it was the first kind touch, the first understanding she had experienced since Lhiannon had gone, she felt the throttling vein in her heart shrink slightly and she cried even more.

'My dear little needlewoman, it's time we put some plans in place as you don't need to stay here any longer.'

'But how? The doors and gates are locked. Even if I should manage the impossible, Luther is always close by. There is Huon, the Ravens, huh, I would be easy game.' Adelina took a soft linen kerchief and wiped her tears, her eyes red-rimmed and overbright as she felt on the brink of another watery bout.

She busied her hands with the mess on the table, throwing the knotted threads into the fire and folding the silken cloth. Despite her distrait, she took inordinate care with the hoops of insects and flowers, the components of the last part of the robe – like an artist who washes his brushes with tenderness, to place them in a jug safe from harm's way but where they will be ready for the next onslaught on the artistic piece.

Thunder and lightning crashed about outside and she dispiritedly took up Severine's box as it was revealed under a scrap of fabric. The middle of the black suede lid opened with a tiny gold hook and stud to fold back and reveal its contents lying on white satin lining. 'I am now at my most vulnerable,' she spoke in defeated tones as she tipped the pile of delicate charms onto her lap with a jingle that could hardly be heard over the growl and grumble outside. 'Severine has left me here in the charge of Luther and he has made no bones about his intentions. He touched me intimately and I have a fear Severine wouldn't care if he has his way, in fact I think she would find it amusing to have me so debased. At the risk of being indelicate, the last man I slept with was the love of my life who is now dead. To have that despoiled, that sensation which I can even now recall,' she began to cry again. 'To have that expunged by the rutting of that brute, I would honestly slit my wrists!'

Gallivant had pulled a coffer next to her and grabbed the kerchief to wipe at the tears. 'There's absolutely no need for such action. He can't harm you while I'm here. I'll be your armed chaperone!' At this Adelina cocked an eyebrow, even in tears. He tapped her arm in his fey way. 'Just because I don't carry a weapon, it doesn't mean I can't be fearsome. Did you forget I'm Other? Now let's look at these little oddments.'

The charms were beautiful – a tiny cuckoo clock with working weights and chains, a diminutive beer mug with chaste patterns and an opening lid, a petite pair of working scissors, a bijou cottage with a door that opened and many more. Oh, a minute Travellers' van! Adelina sucked in her breath... so many memories! And look! A small Raji oil lamp of the kind Aladdin would be sure to have held.

Gallivant had been watching her, all the time puzzling how he could remove her from the room. One would think it would be easy for an Other, a mere question of a spell, mesmering her far away. But no, it was much more difficult because he couldn't manage such large-scale glamarye. Somehow he must mesmer the keys and get Adelina to the stable and the horses. But she would have to leave the robe and all her possessions behind. He shifted on the coffer. 'Adelina, what did you plan as your retribution? How were you planning to avenge Liam and Kholi?'

She looked up from examining the lamp. 'On the good days I hoped to somehow take her prisoner, deliver her to the Courts of Veniche for judgement.' Her face had the bleakest expression and the thunder continued outside, a grim accompaniment to her base words. 'But on the bad days, the mad days which far outnumber anything else, I have visited every kind of rough justice on her that I know. It's usually bloody and painful and as I think on it, my soul shrinks to a pinhead and I might as well be dead myself! Gallivant, I'm a Traveller, we're kind folk, we sew. We do not kill and nor are we ever brutal!' Panic slid across her face as once more he saw her teeter on the balance.

'Hush now, hush.' He brushed her arm and stood to wipe a warm hand over the creased forehead, the gentle mesmer a form of calming. 'What have you there, is it what you need?'

She glanced down at the tiny lamp lying in her palm. 'Yes, yes it's just what I need. A little polish to lift the tarnish and I can sew it on.'

CHAPTER TEN

Dawn came early at sea. Phelim turned the dory slightly and the swift southerly scooped it up on wings and progressed it a goodly distance by the time Adelina had been taken to the garden. Far out to sea, the sailor passed Polcarrow, Zennor, Porthcawl and Mevagavinney, blithely unaware the Ravens of Mimring had spied to Severine's satisfaction, smelling only Færan, the true identity of the individual mattering little.

The boat skimmed the surface as if it flew. Dolphins and flying fish kept pace and muttonbirds flew in mighty flocks, colouring the sea grey with their shadow. Phelim was coiling extra ropes neatly on the floor of the boat when he heard the faintest grumble. He hoisted himself up on the stern seat, an arm over the tiller and concentrated his gaze on the starboard horizon.

On the coast, storm clouds swirled in an ugly tower. Grey and black rolls layered upwards into the cumulus that indicated a storm of unseelie proportions. Above the swish and sweep of wave and the singing of the southerly in the shrouds of the dory, thunder rumbled from the Styx, Huon's lair. Phelim's heartbeat quickened. *The Wild Hunt! I have been marked. They know what I am and what I carry.*

He looked to the sails as they began to rattle and flap and hauled harder on the sheets, pulling the sails tighter, turning the boat a little more to try and catch the wind that had begun to die behind him. He cursed in unbidden Færan. *The wind drops out!*

The boat began to lollop. The sails flapped and the boom swung dangerously. Checking the east again, Phelim could see a faint dark line on the ocean and guessed that a weather change was about to overhaul with eldritch speed. With equal speed, a feeling of gross impending doom settled in his stomach, sparking a surge of urgency.

He grabbed the oar and paddled as hard as he could on the starboard side and then pushed and pulled at the tiller trying to turn the boat away from the oncoming windstorm. If it hit broadside he was finished – thus the mortal inside him reasoned as he struggled to shift the boat. The sails had begun to crackle crisply as the forerunner to the gale licked at them but Phelim let them out a little more and the tickle of the wind flipped the boat with a snap so it was now facing hard west and the storm would hit dead astern. But he caught himself in mid mortal thought and spoke aloud with disgust. 'But I am Færan, unless it's my bane I can't die!'

Never cowardly or beaten by obstacles, he jammed his knitted cap down harder over his ears, grasping the tiller and grabbing for the main sheet. Behind him on the shores of Trevallyn, thunder vibrated and a deep black rain band could be seen thrashing the coastline. As the wind hit the sail and filled it with a sharp, ear-splitting crack, the lightning flashed to his rear and a massive swell began to undulate across the ocean. The dory sliced through the water and the wave-cap flew, drenching him and flooding the insides of the boat. He reached down between his feet to the stern and pulled at the cork bung and it floated free on its fragile string to lie in the bilge creating a self-emptying drain as the dory made swift passage. Sure enough, the water disappeared out the back but only to be replaced by more and then more still.

Galeforce winds kicked the waves to threatening heights. If Huon didn't catch him, he would be blown so far to the west it would take a lifetime to return to the sea-lanes that could get him to Veniche. *Oh Ebba, if you have a prayer for me, send it now.* He fixed his grasp tighter on the helm.

In Mevagavinney, the storm beat at its violent peak. Lightning lit the harbour with ferocious strobes and thunder rattled the glass in window frames. Plates and goblets fell off shelves and people taking sanctuary behind locked doors could hear slate tiles crashing off roofs onto the ground as a tumultuous wind swept destruction before it. Had they looked out of the windows instead of cowering by the cold hearths, they would have seen twisted grotesque shapes: horns and antlers and arms wielding cracking whips. Then again, it could have been the stripped branches of the oaks, the elms and the willows flying and distorting. Eyes closed and fists grasped talismans and made the protective horn sign so who could tell?

Adelina perhaps? Hearing the sound of bestial baying and feeling goosebumps rise on her skin, she threw the little charm on the table and rushed to the window. Gallivant stood behind her, his hand resting at her elbow. 'It's an evil day, Stitchlady, an evil day. For there he goes, the antlered one, with the Hunt.'

Adelina stared at the sight sweeping across the darkened sky in the scuds of the tormenting wind: the antlers and the muscled torso astride a mount which pawed the air as it reared, the cracking whip and the baying dogs all an intrinsic part of that thunderous blow. 'Aine help Lhiannon, Gallivant!' It was less than a whisper.

In the woods behind Mevagavinney, the horse with the back as broad as the unseelie Cabyll Ushtey had added his frantic shrieks to those of the Hunt and the wind. Nobody heard the frightened animal, the one who feigned bravery but who found heights and other things sometimes just too much to bear. Calling for his precious Adelina, he received no response. Fear endemic to the horse, ever the hunted and never the hunter, spread through his body. Like Ana light years ago, the thought was the same: fight or flight? He charged at the yard fence as thunder and lightening exploded all around. Lifting his great body, he half jumped, half crashed through the post and rail timber. And as he attempted to put distance between he and the storm by fleeing northerly, a massive flap of flesh hung from his shoulder where it had been ripped, the muscles and ligaments torn and pouring blood. He pecked in his stride, regained his footing and galloped blindly on.

As Hurle's Ride spread terror across the sky, I cursed at the risk Lhiannon had taken in even knowing me. Sometimes I wonder if in an instant, I had selfishly

placed her in the space left by Ana. By force of circumstance, by my loneliness and desperation, I viewed her as my sister-friend on this tormented journey, not just some stranger who passed through my life.

I can tell you, I don't want her to be a stranger that passes through. Ana passed through and the pain of her passing was terrible. Is that what will happen to Lhiannon?

Now I think on it, all who have entered my life and whom I have had affection for, even loved, have gone. Ana, Liam, my Kholi. And I couldn't bear for it to happen again. Not another one. It makes me terrified to make new friends, to open my heart to them. Perhaps I am a poison, a blight... a bane.

Should I allow the hob into my life or shouldn't I?

Is Gallivant at risk by knowing me?

It is important you see the way my mind works.

CHAPTER ELEVEN

The terrible chase scattered foam and wave before it. At the centre of the swirling cloud mass, at the hub from whence came deafening thunder and crashing lightning, at the source of the gigantic swell that battered the little boat, Huon the Hunter galloped through the skies.

Phelim sailed with mortal desperation and that which was Færan was subsumed by twenty-eight years of living as Ebba had raised him. The mainsail had shredded to ribbons and all he could do was hold onto the tiller as hard as possible to keep the wind behind. He had laid out most of his ropes in lines at the stern to anchor the vessel to the swell to prevent it yawing. But the waves threatened the craft – mountainous peaks which the doughty boat climbed to view the ocean ahead as if from the top of Mount Goti and then a slippery slide to the trough where to look up at what was coming was to face death and damnation.

But crashing now upon him, breaking like a wave from above, was the realization he must let his Færan instinct guide him, open himself up to it, allow it to take hold, quash anything mortal. For it was Other against Other and he would not be beaten. The tiller ripped in his hands and he yanked with all his strength as the waves conspired to turn the dory broadside and as he pulled, his eyes, wet and stinging, opened wide.

Looming out of the rain and spray, dark and huge as the waves, was a landmass threatening to smash him against its rocky shores. Waves hit its northern end, crashing the length of shore as if the landmass itself was sliding broadside to the storm. *It's moving! The land is moving.* Phelim almost lost hold of the tiller. *What is it?* His mind reeled until he remembered another of Ebba's mysterious revelations from his childhood.

Hy-Breasil! The Sacred Isles, the twin islets! His Færan mind working fast, he reached for a gaff hook from the watery morass in the bottom of the boat and wafted a hand over the helm, the tiller growing, unfurling like the branches of the strongest tree to fix in position and free Phelim's hands for other life-saving tasks.

Tying a rope to the shaft of the gaff, he hefted the whole to his shoulder, mesmering the weapon and swinging back and then forward to loose it like the athletes from the ancient legends. He lost sight of it as the boat sped down into the trough of the wave but knew by the rope's slack that his glamarye was weak. He dragged it in as furiously fast as the storm swell would allow.

The boat wallowed in the trough momentarily and then climbed again. At the peak, Phelim spied the landfall with a black hole yawning like a mouth opened wide, and he aimed again. The gaff flew, the rope trailing behind, along with a vehement mesmer. Just as the dory began to slide down the slope, the boat gave a slight tug and Phelim whooped and started to pull. He continued to drag and felt the vessel turn slightly to nudge diagonally across the waves in pursuit of its anchorage. Faster he pulled, using every bit of his strength.

Huon roared as he observed his prey slicing away from his grasp but Phelim, arm over arm, hardly dared face his nemesis. The distance between the boat, Hy-Breasil and what was patently a cave narrowed. That entrance, the door to safety, lay on the southern tip of the island and as the rope grew shorter, Phelim noticed the twin isle slipping back behind its partner, so that his own craft would have to slide between the two. A glance over his aching shoulder revealed Huon within striking distance, the hounds filling the sky deafeningly with their baying, the whip snaking forward to grab the mast.

Phelim could smell the dank air of the cave, as breath after exhausted breath, ribs aching, chest and arms pumping beyond any sort of mortal endurance, the rope shortened. In seconds, the bow touched the cave entrance.

Huon and the hounds flung themselves after him, faster than the wind and waves. Unintelligible yowls of frustration vied with the crack of thunder and a whip snaked out, wrapping its pliant length around the mast like a basilisk coiling around its prey, the plaited whiplash stretching taut as the dory was flung inside the cave by a wave surge. The twin island shifted fast towards the rocky entrance, slamming viciously against the cliff walls – breaking the whip leather, sealing the entrance of the cave and flattening the few of those red-eyed hounds who had tried to enter the sacred confines behind the dory as clods of dirt, shards of stone and pieces of seaweed fell into the boat.

Waves smacked noisily against the walls, back and forth. Of Huon and the Hunt there was no sign. With each run across the cave, the undulations lessened until they whispered. Phelim collapsed to the seat breathing harshly, his head hanging in his blistered and raw hands. *So that is how it is done? One mesmers in anger?* But there was no answer to his confusion. All he could sense was moist darkness and wondered tiredly if he had merely exchanged one danger for another.

Don't sit like Phelim, I haven't time for you to rest! You must hasten on to the next books for there is yet more of this story. Phelim begins to discover another side to himself and I, perhaps I am yet to discover an alternate side to my own. It scares me, I feel as if I stand on the edge of some phantom crevass, one step in one direction to safety, the other way to doom.

You will notice that I have placed a red-shaded dragonfly high on the centre back seam, between the shoulder blades. If you very gently ease the organza wings up you will find a flimsy tissue pamhlet there. And there are six other dragonflies: remember I told you I had designed seven stumpwork models of the real thing? With each of the dragonflies, you will find a similar leaflet. Read them in the exact order of the colours of the spectrum. Order is implicit in the revelation of this story, simply the difference between life and death. You shall see!

CHAPTER TWELVE

Severine had ridden out from Mevagavinney just before the storm had hurtled across the fishing village. The house she left was in order, the embroiderer quiet. Luther was more than capable of handling anything untoward.

Her fingers tightened on the reins as she dragged her horse to a stop at the edge of the Styx, close by Huon's Tor. Her ice-floe eyes sought the streaming pack of hounds far over the ocean, the howling intrinsic to the gale's roar. Her hair escaped from its net cawl in the slipstream wafting behind the unseelie horde and her skin rose in excited bumps in the crackling atmosphere. Her mare danced fractiously, unnerved, feeling the rider's excessive arousal. It gave a half rear and Severine laughed as she whacked the mare on the neck with her whip.

Yes! The beauty of it all was that *this*, this dominion over beasts like Huon or the Ravens was what she was due and more after the years of patiently searching and learning. She turned the mare toward the darkling forest, its shadows undelineated in the blackness of that awful afternoon. *Oh I am due! I invested my life in searching for those dreams. I was undaunted by the sheer heights I was forced to climb. I know they say the depths I plumbed, but so what, the end result is the same so how does the method matter? I have dominion! I have the four shreds of washi paper with their spider scrawls of lore and I have dominion! And when I have that Færan chit, that bitch with my souls, then I can tread the final steps to greatness. Is it not the apogee of greatness to be immortal?*

Severine's mind began to quicken. *But then I must find the Gates to Færan, for what is the point of everlasting life if one must surround one's self with ugliness?* She thought of the cobweb man towards whom she now sped and of Luther. *Dispose of them, for they are not lovely and shall despoil my domain, and it* shall *be my domain to do with what I will!*

She felt no guilt or wracked emotions at the thought of ridding herself of those on whose backs and shoulders she had climbed to reach such heady heights. Why keep something one no longer needs? Ugly clutter is unseemly and the sheer awfulness of Luther and the cobwebman had no place in the life she envisaged. Færan lured her with its beauteous bait and she belonged there, more than the tawdry world of mortals.

She had a hunting lodge in the Styx: a secret place built of interlocking wooden beams and draped and covered by ivy and wild clematis. It was lost in amongst the tall timbers, so easy to pass by. Her cobweb man lived there occasionally – when she had cause for him to be close. He manifested from as far as Veniche or further just by a certain call she must make, the rubbing together of coins, but such are goblins, obsessed with gold, silver, gems of all sorts. What they did with it she didn't know or care. But glittering stuff to them was like air to a mortal. *Ah, wouldn't he love Færan!* She had heard the old wives' tales that even a witch wouldn't allow a goblin by the fireside so disreputable were they – prone to nightmare weaving and luck-spoiling. But she had never had a nightmare in her dealings with the goblin and in truth her luck improved by the hour, for was it not fortuitous she had found the Færan charms? Nothing, not a thing, was beyond her reach.

She slowed her chestnut mare to a trot as she eased along a forest defile. At a blackened stump, she turned into another lesser-marked track and presently entered a glade lit by the weak sun that had followed on the thunderstorm's heels. A grey trow came forward to take the horse's reins and led the animal off to a small barn behind the lodge.

Severine strode through the door and flung her whip on a table in the room. It was an unassuming place of mellow timber with antlers clinging to walls, horns and walking sticks by the door and a vast fireplace. The large room housed a stair that led to the floor above and a ground floor passage hastened hungry feet to the kitchen.

She slammed the door behind her and within seconds the cobweb man had sidled down the stair to meet his mistress, the woman who controlled him by the expedient of greed for gems and precious metals that worked on him like the worst possible addiction.

'Madame', he mouthed, his unctuous hands folding over and over as if forever washing them. Sly downcast eyes examined the floor and his odd brown robes fluttered and waved like the torn filaments a spider leaves behind when it quits its web. His wrinkled face had more to do with the kind of unseelie life he led than his age, for when Severine left him to his own devices, he would track unwary mortals and without the necessary greasing of palms with groats and gelt, he would indeed whisper nightmares that could send a man mad or cause luck to change.

'Ah Gertus, you are here.' She had no urge to address his face, merely walked round the room straightening things, picking up objects. 'Huon is even now fetching the souls. But this you have no doubt surmised.'

The goblin nodded his head, his expression obsequious.

'So... I want the locations we have talked of. Show me what you have found.'

The hand washing became frenetic. He licked his lips and shifted from one foot to another, a lock of greasy hair falling from behind his ears. 'Madame, I have spent days and nights examining the lore and travelling hither and yon. Hours and days.'

'And?' The single word cracked into the air.

'Madame, I found a series of clues that contain neither word nor map. They were much deeper in that same crevass where we found the ring and the washi cantrips.' He giggled, a sycophantic weak chunter. 'The Færan thought to hide their lore for posterity when they buried it in the Abyss but the earth will always spew out what it doesn't want, goblins know this better than anyone. I found this,' he pulled a small box from deep within the folds of the cobwebs. 'It was under the mouldering body of a Raji trader who had gone wide of the Stairway and fallen to his doom, deep deep, so deep.'

'Yes, yes!' Severine grabbed it in her long fingers and turned it over, looking for the opening. 'How does one open the thing?'

'A word, milady, a word.' He folded his hands and stared at the woman who would be immortal and whose patience snapped with one exclamation.

'AND?'

'*Oscailt amach!*' His gutteral voice shook as he cowered in front of her, the box in her hands flipping up its lid. She took it to the window to examine the contents, Gertus staying well back, cogniscent that sunlight is the bane of all goblins.

'What in damnation is this?' She pulled each object out and slammed it on the table, underlined by her livid words. 'A stone from a fruit... a grey stone... a brown stone... a yellow stone! What? Someone's pathetic mineral collection mixed up with the detritus of their lunch? What use is this, what use?' She threw the pebbles to the floor. 'I want specifics Gertus, and I want them before I leave! You have tonight only. I want to know where the Gates are by tomorrow morning.' She swept up the stair, her hunting coat rustling as it streamed behind her, the goblin wincing as her chamber door slammed.

His wrinkled brow produced a new array of folds and sweat began to bead. He had read everything he could find and could not interpret the pebbles. So well protected were the Gates by the Færan, he had never heard a whisper of where they could be. Never. No one, mortal or Other, had ever been able to find or penetrate their retreat. But the answer lay in the stones, of that he was sure and he had no intention of failing in this task. Too much to lose and everything to gain, he thought, fondling one of Severine's shiny geegaws in his pocket. Picking the stones up and replacing the lid of the box, he crept to his room.

CHAPTER THIRTEEN

'It must be close to dinner. My belly burbles.' The hob pulled his feet down from where he had them propped on the window-seat. He had sat patiently stitching the last couple of hours, Adelina having been encouraged to teach him how to embroider berries. Now he had accomplished it with some relative success, he had a desire to make a vest. Adelina didn't feel like quelling his enthusiasm because in fact he was quite proficient... for a male.

'I'm not hungry.' She bent over the fritillary leaf she had applied to the gown. It wouldn't bend properly over itself and she risked losing the firm shape of the wire if she fiddled much more.

'Well milady and how stupid would it be not to eat everything laid before you? You need to keep up your strength.' Gallivant placed his small hoop on the table with pride, waiting for Adelina to comment. She glanced up.

'It *is* good for a first effort.' Compared to Ana, she thought, who was quite brilliant, who *had* been quite brilliant. 'No, I don't want to eat because Luther brings the food to my room and I don't want him to have any excuse to come near me.'

'Pah! Don't be a ninny! I can sort that out, never you mind.' Gallivant was in one of the brash moods Adelina felt so typified his Otherwordliness. Reality was surely only something he grasped on the rare occasion. As he spoke, as if to underline Adelina's thoughts on his usefulness or otherwise, the door rattled as the key was turned and Luther entered, bearing a tray.

Adelina froze. The brute's expression was unreadable but he had washed and used some sort of woody fragrance and his clothes were fresh. Her heart sank.

'Well then, embroiderer. I had cook send up some smoked salmon and a potato salad with capers and she has given you some fresh baked bread and butter. And she made you a Queen Pudding and used some raspberry jam under the meringue she said to tell you.' He kept up the gravelly patter as he put the tray down and laid out the food. Gallivant, invisible, noticed the ruddy flush on the fellow's neck and wisely deduced the potential for trouble. 'I brought you up a bottle of Madame's finest wine which I thought we could share, yes? A glass for you and a glass for me?' He busied himself with the cork, using an ugly knife from his belt.

Adelina, her heart pounding, eased herself from the table and edged away. Closer to the open door and closer. One more step... and she was through! She ran down the curling stair.

She heard the curse behind. Curving round and round until she got to the bottom, to the massive cedar door which led to the garden that she had forgotten was walled, enclosed, surrounded. She pulled on the latch and shook it and pulled again, hearing Luther's steps slowing, realising she was trapped and had nowhere to go. He rounded the corner, his face blotched with anger.

'*Bitseach!*' He grabbed her arms. He twisted one up her back so that her shoulder and elbow wrenched painfully. 'Here I was trying to be pleasant, trying to do something nice for you and you repay me by running out on me. Adelina, that's just not acceptable!' As he articulated the last word, he yanked her arm brutally further up her back and pushed her ahead of him back up to her room – her room which seemed empty of Gallivant, her room where the wretched robe lay across the table, mocking and teasing. She felt such rage and fear, all melded together in a sticky morass from which she could separate neither one from the other.

Luther kept pushing her past the table toward her bed and seeing her situation for what it was she allowed the morass to bubble over. She began to fight and kicked back hard, missing Luther's groin by inches and dragging her fingernail down his cheek to rip it open and lay it bare, gore dripping.

'Bloody *BITSEACH*!' He jerked her body hard and naked lust and excitement at her rebellion rippled across his face as he threw her onto the bed. He licked his lips with a red, wet tongue, grabbing her flailing hands with one giant maw of his own and twisting them above her head, his heavy body pressing her into the covers.

Gallivant had been behind the door and had crept forward as Adelina fell back on the bed. He had debated what he could do as she ran down the stairs, knowing his skills were to create mischief not mayhem. But he had been entrusted as a companion to the mortal. 'Sink me,' he sighed petulantly.

He passed his hand across his front in the universal method of mesmer, focusing all his attention on Adelina, knowing he must get Luther away, get her safely out of his clutches. Besides, he had a feeling...

A churning began in Adelina's belly, a burning ascending to her gullet and just as Luther brought his lips to her frantic face, she vomited – a stream of all that was old and foul-smelling of her breakfast and lunch launched itself over his face and clothes. He shrieked and jumped away as Adelina sat up and continued to vomit and retch, the room filling with the sour smell. 'Aagh! Gah! You foul little whore! What is *wrong* with you?'

But Adelina had no answer and continued to retch until the tears streamed down her stained face and she thought her insides would become outsides. Luther hurried to the door.

'You! You'll pay for this! By Behir!' He glanced down at his clothes, trying to stop retching at the smell and then rushed from the room and dragged the door behind him. In the silence that followed, Adelina's gasps fading as the vomiting eased, she heard the lock turn and rolled over on her belly and began to cry.

'Well you could thank me!' Gallivant wafted his hand repeatedly as if to remove a particularly bad smell from under his nose. He grimaced.

Adelina lifted her head blearily. 'If this was *your* mesmer, *your* idea of saving me,' her head collapsed back down, 'then I am speechless.'

'Oh don't be so woebegone!' Gallivant waved his hand again and Adelina felt the nausea recede rapidly. More wafts and the room righted itself, a small fragrant whirlwind rushing over everything, cleansing, cleaning, refreshing. In minutes it was as if it hadn't happened. The lamps glowed and the room was again the plain prison for an embroiderer and her work. Outside, an owl hooted and the seabreeze wafted through the window.

'Why couldn't you have mesmered him instead of me and then we could have taken the keys while he was wretched and be gone?' Adelina tested her legs in case she should feel weak.

'Because as you discovered, we wouldn't have got very far. My skills are not,' he had the grace to dip his head and if Adelina had looked in the low lamplight, she would have observed an embarrassed blush spreading across the baby cheeks. 'They are not like Færan skills. I cannot do what they do. I'm a hob. I shape-change and create a little mischief and if I like someone, I can be a friend and help in what little way I can. I'm sorry I didn't perform to your expectations.'

'Gallivant, I'm sorry. I owe you such a debt. You stopped him,' she looked at him, her eyes swimming.

'All's well that ends well, because that's the thing you see, I have a feeling...'

He had a feeling.

He was a funny thing, Gallivant, different from the other of my strange acquaintances, like a babe learning his way. But he was good company, he had a way of making me laugh, was a cruel mimic and a good storyteller. And he was carrying out Lhiannon's orders to the best of his ability. He was keeping me company and in his own way, he was keeping me safe. If I had been a little less traumatised that night I would have pursued the issue of his 'feeling'. As it was, I jumped when I heard Luther's voice shouting there was a bucket, mop and hot water outside and finishing with a trail of threatening obscenities. I went to the door and reached out a hand. The thug covered his nose and mouth and looked away muttering 'take it, take the bloody stuff' *and beat a retreat, locking the door as he went.*

I turned to Gallivant but he had gone and so I climbed onto my bed and lay back, allowing thoughts of Kholi's love and affection to fill my mind, overflowing to every dark, damaged corner, to lull me to a deep, unbroken sleep – the first for many weeks.

CHAPTER FOURTEEN

Severine had taken a meal in her chamber at the hunting lodge and now sat in a rocking chair by the window, gazing out at the night-shrouded Styx Forest. The chair suited her mood. For someone who was always frenetic, always in agitated motion, this allowed Severine to sit, to be in motion and soothed all in one.

It was a graceful piece of furniture, for if Severine had anything worthwhile, she had an eye for good pieces to fill her houses. The chair came from a folk market in Trevallyn and suited the lodge, the timber mellow with age and the arms, seat and back lovingly upholstered in excellent canvas work: a tapestry of fruit and vegetables, no doubt stitched by a Traveller.

Her forehead creased as she pulled at the weave with one hand. In the other, she had a piece of silk and she took her agitated fingers away from smoothing the wool in the canvas work, to smooth out the silk. It was a tiny piece of Adelina's discarded embroidery. A pansy – inky violet and yellow with a leaf in emerald green. Crawling across the leaf was the ubiquitous ladybird and under the leaf, directly on the silk, a black money-spider sitting in a silver web. The work was perfect and yet Adelina had consigned it to the rubbish. Why? Severine knew the truth of her own embroidery skill, its ragged unevenness, its lack of finesse. So why would Adelina throw something this perfect away? Severine growled. What was it about the wretched woman that so disturbed her to the point of murder? Jealousy? She tipped her toes against the ground and set the chair gently rocking again, rejecting the idea of such an infantile emotion. Scrunching up Adelina's rubbish, she consigned it to the papier-maché bin beside her.

Next door, Gertus would be bent in a cobweb huddle over the stones, trying to decipher their meaning. She smiled the cold smile that never reached the grey orbs and barely reached the corners of her lips, lifting a crystal goblet to sip the gold wine inside.

She drifted on nostalgia, contentedly reviewing her thrilling ascent to this point. Not long after Gertus arrived in her life, she had fretted about the Count's disgustingly voracious need of her, as if the sexual act defined his manhood. Luther, her public manservant-private assassin, solved her problem. As she bemoaned the old man's compunctions one day, Luther gruffly offered a way out. That night, after giving the Count a warm glass of milk laced with enough Belladonna to stop an ox, Severine lay in bed listening to the old man's breathing becoming rasping, erratic. He clawed his way to her side of the bed and she jumped out to stand and watch him with ice-cold eyes. He knew. Oh he knew as every sinew, muscle and nerve screamed in his silent death-throes, that his wife was a murderer! His eyes stared back sightlessly in the end, and she waited for some measure of emotion to bite – guilt, horror, dismay, even sorrow. Instead, euphoria swept like a wave of applause through her body, affirming her dreams and the process that must secure those dreams. It hadn't hurt at all. She knew she could do it again.

Where did this vein of coldbloodedness come from? She shrugged her shoulders at the empty room. She didn't care except to thank the Fates she'd been blessed with such cool carelessness because it made everything easy. It also marked the massive difference between her and her confrères. Changling indeed!

So there she was. Wealthily widowed and with two servants literally worth their weight in gelt!

The evening Gertus happened into her life, not long before the old Count had 'died', she couldn't sleep. Slipping from the despised marital bed, she had wrapped herself in a silken shawl and crept quietly along the darkened corridor of their Veniche palazzo. In the moonlight filtering through elongated windows, dreary, equally elongated and bearded faces of be-decked ancestors peered down at her and white marble busts on carved plinths glimmered in the moonbeams slanting across the terrazzo floors. She was bare-foot and proceeded like a silent wraith to the library where were her favourite tomes. She was lured to the presence of stories on Others like those lured by the poppy.

But a queer glow stopped her in her tracks. Flitting about inside the doorway of the library, like the Teine-Sidhe, was a golden light. Severine's breath caught as she crept quietly to the door.

A strange figure slipped from one wall-hung picture to the next. Lifting them, looking underneath. Moving on. Then to boxes, lidded bowls and caskets. Opening, closing quietly. But becoming anxious. Swearing as each item held nothing – some quaint, gutteral language.

It's Other! Severine's heart jumped. He's a goblin looking for jewelry, gems, whatever! He approached the door and she slipped behind an arras, briefly laying her magnificent black pearl and diamond betrothal ring on the chiffonier where it caught the light of the moon and glimmered in a particularly eye-catching manner. She held her breath.

The goblin passed through the door into the beautifully decorated corridor and paused, his nose twitching as if sniffing a scent. Slowly his head turned and his eyes scanned the furniture against the walls. The diamonds winked and the pearl gleamed like dark satin. The goblin's breath gushed as his hand reached out.

Severine grabbed. Hands like iron cuffs fastened on the unfortunate's wrist and he shrieked. 'Be quiet and you shall have more.' Severine's urgent whisper cut through the cry like a wire through cheese, the word *'more'* filling the brain of the unseelie sprite.

'Like what?' His globular eyes narrowed.

'This?' Severine pulled the oval opal pendant, as pure as milk and filled with red and blue veins of fire, from the neck of her fine lawn nightgown. The diamonds surrounding the gem were a carat each and the goblin's eyes stretched. He reached his other hand to touch it.

'No! You work for me and I will pay you in gems and gold. No work, no touch.'

The goblin moved backward away from her, all the time eyeing her off, gauging the price of the passion. His hands wrung themselves over and over. 'As you say. A payment up front though.' He bent his head in a quasi obeisance.

'The ring?' Severine held the pearl and diamond geegaw out.

'Mistress,' he smiled the way a sycophant would, the wrinkled fingers closing over the ring. 'I am your humble servant.'

They had come so far together and now he was next door sliding not precious gems but arcane stones around under his fingers, trying to find the gates to what Severine perceived as her long lost home – the world of Færan. She rocked back and forth.

CHAPTER FIFTEEN

Wood knocked against wood, a dull sound but repetitive enough to wake the sleeper in the dory. Phelim raised his head from the stiff, blood-encrusted hands that had been his pillow. In the gloaming he glimpsed a jetty, a small construction the width of a man's shoulder. He rubbed his bleary eyes and lowered his head.

But wait! A jetty! Gloaming!

The dark cavern glowed with small blinking, flitting lights which beckoned to Phelim, enticing, leading away into darkness.

He warred with himself, wanting to sleep but knowing he should move. Every part of his body ached and placing a blistered hand to his head, grimaced as it came away smeared with blood. Feeling more carefully, he fingered a gash amongst his hair, three or four inches long. Immortal or not, he understood he must tend his injuries and rest and that a dank, dirty cave was not the place for such ministrations. The flickering lights waxed and waned and Phelim pulled himself tiredly out of the boat.

As he bent to grasp the line to moor the dory, it snaked out of its own accord and wrapped itself thrice round a pole and then looped under and over into an unslippable knot.

'Phelim, son of Ebba,' the irony echoed as he spoke aloud. 'This is *such* a voyage of discovery.' He stepped up the well-lit stair, the lights brightening as he approached and fading to darkness after he had passed. The broad stairs were cut into sandstone, the walls mellow in the light, and the air occasionally wafted a fragrance despite the dankness of the sea air – a promise of something.

He pushed a heavy studded door ajar and a soft breeze teased with the smell of meadow and brook. Dawn had broken and the light was as gilded as that of the cavern glimmerings, but wider, dusting everything and a riverbank lay ahead, clothed in thick grass and wildflowers. His confusion grew – that such a paradise should exist so close to the mayhem of oceans and storms. The waterway before him stretched in a broad swathe and was edged with the eddying branches of willow. He could hear Ebba's voice, another poetic verse designed to educate Phelim beyond the language of the farmyard so long ago.

'*Willows whiten, aspens quiver,*
Little breezes dusk and shiver
Through the wave that runs for ever
By the island in the river.' Ah Ebba, so apt he thought, for in the middle of the watery sward was such an island, covered from end to end in a forest of willow, aspen and beech.

From further along the banks a musical sound invited him on and he walked to a glade, close enough to the river to see and hear the chuntering of water over rock but far enough away for the meadow grass to be dry and pleasant to sit on. A feast had been laid out and Phelim looked for servitors but there were none. Despite his stomach churning with forboding, he took a wedge of cheese and bread between cautious fingers. Encouraged by the flavour he drank wine, finishing the meal by eating fresh apricots and figs, the like of which he had never before savoured. Lying back on the grass, he pillowed his head on a fallen log and sighed, concern momentarily abandoned.

Phelim of the Færan, he thought. He closed his eyes and the sun warmed him, the words '*of the Færan*' resonating through the soporific glow. Nothing he knew of the Færan could make him glad he was one except for the valour of the Færan girl, that fated lady of the souls. She had been exceptional, of that he was sure as he pieced together her journey with the fragments from Ebba's urisk. *But I am more mortal than Færan. I am! It's what I know, what I prefer. And I miss Ebba. More than I could possibly imagine.* The gentle silence of woods and water filled the surroundings and he found that he could forgive his stepmother and despite the agony of his displacement and subsequent confusion, that he loved her for her care and ultimately her honesty. But his equanimity lasted only a minute as he ran eyes over his surroundings.

Hy-Breasil – he had heard the fisherman talk of the Floating Isles but no one had ever returned to tell of actually being in such an enchanted place, for when did mortals ever return from the Other world with sanity enough to explain or discourse on anything, if they returned at all? Hy-Breasil was well known in legend, believed to be a sacred place in the Other world. Perhaps, he thought, it is an Other paradise where the souls of the departed come to everlasting peace and rest.

Then perhaps I am dead! Phelim's repast of earlier sank heavily in his belly. *But no, if I were dead and in such a place as this, then I think my purpose would leave me and I would rest in peace. I would not be deliberating the whys and wherefores of my situation.* He sat listening to the sounds of birds, the water and the breeze sighing through the trees and a slight niggle itched the former shepherd like fleas in a dog's coat.

What if the Isles are more sinister? What if I am stuck here and can never get off? He fingered the chamois bag. *If this is an Other Paradise, could I not just release them now? Why continue on a journey that promises to be fraught when I can just open the bag, go back to the dory and return the way I came.* He fiddled with the knot of the cord.

As if they read his thoughts, the souls and the bag chilled dramatically and he shivered. He pulled the cord over his head and thrust the bag beside him, preferring not to think on the contents for if he did anger would spew forth that he should be forced from his home in the pursuit of some sort of Fate for which he cared nothing.

Silence swallowed him and eventually he dozed in the warmth of the morning. Bees buzzed and butterflies flittered but there was no sign of any other like himself, man or woman. It was as if he and he alone was the only person on the Isles.

He woke an hour later and lay still as he oriented himself, watching the sky and clouds, glancing at the sun. How strange this place is, he thought as he sat up. No sign of a living soul, nor dead and yet I am served, but by whom? He tried to hold the thought and think on it, but a roaring of water in the river drew his attention.

The noise of rapids rushed from the upper bend and with spume and froth and the violent coughing of the river against the banks, an eddy shot downstream, rippling, swirling, sucking everything that floated into a vicious vortex. Bark, flowerheads, leaves, feathers, all spun frantically and then disappeared in the corkscrew of the whirlpool, leaving nothing behind. Having demolished all in its path, the unseelie current smoothed itself until the river was a calm swathe burbling through the meadows. He wondered if the island had its own way of speaking: *Phelim son of Ebba, cease this chitter-chatter! You are here. Let that be an end to it! Rest and enjoy what you are offered and do not offend.*

The cloying salt on his face and arms itched him and a swim on the river edges tempted him so he slipped down the riverbank, discarding his stiff clothes. His shoulders and hands throbbed with weals from the rope and on his cheek a deep gouge from the split tongue on the end of Huon's whip oozed blood, whilst the gash on his head had dried his hair in clotted lumps.

He waded into the river and allowed the now gentle eddies to wash over his naked, bruised body, unafraid of the secret currents in the deeper water, as he had been a strong swimmer from childhood. Thus he closed his eyes and the cool stream slipped past his skin like silk against flesh – seductive and erotic. When he eventually glanced upon his arms, he was unsurprised to see the scarring gone and slid a hand along the unblemished musculature of his shoulders. In the same way that he had been unperturbed when Lhiannon had 'vanished' her kayak, knowing deep within that such things were right and proper, so he expected such glamarye to manifest in this place. His cheek when he rubbed was scar-less but rough with a day's growth of whisker and his scalp as smooth and firm as it had been when he left home. He snorted softly and heard a low laugh.

'Strong powers, Ebba's Phelim.'

He dashed for the bank and flung on his breeches, a coy blush creeping up his cheeks as the woman's melodious voice flowed from beneath the willows. There followed a faint chuckle. 'Do not be shy. I am beyond your charms. Although I see how well formed you are and how easy it must be to love you!'

'Where are you?' Phelim hastily pulled on the rest of his clothes, aware of their new softness but too concerned to waste time in examination. 'Show yourself!'

'Why, Phelim? It is enough that you have a voice to commune with.

And we have much that we must talk about, so rest you easy. It is not necessary that you see me.'

'I'll not talk with anyone who is afraid to show me their face. Adieu.' He thrust the cord of the bag over his head and tucked the chamois under his shirt against his bare chest and began to walk away from the river toward the door of the cave. As he took a step up the incline, a searing burn arced along his ribcage and he grasped at his shirt as if to fling it and the concealed bag from his body. 'Aine!' He winced with the awful pain as the pouch pulled away from scalded, gummy skin.

'Ah. So the souls tell you that you must listen when you are spoken to. Hearken, Phelim.'

Phelim slumped to his knees, breathing hard, trying to hold the bag and the folds of his shirt away from the deep burns. 'Then speak, for if you are the kind who must torture and burn to make your point, I would prefer it was over quickly.'

The amorphous voice shifted to come from in front of him, further up the slope toward the door. 'Go back to the river, Phelim. You will find if you step back the pain will ease and you will be of a mind to listen.'

He felt a rush of something soft and pleasant flowing past him and heard a rattle as if a breeze blew through the dry seed cases of the trees so that he was reminded of the crushed rustle of a piece of Ebba's favourite taffeta that she had hung over the back of a chair. He turned and stepped back down to the river, the burns fading in intensity, until as he stood on the banks, it was as though nothing had happened. Rubbing cautiously at his side, he cast an intense look over his surroundings, thinking he spied a dark shadow under a swathe of willow.

'Sit, Phelim. Be at ease. Nothing will hurt you now and we have much to say.'

'So you said. And yet I can't imagine what I would have to say to a disembodied voice that has neither the courage nor conviction to show itself.'

The voice laughed with delight, a sound that caressed every sense Phelim possessed. 'They chose you well, my friend. You have backbone.'

The voice once again came from behind him and he turned to look, his body shivering with trills of fear and excitement. 'Who chose well? What do you say?'

'You do well to fear me, Phelim. Because I can do as much as the souls or worse if I choose. But I think we can be friends so shall we relax?'

He looked up from where he had sat on the edge of the riverbank and spied a pair of delicate feet clad in dark Raji ankle boots, their upper edges touching the folds of a full skirt. At his eye-level, the skirt was embroidered with silver trees which were frosted as if by star and moonlight and as he gazed at the detail laid against an indigo background, the daylight surrounding him darkened until he could tell neither the sky from the skirt and felt himself falling into dark blue almost black heavenly depths. The sky as he raised his eyes further, became studded with stars and swathes of delicate cloud and as he looked up further still, a pale face stared down, as pale as the moon and as lovely, the woman's hair drifting like dove-grey mist, this way and that, whilst stars glittered and flickered in the celestial mass. Was it a woman, or was he asleep? Did he lie on the grass in the night and stare at a face or at the moon?

'Are you Færan?' he whispered. 'Are you Other?'

She smiled down at him.

'Are you the Lady Aine?'

'I am who I am, Ebba's Phelim, and it matters not one jot in our conversings. Rest easy now and we shall pass the time.'

'Why? What do you have to say?'

'Ah! The nub of the matter.'

Something cool rustled over his hands as they lay in the grass and he heard again the crisp crush as if someone sat by him but when he looked he could discern only the night sky, the stars and the beautiful moonlit face. 'You have said little over much time.' He tried to be masterful. 'I am waiting.'

'Then Phelim, son of Ebba, shall we talk about prophecies?'

Prophecies and Fate! I hated that Fate had brought Ana and Liam together and I despised that Fate had split them apart. I cried that Fate brought Kholi into my life to then remove him so cruelly. All our lives appear to be at the whim of Fate the shatranj-player, as if he or she were an aliyat and we the ivory and obsidian pieces moved without care around a board with the sole purpose of entertaining... and winning. Fate be damned!

But another manuscript is finished. And by now I imagine you will already have the tweezers, the thread, the needle and the scissors to replace it and any others, so we shall move on. Seek the acid yellow silken petals of the dandelion flower. Under each of the two flowers and the bud, there are small yellow books. And underneath the wings of the lavender and terracotta butterfly, another – dyed to match the fanciful wings, everything camouflaged and secret.

CHAPTER SIXTEEN

'Prophecies! I would prefer not! Some soothsayer has practiced his art and now my life is turned upside down.'

'Your life was turned upside down the day your real mother left you by the sea.'

Phelim was silent. He had not yet had time to wonder what his life may have been if he hadn't been mislaid. Did he have a father, brothers and sisters? Had his mother met her bane? But what did it matter anyway? His life was the one Ebba gave to him when she held him in her arms that fateful day and he was without doubt better because of it. 'To a point,' he replied to the woman and expounded his most recent thought.

'An interesting choice of words, Phelim. '*That fateful day*' you say and yet what you don't realize is that one cannot change Fate. It is immutable. In the stars.'

'Spare me! Would you tell me my future has been reduced to a bit of augury or card-turning?'

'No. More serious than that. Listen to me and hearken. Every individual in this world has a span of life that they are destined to live, some with more éclat and danger than others. But no matter what, it is written! Most never find out their Fate or if they do, it is too late. And if they are fool enough to try and change it, they destine themselves toward the proving of a prophetic end. It is the way of life. Unalterable. The prophecy that hangs about you, Phelim, will help you find what part of your life is truly your destiny. You shall discover what you fear is lost.'

'Do you mean that I will return to my mortal life?'

'Ah Phelim, your destiny is for you to discover. I am merely here to offer you some timely advice. It is the souls that propel you toward your destiny. Deny it till you are breathless but it will not change. It is also your destiny that you are honourable. A promise was made to a dying woman that the souls would be taken to Jasper of the Færan. Even then the Fates were conspiring to push you toward your destiny. The prophecy, seen also by Jasper, is that you are to be saviour and perhaps even avenger.' The pale face and the rich voice settled over him like a dream.

'It sounds like a bard's heroic tale,' he scoffed, 'and I can't envisage how I could possibly fulfill the lofty ideals of which you speak.'

'You are halfway there already, Phelim. But you have emasculated Huon, and the huntress, Severine, will not forgive you lightly. Your advantage is that neither Huon nor Severine realise *you* have the souls but she is clever and may deduce it eventually. Trust me Phelim, when I say that you shall take the souls further, that you will do what you must and that your reward will be finding what you thought you had lost.'

Phelim sat digesting the enigmatic words. 'With respect, Lady, you have said a lot and revealed little. Methinks I could have gone on without your words.'

'I think not. You had forgiven Ebba and were as like to turn around. And then you would have delayed everything. Better that I encourage you to accept what you cannot change and urge you to use your wisdom in moving forward and to move forward with speed.'

'Then I shall, albeit unwillingly, and you should know I do this only because Ebba promised a dying woman that it would be done. Show me the way off this island and I'll be gone. The sooner gone, the sooner I can return to my home.'

'Patience Phelim, son of Ebba. You must rest first.'

There was a rustle and Phelim guessed the woman levered herself to stand. However looking up he saw nothing beyond the ever-deepening night-sky and the mesmeric twinkling of stars.

'Phelim, I will tell you one more thing. There are two men of whom you should know. One is the Dark Haired Man. He exclusively serves the baser side of Færan. He can abduct the heart and mind of any he chooses and will encourage them to mount behind him and they shall never be seen again. And there is the Red-haired Man, who for no reason other than he is a good man, will protect those mortals that he finds. You shall meet them in your journey and I bid you to beware because the choices you make at that time will determine the path you follow to your destiny.' The woman gave a sigh. 'You must be tired. Sleep now. Let the soft dark of night erase your troubles and let the light of the stars and the moon protect you until you wake. Good fortune.'

Phelim heard a shivering sound but as he sank into a dreamless sleep, the vast indigo heaven wrapping around him, he would never know if it was skirts he heard moving away or merely the blowing of a welkin wind, rattling the leaves and buds around him.

Far from Hy-Breasil, a horse stampeded in blind panic – tripping, stumbling, leaping logs and ditches with all the power of huge legs and massive hindquarters. All the while the blood flowed in a stream down his shoulder, past his knee, to cover the fetlock in a shining, sanguine stain. The flap of skin, muscle and tendon was covered in dirt and the first throes of infection began to course rapidly through his body.

He stopped when he smelled water and drank, shivering and sweating. He would doze, a fetlock resting, head turning unconsciously to bite at the injured shoulder. The pain would wake him with a start and he would bolt again, aware of the flash of lightning and the growl of thunder in the far distant cauldron of the Styx. This was the horse who though valiant and loyal to Adelina, trembled on the heights of the Celestine Stairway. Thunder likewise induced deep-seated anxiety. Fear goaded him on and by the time Phelim had sunk into sleep, the exhausted horse was as far from the hateful storm as he could be. He stood shaking as the once proud head hung low, as his breath gushed through red, distended nostrils and as the dawn light softly crept amongst leaf and tree.

Adelina had woken with a disquiet of her own well before the dawn. Her eyes had ripped open and her heart pounded like Ajax's hooves. Immediately she recalled Luther's attack and leaped from the bed, rushing to the window. 'I can't stay here,' her fist crunched into an agitated ball and she pounded the windowsill. 'I have get away, get Ajax and run for my life. I must!' Her voice bounced around the dark room.

'Well, I must say I am pleased you have at least come to a firm decision,

Adelina. Like I said, your equanimity has been surprising.' Gallivant appeared by her side at the window. He noticed she was shaking. 'What's amiss?'

'I don't know. I was in a dead sleep and I woke suddenly as if the Hunt were at my bedside and I can't shake the feeling. I just have to get away, Gallivant.' Adelina cast a miserable look at the hob. 'And I don't know how.'

'Ah, well I think I may be able to help. I have had a thought you see.'

Oh yes, Adelina surmised miserably, the hob has had a thought.

'Now let us not stand in the dark. Light the lamp.' He bounced around cheerfully, passing her a glowing taper from the hot coals of the hearth.

Adelina held it with trembling fingers to a small table lamp and sat herself down, for indeed she felt weak. Gallivant noticed and to divert her, offered a suggestion.

'Write or sew, Threadlady. Occupy your mind, for I have a task I must undertake but I will be back as soon as I can.' He looked at Adelina's pale face. 'Shall you be alright?'

She nodded her head faintly, copper hair falling everywhere. And before she could ask where he must go he was gone, leaving a space for lonliness and agitation to fill. She picked up a pen and a piece of washi paper and began to write. Every night of her stay in this wretched prison she had spent detailing her journey and secreting it behind the embroidered stuff of the robe. It was in truth one of the few things that gave her any satisfaction – that every single thing that had happened since the day of the Stitching Fair had been laid on paper, like bricks on a pathway, all the while leading to Severine's downfall. It was what she hoped with every vengeful fibre of her being. She let the pen fly across the page.

Severine had slept like a baby until the trow's hand scrabbling at her door woke her. Candle-like fingers of light poked under her drapes suggesting dawn was close and she bade the creature enter. A message was passed and her howl echoed throughout the lodge, causing trepidation in all living things, so like a banshee was its pitch. She hastily dressed and flung herself along the corridor to the cobweb man's room and threw open the door to the dim space lit only by a candle which had slumped in a melted heap on its holder.

'And?' Her voice froze the air on the room and the goblin pulled his tatters tighter round his body. He began his handwashing.

'Well Madam, I have pursued the puzzle all the night. Wracked my brains I did. All the while the stones caused my fingers to tingle and I thought they were tell...'

'GERTUS! In the name of Behir, will you get to the point!' She stormed across the room to the table by the window and picked up first one rock and then another. 'You had best have something for me goblin, because I have just had a message from an Other of your ilk, as unseelie and wanton as yourself.' She threw the rocks down. 'The great and invincible Huon has lost my souls Gertus, lost them! And now I am forced to chase after them myself. Either that, or you get me into Færan where I can find a soul surfeit, where I can use the ring and help myself to all Færan has to offer.' She turned quickly to the cowering goblin. 'Do you see now? I must have the details!'

She fixed him with her grey eyes and the obsequious hands rolled over and over as the unctious voice began. 'This stone, Ma'am, I felt it till my fingers ached.' He fingered the pitted brown rock. 'It is volcanic. From some deep basin that has become dry and bereft of moisture, somewhere where the sun has baked and burned and boiled and where some acid has etched pits and craters in its surface before Time even began. There is only one such place in Eirie, milady and that is in the Raj.'

'Of course! Fahsi! The town is built over a dried out basin. I remember! The river changed its course centuries ago.' Severine smiled, ivory teeth bared, eyes glittering and a sharp tip to the thin, red lips. Suddenly the day had hope. 'Gertus, I am proud of you! And?'

'Now the grey stone.' He held it out to show her. 'See how perfectly ovoid it is. And how smooth? It is like the touch of Færan silk on the skin. And see the paler undulations of colour melded through the stone. This, Madame, is a sea-stone. Washed and rolled by aeons of waves and as such, one has to think of which coast has such grey rock. Trevallyn is walled with sandstone on its coast. Veniche has no real rock as we know it. That leaves the Pymm Archipelago and almost all the islands have a granite shore. Except for one.' His expression of self-congratulation drew his chin back into his neck and his eyes became sly, the lips stretching into a thin smile.

'Indeed. And that would be?' Severine humoured him. Perhaps he was worth the weight of precious gems she had turned his way.

'Foula, madame. Foula is as grey as a stormy sea day. Remember the story of the Mermaid of Foula? In order to have a soul, she was told she would have to renounce the sea. And when she couldn't do that, she sobbed and sobbed and her tears stained the rocks and pebbles of Foula to the grey they are today.' Gertus held the rock to the candle, the soft grisaille shining in the glow of the wick.

'Oh my friend! You do very well.'

Outside, the forest birds had begun to sing and the light around the edges of the window drapes was stronger. Gertus preened like a cock, his ego climbing like the comb of said rooster to stand erect and proud. He smiled a self-important smile.

Severine picked up the third stone. A pale yellow rock that left a faint ochre stain on all who touched it.

'What causes this, Gertus? It flakes like...'

'Paint, mistress. And I think it is just that. Underneath is a red clay-like substance, maybe from bricks I am guessing, and this too is only a guess. It is from Veniche.'

'An inspired guess! Veniche! Now we have only to isolate the building, a not impossible task, I think. But what about the fruit stone?'

Gertus swallowed. His mistress seemed mellow enough but she was an expert at the volte-face. 'I don't know. Someone's dinner perhaps?' He laughed selfconsciously at his own joke but swiped the grin when he saw his mistress's expression. 'At any rate, if one assumes that the Archipelago, Veniche and the Raj are the sites of Gates, it would be fair to assume the last would be in Trevallyn. As to the stone representing this? It may, it may not.'

As Gertus expounded so Severine's mind had racketed ahead. She didn't really care if there was a gateway anywhere else now she knew there was one in Veniche. It would be a matter of a day to find the building with that distinctive ochre paint and then? Suddenly Huon didn't matter because if Lhiannon and her little boat made for Veniche, then she made for the Gate. A glut of souls presented themselves as if they were served on a platter.

She turned to her gnome, fingering the swathe of damask drape as she did so. 'Ah Gertus, what a help you have been.' She smiled. 'I can't imagine how I would have done any of this without you.' The gnome washed and re-washed his hands, excitement at just rewards lubricating the exercise. Severine flicked the drapes open with a rapid swish so the sun streamed in, a golden shaft pouring along the floor, a chasm of brilliance that had the gnome screaming as it touched his feet. With excessive speed, a stain of grey sped up his legs, hardening, solidifying. His horrified expression froze in a layer of stony resin, to be screaming for posterity.

'Gertus, Gertus,' Severine smiled mildly. 'Gnomes to stones, dear man, gnomes to stones.' She scooped up the pebbles and placed them in their little box and without a backward glance she strode out.

On Hy-Breasil, Phelim had wended his way back to the cave, the bag warm against his ribs. One part of him was energised at the thought of his journey and eager to be away. The other less adventurous side grieved for a way of life he had loved, viewing the lonely immensity of his task with disquiet. Forboding weighed the boat down as the rope untied itself and the bow swung to the entrance.

CHAPTER SEVENTEEN

'Right, I'm back.' Gallivant bounced around the room on his matchstick legs, a damask coat covering the excessive brightness of the silk shirt and cuff.

'Oh, that's good.' Adelina responded dryly.

'Well, you could be happier! Honestly Stitcher, sometimes I despair of you!' The hob's pleasant mouth drooped slightly and Adelina looked up from her worktable. It seemed hours had passed with Gallivant gone. She had finished writing, shrunk the manuscript and sewn it into the body of the robe, and completed another silk scene on the gown. Breakfast had not appeared – a punishment she was sure – and she was as grateful to Aine as she would ever be. The thought of the over-sexed and angry Luther appearing once more in her room was too much to bear. She fingered the bruises on her arm where he had grabbed her.

'Despair away, hob, but I am not happy and as like never to be happy again so don't give me more grief than I am already drowning in!' She threw down a handful of hoops and stalked to the window. 'Hell and damnation, I want to get *out* of here!'

Gallivant ignored Adelina and leaned over her worktable. There were two neat piles on the table, one bigger than the other. 'What are these?'

'They're the makings of the last two elements on the robe. Only two to go Gallivant, and I am done. The larger pile is the design for the middle back. It will be a an eyecatching centrepiece and I have no doubt Severine will be furious at my choice of subject but it hardly matters.' She walked back to stand beside Gallivant and looked down at her work. 'It's hard to believe isn't it, that my life ends with the last stitch I place on that robe. I am effectively embroidering my own death warrant.'

She moved away and sat in an elegant ladies' chair by the fireplace, whilst Gallivant folded himself onto the tapestry-lidded coffer. 'You think she will kill you?' His face was as serious as Adelina had seen it, a furrowed young brow and a turn of the lips.

'Of course, killing comes as easy to her as burping to you or I. The point is that I'd have outlived my usefulness and she couldn't let me go because she despises me. Besides, she would hardly want me to shout her perfidy from the rooftops. So you see – my life is measured by each length of thread that I cut. My life and Ajax's.'

Gallivant jumped up in his energetic way and went back to the robe on the table. Adelina joined him and picked it up, carefully slipping a hanger through the armholes and placing it on the hook on the side of the armoire where Gallivant examined it, finger on his lips and one elbow cushioned in the other hand. 'It's beautiful, you really are an artist.'

Adelina scrutinized the garment with gimlet eyes. 'I've grown to hate it. It's bright, unsubtle and represents pain, hatred and humiliation.'

'I think you're too hard, Needlewoman. And too subjective.' He held up the part of the hem with Aladdin. 'Look at him! This is my favourite embroidery on the whole robe.

'Well, that rather proves my point. It's bright enough to catch your attention and I didn't do it anyway! Ana did, I merely applied it.' Her mood darkened more.

'It doesn't matter. It sits perfectly. Anyway, where is his lamp?'

'The charm is by the bed but it's filthy dirty.'

'And how fortuitous I returned.' He slapped a dented tin on the table and a soft piece of rag. 'I pilfered some paste from the kitchens. Why don't you clean it now? I should like to see him hold the lamp in his little hand.' He pushed the rag into her fingers and opened the lid of the tin.

Adelina shrugged and grasped the charm, working the cleaning paste into the murky gold as Gallivant peered over her shoulder, watching as she began to burnish the tiny object that could be so easily lost in the folds of the cloth. Within seconds it was done and when held to the light by the tips of Adelina's fingers, glistened and gleamed. She threaded a needle with some silk.

'Are you going to attach it straight away?' Gallivant picked the charm up and cradled it, examining every inch of the bauble.

'Well, yes. Isn't that what you wanted me to do?' Adelina's temper crackled, the fuse smouldering and even her understanding of the importance of Gallivant to her sanity could not prevent sharpness in the voice.

'Um, yes, but...'

'But nothing! Give it here.'

'No!' The negative burst into the air like a pricked balloon. 'I mean no', he said more equably. 'Look, there is still paste here, see?'

And indeed, right at the join of spout to bowl, a tiny smear of white remained. Adelina grabbed the rag, found a corner and manoevred it back and forth over the gold. 'There', she tipped her head at the hob. 'Happy?'

But his eyes were fixed on the charm. 'Adelina, your little wand! Quickly!'

'What?'

'Adelina! The wand! Enlarge the lamp! Just do it!'

Adelina had never heard such terseness in the hob. Perhaps when she had spurned his initial overtures of friendship, but not since and it was enough to make her reach for the miniscule wand embedded in its wooly ball, and to tap the charm.

'*Grow bigger and be,*
For I must see.'

But there was nothing to be observed in the opaque fog that completely surrounded the table and caused the hob and the charm and everything within range to disappear before Adelina's eyes. She coughed in the humid air and when she ceased, a voice that was deep and resonant and full of exotic echoes, spoke to her.

'Memsahib, a thousand, a million gratitudes! You are my saviour, light of my life, queen of my dreams.' The figure in front of her touched his brow, his lips and his middle and bowed. 'Your wish is my command.'

'I knew it', said the hob smugly, clapping his hands. 'Sink me, I knew it!'

Dressed in black Raji suiting detailed with fine silver embroidery and narrow trousers which ended in a pair of quaint slippers, the fellow who smiled at Adelina had a powerfully carved face with the darkest eyes and equally dark hair which flopped over the forehead. His mouth widened in a friendly smile revealing teeth... well, there had been only one other whose teeth had been as white. Memories rushed through Adelina like a scouring wind.

She sat with a thump, her legs caving. Gallivant grabbed her hand and rubbed it. 'Adelina, Adelina!'

The figure stepped forward and knelt by her side. 'My pardon, memsahib. I had no wish to frighten you.' His touch filled the empty corners of her soul and the shadow of her faint receded like an ebb tide. 'My name is Rajeeb and I am your djinn of the lamp. My Lady, as you can see, you have released me from a very cramped prison. And whilst I did say your wish is my command, I must qualify that.' He stood and brushed the fibres of the rug off the black silk of his knee. 'I can grant you three wishes and then my debt to you is paid and I can once again wander free in the Raj.'

Adelina found it difficult to work her lips and when her voice emerged it was cracked and burning with raw memories of another Raji. 'There are no such things as djinns!'

'Say you? And what then happened with Aladdin?'

'That's a legend!'

'I fear not, dear lady. It is history and fact. Besides, are the good folk of the southern, eastern and western reaches of Eirie entitled to Others but the Raj is not? Fair mistress, you are either woefully naïve or despicably arrogant.'

Gallivant, disturbed at the frown between the djinn's eyebrows, rushed to the side of his charge having heard bawling and uncouth noises below. 'She is naïve. I have always said so *and* she has a mouth as loose as a starving man's belt. She doesn't mean ill. Now tell, what are the three wishes she should have?'

'That is for the Memsahib to decide.'

'Adelina', Gallivant grabbed her hand and shook it. 'Quick, think! Listen, Luther is coming and he will take his revenge. He is full of the grape. Do you wish the lout to part your thighs or do you wish to leave? HURRY!' Fear for his friend made the hob's voice rise to a falsetto as he jumped from foot to foot.

She heard Luther's obscenities from the bottom of the stair and began to tremble, realizing this was her only chance, a chance where she *had* to trust Others and accept their help as Maeve had said. 'To go, I wish my horse and I to go. Now!'

'Two wishes shall be done. And the third?'

She tried to think clearly, her ear on Luther's noise, her mind slowing as fear took over. 'I don't know.'

'ADELINA!' Gallivant hopped about grabbing the robe and the wand and the objects on the table, including the djinn's lamp.

'Lhiannon!' The words exploded from the Traveller's lips in a rush. 'Help Lhiannon!'

'It is done. Prepare yourself.'

'Wait!' Gallivant grabbed a leather satchel. 'Quick! Shrink everything.'

Unquestioningly Adelina did as she was asked and the hob squashed all the minnikin things into the bag and flung it over her head. Outside they could hear swearing as Luther tried to fit the key in the door and dropped it.

'Now!' Gallivant yelled.

As the key turned, a puff of fog filled the room briefly. As Luther pushed the door open, the hob vanished through the walls.

He stared.

The room was empty.

CHAPTER EIGHTEEN

'Where are you, *bitseach*?' Luther launched himself to the garde-robe and flung open the door but it swung to an empty space. He bounced off the frame and staggered back into the room, an unasked-for sobriety beginning to trickle through his blood vessels as he swung round in a circle, noticing the robe had gone. 'I'll find you, woman,' he roared, 'and so help me I shall make you rue the day you decided to cross me!' Then he remembered the horse and raced to the spot on the edge of the forest where he had left Ajax. The smashed rails and a short trail of broken timber gave him brief hope that he could follow but Huon's storm had washed everything free of indent and any trail had become slick with mud.

He bellowed, the reality of his predicament filling every pore of his being. Adelina and the robe had gone and in his charge! By Behir, he should just slit his own throat this instant! Returning to the manor, he thought how apt, how ironic it should be that the staff should tell him Madame was back early and in the most odd mood. Luther fingered the dagger at his belt. A quick stroke and it would be over. But for whom?

The glimmering lights had disappeared, leaving the cavern as dark as Hades. Phelim's dory wallowed in a slight slop close to what he perceived was the entrance. Disconsolately he sat and wondered what he was supposed to do to get out. *Mesmer? Is that how it should be?*

A loud grating filled the air and veils of soil and dust from scraped rocks fell about him as the cavern yielded a piece of daylight. Ever widening, a mouth yawned to make an exit as the two isles slid apart. The dory glided through, disquieted passenger at the helm and within moments had floated beyond the shadows of the islands.

Looking back at vanishing Hy-Breasil, Phelim longed for the familiarity of his pastoral life and for Ebba but the souls burned with icy coldness against his side. Unwillingly he reached for the ropes and hoisted the mainsail, unsurprised to find the canvas whole again. As he had been unsurprised to see the damage on the boat itself completely mended. But whereas before he accepted such things as unconsciously right, now, under duress, he was annoyed at the slick secretiveness of it all.

The watery sun with a vestige of opalescent sea mist hung directly overhead, thus he assumed it was the middle of the day. As to where in this wide west sea he now floated, he had no idea. He allowed the breeze to feather his mainsail and push him slowly ahead. He assumed that some eldritch current bore him north and so he surrendered his boat to its ministrations.

There was food in the bottom of the boat and a bladder full of water but he touched neither, unable to stomach anything. He twisted a rope tightly around the tiller to fix his course and then he abandoned himself to the mother-like rocking of the ocean beneath him. He wanted night to fall, the better to chart the rest of his journey but at the moment his anxious mind wandered haphazardly along the paths of his past and future.

His life till now had been safe and as predictable as the seasons. He reveled in his work for the Squire – not for the Squire's sake but for his own because Ebba had taught him to take joy in small things, for the small things added up to something truly remarkable. He had no higher aspirations – why should he? He was as fulfilled as someone who loved the land and its response to the seasons could be. But was fulfillment enough? According to the Færan patently not because they believed there was always something better, bigger, more perfect.

Finding out he was Færan had destroyed his equilibrium. It opened a gaping hole in the fabric of his life as surely as if a giant had rent it. What does it feel, he agonized, when someone loses their identity? He thought of a tree in a fierce autumn gale – the bright red and yellow leaves disappearing until only the nondescript twig and branch remain, leaving nothing by which to identify it. He thought of a man without memory. A man without recall is nothing, thus how does he become something? He had no memory of Færan, so how could he *be* Færan? He floundered in the purgatory of No Man's Land – neither mortal nor Other and everything he knew of the Færan, every snippet, every tale made him want to scream to the stars, *never!*

The dory flew across the wave and it seemed to Phelim he flew toward a life he wanted least. He craved to turn and head for home but the souls rested against his side and burned coldly into his skin each time he thought thus and he felt they punished him for his reticence.

The graceful shape of a black swan winged its way over him, to bank and turn the way it had come. Briefly as he glimpsed the bird, his heart lightened as he realized land was close and he allowed the sea and the breeze to speed him on.

'How? How did she get away?' The high-pitched voice strangulated with suppressed emotion.

'She could not have got out without help.' Sweat beaded on Luther's heavy upper lip. 'And that help could only be Other because I have the key round my neck at all times. No trail, nothing. It *reeks* of Other meddling.'

Severine turned away from Luther. If only a stiletto had been handy! But a fear twitched at her fingers and behind her knees, making them tremble. For the first time ever, she felt the weight of the whole Other world pressing down.

When the Swan Maid and the servant-girl had flown away with the souls, she suspected she was pitched against Others but she had pushed the thought away, deceived into a false security in the guise of Huon, of the Ravens, of Gertus. Now, to have an intimation of Adelina being helped by Others, that they allied themselves against her, meant difficulties on a wholly different scale. For if nothing else her years had taught her of the immense power of the Other world. She tried to speak, her mouth dry and tacky, the words cracking.

'Leave me, Luther. Leave me before I heave a knife through your breast. Pack for Veniche because we shall leave in the morning and I need to make haste on the road.'

Luther slunk away but she called him back from the door. 'Luther, you will redeem yourself in Veniche.' Severine gathered herself, fear transposing to anger. 'You will seek and search and when you find Adelina – for have no doubt that is where she has gone – you shall retrieve the robe and bring the bitch to me. She was the bane of my life when we were young and is twice that now and I want to be rid of her.' She twisted her hands together until the bones glistened white. 'She will beg me for her life and then you shall cut her throat very slowly!'

She heard the latch click as Luther left and subsided with a rustle of violet silk onto the stool near the fire. Why had she let him go unscathed? The goblin had been despatched for less. Did she need him because she was afraid?

Fraught, she tried to clear her head and begin to plan. *The souls are again on the high seas. I will set the Ravens on the trail between Veniche and the last point at which the boat was seen! By Behir, I wish I'd known the maidservant had been Færan! I would have used the ring on her, sucked her deceitful soul right then and there and at least had something... something!*

And Adelina? Other help or no, she also headed for Veniche. Had Luther not heard her chattering to that miscreant maidservant that the Museo waited for a masterpiece from the embroiderer? There was absolutely no doubt in Severine's mind that while the Traveller was in Veniche, she would deliver the robe to the famous gallery. Her ego, so full of itself, demanded it!

But wait! Might there not be other eldritch champions with Adelina?

So what, Severine sighed, relief rampant, I have the ring, the ultimate weapon. Perhaps I can mesmer? *Could* I mesmer? For a moment, a moment only, she chastised herself for removing the goblin from her life. He would have been able to explain the charms to her in more detail – those valuable strips, folded away in their casket.

But then, she thought, am I not Severine the changeling? I who studied the Others and their lore all my life? What could the goblin tell me that I don't already know?

Nothing!

She stood and brushed her hands together as if removing dust and dirt, composed again, doubt and fear pushed into the darkest corners of her mind.

The djinn deposited Adelina on the edge of a forest. She stood unsteadily for a moment, waiting for her head to catch up with her body.

There had been a puff of mist smelling of sandalwood and then she had felt as if she fainted. Sounds converged and then echoed away into a roaring distance. She had shut her eyes at the vicious vertigo and allowed herself to fall. After that she could remember nothing except a broad chest in a Raji tunic supporting her head and strong arms around her as she struggled to find her feet. 'Is the Memsahib well now?'

Rajeeb's deep voice soothed her ruffled spirits. She was unsure if it had been the journey or the presence of heart-breaking memories that disturbed her equilibrium the most. She pushed at her support ineffectually. 'I am,' she responded crisply, 'thank you.'

'It is my pleasure, madame.' Rajeeb led her gently to a log, encouraging her to sit as he continued to hold her hand. 'I was in your debt as I had been in that little lamp for millenia. I was placed there as a punishment because I ran away with a mortal serving girl. My family were djinns of the highest rank who saw me as their shame, and my father gave me a choice, once he had turned my beloved into a pillar of salt: to be a djinn his family could be proud of, causing death and destruction, or I could be imprisoned in the lamp. I chose the lamp because I didn't care about life after I lost my love and because I knew confinement would be better than living by that dark paternal side for infinity.' He grimaced. 'So you see, you and I share a similar pain, that of love and loss and confinement. I hadn't realised my esteemed father had shrunk the lamp to a piece of jewelry. Huh, such is life.' He smoothed his fingers over Adelina's hands and then shrugged with profound equanimity. 'So! You are my saviour as I have said and no doubt you wonder where we are. We are on the edge of the Luned Forest.' He waved his arm. 'And you will no doubt wonder why I have brought you here. You asked for your horse. He is here, Adelina.'

The Traveller opened her mouth.

'Stop,' the djinn placed a finger on her lips. 'You asked for your horse to be with you but he had already gone when I went to mesmer him. Nevertheless, in the way of a djinn I found him here. Remember Adelina, you asked for you and the horse to be away from your prison. Simply that. They were two of your wishes. Your third was for Lhiannon's safety. I have carried out your first wish, you are away from the soul-thief. Your second wish? You will be with your horse. I leave now to enact your third wish.' Rajeeb touched his brow, his lips and bowed over the hand that touched his middle. 'Follow the path!'

With a waft of sandalwood, he was gone.

CHAPTER NINETEEN

Adelina stood listening to the chorus of birds, frogs and insects as they blended in a quaint but charming harmony. She envisaged a map in her head, the better to determine how far from Severine she was and savoured her freedom for less than a moment before running down the path calling to her horse, the leather satchel with the robe and a few sewing implements banging against her hip.

She entered a clearing surrounded by a circlet of leafy elms whose shadows were deep and protective on the outskirts, providing shelter for the needy. Close by, a freshet trickled with enough clear water to salve the driest thirst and in the sunny centre of the glade grew a patch of rich clover which could satisfy a hungry animal. A perfect place to rest and re-gird one's self. Which made it all the more poignant when Adelina skidded to a halt, to see an ailing horse lying on its side, gasping, and with dark patches of sweat on shoulder and flank.

'Ajax!' Adelina flung herself to the side of her beloved friend. Recognising the voice, the stallion raised his head and nickered, then flopped back, the wet mane straggling in the grassy growth under the trees. 'Ajax,' she whispered as she knelt by the horse's neck hugging and kissing, her hands running over his wet neck and nose. As she stroked, she found the suppurating wound on his shoulder. She knew by the size of the foul smelling injury that the poison had gone deeply inwards and threatened the horse with death and instantly she knew why the djinn had warned, perhaps not so ambiguously, that her three wishes had been clear and irredeemable. Because truth to tell, she would swap the Farean

Lhiannon's life with Ajax's at the drop of a hat.

She grabbed her kerchief and bathed it in the cool water to sponge the great animal's head and clean the wound. But she needed wadding, a knife to open the wound and drain it, fire and medics. She needed help!

She ripped off the satchel to find her scissors and then pulled a corner of the shrunken robe from the leathery confines. The crane's head scissors opened with a cry that aroused a million memories as she slipped one blade under one side of the robe and brought pressure to bear on the handle, all the while thinking, another of my loved ones to die!

'No, no!' A high-pitched voice shattered the peace of the glade and the scissors fell from Adelina's grasp, Ajax's eyes flying open and then closing again as he rasped. The Traveller turned in fear, nerves on edge, emotions raw.

Gallivant stood on the edge of the clearing. 'No! Don't cut the robe, Adelina. You mustn't!'

'I need wadding Gallivant, and I need a knife. Have you a knife?' Her gaze sharpened as she looked at him. 'How are *you* here?'

'Later. I will tell you later. You need spaghnum moss, wads of it, it's a great healing medicament, full of the enchantments of the Luned Forest!'

'Of course!' Adelina's voice shook with frustration and alarm. 'And look! I have it here in my hand! Gallivant help me, where do I find it? Quickly!'

Gallivant grabbed her and pulled her to the side of the freshet. 'Here! See? Look, masses of the stuff!' He began to pull hanks of the moist moss. 'As it dries we shall put a fresh load on and then more until the wound is clean.'

'Will it work? He's all I have...'

'With respect Adelina, you have no time for watery expressions of sentiment! Just tend to your horse. Hurry, use your scissors and ease the wound open. It will hurt but you must allow some of the pus to run and then you must cram this stuff in. Remember the old saying, *if it's pus, let it gush!*'

Adelina grabbed her scissors and with murmurings of endearment to Ajax, she slit the wound open. The horse reared his head as the blades entered, shrieking wildly, but Adelina spoke above his pain and as the foul infection dripped out, she packed some of the moss into the offensively fragrant wound. Gallivant wet some fabric he had whipped from his pocket and wiped around the horse's face and dripped moisture in between the huge teeth, onto the dry tongue, a placebo to be sure but it helped Adelina to see they did something.

The small glen echoed to the grating sound of the horse's breath. Adelina sat with Ajax's head on her lap, crooning sweet nothings as the tired ears flipped slowly back and forth. In time the sun had moved to the western side of the glade and Gallivant had continued wiping and squeezing water.

Close to dusk, the animal's breathing changed, becoming quieter.

'Is it less laboured do you think?'

'Yes, it is.' Gallivant sat back. 'Cover him with something. He will chill as the sweat dries.'

Adelina could think of only one thing she had big enough to cover the horse's back and with a gasp from the hob, she dragged forth the magnificent robe, enlarged it and laid it with all its silken art-work over the animal. For her it meant nothing more than a way to protect the only thing she had left to love. The robe? She would make another.

The two companions began to relax a little as they observed the sweat drying in crusty rippled waves on the horse's coat where it showed beneath the gloriously decorated stable-rug.

'Amazing little mosses, are they not?' Gallivant had washed his hands in the stream and resumed his seat by the embroiderer.

'By Aine, an understatement.' She looked down at her clenched fingers. She was so tired and sighed as she prayed silently. *Please Aine, Mother of the World, allow my Ajax to live. I will give up my oath of revenge and be compassionate for the rest of my life, should you grant me such a wish. I promise.* She prayed with her eyes squeezed shut tightly and ran her hands, over her face as tears trickled down her cheeks.

'Ajax is just this far,' Gallivant measured a tiny distance with his thumb and fore-finger, disturbing Adelina's prayers, 'on the right side of the death line. I believe the healing should work.'

'But it *is* working, I'm sure. Look. He has stopped sweating and his breathing has settled. I think it will be alright.' She was quiet for a minute then turned back to the hob. 'Don't you?'

'I think so, I do. We must be patient.'

'Mercy, Gallivant, it's as well you came. How did you? Tell me.' Adelina's hand smoothed ceaselessly over the neck and forelock of the horse.

'Rajeeb. He gave me a wish because he said cleaning the charm had been at my instigation.'

'And you did say you had a feeling, didn't you?'

'I did.' The hob grinned engagingly. 'I saw an odd script engraved into the charm and was sure it was Other but done in that angular Raji way. And I just thought to myself, *what if*. I mean we had everything to gain, if only a clean charm. Anyway, I appropriated the paste and when you rubbed it in and then polished and nothing happened, well sink me I was so upset because my feelings aren't often wrong! But then I saw a little dusting of dried paste on the spout and I thought, *just once more*. And you didn't see but as you finished, a tiny thread of smoke eked out of the lamp and I started yelling for the wand. And then sink me if it didn't all work!' He splayed out his hands and shrugged his shoulders happily.

'And so you wished to be brought here.'

'Indeed.' He grinned, a self-satisfied, *aren't you pleased* look.

Adelina gave him a grateful but cautious glance. 'Gallivant, it's more than heartwarming that you wished to be with me and I'm unbelievably grateful for your help. Ajax would have died without doubt and I can never return the favour I owe you.' She stopped and looked at the salty ripples over the horse's coat. 'Actually perhaps I can!' She took a breath, 'I must go on alone.' Steely and determined, the tawny eyes indicated she was not to be convinced otherwise. 'You must surely realise everybody who is close to me ends up dead or injured. I'm a kind of poison. No, don't. It's true.' She laid a hand with firm fingers on the hob's arm. 'Look – Ana, Kholi, Lara, Liam. Aine knows if Lhiannon is still alive. My parents. Even Ajax is not immune. You see? So I forbid you to come any further with me. You must turn away now, soon, before you are tainted with whatever eminates from me.'

Gallivant stood up and walked to her satchel which lay spilled open and began dusting off the shrunken implements: needles, wooden spools of threads, packets of wired petals and insect wings, observing the seeds of depression sprouting leaves and tendrils in Adelina's words. 'Your parents died normal mortal deaths. It happens. Kholi was murdered. No no, there there.' He touched her gently on the shoulder. 'Ana had an accident, indeed so did Ajax. Lara and Liam had something an insane woman wanted enough to kill them for and Lhiannon is alive until we hear otherwise. Yes, you are a common denominator but you stretch a very long and if I may say, somewhat self-indulgent bow to intimate you are the cause. And sink me, as to my accompanying you, it's as well I am of an age and attitude to make up my own mind what I do. I will come.' As he issued these last words an ear-splitting bellow came from outside the copse, as if an animal was being squeezed empty of all the air in its body, like the bagpipes, thought Adelina, that some of the islanders play. Gallivant, who obviously loved bagpipes, smiled and ducked behind the far tree to re-emerge pulling a rope with a recalcitrant donkey tugging firmly backward. The hob smiled beatifically. 'Isn't he beautiful?' The ass roared back moodily. 'He's my ride.'

Speechless, Adelina couldn't help grinning as Gallivant tried to turn the beast to the middle of the clearing with the animal swinging its haunches to the hob and lashing out with its hooves. Thereafter, every time Gallivant made a move the haunches would swing and the hooves would fly.

Adelina eased the head of her peacefully sleeping horse aside and walked over to the donkey. 'What's his name?' She held out a hand and the animal paused in its circling and kicking to sniff and lo, to lick!

'Ouch, don't know! Oof, that was close!'

'Well, I think you should call him Bottom, because patently that is all he wants to show you. Here Bottom, good man,' she grasped his bridle and clicked her tongue, tugging gently. 'Come up, good boy.' The donkey lowered its big head and twitched the long loopy ears. Swishing a grey tail, he followed Adelina equably to the patch of clover in the centre of the glade. Adelina patted him as he chewed, his eyes blinking as he batted cow-like lashes at her.

'Easy, you see.'

'Huh!' grumped the hob.

They built a fire and lit it with a flint from Gallivant's vast pockets. Another such space provided bread and cheese and some dried figs and they drank their fill of the crystal stream that chortled happily by their sides.

'Where do we go, Adelina?'

She looked up in surprise. She had hardly thought that far. It had been enough to leave Severine behind and to find Ajax. The horse was feeding, resting a feltlock. When they had lifted the wad of moss, the wound had shrunk to the size of a scratch and was clean and clear. They re-attached the compress and were now heartened to see the two stallions – one large and handsome, one small, flea-bitten and with an over-large head, grazing peaceably on the clover. She gave the question some serious attention. 'We are close to the Marshes, I think.' She scratched her head. 'We could leave the animals there and go on to Veniche.' Her words began to gain momentum. 'Yes, that is what we shall do. I am of a mind to see Lhiannon again. You shall use your Other friends to find her, yes? And then I will be happy. To know Liam's soul is almost home and that Lhiannon is safe.'

'What if Severine comes?'

Adelina's face grimaced. It was evident she had given no thought to the woman. 'I have no idea. I don't know.'

'Ah well, shall we cross that bridge when we come to it? Can we sleep now? It's been a mile long day.' The hob burrowed down by the fire, wrapping himself in his capacious frieze-coat. Adelina leaned back against the tree and warmed by the flames, stared into their jumping yellow flicker. Aine, Mother of the World, she thought, you have given me back my beloved Ajax and I promise to fulfill the bargain. Compassion...

Do you understand why I made that pledge of compassion to the Mother? Why my oath of revenge hangs in the balance?

Imagine you have lost everyone you hold dear, everyone except a beloved pet, a dog or cat perhaps, that has been loyal, loving and by your side forever so that it knows every paltry idiosyncracy you have and yet loves you unstintingly still. Imagine that this one living thing is all that separates you from a dark chasm of unmitigated lonliness, one that terrifies you with its unknown depths. Perhaps you think I exaggerate but ask anyone who has been in that position whether they would make a pact with the most unseelie of this world to keep their beloved friend alive. They would, I know – in a heartbeat.

I asked Aine, the Mother of the World. Whether she believes in my promise and takes pity on me or whether she sees me as a weak-willed mortal, time will tell. I hope she takes pity on me anyway.

CHAPTER TWENTY

Severine sipped slowly at a glass of rich, garnet-coloured wine from the vineyards on the north-facing slopes of Trevallyn, musing.

Adelina – Adelina of the tawny hair and the luscious skin and body.

The atmosphere in the room filled with poison, like the invisible sulphur mist from the deadly swamps on the outskirts of the Marshes. Never had Severine been ignored, taunted, disobeyed and finally humiliated as much as by that whore, Adelina.

Time now to strike, to teach the woman a final lesson. Adelina must die. In truth it had always been intended anyway. The only difference now was the level of pain to inflict, for pain must be implicit.

She sipped again, savouring the strong flavour. All trails led to Veniche, that cradle of civilisation on its watery canals. And she was content for Veniche was her home. She knew every canal, every piazza, every small island and village in the laguna better than her protagonists.

The Færan girl, had she such detailed knowledge? And Adelina? It wasn't often the Travellers visited Veniche. They disliked leaving their vans behind on the mainland. So would Adelina be ignorant as well?

Severine ran her finger around the edge of the crystal goblet, round and round so that a screeching resonance filled the room. Of course they wouldn't know the city like she did. This episode of inconvenience would be concluded quickly. It would be a matter of posting Luther at the Museo where he would trap the embroiderer as she delivered the robe. And the Færan? She was heading to Veniche to be sure, this the Ravens would confirm. But she, Severine, had plenty of time to locate the source of the red-clay brick with its yellow paint. Why, she had architects and tradesmen by the dozens that she employed and could prevail upon.

She stood up and wandered to an inlaid card-table on which stood the pretty casket housing her incalculable treasure. She lifted the lid and began to unfold the papers, mininscule ribbons that whispered in her hands like pieces of delicate silk organza. Here lay four strips of Other wisdom which could control a Universe. Of course one mesmer she now utilised, intrinsically tied as it was to the soul-syphon. But the others – they were yet to be put to their diabolical use.

Gertus had told her these old mesmers had largely been allowed to fade from memory in order for the world to survive intact and in peace. To all intents and purposes, he had said, memories had faded enough for the lore to be the stuff of legend.

Legend? There was stuff here that could enable her to best the world in a heartbeat. How could eracing such empowerment be for the greater good? Such eminence was surely sacrosanct! She folded the papers. She had thought of how to hide the documents from none but her own eyes. There was a glassmaker...

She poured some more of the vintage drop into the beautiful goblet made by the self-same artisan. It was a smooth vessel with a finely etched design along the rim, like one of Adelina's looping stemstitch grapevines. More relaxed after the disasters of the day now that she had regained control of the situation, the Contessa lay back on her chaise-longue, musing that in actual fact to have all the major players in the one place at the one time could only be to her advantage. Luther had said the packing was complete and she had given instructions for the two of them to leave before dawn. She closed her eyes.

'You know, Gallivant,' Adelina murmured as they sat on the backs of their mounts the next day in the milky light of early dawn, 'what it is like when you tip a jigsaw from its box onto a table. Hundreds of fretted pieces of wood that must be cunningly, craftily joined to make a picture – that is how I see Severine. She is made up of hundreds of different interlocking pieces that make the whole.'

'But it is certainly not a pretty picture. Sink me Adelina, jigsaw indeed!'

The hob eased his rear in the small saddle.

'Oh, believe me. I'll wager that she can be as charming as she is a viper. As erudite as she is poisonous, that she is elegant, a benefactor of the Arts, of the Opera, the Painters' Guild, the Sculptors' Guild, of the Museo. Then there are more pieces of the jigsaw – she lives under the total misapprehension she is a Færan changeling – my fault of course.' Adelina warmed to her theme. 'And then there is the side of her that craves immortality, which is a conundrum in itself. Would not the very point of her being a Færan changeling mean then that she is also already immortal and therefore not in need of the souls at all?'

Gallivant didn't answer, allowing Adelina's loquasciousness to continue.

'It seems some part of her believes in the need for this quest for immortality, along with the confused belief she is a changeling. With the additional obsession of learning all she can about the Others, an obsession which shrinks neither from death nor maiming! I tell you, hob, it's a quagmire, this delving into another's mind! *My* view is quite simplistic – I think she is insane, for surely the killing of another, the wanton taking of a life, is insane.'

Gallivant said nothing and the movement of Adelina's horse rocked her gently. She mused silently that Severine's insanity had pervaded her waking and sleeping dreams for too long. Now, with Ajax well and freedom a commodity to be cherished, she realized she needed less and less to think on the woman's state of mind or to stoop to the woman's level and kill. *It is what I wanted to do. I wanted revenge. But is that not a form of insanity?* She fidgeted on Ajax's back. *I feel the weight of Others on my shoulders: the Swan Maid, Gallivant, Lhiannon if she still lives, Jasper... even Rajeeb. To avenge their losses. Aine knows I told them I would. And a word to an Other is a pledge. The only way to avoid it is death – one's own.* She gave a heavy sigh. *I am sorry for Liam's and Lara's demise and for how they died but I am not Other and I cannot avenge Other deaths. I am mortal and can only think of avenging one death, a mortal loss – my Kholi, and even that makes me uneasy and ill. And perversely, as my freedom grows and time distances me from all those macabre happenings, I find I can reason again and I can rationalise.*

Her cogitations were finally subsumed by the light and beauty of her surroundings and she surrendered to their charms.

The Travellers' way filled my veins again. To be sure, if I met Severine again and she goaded me, I would find it easy to slit her throat for the death of Kholi but I have another pledge I must keep in mind. As I wandered the trails of the Luned Forest with Ajax, his mane blowing in whatever little welkin wind chanced our way, I thanked the Lady that we walked together at all, remembering my promise to Her. And it is that pledge that I must adhere to no matter what. You shall see.

So, more booklets concluded and thus we must continue searching for the rest. You must follow the bees from the yellow dandelion flowers to another bee bothy. Remember how I told you it took me hours of weaving honey-coloured thread? Well, this one was exactly the same – tiresome weaving, under, over, over and under. Feel inside and pull out a thick little suede book. Enlarge and read on.

CHAPTER TWENTY ONE

Phelim had fallen into a deep sleep, rocked by the boat like a baby in its cradle. After seeing the swan and realising land was close, the tension filling him had dissipated and he relaxed his head onto the bent arm as it draped over the tiller. He thought as he drifted into sleep that perhaps Hy-Breasil was a blessing after all, having carried him safely against wave and wind to the north, to release him in a place where he could more easily find his way to Veniche and the Gate.

Once, when a knocking at the planks at his feet had woken him briefly, he lifted his head and in the light of the moon saw pairs of eyes gazing at him. Three roanes hung over the port side, the moon glinting in their silver hair, the night light casting up a phosphorescence from their creamy breasts. They murmured, a sultry seductive tone belying the downcast eyes. 'Join us, handsome one. Let us take you away, let us spoil you, let us love you.'

Phelim shook his head. 'Begone. I am not for you this night.' He waved his arm so the dory lifted its port side to flick them away like a dog shaking off water. He watched them as they gazed back at him and heard their whispers, *such a face, such a body!* He blushed as they flicked up water and dived as one into the deeps.

He stared at what he hoped was a horizon, aware that Færan mannerisms had once again come upon him unasked for and unexpected and was unable to reconcile the thought comfortably. Unconvinced that passage into his Other life should occur so seamlessly, he tipped his head to the sky and marked off the constellation, charting his position to the far north

– perhaps near the Marshes. He was mildly content and allowed the light breeze to push him on as he dozed again. Thus he did not see three avian shapes creating a black chevron against the dark sky.

The Ravens marked the tiny boat, saw one figure lying on its floor. From on high the hair was covered with a cap and the body concealed under a dark jacket but the scent of Færan the birds could determine from miles hence, the same as they had smelt close to Maria Island. They banked and headed east with their intelligence. They believed they had found the target a matter of days from Veniche. The mortal woman would be content.

The moon had reached its zenith and was preparing to descend when the dory bit into the shingle of a beach as a gentle wave lifted to cast it ashore. Withdrawing, the water left half the boat dry but the stern still wallowed and it was the zigzag motion of the toying wave that finally woke Phelim. At the end of the beach, low wind-beaten tussocks led into a fens filled with salty water and seagrass, but the shepherd could determine little more by the light of the moon and decided it was more judicious to wait for dawn and a brighter perspective. He furled the sail and set about collecting wood for a fire, the pre-dawn air being chill. Leaning with his back to the dory, his feet to the flames, he chewed on some cheese and apples, sipping from a bladder of water from Hy-Breasil.

'Thou art content, Phelim.'

He jumped up, grabbing the gaff hook and holding it firmly.

'Thou needs no weapon when thou talks to myself, Færan.' On the other side of the fire, a slim, black column of a woman stood warming her hands. 'It is brisk. Winter approaches the northern climes with speed.'

'A swan-maid!' He was struck by the woman's white beauty, accentuated by the soft drift of her black satin dress and the heavily feathered ebony cloak.

'It is rewarding to know all thy senses are still intact. A swan-maid indeed. Thou hast Maeve in thy presence. She would talk with thee.'

'It was you who flew over the boat earlier.' He was about to say he was grateful for the hope she had given him that land was not far distant but in her habitual, dismissive and sibilant way, she cut in.

'Thou art observant! But tell me Phelim of the Færan, do you have a fellow passenger, a Færan woman?'

'She could not come with me.' He ignored the pointed question, replying with one of his own. 'How do you know me, know that I am Færan? I hardly know myself.'

'I saw thee with roanes. Thou art Færan and look familiar.' But like the best interrogator, she returned to the subject of her concern. 'Tell Maeve, Phelim, I ask thee again, where is Lhiannon? My sister heard thy stepmother and her urisk friend discussing the souls but they did not mention the Færan woman.'

He looked at Maeve. The brightness of the flame hid her intent eyes from his gaze but she stood immobile, immutable it seemed. He took a breath. 'Lhiannon is dead.'

The swan-maid hissed and her head turned to the side so that her long gleaming hair fell as straight as a die in a waterfall cascade over one shoulder. 'How so?' The words spat forth.

'She was killed by a bite from a tiny poisonous octopus on Maria Island. My stepmother and I tried to save her to no avail. She said it was her bane and for us not to be grieved.'

Another hiss and she glided quickly and quietly around the fire to stand directly between he and the flame. 'Then have thou something of value the girl carried?'

He forbore to reply. He had limited knowledge of swan-maids, apart from the legends Ebba had told him – they showed themselves rarely to mortals. Could they be unseelie? He hoped his newly acquired intuition would not desert him at this crucial moment. The swan-maid laughed, a haunting cry like a waterbird. 'Not so Færan then! Thou art afraid to answer! Think thou I would take souls from thee? I who helped Lhiannon escape? Stupid man! Thou needs to be more at ease as thy new self, Maeve thinks.'

Her amusement, her condescension, bit into Phelim's mood and he snapped back. 'Yes, I have the souls. It was Lhiannon's dying wish that they be taken to Jasper at the Veniche Gate.' He sat down. 'Frankly I don't know why if he is all seeing, he doesn't come here to me and retrieve the souls. Already the journey has cost a life and perhaps there will be more. I fail to see the value of happy *dead* souls when live ones are more important. The woman who wants them is sure to know they left from Maria Island.

She will no doubt be trying to track the boat down as we speak!'

'Phelim has not yet developed understanding of Others or he would be sympathetic of our needs.' The look she cast on the shepherd was filled with a disgusted impatience. 'Maeve hopes thy maturing is not long in coming for if thee has *thy* soul stolen, then shall thee understand the black pain thy Færan peers suffered, pain all Others would avoid or ameliorate, should it happen to loved ones. Elders say it is like pain of a thousand lashes or pain of constant suffocation. Some texts say it is like pain of disembowelling. Has Maeve made it clear for thee?' She sneered, her beautiful mouth straightened to a dark red line. 'Nevertheless, thou art correct in thy earlier thoughts because foul Ravens even now fly to the Soul-Stealer with thy whereabouts. Maeve thinks they mistook thee for the girl in the little boat. But – as Maeve said – stupid man! Whether it is thee or Jasper who takes the souls from this point, even me let it be said, the Gate in Veniche must be entered. Maeve thinks that is where Soul-Stealer shall wait. Maeve has spoken to Jasper. The more Others at the portal the better to confuse the issue. But it shall be thee who takes the souls, Phelim. And it is fitting because thou art Færan, even if thou art ignorant of Færan ways. Rest easy, half-time mortal, there shall be many Others there as well. The woman shall not win.'

'Why don't the Others just kill her? It seems you all require revenge.'

'Indeed, it is what Maeve asks time and again.' She sighed. 'It is because a mortal has demanded the right to her death. The Threadlady…'

'Adelina!'

'I see thou knows the story. Indeed, Adelina. Maeve offered her Other help but she spurned it.' The swan-maid snorted, an ugly sound from the beautiful visage. 'The woman may well be killed by Adelina but she will not suffer. We would have her suffer deeply as a message to more of her ilk to leave what they can never understand alone. A warning, dost thou understand?'

Again the two sides of Phelim warred with each other. The mortal side cringed from the outrageous cruelty of the swan-maid's revelations. The Other side calmly agreed with her. He remained silent as each side battled for supremacy.

'Thou art a deep one. Thy thoughts are thy own!' Maeve laughed, a short hooting sound. 'So! I shall direct thee.' She turned and pointed. 'Behind thee is the Fens. There are streams and rivulets lacing through seagrasses and one in particular is deep enough for thee to take thy boat all the way into the Marshes. Better to leave the open sea now Ravens have located thee. Soul-Stealer will not expect thee from the Marshes. There thou can find a Veniche-bound boat and make for the Gate. The portal Phelim, is...' she bent and pretended to whisper, the softness of her breath tickling and tantalizing and she finished by licking the cusp of his ear. She laughed as his head bent unconsciously to hers. 'Dost thou think Maeve wants thee? Ah, sadly for thee, no. And dost thou think Maeve would know location of Færan Gate? Huh, feckless Færan trust no Others and will not share secret. Thou must find it thyself!' She laughed again as he jerked his head away, cheeks flaming.

'I...'

'Thou are not yet comfortable in thy Færan skin, Phelim, half-time mortal. It will happen. Now follow Maeve's directions and trust her when she says Others will be there to help.'

She rustled the cloak of feathers, like a bird shaking itself down and before his eyes she became a black swan and pushed herself into the brightening sky, uttering a call to usher in the dawn.

CHAPTER TWENTY TWO

Phelim set about unpacking the dory, unloading the food. Everything that would threaten the boat's lightness and therefore its passage through the narrow channels of the Fens was cast aside. Inevitably all that was left was an oar, the gaff and himself as he towed the boat along the shore to the opening of Maeve's channel where he tied the craft to a log.

He heaped the ditched goods and then stood wafting his hand over them, allowing whatever Færan mesmer came into his head to do its job. The objects faded before his eyes – just disappeared, no dust, nothing to indicate that they had even been and he could not help the flicker of surprise then pleasure, almost a conceit, that coursed through him. Huh, he thought, and was not unhappy. He listened to the ocean waves for the last time and pushed off inland, the reeds and brush closing over his secret path, insulating him from the crisp rattle of the coastal wash.

He poled the dory as if it were a punt, using the oar deftly off the stern of the boat, kneeling on the floor the better to conceal himself. The smell of the pale gold and green grasses and the peat that lined the banks wrapped itself around like a blanket as he ventured forward. He saw dragonflies and damselflies wafting in the early light, hovering, almost still and then darting erratically sideways. Ahead fish leaped, concentric rings casting out, and underneath him a writhing shape undulated past. The sun warmed and he threw off his coat, holding it below the water until the sodden mass sank to the floor of the channel. The retrieved souls hung by his side under his shirt, a constant thorn, reminder of an endeavour he must bring to fruition.

He thought about himself in the quiet of the Fens. He was the same but different – like a boy who overnight has entered adolescence and awakes to find a cracked voice, a gawky body and pustules in amongst the stiffening hair which signifies whiskers. Inside, the youth still feels like the boy but moody, introspective moments remind him that a man is lurking beneath his uncomfortable skin. Part of him buzzes with excitement, part of him would rather meet a Red Cap than deal with it.

The air of the gentle shepherd hung about Phelim still – one who had never traveled, whose hearth and fields were his world and all he wanted from life. The thought that he could dispatch Other spirits and mortals at will made the gourge rise in the 'half-time mortal's' gullet. The shepherd's side of him was afraid, afraid of all the Others he had ever heard of. At the same time, the Færan would remember Hy-Breasil, the swan-maid and the souls resting as heavy and cold as lead against his chest as he headed towards Veniche and he would become energised.

Light in the Fens rarely changed: a wash of pale greens, faded blues and golds. Only in the early evenings and mornings were the colours flamed like opals with a vermilion fire. Waterfowl clucked and called in chorus as Phelim guided the craft along the varied watery lanes and slowly the landscape began to change.

Twisted and broken crack-willows shaded inaccessible banks. There were signs of life – holes for water rats and otters and once a fisherman poled past, dressed in the green of the Marshes. He raised a stumpy finger to his forehead by way of greeting. Otherwise no word was spoken and the peculiar quiet of the Fens pervaded all.

Further along a wider canal, larger trees graced the banks. Weeping willows and large ferns, mahoganies, blackwoods and bay trees shaded Phelim from the watery sun as the craft poled ever deeper into a thickening shadow where cobweb-like skeins of marsh moss hung from the trees. The sound of a frog chorus, the secretive calls of the mopokes and wood pigeons, the occasional cooing of doves and a chittering which warned of Siofra filled the silence and reminded Phelim that he had entered the Marshes, an enchanted place.

Despite the cold ache at his side demanding he move on with speed, he drifted and spied a tiny slip of river sand lit from above with an aureole of sun. Just wide enough for the dory, he pulled it on the shingle and sat with freshly washed hands against the bole of a myrtle tree, its starry white flowers dropping beside him. Tall water iris and plantain hid him and solitude surrounded him – until he heard voices – male and female. By the *frisson*, he guessed they were Færan.

'You shouldn't have left her mesmered. It was unkind and she could be prey to anything.' The woman's voice was well modulated and there was a tinge of disgust in the tones.

'*She* shouldn't have been fool enough to spurn the advances of a good-looking fellow like myself. And besides, it was only a partial mesmer.'

The man's response showed a touch of self-mockery and Phelim suspected he teased the woman. He remained hidden and presently the voices moved out of range, their horses' hoofbeats fading into a faint thud and then nothing. He realized that somewhere close by, some poor mortal girl had been the butt of an idle game and left half-mesmered on the edge of a dangerous waterway, unable to move and at the whim of any unseelie Other who passed. Aine he thought, turning to track along the way the specious couple had come, they might as well have signed the girl's death warrant!

As Severine and Luther galloped through the forests of the Styx, over the moors and into the Luned on their covetous hunt, they ignored the beauty of the hours of dawn. Nor did it occur to Countess di Accia, as garnet coloured autumn leaves trailed in her wake, that she was re-visiting the scenes of slaughter. In the Styx Forest, amongst shadow and subfusc, a grey stone statue of a gnome screamed into infinity with clawed hands shielding terrified eyes. In the Luned Forest by the side of an eldritch rill, where tricksy sprites spied with sly eyes, a dark rusty stain, legacy of a mortal death, was concealed by crisp, fallen leaves, and the place of Liam's death was marked by a frost white shape burned into the ground.

On the other side of the Luned, two people ambled towards their destination. There was no doubt that if Ajax had not led, Bottom would never have followed. As Gallivant approached him early in the day, when the only sound had been the soft chirrup and whistle of forest birds, he wailed like a banshee until Adelina spoke to him, fondling the lop ears, kissing the velvet nose, explaining the hob was gentle and kind.

'Tell him while you are at it, that another wail like that could give us all away.' Gallivant was miffed – Adelina's ability with the animal irked him.

'To whom? At best he sounds like some lost donkey, at worst a werewolf and as this is the Luned, it is what one would expect. Didn't you hear the hobyahs just before dawn? They sounded perilously close.'

Huh! Hobyahs – creatures of nightmare that feed off fear. Indeed he had heard them! Waking him from a doze when he should have been alert and minding Adelina.

The fire of the evening had burnt to coals that flared as a sulky night breeze blew through their encampment. Gallivant dozed with his back against a tree, his body in shadow from the overhanging branches. Adelina stretched out under his riding coat and the bruised red glow from the coals lit the planes of her face. She tossed and turned although the hob was unaware, his eyes having drifted shut earlier.

She said later that she had been dreaming of Kholi, seeing him on that last day as he struggled in Luther's grip, feeling the bite of the garotte as tiny beads of blood sparkled like rubies along the arched, taut line of the straining throat. Adelina wailed in her dream but around the encampment it came out as a strangled moan, as if something equally fatal had pressed against her own air-passage to throttle her. In the dream, Kholi's throat was slowly sawed through as he yelled after Severine, *'you'll find out!'* As she strode away, Luther delivered a quick coup de grace and Adelina screamed and screamed, feeling the pressure on her own throat increasing.

The hob woke as he heard Adelina threshing. Jumping up, he threw himself against the hobyahs who were trying to crush the throat of their victim. He thumped them about their heads, calling a mesmer so the rowan branch which he could not lift but which he could cause to fly through the air, beat hard against one head and then the other.

Adelina's eyes flew open and the nightmare sped into the recesses of memory as fast as the howling hobyahs ran off to the trees and away. Sighing, her eyes closing again with a sleep mesmer from the hob, she slumbered, this time placidly because at great discomfort to himself, Gallivant had kept Adelina safe, surrounded by rowan and hazel twigs and chains of daisies and hypericum flower. He had slept little and was somewhat sour this morning.

And so they proceeded at an ambiguous pace – Ajax walking slowly, Bottom trotting along behind on his delicate hooves. Only Gallivant sensed the ugly shades of the Luned as memories drifted on the woody zephyrs, something he forbore to mention to Adelina.

He felt a need to hurry her on. To get to the safety of the Marshes where they could blend with the mortals there. A spasmodic welkin wind, cousin to the zephyrs, swirled on the outer edges of their trail, lifting leaves in a spiral and warning the hob, as it would have warned Ebba, that Severine was not far away.

'See how the trees change, Gallivant? They thicken and are decorated with veils of moss. And the ground is wetter with more streams and rivulets. The smell is richer as well, the air more humid. It's a secret place.'

An air of contentment wrapped Adelina in its care. After the grief and pain of her three months imprisonment, even allowing for the absence of Kholi, she felt lighter. Her legs stretched wide around the vast middle of her beloved Ajax and she felt more secure than she had for ninety-three days.

'A safe place. There are stables on the outskirts of the town and we can leave the animals hidden.' Gallivant's serious voice hung under the misty moss. 'I know the Marshers and they are kind.'

It was true. I felt more at ease, as if the strange humid airs of the Marshes sustained me. Eldritch to be sure. Severine and memories of despair seemed far away on the other side of the world and I sank into my new equitable state, deliberately not drawing up unsettling thoughts, keeping calm, looking forward to Veniche and possibly seeing Lhiannon. But as I grew calmer, the hob became more edgy, as if a doom hung over his shoulder and he would not talk to me about it and I confess I was glad.

But all that aside, you must search for the next books.

Look for the bees again and follow them to the Herb Robert that you will recognize from our medicinal and kitchen gardens. The three pink geranium flowers have eighteen separate wired petals and they hide two journals and the silky blue butterfly hides one. The butterfly is rendered in a fine, lustrous Færan thread. It is a thread I compared to Liam a lifetime ago – superb, but capricious and with a mind of its own.

I shall tell you this for free my friend... should you ever reach a perilous stage in your life where you need to sort out the mind's wanderings, write a journal, it helps sort the good from bad.

CHAPTER TWENTY THREE

The girl sat frozen, completely immobile. All except for her head, which Phelim could see was turning. She was pale, a spasmodic shudder shifting her shoulders, her eyes darting in the direction of every noise. He concealed himself under a willow with its trailing, leafy branches, standing amongst the elongated leaves of the spatterdock lily that reached to his waist. He was captivated by what he observed – by the girl's smooth face and by her comely shape. She was dressed in the dark fustian of the Marshes, a pair of tight trews tucked into eelskin boots and a seaweed green sweater over all. A broad black ribbon anchored her silver hair to her forehead and the bulk of the beautiful swathe hung down her back and curled at the bottom. In the river breeze, tendrils blew about her face but she was unable to wipe them away. She turned her head into the zephyr to free the strands and turned back again, all the while an element of anxiety and tremulousness shadowing her face.

Phelim parted the willow fronds and slid his eyes over her fine visage with its gently moulded cheekbones. Her brown eyes reminded him of chocolate and her lips trembled as she surveyed her predicament. And as he continued to examine this ripe young thing, a mist began to trail around his shoulders and arms and a black waft of some malicious spirit slipped up his veins and into his soul and heart.

He jerked back, the willow sliding from his fingers, turning to source the unseelie thing that darkened his very existence to such damnation. But there was nothing. Just a ray of light from a willow-strangled sunbeam leading to his hidden position amongst the branches. Nothing else. No spirit, no shade – no shadow.

Phelim of Merricks, son of Ebba, sucked in his breath as he stared at the space behind him. He should, like any other living thing, have a shadow. But the grasses and plants lay naked. No darkness there, no graphic outline, nothing to anchor his mortal body to the ground of the real world. Because Phelim wasn't mortal and needed no earthly anchor, he could exist in two worlds. As the horrible realization filled half his mind, the other half chuntered a wicked, sadistic laugh and the darkness that had entered his veins solidified.

The girl heard the laugh and looked in the direction of the willow, her breath coming in sharp little gushes. Around her the birds stopped singing, the air filled with expectation.

Phelim's eyes focused completely on the girl and he could almost feel his pupils dilating to vast ebony saucers so that he knew, should she look into them, she would be in his sway and unable to deny him anything. The thought excited him, giving him a sense of power.

His mind filled with sweet, beguiling words the better to woo her and his body hardened and stiffened with fierce desire. He took a step forward and crunched a twig and the girl uttered a strangled yelp as sharp as the snap of that broken branch. The air by the riverbank filled with the *frisson* that is Other and which smacked of disaster as Phelim appeared through the willow, the delicate branches trailing over his shoulders along with the eldritch mist. The fear in her eyes goaded the Færan – for Phelim had become the Ganconer, the Far Dorocha, the Dark haired Man.

But as the girl uttered a more piercing cry, a miniscule part of the half-time mortal's soul opened up and conscience crept out to stake a toehold in the struggle threatening to rent Phelim's mind apart.

By now the girl could see him fully – tall, his black hair curling on his collar, his magnificently carved face filled with the intent of seduction, his mouth desirous of kissing. His eyes pinioned her to the spot like a fish on the end of a knife and she squirmed, longing and fear intimately entwined. But she could not move, trapped in the mesmer like bait on a hook.

Phelim heard her cry... that part of him that vaguely remembered being mortal, and disgust at his hard sexual needs, sympathy for her fear, pity for her misplaced desire welled up into a miserable fount. He moaned, fingers crushing into the hard palms of his hands as the Ganconer walked on, whispering precocious and daring love-talk.

The girl watched him with trepidation. She wanted him but she feared him and the expectation created trills of desire. She heard his words, uttered with such cunning devotion as he approached and she lusted like a thirsty mortal craving water and all idea that she could die from such surfeit melted from her willing body.

Within Phelim a battle raged. Gratification or not!
His heart ached and with a final effort, Ebba's upbringing grabbed the Ganconer by the neck and squeezed to the point of extinction. His body softened, the sexual urge shriveling, shrinking, disgust pushing back the darkness.

Tears of realization fell down the girl's trembling cheeks as she watched the mist dissolve from Phelim's shoulders, his shadow stretching away from his toes as he slumped to his knees, sweat beading his forehead.
'I'm sorry,' he whispered, birds beginning to chirrup again. 'I wouldn't hurt you.' He wafted his hand and her frozen lower limbs loosened. She wrapped her arms around, protecting herself from what might befall her as he continued in an anguished voice. 'You should not be here on your own.' He turned his face away as he spoke.
'Are you the Ganconer?' She kept her distance but there sounded the faintest wistful tone as she asked.
'The Ganconer!' Phelim could hardly bear to mouth the name. 'The Ganconer is every Færan male who would seduce a mortal woman. If I am desire, then I am the Ganconer, I am what *you* desire!' He could hear the words falling from his lips but could scarce believe them as though his mind and his voice were two different people. 'Every Færan male is desire.

If you see us we can beguile you to the point of death. Tell your friends to beware or they shall be weaving their shrouds by nightfall.'

'But you didn't touch me. Why? Am I not attractive?' The hurt face begged to be stroked and the man in front of her took further steps toward her.

He smiled faintly and sighed. '*Muirnin*, you are lovely. Too lovely to waste your life on a Færan dalliance. Lovely enough to belong to a mortal man who will cherish you as his wife and the mother of his children until you are old.'

She looked longingly at him and turned away, stopping momentarily as if to thank him although she no doubt knew to offer gratitude to an Other was to offer offence of great magnitude. Instead,

'I know who you really are!' She gave him a grateful smile. 'You're the Red-Haired Man. I see it in your locks now in the sun, a faint wine-coloured tint here and there. Is it not true that you warn us against your race in the most altruistic way? That you lead us to safety from what harm could befall us, warn us against the Færan way, bless us so that we shall not be abducted?'

Phelim heard the Lady's words. *The Dark Haired Man and the Red Haired Man – you shall meet them on your journey. Beware.* 'Dusk approaches. If you want to avoid my brother the Dark Haired Man who is the chiefest abducter, who is silent and powerful and cruel, then you must hasten to your home. Begone now!' He turned his back and walked to the willow, casting himself invisible as he passed into the waving shade, only to turn and watch the girl secretly.

She stood looking to where he had disappeared, rubbing her forehead and shaking her head, but hearing a horn blowing faintly far away, she turned and hurried toward Ferry Crossing and Phelim's most immediate destination, her words flying behind her.

'I met the Love Talker one eve in the glen,
He was handsomer than our handsome young men,

*His eyes were blacker than the sloe, his voice sweeter far
than the crooning of... pipes in Coolnagar.'*
Silence swallowed the rest of her poem and birds filled the space with prettier music.

CHAPTER TWENTY FOUR

The girl's descriptive verse had pricked every part of Phelim. The Dark haired Man! The Ganconer! If he had not battled the monumental darkness of desire that had been as blood to his body, then the girl would have lain with him. Færan would say it was not rape because she would have wanted it as much as he, but Phelim knew she would have been befuddled and beguiled and at a complete disadvantage. Afterwards she would have remained numb to anything but the fantasy of love, her desire eating away at her body and mind as she searched every face for that of her Ganconer. Deprived of satisfaction and gratification, she would pine, becoming listless, refusing to eat.

Sadly, she would in her wiser moments realize she was fading and, choosing death with love, rather than life without, she would spend night after long, cold and loveless night weaving her shroud and laundering it with a basin of bereft tears, ever alert to every noise should the Ganconer return to her door. But the Ganconer never returned and many a girl had pined to death, white skin and sharp bone.

Phelim closed his eyes at the image of what he had so very nearly caused, utterly cogniscent that the path of the Dark-Haired Man, the Far Dorocha, was the path of damnation. His legs trembled with weakness as if he had trod for years all over the world and his scalp almost split apart from his head as if an axe cleaved it, so great had been the battle with his Other side. He rested briefly, slumped in the willow's womb-like shade.

This then had been his coming of age. The girl saw him as Færan, with all the attributes and abominations mortals believed Færan could possess. He was struck dumb. No longer of the world of men! How had this happened so quickly! It was as though Ebba had opened a weir-gate when she had told him and all of his previous life had sluiced away!

And what would she feel now? Would she still love him as the son she had raised? And the Merricks people? They would despise him and be afraid, he was sure. His man's heart, twenty-eight years of age, cracked a little. The girl had stared at him through eyes that were cautious and unsure. This was how it would be – everyone distrustful.

How angry he was now! Angry at himself, angry at the girl, angry at Fate which had contrived to throw a large stone into the calm pond of his life and set up a thousand uneasy ripples. Turning him into the very antithesis of what he wished to be.

Fulsome, woody silence surrounded him, pressing down on his neck and shoulders and he heard the sarcastic chunterings of sprites amongst the undergrowth. He thought of the girl and sought to follow her to her destination to see her safe, but decided to give her a few moments to get ahead as he didn't want to alarm her. The mocking whispering became louder as he waited and he spun around, fury filling his veins. Fate now stretched before him, illuminated and gilded in the gaudiest way by all the wretched tales he had ever heard of Færan from mortal lips. A never-ending lifetime of loneliness, an infinity of being misunderstood.

His experiences of the past few days erupted into a fount of angry melancholy as he railed against his predicament. The unwanted knowledge of his ancestry, leaving his home, the death of Lhiannon – too much too soon, even for a man of his age. So much of his life had been spent comfortingly in the knowledge, the surety, that his days would be spent like other men – working, laughing, eating, sleeping, crying even, but all shared within the close circle of the Merricks demesnes. The awful belief that such communal warmth was now lost to him forever – for it was, they would never countenance a Færan living in their midst – cut him to the very quick of his soul. He picked up a fallen bough and with a rising crescendo of roaring, flung it into the shrubbery, occasioning a shriek from whoever dwelled there.

The souls burned cold and with no comfort into his side.

Unwillingly and with no excitement and with the knowledge he had no choice, he followed in the girl's footsteps.

Adelina and Gallivant had reached the outlying steading of a Marsher. Known to the hob to be a kind man of understanding, the hob prevailed upon Adelina to ask for a secret stabling of their mounts.

'How do you know this man to have such integrity? Surely all mouths become indiscreet with money?' She was leading Ajax by a loose rein along the narrow towpath at the side of one of the many shaded rivulets that laced through the Marshes. Gallivant and Bottom followed, the donkey snatching at sweet mouthfuls of river-grass, a long seed head hanging out of his mouth like the pipe of some grizzled old shepherd.

'I know of the integrity of the house Adelina, trust me. He has had dealings with Others before and trusts us as we trust him.'

She had noticed the hob had become ever more serious of late, dour and crisp, so that she wondered if they had exchanged persona. But he *had* contrived her escape so she could do nought but listen and be prevailed upon by his advice.

She left her horse at the edge of the path and proceeded along a raised walk to the door of a house perched four square on thick pylons over the water. At her knock, a rosy face answered and a bewhiskered mouth smiled when she politely asked for stabling. 'Course I got room for your beasts and they'll be well hid. It'll be for the best. Come with me.'

She followed the Marsher back along the walkway to the towpath and gathering Gallivant and the rides on the way, made for a solid barn with wide swinging doors and positioned on an isthmus of land between rivulets. Myrtle and blackwood and skeins of marsh moss hid it from prying eyes. Inside stood a solid gentleman's hunter that nickered pleasantly from its stall. Two stalls stood empty, the third of the four-stall barn filled with a toffee-coloured house cow, who broke from contented chewing of a wad of lucerne to turn and low at them, her eyes fringed by thick lashes. The Marsher trotted back and forth with arms of hay and pails of water. 'Stick 'em in the stalls. They'll be safe while you do your business and when you're ready, come back and they'll be waiting.'

'It's very good of you, but I'm not sure how to p...'

Gallivant reached in front of Adelina and passed over a small clinking black bag. 'That's to be going on with.' He smiled a serious, 'business is business' smile.

Adelina looked at the hob curiously – just *where* did he get *that* from, the money and the manner?

'Nay.' The fellow passed the jingling bag back. 'Pay me when you're done. I prefer it that way. There now, look at that, they're very happy!'

And indeed the two animals had pushed noses deep into the meadow-sweet hay and betrayed no concern whatever as their owners left with the Marsher.

'I don't know how long we'll be.' Adelina shook hands with the man who reminded her a little of Buckerfield.

'If you follow that path', the Marsher pointed slightly north, 'that'll get you to Ferry Crossing in next to no time.' He looked at the sky that was beginning to darken. 'And not a moment too soon. Now winter approaches, the nights are drawing in very hasty. Alright then, be off or the bogeys'll get you in the dark.' He waved as they moved away. 'Cheerio.'

Their feet echoed on the hard timber planks of the boardwalk. In single file, passing the occasional journeyman walking in the other direction, they proceeded carefully for there were no protective handrails on either side. I'd not like to travel the walkway in the dark, thought Adelina, despite the *torchères* placed every few feet. She looked at the dark green depths to either side and fancied she saw the leering faces of fuaths of all kinds, male and female.

'Well, Threadlady,' the hob spoke from behind, sensing her unease. 'You wanted to go to Veniche and you must pass through the Marshes to do it.' It was his turn to be ascerbic. 'I just can't see that this little escapade will accomplish anything, Adelina!'

'I want to see Lhiannon, hob, to know she is safe. I owe it to her because she tried to keep me safe. Besides she gave me *your* friendship, I am obliged to her for that if nothing else. And I've told you before, I have this feeling that all who know me are...'

'Fated to die, I know, I know. Sink me woman, it's ridiculous! And I fail to see how you being near the Gate, which I might add is another problem, is going to help with anything. Adelina, forgive me, but you *are* mortal and will be more of a hindrance than a help with this quest Lhiannon must carry out. Other business is best *left* to Others, trust me.'

'Well pardon me for caring, hob!' Adelina muttered under her breath. She strode along, bigger steps that caused Gallivant to trot to keep up. 'And *sink me*, why is me being near the Gate *another problem*.' She mimicked his tone as she posed the question. Behind her she heard a tired sigh and slowed down.

'It's not exactly you being near the Gate that's the problem, Adelina. It's... oh, it's that I don't exactly know where it is in Veniche. No one does except the Færan. So you see, this whole thing is a bit of a wild goose chase during which you lay yourself open to discovery and, let's not be coy about this, death because we will never find Lhiannon I'm sure and if Severine chances upon you, she will snuff out your flame,' he blew a breath out sharply, 'just like that!'

He stopped and she halted as well and turned around carefully because she didn't want to overbalance into the arms of the Nökken. She took a step toward the hob and hugged him. 'You're right, I know. But Gallivant, I have been such a victim and I think to myself of all whom I loved and who have displayed such outright courage. I must be brave too because I have still to exact a reckoning of sorts, don't I? And if I could just know Lhiannon is still alive it would give me such a boost. Please try and understand.' She took his slim hands in her own and squeezed them. 'Look at it this way if you like. I am a woman and a mortal into the bargain, so nothing much I say is going to make any sense, is it? We are not regarded by Others as the most clear-thinking bunch, are we? But I can tell you this – I am aware there may be danger and if you can bear with me knowing that I might be your poison as much as anyone else's, then I would rather have none but you by my side and at my back.' She smiled the golden smile that so charmed Buckerfield and had brought Kholi melting like Goti tsampa in the Raji sun, to her side.

The lights along the boardwalks lit up Ferry Crossing, little golden will o' the wisps, delicate, pretty and enticing... The lamplighter proceeded through the unusual town calling *'light time, night time'* and children circled around him like moths to the flame. The lamps created yellow patterns on the water meandering through the Marshes, shivering and wavering in the light evening breeze that wafted between the piers. In places undisturbed by the dancing night airs, one could look down and think a depository of topaz or bullion lay below the surface. It could be a trap for the unwary, thought Adelina, designed to draw some negligent, greedy mortal into the waters of the Pealliadh or the Addanc and from there to their deaths. She shivered.

To her left and right, boardwalks led to four square wooden buildings on thick wooden pylons and with skillion rooves and finials which in daylight would have revealed the carved shapes of marshbirds. And by way of an address, that is how one found one's way in Ferry Crossing: to the House of the Swan, the House of the Egret, the House of the Moorhen and so forth. Gallivant led the two of them to the Inn of the Thrush, a comfortable hostelry on the seaward side of the town and whose rooms overlooked the broad sweep of the laguna. One could stand at night and look to the north over those waters and see a hazy aura of light cushioned by the horizon – Veniche, its glow beckoning and enticing.

CHAPTER TWENTY FIVE

The girl had led Phelim unwittingly through the Marshes towards Ferry Crossing on the edge of the laguna. As he walked through the woods, he thought back to one of Ebba's acidic comments on the Færan.

'To be frank,' she said as her knotted fingers slipped over Grimalkin's white fur. 'I think Færan are extremely content at being what they are: self-indulgent, arrogant, utterly oblivious to the damage their games cause. And they are never involved in *serious* business: life is ever the pursuit of one light moment after another at the expense of anything that lies in their way.'

Phelim now examined this. Never one to be less than courteous, gentle and empathetic, he found Other reputations sticking to his hide like wet clay to a farmer's boot. Contrary, perturbed at being Færan when he wished to be what he had always been, that part of him that had been coaxed and groomed by his mortal stepmother fought to be free of the Færan slur. The memory of the girl's expression as she faced him earlier had filled him with distaste and despair. He hadn't asked to be Færan and he wondered if the Færan woman and her bag of souls had never entered his life, whether Ebba would ever have told him the truth. He could hear her loved voice so clearly in his mind and he recalled the only thing she had ever said of Veniche, his destination.

'Aine Phelim, it's wet and smells of mould and damp and is like to bring on an ague. Pretty if you like the light on the water and the gracious buildings but I'm for the open spaces of woods, sea and sky, where I watch a linnet fly free and not cooped in a gilded cage. For me, Veniche is a big gilded cage! Mind you, they make superlative glass. I always regret never buying a millefiore paperweight. Those little objèts looks as though the Færan have scooped up a field of wild flowers and shrunk them to minikin size and placed them under glass.'

People ebbed and flowed around him in rivulets as wide as the walkways. He relished the sights and sounds, the colour, the wide palette of green as the Marshers hurried about their dusk business. He thought it was like looking across a coppice of leaf and bud in springtime.

Except for that flaming autumn shade...

His eyes grasped at the colour, the tint of a new-minted groat, gelt that most rarely see. And thus Marshers turned and looked curiously at the woman as she pushed against the flow, a thin, elfish fellow guiding her.

Phelim's eyes rested on the downcast face and as he observed the tawny hair and softly tinted skin, he was struck by a gentle pain under his ribs where the chamois bag rested, warming like a heart that has found true love.

Around him, as the unusual pair approached, the sound of cheer and gossip hummed. The odd mild call echoed but everybody seemed equable and polite so that when a harsh, wild shout split the ambience apart, the woman and her friend were galvanized as if by a bolt of lightning.

'*Bitseach! Bitseach!* I'll get you!' At the far end of a walkway, a bald-headed ruffian screamed and the woman's head flew up, her companion dragging a dark hood over her hair and then pulling her along until they were level with Phelim.

He stepped aside, the woman's magnificent hazel eyes meeting his and he saw how they overflowed with fear and how tears made them sparkle. The fellow pushing her hissed, 'Come on, Threadlady! Down here, quickly!' And as he dashed past, the *frisson* that is Other vibrated between he and Phelim.

The agitated atmosphere sparked as people called and jostled like birds disturbed, the Marshers disliking the aggressive shouts from further along the walkway. But the thug continued to yell, battering his way through the crowd and Phelim watched as the hunted couple dashed down a dark walkway, under the shade of large overhanging eaves.

The ruffian had cold grey eyes Phelim observed, with nothing but death and misery in their far reaches and the fellow's mouth snarled as he shoved aside men, women and children.

The chamois bag become colder during the fracas, chilling until it burned Phelim's ribs with frostbite, and all that was Færan in him once again flooded effortlessly to his fingertips and he cast himself invisible, waving a hand at the walkway down which the lady and the hob had disappeared so that it shape-changed into the vertical boards of a blunt-ended building. His leg came out as Luther rushed by and the fellow tripped, crashing to the walkway, his chin striking the ground.

Gallivant glanced back.

That fellow, the one with the *frisson,* he was Other to be sure! Færan? He hadn't got a good look, hustling Adelina as he had been. Now he saw Luther trip and fall over something, his chin crashing heavily into the timber of the walkway. And there was something about the way people walked past their own hiding place as if it didn't exist, that made him wonder at their good fortune.

'Gallivant,' Adelina shivered, her face pale as a shroud, 'how did he get here? I didn't think he'd find me so soon. Aine help me!'

'Hush Lady, hush! We are honestly as safe as if we are on the other side of the world. But we must be careful to cover your hair, it's like a beacon. Oh, look Adelina, sink me, look at that!'

At Phelim's feet, Luther moaned. People bent to help him stand but he brushed away their concern and holding a linen square to his profusely bleeding chin, he shouted. 'Where are they, did you see them? The woman with red hair and the man! They went down that way!' He pointed at the bare wall in front of him. People shook their heads and their mutterings provoked him further. 'You must have seen them! They were so obvious. Are you wretched idiots blind? So help me!' He spun around in a vortex of rage.

A brave man, taller and broader than Luther and whiskered with importance, took Luther firmly by the arm. 'Sir, you have hurt yourself and given your head a resounding wallop. There was no red-haired woman and you see, this building has no entry from this walkway.' The man bent and sniffed at Luther. 'I think you perhaps had a little too much wine earlier and perhaps you imagine things. Either way, you must get that chin doctored because it is split open like a watermelon. Come now!'

Luther jerked his arm but the man held fast, and turning a last, angry and baffled look at the wall and seeing blood dripping at his feet, he finally allowed himself to be led away.

The House of the Pee-Wit hung over the water, the patron welcoming Phelim pleasantly and giving him a room overlooking the gold-tinged water of the laguna. Much later, bathed and fed and with a promise his clothes would be clean by morning, he took his tired body and his over-filled head to the pillow. Outside he could here the small slap of wavelets against the piers of this town above the water, and in the distance, the sound of frogs and crickets and the odd nightbird. Occasionally there was an unseelie shriek and he would automatically perform the horn sign and catch himself ruefully.

He drifted in that delicate state between dozing and sleep, content for a few hours to let introspection and examination disappear. Færan or not, exhaustion claimed him and he surrendered himself quite readily to sleep when it came, glad to forget for a moment of the chameleon changes of his life and the results such changes may incur.

As Gallivant was I know not where, in the room I shared with the hob at the House of the Thrush I was making a fulsome discovery. There was a full-length mirror and after a bath, I had stood surveying the body that had been immured in prison for three months, suffering the agonies of grief and depression and all the nausea and loss of appetite and bodily changes that such conditions entail.

One would assume I would be thin and drawn.

Except I was not.

My thickened waist and heavily veined breasts told me one thing alone.

I was pregnant.

I smoothed my hand over the gently swelling belly, stroking the child of the Raj who lay safe and cocooned in the dark. I guessed I had become pregnant that fateful morning when Kholi and I had made love quietly and frantically, with Liam drugged and asleep in the pavilion in the throes of his own awful grief.

On that same morning, Kholi Khatoun, the love of my life and father of my child, had then dressed and gone hunting the Fates and Death.

CHAPTER TWENTY SIX

Excitement filled Ferry Crossing, tangible like a breeze across the skin. Today was the day of the Festival of Water Dressing, a symbolic appeasement to the spirits of the water because everyone knew that water was the mainstream of life and fertility. The Festival took place at midday and all the unattached maids of the town were to execute the Dressing at the wharves, appropriately garbed in white gowns embroidered all over with floral patterns.

Drifting along the boardwalks like so many veela, the young, nubile girls of the town carried baskets of botanica of every conceivable sort, and pieces of glittering quartz and river shells – all for the Dressing. Awaiting them was a large square of sand lying on a stretched canvas on which the floral and woodland offerings would be laid to make a picture of colour and texture. The whole would then be lowered onto the waters of the laguna, to float away to the spirits' homes ensuring a bountiful year to come for all the Marshers.

Phelim walked to the bottom of the stairs in the House of the Pee-Wit, turning as the mistress of the house called out. 'Master Phelim, you would do well to hasten to the wharves and secure a spot for yourself to watch the festival. It is a charming event and very mystical for us. We need the Others' beneficence for another good year.'

Phelim thanked her and wondered what she would think if she were aware an Other stood right now in her house. He expected no great joy and substantial hysteria and thus found it politic to move out to the walkways and thread his way with the crowd to the site of the festival.

The waters of the laguna were still and boats lay swinging lazily across their reflections on their moorings. Oystercatchers, plovers, gulls and gannets swirled overhead and behind the seaward hub-bub one could hear the ever present frog chorus from the Marshes. Maids in virginal white passed Phelim with their cornucopia of flowers, seeds and mosses and their families and friends greeted each other and chatted as the wharves settled for the business of the festival. It was almost midday.

People pushed politely in order to get a good position by the rails – amongst them Gallivant and Adelina, her copper hair hidden in a floral headscarf tied Traveller fashion, her burgeoning body clothed in jodhpurs and sweater and a green coat. The clothes were by her bed when she woke. Gallivant presumably had been up to more mischief as he strove to care for his charge. He stood by her side, watching the crowds and moved sideways for a tall, good-looking chap to squeeze in and he smiled so Gallivant smiled back, the chance to speak lost in the press of people.

Adelina's attention was fixed on the interloper. Her heart hammered and she went to speak but a whistle on the water broke in and all heads turned.

A handsome varnished galliot pulled away from one of the wharves. Oars were seen to rake the water and a chant broke out over the top of wharf noise, the prow of the boat swinging as oars feathered to turn the craft north. Then, with a series of shrill whistles that scarified Adelina's spine, oars struck the water in unison and pulled, propelling Severine and a murderous Luther towards Veniche.

Adelina's hand had grasped the hob's sleeve as she recognised the passengers. Her nails dug into the fabric of his coat and had he been able to hear above the whistles and the hum of the crowd, he would have heard her speaking to no one in particular. 'As Aine is my witness, Severine, I hate you!' She couldn't help the sob which racked out as with her other hand she shielded her belly. 'I hate you and you will pay. Somehow, somehow, you will pay!'

The dark-haired stranger had seen the angst on her face however and had heard the cursing but before he could speak to her, she and her partner – the skinny hob in the vast riding coat with the capacious pockets – had withdrawn into the milling crowds and Phelim's attention was drawn to the lower deck of the wharf where a soft lute had begun to play, now the galliot had disappeared into the northerly distance.

Adelina hurried against the flowing current of the crowd. She wanted peace and some time to calm herself. The stranger had started it. He had a look of Liam she was sure, only he was a little taller and broader and his hair was darker. She had almost spoken to him, although what she had wanted to say was ridiculous. Are you Liam's family? Mad! But the whistles had started in the galliot and there had been no chance because then she had seen Severine and Luther and her heart dropped through her boots, the idea of compassion and empathy disappearing in an instant. All her fears and anxieties had rushed headlong and here she was, tearing backwards and forwards along boardwalks with the hob trying to keep pace and asking what was wrong.

She rounded a corner and could run no further. A square lay in front of her, if one made of water could be called such – a liquid space surrounded on all sides by ranks of tiered seating on walkways and in the middle a floating pontoon anchored at each corner. Above the water a system of high wires and trapezes were strung and an acrobatic troupe practiced for the evening's festivities. She sank onto one of the lowest seats. High above her, two trapeze artists swung rhythmically back and forth and with a distant '*hop-la*', one somersaulted into the other's waiting grip. On the pontoon, troupe members mimed fear and then joy as the manoevre was completed without incident.

Gallivant hurried up panting. 'Sink me Adelina, what's amiss? You took off as though your pants were on fire!' He sat and fanned his face in a dramatic way, expecting some response from her. When silence ensued, except for the '*hop-la*' on high, he noticed the drooping expression and the watery eyes and thought, oh Aine, here we go again! The thing is, he raged, she has every reason for the tears and the thwart emotions. Not just because of all she has been through but because...

'You think you have grief under control and that life is more balanced,' she spoke unevenly as she lifted the fraught face to watch the trapezes swinging back and forth. 'But suddenly something happens – you see something or hear something. Aine, even smell something and the world you have built shatters again. Like a pane of glass or a mirror. Tinkle, tinkle, tinkle.' She made a movement with her fine long fingers, drifting her hands down to imitate the glass falling. 'And you know if you are ever going to survive, you have to pick up every shard and glue it back together and begin again. And it hurts, oh how it hurts! Because every shard is a memory and every memory a pain. And all you really want to do is tip it all in a bucket, like so much cullet, and forget about it.'

Gallivant sat next to her calmly, neither taking her hand nor speaking emotively. 'I saw her and I saw Luther. At least we know for sure they will be in Veniche and can be on-guard.'

Adelina lifted her hand to her stomach under the coat and rubbed and then reached for the hob's hand and placed it on the subtle mound. 'Do you feel it, Gallivant?'

He kept his fingers still and beneath them he felt a tremor, a fluttering like butterfly wings. He sat very quietly until the soft agitation ceased and then he lifted his hands and slipped them into the caverns that were his pockets. 'At last you have realised, Madame Needlewoman!'

'You knew?'

'Adelina!' He couldn't help being dismissive. 'Of course I knew – the nausea, the loss of appetite for anything other than a dry piece of toast. And later, the bloom on your skin! Aine, girl, you glow like the Tan Ellyl.'

'I thought I wasn't well because of shock, because I was depressed. That I grieved. That the trauma of everything had upended my regular rhythms.' She shrugged her shoulders, explaining away her ignorance.

'There is no doubt it did. You still grieve. Patently. The symptoms of both are similar. Curious isn't it? That such a wondrous event can present with the same awful feelings as the most shattering loss. But all that aside Threadlady, you are pregnant. And I for one am glad.' He bussed her cheek with warm lips but she was serious as she sat back and tipped her head to the trapeze again.

'It is a life, Gallivant. Kholi's child.' Her expression was cold, filled with none of the joy he hoped for. 'And she, *SHE*, killed the child's father and I want her to pay! An eye for an eye and yet I am a Traveller and should be compassionate.'

Quiet wrapped itself around the couple as the troupe disembarked from the wires and pontoon and presently the only sound was the ubiquitous frog chorus and the slapping of water against the piers of the walkways.

'She needs some old fashioned Raji treatment.' The hob's voice funneled up from the standing collar of his coat where he had dropped his chin to rest on his chest.

'What do you mean?'

'During the upheavals of centuries ago – aeons before you were born, Adelina – the Raj was an unusual place, as filled with art and culture as it is now but with inordinate brutality. They would bastinado, ganch, flay. And I ask you... she has murdered not just once but three times at least, of which we know! Huh, milady! You may think I am utterly evil but nothing, nothing at all, is too nasty for her. Or Luther!'

'Don't Gallivant! Not in front of my child. I can't bear it. And I can't bear that I must become a murderer as well.' She gave an enormous sigh as the hands once again began to rub circles over the mound. 'I must go to Veniche and it seems I have a number of things to do, doesn't it?' She began counting her fingers. ''Finish the robe and take it to the Museo for I want it to be seen and my story to be found so you must clean it for me somehow. Number Two, I want to know Lhiannon is alive, that Severine hasn't murdered her, that I haven't in some way pre-disposed that brave girl to an untimely end. And three?' She sat for a moment tapping the third finger she held up with the index finger of the other hand. 'Aine forgive me, it is revenge!'

Three little books finished with so much said and so much still to say. I feel myself in the throes of something momentous. I suppose it could be the birth of my child, after all is that not the ultimate achievement for most women? But in this instance, while I can hardly wait to hold Kholi's child in my arms, I feel that is not the momentous thing I mean. There is something else, as if the whole of my world might shift and it scares me. Travellers have strong intuition sometimes and something tells me there is a change coming.

But perhaps we should read on.

Continue to the second last design on the robe. Here you will find the deep indigo purple of the Bittersweet flower. It is of course known colloquially by another name, 'Deadly Nightshade', because its toxin is quite fatal and in its time has been used to counter unseelie Others in their actions. I tell you, as I embroidered the deep violet petals with the yellow stamens, I would have liked to make a deadly infusion of the flowers and feed it to Severine in some of the wine to which she is notoriously attached.

But I wander in my pregnant angst. Under the two flowers you will find two more books and underneath the delicate viridian butterfly another. The embroidery itself is a simple exercise in overcasting, satin stitch, and blanket stitch – nothing special but the effect is there – a flower the colour of a night sky when unseelie spirits fly from barrows and sidh.

Read on.

CHAPTER TWENTY SEVEN

The lute filled the afternoon air with its delicate melodies. The fine plucking, joined by the descant of the maids, produced a harmony that warmed the people's cockles and the afternoon passed with soft and beguiling entertainment. As the maids danced dainty steps, Phelim's attention drifted again and again to the full-flowering beauty of the Traveller. There was something about her... interest stirred.

The lute notes faded on the breeze and a harp filled the space with soothing cords, the maids stepping with their baskets to colour the canvas and its surface of sand. A picture took shape – the magnificent face and naked body of a sprite depicted with leaf and petal. She could have been the Lady of the Marshes, a veela – any sprite who must be appealed to in her watery home, for this was a gift to the water, a dressing of great beauty and if all the spirits were satisfied then the Marshes would be a safe haven for another year.

Finally to the fading notes of the harp, one maid with silver hair whom Phelim recognized, lifted the canvas and carefully laid it on the water. The Marshers placed small floating candles alongside and the picture floated on the ebb tide as a silence ensued, albeit with the inevitable frog and cricket chorus.

Eventually the waters conspired to pull the whole masterpiece below the surface and the Marshers cheered, for truly did the sprites not take it for their own? Clapping burst forth and the crowd began to make their way to the foodstall before heading to the water square where they would spend the night watching the acrobatic show.

A voice at his side caused Phelim to turn. 'What did you think?' the patron of his inn enquired politely.

'Haunting and beautiful, the water spirits would be churlish to think otherwise. I'm grateful your wife told me of the festival, it would have been disappointing to miss it.'

'Come with us now to the water square and have some food.'

'You're very kind but I must make my way. I'm late for my business in Veniche. Tell me, when does the next ferry leave?'

'During the acrobatic display. Must you go?'

'Sadly, but once again I'm grateful and have left a bag of gelt on my bed.'

He shook the hand of his host and as he turned away, seeing the man's surprise at the *frisson* surging up his arm, Phelim wafted a gentle mesmer so that by the time he was lost in the crowd the fellow had forgotten that he had even stayed at the Inn.

The Palazzo di Accia stood umber and candle-lit in its position amongst the homes of the rich and infamous of Veniche. At its feet the Grand Canal lapped delicately, like a cat with a bowl of very rich cream. The water traffic drifted back and forth although at this hour when dark had truly settled and a cold mist had wound across the laguna to fill the alleyways and smaller canals, it was dwindling to the doughty few – gondolas ferrying people to and from dinner or the opera, the theatre or some government reception. Women stepped into and out of the boats wrapped in stoles of taffeta and satin and men merged with shadow in tailcoats, the light of a flambeau catching the bright white of frilled shirt and silk scarf.

Severine felt a huge surge of relief as she surveyed her home, the epicentre of her power. Here she felt confident, strong, in control. Somehow over the last few days that omnipresent sense of infallibility had teetered. It started when Luther had told her Adelina must have had Other help to escape and her ego, her confidence in her ability to achieve her goals had cracked ever so slightly.

Surely this was why she needed to be immortal. To never feel insecure again, to know that nothing could ever harm or that one's plans and dreams could never be foiled. This was the fundamental reason for her desire for

Adelina's murder. Because she, Adelina, would appear to have the aid and support of Others by being nothing but herself – no force, no bribery, no blackmail. Just herself! Whereas she, Severine, had needed to claw her way into the consciousness of the Others and the thought was as bitter as gall. For one tiny moment, the idea that she was a Færan changeling suddenly seemed improbable. Her heart skipped a beat and she paled.

She stalked back and forth in the salon, hands clasped tightly in front, muttering to herself. Did they laugh, these Others? Did they think her fatuous? By Behir, if they did not live in fear of her perhaps they should! Gertus had been killed for far less, Huon had been diminished by her threats. She pushed the battered ring up and down on her finger.

The ring, the soul-syphon! She had forgotten!

'If you laugh, if you think I am not serious, then *Others*,' she sneered louder still, 'know you are so very wrong. And a message for you Adelina – I *always* intended for you to die, but now your death shall be full of such exquisite pain. I want you to beg me, *BEG ME,* to allow you to die.'

She threw herself down on a chaise and looked around the elegant room. It radiated wealth and largesse. An ormulu clock graced a marble mantle and slight tables were covered in Raji cloisonné. A secretaire stood against the wall between windows as high as the gilded and fretted ceiling and the paper strips lay on its inlaid surface, drawing her towards them. As she handled them they rustled, reminding her she must conceal them with speed!

Luther had unpacked in the rooms that were his apartments on the second floor. The windows opened onto one of the canals and when he stood on his balcony he spied the gondolas poling back and forth, lit fore and aft with lamps and he could see the small bridges that joined one side of the moonlit canal to the other. On a table between the open doors to the balcony he had laid the tools of his trade – rapiers, a whip, pistols, powder and shot, and the silent and deadly arsenal he loved most – daggers, poniards, stilettos and the garotte.

He picked up the latter and in the light of the lamps in his room, fingered the wooden handles and took a twist of wire around each knuckle. He stretched the wire a little and listened to the faint 'ting' it made as the ruckles and twists from where it had been curled in his saddlebag gave way to the tension.

The image of Adelina filled his mind. He *had* seen her at the Crossing, he swore it was her! He would recognise that hair anywhere. The price he could get from the wig-makers for a fall of such vivid hue would be stupendous, the colour so rare. Even he could admit that.

He had kept the sighting secret. He couldn't stand more vituperation from Severine. He had his own ideas of how he would entrap Adelina, no need to involve the Contessa. No, the red-coated bitch would surely require threads and other tools of her trade and so he would position spies at each of the six haberdashers of Veniche and she'd appear eventually. And when he found her, he knew exactly what he would do and there was an end to it, he didn't need the madwoman downstairs telling him what and how.

He had been an assassin long before he came to her employ. Working throughout Eirie, always for large amounts of gelt, dispatching targets secretly like an unseelie shadow. He smirked. He was better at his job than any Other he knew of, the best. There were plenty of sad souls flying across the land who could attest to the fact.

As to Adelina? She had refused his advances, ridiculed him, emasculated him. He tightened the garotte. He would never forgive her because he had a livid scar down his cheek from the bitch's nails, he had a cut chin from his chase in Ferry Crossing and his groin hadn't stopped aching since she was spirited away. No one had ever injured Luther the Assassin. EVER! He thrust his fists apart and the garotte straightened with a musical 'twang.'

'This my pet', he told the room at large, but really he was talking to Adelina, 'this is for you.'

CHAPTER TWENTY EIGHT

Adelina would not sit quietly and rest. Agitated, eager to get to Veniche, she harried Gallivant to the ferry wharf where they paid fare and sat, two lone passengers, waiting for the appointed time of departure. They could hear the appreciative crowd at the water square watching the acrobats and just like the Fire Festival so long ago, Adelina could hear the tabla creating an atmosphere with its pulsating rhythm. She wondered what the acrobats wore. Somehow the thought of black and gold from the mountainous fire celebration didn't fit. The silver sparkle of the water and the chiaroscuro of the Marsh trees in the background required an entirely different palette. In her imagination, they tumbled and turned with silver sequins and strobes of pale green and blue, cosmetics in soft marine colours of celadon and ice – a liquid fantasy as they swung and balanced and flipped like flying fish jumping or drops of water sparkling.

Lost in her dream, only the ferry rocking disturbed her. Another passenger walked down the gangplank to take his seat in the small galliot. The rowers sat in pairs deeper in the hull on either side and chatting quietly, inviting each other to drink at an oarsmens' tavern in Veniche to celebrate the end of their shift and a long muscle-bound day. They fingered their calloused hands, flexing their prodigious muscles and rolling wide shoulders. The rowers of the seas of Eirie were highly regarded and earned good money for theirs was the strength that kept the maritime coasts afloat.

A small whistle blew once and Adelina could see there were only three passengers: herself, Gallivant and the stranger. The rowers on the port side sat waiting whilst the starboard side feathered and swept gently to bring the bow of the boat around and then with another short burst of the whistle and a command from the ferrymaster, the rowers pulled, the keel cutting through the water.

The passengers turned and watched Ferry Crossing recede. Above the skillion rooves of the buildings, they could see the high wire apparatus at the water square and hear the roar of an appreciative audience punctuated by laughter at the clowns who no doubt sought to wrest attention from the aerial athletes. Gallivant stood to stretch his legs and walked to the stern, keeping clear of the rowers' deck as they pulled rhythmically but silently through the water. He thought how much more pleasant it was than the shrill and constant whistle of Severine's galliot which had torn the mellow Marsh sounds apart.

He leaned with his hands on the taffrail, watching the phosphorescence froth and cream as the ferry coursed across the laguna. He was sure he saw faces under the surface, luminous and pale green and with sharp teeth as they smirked at their earthly Other brother.

'Merrows?'

The Goodfellow turned, a fractious hand to his chest. 'Pardon sir? You startled me.'

'Merrows?' The fellow indicated with a tip of his handsome head to the water beneath.

'It would seem so, yes. Sir, I believe we owe you thanks...'

Phelim shrugged. 'It's of no account. I didn't like the ruffian. Tell me, you're a Goodfellow, aren't you?'

'I am and you are a Færan.' Gallivant replied politely.

'It appears so. Strange there should be two Others travelling on the same boat to Veniche at the same time.'

'Indeed.'

'My name is Phelim. I haven't been to Veniche before.' He smiled as he admitted this to the hob.

'Neither have I,' Gallivant could not prevent a rueful note slipping into his voice. It worried him no end, the ignorance he had for the place. How could he protect Adelina in such ignorance? The Færan's voice broke in upon his anxieties.

'I know nothing of the city at all and confess it readily. Does your companion?' Phelim looked across at Adelina, whose eyes were still on the shrinking sight of Ferry Crossing.

'No. She has never been. She's a Traveller and wishes to peruse the markets and such. I am her Goodfellow, so I must accompany her.' Must I really, he thought? If I am Other, I owe mortals nothing at all. I am a free spirit. And yet Adelina draws me like a bee to nectar...

As he spoke, he saw his charge turn her head and look for him. Watched her eyes open wide as they fixed on the tall Færan next to him and as the flare of the lamp lit the man's face, he saw her blanch and he stepped back. 'Excuse me, milady needs me.' He turned quickly and returned to the passenger seats to forestall any drama as he could see emotion beginning to brim. 'By the way, my name is Gallivant.'

In the dark of night, the laguna shone like beaten metal the further they moved away from the flickering torches of Ferry Crossing. Adelina's hand crushed the hob's in her own, occasioning a wince. 'Adelina, everybody in the world has a match somewhere. Please calm down. Think of the babe.'

She looked at her friend and realised she was being ridiculously overwrought, for what did it matter if there was someone who looked like Liam. It only mattered to her, surely. It was her equilibrium that was upset, no one else's. And what could the poor man do about it anyway? He couldn't help his beautifully carved face. She felt her child wriggle and slide in the dark of its nest and she slid her hand under her coat to smooth and soothe, the very act calming her as well.

Gallivant watched the stranger walk back to his seat, an air of lonliness hovering about. He would like to have invited him to sit with them but the irrational outbursts from Adelina put paid to that. Besides, the fellow *was* Færan.

The ferrymaster's voice broke into his thoughts. 'Did you realise the Days of the Dark will begin in Veniche at midnight.'

'You say?' Gallivant acknowledged.

'You will have a brief time to find lodgings and then you will see the lights go out and for three days and nights, the city will be dark. During the day, it is clothed in black and serious and at night nothing will light the way. If one has to travel the canals in the evening it is dangerous, mark my words. And then at midnight on the third day, at the final stroke of the town bells, the city is lit and Carnivale begins. Thank Aine!' The man grinned. 'And then one drinks and parties furiously!' He moved away and watched his oarsmen, balancing against the sway of the boat as the oars dragged through the water.

Adelina had heard him. Damn the heavens above! It would be hard enough *with* light let alone without. She asked herself once again – did she really have to do this? Go to the Gate and make sure Lhiannon was safe? Oh Aine yes. Yes she did! She wanted to know not everyone connected with her was tainted with death. Otherwise what future for her babe? And what of the robe? Would it not be a wonderful thing for the child to grow up knowing its mother's artistry hung in the gallery amongst the Masters' works? It was all she had to give her baby. After all, there was no father.

Then there was 'the promise'. But did she mean the promise to exact revenge or the promise to Aine? This uneasy thought circled round and round in her head until it ached and until the stranger's mellow tones filled the watery silence. He spoke to the ferrymaster and Adelina's thoughts hauled to a halt as his words reverberated in her ears.

'Tell me sir, you know Veniche well. Can you tell me where the Countess Severine di Accia lives?'

The lights of the canal city danced along a yellow road of wavelets toward the bow of the ferry. In the moonlit night, the shapes of cupolas and campaniles covered in brass and copper roofing filled the space above the horizon. As the craft drew closer, vast walls winked their windowed eyes at the approaching visitors and balconies with latticed balustrades in the Raji style, legacy of a history long past, jutted out from rendered walls. Striped poles leaned drunkenly whilst others stood in sober lines marking the deeper channels.

As the evening progressed toward midnight, late gondolas slid past carrying passengers home in a race to beat the Dark. Water lapped fractiously at the walls of the buildings, eating away with each fretful slap at the fabric and structure, and here and there was a chunk missing or a crack creeping web-like across the aged facades.

But there was such beauty.

As the ferry negotiated carefully between channel markers and other craft, the passengers sat overawed, even Adelina, and drank it in like thirsty wayfarers having a long dreamed of ale. For a fleeting moment, they could almost forget duty, danger and the delivering up of souls to the Afterlife.

CHAPTER TWENTY NINE

Phelim thought Veniche embodied a city of dreams and fantasies as he disembarked, as beautiful as the woman who claimed his discrete attention. He stepped back as she passed and her eyes sought his as if she knew him and there beat an intangible moment. Then her gaze bent down, the better to negotiate the step to the wharf. The hob on the other hand, gave a half-smile and a nod.

Adelina noticed the smell. Of decay, mould and rot together with the fug of the laguna. The mist ever present on cool nights had twined and undulated around the visitors and muffled the sounds of the wharf and the ferrymaster dismissing his crew.

Maybe because she was pregnant, Adelina's stomach heaved a little and she longed to lie down and rest and not to think about where she was and why and especially not to think about that stranger because she felt something odd all around. Maybe then, when her head was clear and her stomach settled, she could talk to Gallivant about him and why he had mentioned Severine's name.

'Come milady. I have heard of a small pensione. Let's go. You need to sleep.' The hob placed a solicitous hand on her elbow.

Phelim, ever aware of the chamois bag under his clothing, felt it warm from its normally frigid state and wondered why? Perhaps because they know we are close to a Gate, he decided. He watched Gallivant and Adelina disappear into the mist, his eyes fixed on the indistinct shadow of the woman who claimed his attention, struck again by her bereft expression. The ferry master knocked his shoulder.

'They have the right idea. It's cold and close to midnight, you need to find lodgings.'

Pensione Orologio was more than comfortable, to Adelina a tiny little palace – narrow as the House of the Thrush and squeezed between a milliner's store and a men's outfitter. Gallivant had secured a pocket kerchief room with two beds lying affectionately side by side. By squeezing past the carved walnut ends one could find a chaise in front of double doors – the doors themselves like all Veniche doors, leading to a balcony overhanging one of the smaller, quieter canals. The balustrade was fretted and carved in the Raji style and Adelina was immediately transported to Ahmadabad and windows overhanging immaculately tailored gardens where water tinkled and Raji doves cooed and fluttered. It was a memory that pained and so she sank onto the bed as Gallivant closed the doors of the balcony, sealing the room from the damp smell.

She fell into an exhausted sleep and was thus surprised and anxious when her eyes flew open to find the dark room lit by the pallid light of a sickly moon. She could hear the quiet breath of Gallivant, presumably in the bed by her side. Immediately thoughts of Veniche, Severine and her purpose for being there filled her mind and she instinctively and quietly shifted her legs from under the coverings till her toes hit the cool of the aged parquet floors. She pulled on the sweater and jodhpurs from the end of the bed and took her boots in her hands, creeping to the door and praying to Aine the parquet wouldn't creak as it had done when they climbed the stair to the rooms. Her fingers found the elegantly wrought handle of the door and she pushed it down slowly and proceeded to pull – enough for her to squeeze through and begin her search for the Gate and news of Lhiannon.

'And just what, mistress, do you think you are doing?' The door slammed shut in front of her before she could slip out. Gallivant stood defiant as she swung round.

'I thought to try and find the Gate.'

Gallivant's expressive eyebrows shot skywards. 'You did? Sink me, Adelina! And where would you start? You're not an Other, you know! To be frank your behaviour is beginning to worry me. Where's your self-control? You can't possibly go off in the dark in a city you don't know and begin a random search. At any time Luther might spot you. Aine, woman! Have you not thought of your child?'

Adelina had never seen the hob so filled with ire. 'Of course I have, but...'

'Oh but nothing!' He took her arm and towed her back to bed. 'Lie down. Now!' He helped her pull off her sweater and covered her with blankets as she lay down. 'Adelina, I am Other. If anyone can discover the portal's whereabouts, it's me and with complete invisibility if necessary. Do you agree?'

Chastised, she nodded tiredly.

'Then you must rest now for obvious reasons. And let me do a preliminary reconnoitre tomorrow. You can finish the robe and by then I will have some information for you and we can plan. This way *you* are safe and Kholi's child is safe.' Gallivant knew he risked a flood of tears by invoking the father's name but needs must. As it was she smiled damply and closed her eyes. Within moments, maybe even a moment of mesmer, Gallivant could see sleep had claimed her and he heaved a relieved sigh.

He sat guard by the window. Ever since the hobyahs he had been afraid for her, never dreaming he would also have to protect her from herself. He looked at the face in repose. There was an artist in Veniche who painted magnificent madonnas and Adelina looked just like a heavenly madonna, he was sure. He sighed. He loved her deeply – as he would love a sister if he had one. She needed to be guarded – she was too spontaneous and emotional. In addition, the canals could be as full of the unseelie as any other watery place. Satisfied she was heavily in slumber, he mused quietly as he gazed at her in the last moonlight of the night.

'That tall fellow on the boat, the one you thought looked like Liam. I'll tell you something Threadlady. You are very astute. Not that you recognised any familial likeness, I'm sure! But you did recognise Other, the fellow *is* Færan. Sink me madam but the world's an ironic place. We seek the gate and we find a Færan in the process. I wonder if we should have asked him for the location?' He reached over and pulled the covers higher over her shoulders, muttering to the room at large. She was curled like a question mark, protective hands around the belly and the new life, eyes closed, breath regular and calm. 'It's as well you can't hear me. It would just be another wild goose for you to chase and there is quite enough to be going on with!' He lay on his bed, dressed and primed and staring wakefully into the dark.

Phelim had gratefully taken the ferrymaster's directions to a likely hotel and stepped along one alley after another and over some precious little bridges shaped like the humps of Raji camels until he found the entrance of the Pensione Esperia, a place of faded grandeur not far from the Grand Canal where plants hid chipped paint and the parquet, like all Veniche parquet, squeaked and groaned as it was traversed. But it was a clean establishment and had a large room with a garde-robe and twin beds. It looked out over a narrow calle and if one leaned precariously, one could see a bigger canal in the distance.

As he had proceeded along the cobbled alleys, his footsteps echoing from one high wall to another, he followed in the steps of the night watchmen as they snuffed street lamps, torchères and braziers. Phelim wondered if he was entering some unseelie underworld as the lights progressively disappeared. Blackness and shadow festered and footsteps became disembodied sounds, perhaps unfriendly – who would know? In the increasing silence of the Dark a cat yowled and further away a street cur barked half-heartedly in response. Phelim, for all that he was Færan, was glad when he turned into the Esperia – he needed to give the Dark some thought.

He laid his coat over a chair and pulled out the chamois bag from under his shirt to place it on the coffer by his bed. The bag seemed so innocent of interest: scuffed hide, the drawstring faded, stains where he had bled through the frosted blisters on his ribs – such a mundane appearance for something of such import.

He had been disappointed the ferrymaster was unfamiliar with Severine's address. The fellow knew the woman of course but he rarely ventured beyond the wharf on workdays and his own home was on the island of Marino where he led a village existence on the side of the laguna. Phelim had only wanted to know her address so he could avoid it for the danger it implied.

He stripped off his clothes and washed himself before climbing between crisp linen sheets and lying back, muscular arms behind his head. Glancing down, he registered the frostbite against his ribs and thought of the bag and how it had warmed as Gallivant Goodfellow and his Traveller friend passed by. He recalled the woman's face again. She was beautiful – lush and full of promise but with some sort of melancholy that bit deep.

His fingers ran gently over the blisters just as they would if they ran over the woman's face. Touching the rawness as if they were the wings of a butterfly, to patter away the hurt. Looking down he realized there would be more damage as long as he hung the pouch under his shirt. He reached for the glass of wine by his bed and wondered how the woman's hurt could be soothed and what she would think of his Færan ancestry and then he had an absurd desire to tell her if she ever asked, that he was indeed an Other and would deny his heritage, for it made him unbelievably unhappy.

Had I been aware my unfamiliar companion on our ferry trip was Færan, do you think I would have been friendly? For the sake of Liam, for the sake of Lhiannon, for the sake of the Færan silk-seller?

I suppose I would. But it was hypothetical and hardly of concern at that very point in my life. The only thing that truly worried me as I lapsed into a heavy sleep that first night at the pensione was how he could know of Severine? It scared me that even on the ferry I was unable to escape the threads of her web. I determined as my eyelids crashed down to block out the world, that I would ask Gallivant what he thought in the morning.

But now we have just finished the last book of the second last design on the robe. We have entered and exited each godet on the front and back and we have finally reached the enormous design that spreads itself over the centre back seam.

It is the marriage piece and I'm sure you guessed quickly to whom I dedicated every stitch. The bride and groom of course – one dark, one titian and dressed in silks and with lace stitch fan in the hand of the bride – can only be Liam of the Færan and Ana, his mortal betrothed.

There are a number of journals hidden here, enough to finish the story. But one at a time, so firstly go to the folds of the groom's shoulder cloak. As you can see, it is appliquèd to the robe and it is just a question of lifting two or three of the stab-stitches and you will find the book beneath. There are four other books hidden amongst the stitching of my bride and groom and one of them you must not touch, the one hanging from the bride's hand. Please, I beg you!

On pain of death.

You think I jest? I do not! Remember that Færan and Others have become my friends and there is such a charm on that particular book that in fear of your life you must do as I say!

You will find out why at the end of our story and if you are the friend I think you to be then you will pay attention and observe what I have said. Indeed, if you have read the story thus far and you are still with me, you have obviously paid heed from that first time when I requested you read the books in sequence if the fires of damnation were not to be lit.

In any case you have one to read now. So shall we continue?

CHAPTER THIRTY

Dawn arrived like a flood. Moisture ran down windows and exterior walls and the persistent patter and tumble of drops down drainpipes stretched nerves.

The Dark before Carnivale could be a difficult time. Few people ventured out, there was an air of shadow about the city, aided and abetted by the time-honoured ritual of dressing in black. The funereal shade served to heighten the atmosphere and many chose to stay indoors close to hearth and home. The emphasis on darkness inevitably created some expectation that the unseelie might be about in more pressing numbers. Certainly there was a lift in the crime-rate but whether this could be attributed to some eldritch being or whether the offenders were entirely mortal and taking advantage of a situation was a moot point. No one was prepared to argue that by celebrating the Days of the Dark the city was any more or less dangerous than normal. Besides, Carnivale was so good for the merchants' coffers before the Dark began each year, it was highly unlikely it would ever be banned without a massive outcry. It was easier to be aware, to have talismans, charms and potions and to conclude all necessary business before the Dark commenced.

History says the Days of the Dark began hundreds of years ago when the city suffered a famine after years of drought. Rats and mice abounded and disease and starvation were rife. But then had come three days of torrential rain... of gloom and grey and sombre moods where death and destruction appeared at the door and the Bean Sidhe was heard at every second corner. But the days of dripping rain and the accompanying dark shadow had perfected a miracle in the city and its mainland environs. The pestilent and germ-ridden alleys and inns, villas, huts and palazzos were washed clean and crops on the mainland grew.

The next year, a similar period of seasonal rain occurred. Only this time, the citizenry celebrated the end of the three days with a feast. Thus Carnivale grew to become a vast theatre of extreme colour, of vibrant masks and extravagant silk and satin clothes. There was absolutely no effort amongst the citizenry to recognise or placate Others during this festival. This was purely a time for mortal self-indulgence on a grand scale.

So amongst the angst at the diminution in business around the streets and the dislike of the black as Hades nights, there simmered an air of acute expectation and none stronger than in the Palazzo Di Accia.

Severine had been out and about early, rain not withstanding. Dressed in a slick ebony oilskin fashionably cut with vent and tab and with her suitably coloured hair piled underneath an oilskin hat, she entered a sedan-chair and accompanied by Luther, was swiftly carried to the address of the glassmaker on the Calle del Vetro.

Earlier in the day, she had sent to the six master architects in Veniche. Would they kindly attend her this afternoon? Knowing they would never refuse her, she almost salivated – the secret key to the locked gate so close.

Luther held open the door of the glassmaker's, shielding her from the rain with a black umbrella the style of which drew glances from curious eyes. Severine had the forethought to bring it home from a trip to the Raj, ordering several made to match her wardrobe.

'Luther, stay outside. Keep guard and prevent anyone from entering! The business I have is exceedingly private and I don't wish to be interrupted.' She pushed past him and the door rattled shut, the bell chiming like a crystal clapper inside cut glass. Severine proceeded across the floor to a cabinet filled with millefiore paperweights and in her diamond-cut manner, called for service.

A door opened and a blast of hot air assailed the showroom. Over the shoulders of the glassmaker, Severine could see the artisans with their long pipes looking as if they played in some woodwind orchestra. The door slammed shut and the man wiped his sweating brow with a red paisley square.

'Contessa! If I had known I was to be so honoured, I would have dressed accordingly. Please accept my apologies! As you can see I work in the fabbrica today.'

'Signor Niccolo, good-day and please, it does not signify.' Severine's aristocratic manner brought her to an elegant chair and she eased her long coat tails aside and made herself comfortable in front of the eminent display of paperweights.

The glassmaker ran his fingers quickly through his damp hair and untied the singed leather apron, tucking in his striped shirt. 'Contessa, may I offer you some wine?'

'Indeed. Whilst I tell you what I require, a sip would not go astray.' She inclined her head graciously to the side and the glassmaker hastened to pour two goblets of ruby red liquid. She took the glass from him and sipped what was a surprisingly good vintage. Carefully placing the wine on the sparkling counter, she looked up at the man and smiled her most engaging smile but which failed to bring a softening light to her intimidating eyes. 'Signor Niccolo, I am in urgent need of a large order by the eve of Carnivale. Sooner would have been better, but I realise you will need a little time.'

The Contessa's long fingernails tapped the glass surface of the display cabinet, indicating the millefiore paperweights underneath. The glassmaker was reminded of the tapping of a hungry bird's beak and not just any bird. For some reason, the huge beak of a Raven of Mimring sprang to mind. He shivered.

'I require four small, personally handcrafted millefiore paperweights, each one different except for the central flower.'

'Four! Madame!' The glassmaker quailed at the excessive workload. He was a perfectionist and such things took time...

'Please!' She held up an admonishing hand, her manner blunt. 'I truly don't want to hear you say it can't be done. I will make it worth your while sir. After all, you know what it is to have Di Accia patronage behind your business. But I think you are also aware that it would be, shall we say unwise if you didn't accept my commission.'

The glassmaker had watched her eyes grow progressively more frigid as she spoke and he knew that no matter what, he was obliged to work day and night to have this finished by Carnivale. Suddenly the Raven's beak took on an explicit meaning. Goosebumps jumped across his neck. 'Madame, I accept.' He lifted his glass and took a huge draught of the wine.

'Good, as I thought you would! When you have blown and cut the rods for the central flowers, I want you to deliver them to the palazzo, as I have something I wish to slip into the hollows and then Luther will return them to you post-haste. No doubt you think it a bother, but you will have to indulge me: these paperweights are going to mean more to the future of Eirie than you can imagine.' The glassmaker had the sensation that he was a fly caught in spider's web as the woman continued. 'Thus I will require your total loyalty and discretion. If ever the planning and making of these should leak out, then it will be at the cost of your business. Or worse.'

Signor Niccolo remained silent. Thoroughly threatened and not at all blessed by the patronage forcibly dropped in his lap, he assumed the woman had some diplomatic gesture to make abroad. Who knew? The Di Accia web was wide. He also knew none but he could make the paperweights, for his craftsmen were loose-lipped. So the fabbrica del vetro and showroom would have to close with the men on full pay! Aine, she had better make it worth his while, he thought with a slight tremour!

'Signor', she broke into his troubled revery. 'I will pay you five hundred gelt for each paperweight!'

His mouth opened wide and remained open longer than was polite.

'I see it meets with your approval'. There was a noise in the street, her man arguing with someone. She stood and adjusted the folds of her rain-beaded coat. 'Then I shall see you tomorrow afternoon, sir. I have no doubt you will be busy and I have no doubt you will not let me down.' She turned and walked to the door as it was pushed open by a tall individual whose face was concealed by a dripping hat. The Contessa pulled her trailing folds away from his damp wake and scowled at him.

The man held the door open politely. 'Your pardon, Lady.' He sketched a bow. Under his coat and beneath his shirt, a grey chamois bag burned painfully deep welts into his skin. When he straightened, the woman was climbing into a sedan chair, the lout who had barred his way closing the chair's door and walking behind, unaware the man who had argued at the door was the Other who had tripped him up so maliciously and purposefully at Ferry Crossing.

Adelina sat on the chaise, the robe stretched over her knee to appliqué the groom to the centre back. Tiny little stab stitches edged the cloak and around his velvet boots. As she stitched his face with delicate straight stitches, she tried to fill it with expression and animation to bring it to life, for stumpwork is a rendition of reality, not just an artist's vague impression, and therein lay Adelina's skill. She was content to sew. Gallivant had left early, having found her some breakfast and having lit lamps to light the dark corners of the rain-shadowed room.

She felt restful and calm and not at all in an adventuring mood. At one point, she opened the balcony doors and stood shielding her head from the persistent downpour. Leaning out, she observed the umber and terracotta walls, the cobbles shining with moisture, the calm waters of the canals all washed and polished with the rain. The few people she spied were dressed in black in line with the code of the Dark. She returned to her stitching, intrigued with the traditions of this city she had never visited, but was content to let it flow past her like the water outside. The day drifted on with the robe having finishing touches placed upon it and the last few of the books begun and finished, shrunk and concealed.

She hung the robe and began the perambulating inspection that was so much a part of this mammoth task she had undertaken, finding the need for a thread here, a stitch there – and took it down again to sit in a state of such equanimity that she wondered if the hob had mesmered her, the better to keep her out of the city and safe. The thought lasted a second and she shrugged her shoulders to continue her work, the ivory silk cascading over her lap.

The peace in which she had so thoroughly wrapped herself disintegrated like torn paper as the door burst open and a dripping hob walked in, muttering angry invective. He seemed unaware of Adelina as he thrust all his parcels on the floor and as he continued to snarl at the world at large, he dragged off the wet coat and flung it on a chair by the door, noticing Adelina at last on the chaise by the balcony doors.

'Aine Gallivant, what goes? You have cursed all and sundry since you walked in!'

'You may well ask!' He threw himself down next to her, crushing part of the robe under his legs.

'I *am* asking – something has obviously disturbed you. And can you mind the robe?' The air in the room thinned with expectation and already her neck prickled. She had a feeling she knew what he would say...

'It's her!'

I knew it, thought Adelina, her heart sinking to lay itself under her feet on the parquet floor. The woman, despite Adelina's freedom, still had the capacity to reduce the stitcher to the state of victim. She jammed the needle into her thumb in her distress. 'Severine! Then you had better tell me...'

CHAPTER THIRTY ONE

'I was purloining some garments and such for our stay here.' Gallivant rubbed taut fingers over his forehead. 'I found a little glove-maker amongst the glassmakers in the Calle del Vetro and who should I spy guarding the door of one such fabbrica but Luther, with a very sumptuous sedan-chair parked outside. I stayed concealed, it's easy when you know how, and watched and before long a man came down the calle and tried to enter. I couldn't see his face as he like everyone else on this loathsome day, was hatted and garbed against the rain. But I heard his voice as he asked Luther to step aside and I felt a *frisson* drifting across the calle and I knew it was the fellow off the ferry. Anyway he and Luther got into a stiff discourse and he pushed past Luther and opened the door.'

Adelina chose not to interrupt for the hob was wound up like a clock spring and it was easier to let him run on. He clasped his hands tightly together.

'For a moment the fellow stood still but then he bowed and Severine, the bloody woman, swept out like some Sultana from the Raj and climbed into her chair. Now call me odd, call me anything you like, but sink me I'm beginning to see a connection with all these people appearing in the same place at the same time! And if that wasn't enough, I raced across in my invisible way to listen as Severine stepped into the chair. She said, *'Done, Luther. Now to my meetings at the Palazzo. By tonight I have no doubt I will have the location I require and then it will only be a matter of time.'*

He jumped up and proceeded to track back and forth in front of Adelina, the parquet squeaking in animated protest. 'And you don't have to be too clever to work it out, Threadlady! She's after the location of the

Gate, it can only be that. And by tonight, in her own miserable way she'll have it!'

He lapsed into silence and Adelina allowed the pattering of the rain to fill the space left by his voice as she digested this latest revelation. She began to fold the robe carefully, resolving to have the hob clean it with a mesmer as soon as possible. Finally she spoke. 'Gallivant, I've no doubt you're right. Of course she seeks the Gate, as one would expect. And as there is nothing we can do about it until we find the location ourselves, I propose we forget about it – no, don't look like that – just forget about it for a minute. Because there is something else far more important that you said and I think it is more like to help us than anything.'

'And? Tell me!' He threw himself down again. The little chaise shuddered and rocked.

'You mentioned the other man, the stranger from the ferry. You also mentioned there was a *frisson*. Now Gallivant, I'm no ingénue. I know a *frisson* can only emanate from Others, especially the Færan, I have felt it myself in the past. Indeed I swear I felt something of the same from that man when he was at the Water Festival, not just on board the ferry. I chided myself that it was my overwrought imagination but it wasn't, was it?'

'No.' Gallivant bit his lip.

'Then let's assume that he's here because of Severine. After all, he did mention her name. Perhaps Jasper sent him to meet Lhiannon and convey her safely to the Gate. Is it not also entirely logical that he should know where the Gate is? After all he's Færan and they're privy, all of them, to the secret. All we have to do is seek him out, talk to him, explain our predicament and I think he'll help us. He seemed approachable, didn't he?'

Gallivant's heart sank and he cursed himself for his overenthusiastic tongue and his unguarded comments. Adelina was beginning the wild-goose chase – this was the start.

'Yes,' he admitted half-heartedly. If only you knew how he's already helped us he thought, and yes, he is the logical solution to our quandary. Hadn't he thought so himself on the ferry? But he had hoped against all hope that she would give up on this ridiculous idea to seek out Lhiannon, so much so he had indeed placed a hob's mesmer on her this morning just to keep her safe. Sink me, his anxieties rattled his composure, I have *no* chance of getting her away before Carnivale!

'Gallivant, did you mesmer me before you went out?' She asked the question placidly, so different to the Adelina who would have bitten heads off and spat out the pieces. Events had indeed wrought some changes...

'Yes I did! So? It was only a little one and I did it for you and the babe because imagine if you'd seen Severine, you'd have been in a right state!' His expression reeked of righteousness.

She smiled at him, patting his arm and standing. 'I think you were right, the baby and I *do* need to rest.' She put a hand on her belly. 'This child of Kholi's is the most important thing in the world now and I'll try not to jeopardise its safety more than I really have to.' As she walked to the mirror, she began twisting her hair into a tight plait.

'What are you doing?'

'We need to find the Færan and I also need threads to finish the robe – a hank of cream silk and a hank of burgundy silk, I'm sure one of the haberdashers will have what I need.'

'Adelina, you can't possibly go out into the rain! We'll do it tomorrow. And besides you can't wear those pale clothes. I purloined black clothes for each of us,' he reached for the parcels on the floor. 'There is a pair of breeches and a sweater. I thought something a little bigger may be comfortable over your expanding bump. And there's a raincoat and gloves.'

'You have thought of everything...'

'No, not quite.' He looked exceedingly glum, a fitting mirror of the gloomy conditions outside. 'I remembered how abundantly colourful your hair is. No matter how subdued you think your clothes are, when anyone sees your *hair*, it'll be like a flaming beacon to everyone, marking your presence in the town for Severine and Luther. I have no hat or scarf and the headgear I did buy won't fit over the top.'

'And what is it that you purloined?'

He rattled around and found the last parcel on the floor. 'This!' And thrust it into her hands.

She stripped off the damp paper in a second and was confronted with something that could have been Ajax's tail. 'It's a wig, a black wig!'

'And it won't fit over your own hair!' Gallivant picked up the torn paper and threw it into a woven basket near the door.

'Do you really think I'm in that much danger, Gallivant?' Adelina let the fall of black hair sift through her fingers.

'Yes, I'm afraid so, Stitch Lady – more than ever. By escaping from her lair, you've rubbed Severine's nose fairly and squarely in her doings.'

Adelina had pulled on the black sweater and was easing on the black breeches, which although a little big, allowed room for Kholi's child to rest comfortably. 'Then you had best cut it off.' She reached for her dressmaking scissors. 'Now! Before I think on it! Just grab the plait and cut and then tomorrow we're going hunting you and I, and I don't want a word in argument!'

As Gallivant forced the blades of the scissors down, he couldn't help but wonder if it was a bizarre sort of symbolism. Was the hair symptomatic of Adelina's life? Was it going to be cut as short as her hair.

With a dull thud, the thick copper plait fell to the floor.

And so my crowning glory became a piece of waste to be consigned to the rubbish. But you know, I didn't care. I had a few things to accomplish and if it must be done in disguise then so be it. Besides, perhaps the hob's mesmer blunted the loss of my hair a little.

That whole day had passed like a dream because of the hob's charm. Sometimes his intuition surprised me. I think he understood my babe's and my own needs more than I did, myself. Because until Gallivant so wisely put me to rest, I had no idea just how much I had been on tenterhooks.

This day I had been content to lie amongst the feathered pillows on my bed in a somnolent state or to drift to the chaise and calmly embroider another part of that final piece: a stab stitch here, a Veniche knot there. Time took on a different meaning: time to recoup my energies and to work in a calm, almost disconnected fashion. Time for the baby too, to hear my heartbeat at a soothing pace rather than the stormy stampede that had been its accompaniment from conception.

My body and mind had felt the pressure of those two promises – one to the Others and one to Aine– diametric opposites that caused my heart to beat forever in a state of acute anxiety and my head to rattle like bees in a bottle. But Gallivant's gentle mesmer had induced such a tranquil state. I viewed all things from a safe place, almost with ambivalence.

As to the robe – did it have to be in the Museo by Carnivale? No, of course not – because it would have been incomplete. It would not have the final book, the one destined to bring my story to its inevitable conclusion.

I am sure you think you know what the conclusion will be. Then let me tell you this... you would know more than me at this time! For even on this day – so close to the Gate and to Severine, I couldn't envisage how it would end. I knew how I wanted it to end, but Fate often has other ideas.

So the first Day of the Dark ended without me placing a toe outside of the Orologio. Of course tomorrow would be different and as I lay my head once again on the pillows and cupped my hands over my moving belly, I directed my voice at my friend on the other bed as he lay staring distractedly at the ceiling, hands clasped behind his head.

'Gallivant, promise me on your life – tomorrow no more mesmers! I need to finish my tasks, for my own wellbeing and that of the babe. As I promised the Others to avenge them, so you must promise me you will let me do what I must. Please?'

There was a short silence and then the hob's voice answered.

'On my life Adelina, I swear!'

CHAPTER THIRTY TWO

An old man sat in a winged red armchair far away in the Barrow Hills in a house sequestred in the Ymp tree orchard, the Trevallyn Gate to Færan. For weeks he had been frail and depressed, more so as young Lhiannon began her travail. Jasper the Healer chafed to be the avenging angel, to secure the souls himself, to raise the sword of punishment. Instead he was consigned to a chair like some feeble-minded old man in his dotage.

Destiny had snatched the task away, allowing youth and energy to take the place of superior wisdom and experience. Worse – discovering fair Lhiannon's bane had been a bitter pill indeed but as with all else he could do nothing, forcing himself to leave the prophecy to continue its run unimpeded.

He knew Phelim had entered the journey and he knew, the minute he saw a fleeting glimpse of the carved face in his scrying mirror, that Liam's brother had been found and that Phelim must see the prophecy through to its end.

His thoughts rested for a moment with Ebba the Carlin. He could not deny it. Ebba was wise beyond expectation. To have concealed the babe so well and be bold enough to invite the old Færan into groups of infants, into her home! What had she used, what charm? Amber? Calendula? Carlin-tongue? He was impressed, a mortal no less!

Lately though, since Phelim's departure with the souls, Jasper could scry nothing in the mirror or the spheres. Nor had there been visions, despite all manner of incantations. It was as if he were blind and deaf. For days he had existed between the mirror in the spare room and the spheres in his workroom. Sleeping and eating there, briefly visiting the walled garden for mystic plants to add to his repertoire, leaving tray after tray of food merely nibbled at.

Already ascetic, he grew thin and haggard, obsessed with the redemption of the souls and the resolution of the prophecy... so much hung in the balance. Margriet and Folko could do little else but keep the fire banked, the decanter full and trays of bread, cheese and fruit alongside, in the vague hope he would eat more.

Tonight he sat in the red chair, head tilted back, magnetic eyes fixed on the mirror which appeared black and uninteresting. Sighing, he leaned over to fill his goblet and grab a fig and a crust. The taste of the food clung to his palate like ashes.

Ashes!

He recalled Ana's funeral and by bitter association, the death of Kholi Khatoun and most importantly to Jasper, the deaths of Lara the Færan silk seller and of Liam, all in the space of a week, so much grief! So much to be avenged!

He tipped up his head as a flickering of light disturbed him.

The mirror!

The ebony vastness contained by the silver frame cleared to reveal a calle edged by Veniche shops – a glove-maker's, a glassmaker's. Outside the latter stood a splendidly gilded sedan chair and against the door leaned a brutish fellow whom Jasper recognized! The man by the lake, the day of Ana's cremation!

He leaned forward. Rain smeared the colours of the calle and the lout held an umbrella over his bald head, scowling at his environs. Jasper's hands gripped the stem of his goblet as he stared at the fellow, sensing instantly in the manner of a wiseman and seer, that *this* was Kholi's murderer.

A tall, darkly clad man approached through the veil of rain and Luther stepped warningly across the doorway of the fabbrica. But the new customer would not be dissuaded, exchanging terse words, pushing the thug aside with a crafty waft of his hand across his chest. A Færan... was it, could it be?

Jasper stood up, every sense alert, breath sucking in. The stranger stopped inside the door, bowed and the diabolical bane of all Færan stepped past, grasping folds of her coat with disdain. In that instant, relief and anticipation flooded through Jasper, titillating him, whispering of the fight to come.

Severine, Phelim, Luther, the souls! He thrust a fist in the air, a declaration that the glove had been thrown down. But wait, what was that! A movement of something near the sedan-chair, almost but not quite invisible. A hob? Is it *the* hob – the one that had been directed by he and Lhiannon to care for a mortal woman? If it is then one could deduce readily that Adelina must be in Veniche.

Jasper shoved the goblet on the mantle as the mirror faded. He flung himself to the door, the frailty and angst of past weeks slipping from his shoulders like a cloak. Relief that the souls had provided the necessary bait to lure that *bitseach* energized him like a prick from a buckthorn.

'Margriet,' he called, his voice bouncing along the hall walls. 'Margriet, I need food! Folko, pack for Veniche!'

Next morning, the rain continued its rhythmic patter on the shoulders of their coats and hats as Adelina and the hob traipsed down calle after calle. There were few folk about and the town had an atmosphere at once shady and fearful where everyone walked with eyes downcast and purposefully in order to vacate the streets as soon as possible. No wonder, chuntered Gallivant, it's morbidly depressing. The sky hangs on my very shoulders and makes my head muzzy, as if it isn't tired enough! Just before Adelina went to sleep the previous night, she had extracted a promise from him, damn it! And she had said something else. She had sat up excitedly. 'Gallivant! I know what's happening!'

He had groaned a response back, something that sounded like *'g'sleep'*.

She ignored him. 'Bait, Gallivant, that's what it is! Bait! Jasper's using the souls for bait!'

He had refused to be drawn, just humphed and rolled over, but had hardly slept all night as he gave thought to her revelation. She could be right. The souls could indeed be bait. There was no doubt Jasper wanted them returned to Færan where they belonged. But as a trap as well?

He realised Adelina was talking as they walked along the next morning and turned to her, still surprised at the change in her appearance. Gone was the golden Traveller with the russet locks. In her place, a woman with black hair caught up behind her head in a swinging fall. Even her skin tones appeared to have altered with the new hair. Now she was almost as pale as Severine and with the black clothes, she could almost have been the woman's sister but he forebore to mention anything like that to her.

'Gallivant, are you listening? I said when you purloin as you so charmingly put it, are you stealing?'

'Sink me Adelina,' the hob looked mortally offended. 'No! I leave a bag of payment behind always. If the purveyor is honest, then the bag will contain gelt. If he or she is not, then the bag will contain leaves and twigs and such.'

'How often has it been a twig payment?'

'Oh, about half.'

Adelina chuckled. 'Hob, I love you... I truly do. You make my sun shine every day and that's no mean feat. Now look, no Færan yet, but there is a haberdasher's.' She dragged the hob into a cupboard of a shop, the smell of silks, threads and wools exciting her as it always had.

Outside the door, leaning against the wall with a collar up against the rain and a seaman's tricorn protecting his head, one of Luther's spies watched them enter. He glanced through the window and examined the woman bending over the counter to examine the threads for sale. Huh! No red hair, and no Traveller's garb – but then she was the only woman to come near the shop all day! He studied her face. Perhaps I'd best tell the boss anyway. Afterwards, I can go and grab an ale.

'Well, boss. She were pale in the face, quite pale like Madame. An' her hair were black, a great long tail at the back like a pony. An' she were with a shortish skinny fella. An' it looked to me like they bought some cream and red threads.'

Damn! Luther crunched his fists into balls. 'Describe her features to me. Her eyes, her mouth.'

The spy watched his dream of an early drink fading faster than the foam on a mug of ale.

'Cor boss, I dunno. She had nice big eyes, sort of brownish, I think. An' her face were oval and she had a luscious mouth like a peach... kissable like. Her voice were throaty, I heard her speaking to the haberdasher. An' cor, what else? She were dressed in black, but I guess that don't mean much. Oh, an' this here lass were pregnant. About three or four months gone I reckon.'

Pregnant! Well, it can't be Adelina, can it? It was just the way the chap described her mouth... kissable! And her voice... throaty!

'Did you follow her?'

'Aye. She an' the fella just ambled everywhere. Over calle and bridge, until they came to the Grand Canal an' then they sat in one of them coffee-houses an' ate and drank. I thought then I should report what I knew cos there 'asn't been no other woman. One thing, sir – I couldn't make out much of what they said, but I heard 'em mention Madame's name and I heard 'em mention the Others.'

Yes?' Luther's attention pricked up like a dog's ears.

'Just that if they found 'em, the Others yeah, then all their problems'd be solved. I'm tellin' you, the fella didn't look too happy at that.'

Luther threw a handful of coins to his man and sent him off to the nearest inn and then sat at the window of Madame's drawing room. Yesterday had been such a mixed bag of a day – five of the six architects had called, been received and sent packing, the useless idiots, with fleas in their ears. The sixth had spent much longer with Madame and there had been no shouting either.

He ran a hand over the shining dome. The scar stood white and ridged on his cheek and the scab on his chin stood proud and he winced as his fingers touched it. 'Black hair, pregnant, pale, and with a thin male friend, it can't be her. Others, Madame's name, a haberdasher's, oval face and kissable lips... could it be?' He muttered and ground his teeth together, striding around the room. 'Yes or no?'

In his wily way, despite the unlikely description from his man, he knew he couldn't afford to ignore the woman. Something in his gut warned him Adelina was close by in the town. He resolved not to disclose this latest information to Madame. She had been so excited yesterday and it put her in such an amenable mood. He sat recollecting the previous day...

Muffled voices had drifted into the drawing room as the major-domo ushered Madam's guest out through the palazzo entrance and Severine came whirling into the room, slamming the door behind her. 'Oh Luther!'

She had rushed to the chiffonier and poured herself a large white wine from a decanter, drunk it off rapidly and poured herself another. Luther noticed her hands shaking and the bottle made little tink-tink sounds as one edge collided with another. She turned around. 'I've done it Luther, I know!'

He had never, in all his time with her, seen her truly happy. Now the starkness softened and radiance flushed her narrow face, the storm grey eyes becoming dove-coloured. Even her mouth, so habitually pinched, seemed to become plump as it curved, actually curved, up to her cheeks. Normally she was striking, now she was beautiful.

'The architect recognised the flakes of paint. Isn't that uncanny? And do you know how, and tell me this isn't the Fates working in my favour – he has just finished the renovation of the building! Had you and I searched on our own we would never have found it because it is now a completely different colour. But he knew it, he knew it!' She sipped some more wine and her hand became steadier. As always, Luther just listened. 'The Museo owns the building! But better still, I have been invited to the Museo ball, to be held there on the night of Carnivale to open the building. By the Fates, things just drop into my lap! I can find the Gate amongst the crowd of revelers and then I will wait and snap Lhiannon up as she walks through.' She squirmed like a gleeful child with a toy. 'Luther, I can't believe it! By Carnivale, I will have the souls, maybe more than I need and I will have the Gate to Færan. It's truly wonderful!' She had smiled in his direction and he gave a small tilt to his own lips. 'I need you to get formal attire and a mask because you shall be my escort. I need you by my side for this, to do what you have to do.'

Luther, man of few words, knew exactly what she meant and responded. 'Yes, Madame.' And so now here he was about to be consort for the Contessa Di Accia and even better, Adelina was in town. He smiled a thin smile. Life was peculiar sometimes.

The previous evening Phelim sat in the room in the Esperia, the drapes pulled. Such a lost day! He chafed with the uselessness of his journey around the city. Except for the glassmaker's, of course. That had yielded a thing or two of interest. He had purchased Ebba's coveted paperweight with the millefiore, the many flowers, under the glass dome. As he pulled it from his pocket, he could hear Ebba's voice. *'If ever I did go to Veniche there are only two places I would really want to see. One is the Museo and easy enough to visit. The other is the Ca' Specchio, the Mirror Palace. They say it is the oldest and most elegant palace in Veniche but it is in private hands and so I should never gain access.'*

He sat on the edge of the bed recalling another item of interest – that arrogant woman who had pushed past at the fabbrica was Severine, the glassmaker had said *'goodbye Contessa!'* And he *had* seen her before – at Ferry Crossing, and he'd heard the hob's lady curse her with vehemence and fear.

But it was the souls that confirmed the woman's identity. As the woman walked past, they froze deeper than ever against his ribs. They knew! He remembered the reaction of the souls to the Traveller on the ferry and seemed perplexed and excited by his discovery. They sense things, enough for hate and displeasure to make them burn with frostbite and affection to make them warm as a kiss, he thought. I can understand the reaction to Severine, a murderer, but not to the woman on the ferry. Who is she?

Phelim swung his feet to the floor and walked over to the table on which was a tray with a basket of bread, cheeses, tomatoes and figs. A bottle of wine stood next to it and he poured a glass. Strange too, he mused, that her companion was an Other, a Goodfellow who calls himself Gallivant. *I have a feeling about the two of them. The lady with the copper hair, what was it about her? Her bruised eyes, the hob's solicitous care?*

He turned his palm face up and ran his other palm over it, almost as if he caressed something of delicate appearance and infinite value. But then his hands fell to his side as thoughts of his task pushed the image of the woman away.

As each minute passed, he chafed to be done. Leave the Other world behind, become a shepherd again – to feel the wool, oily with lanolin between his fingers, to smell that warm ovine smell, to hear the low bleating of a ewe as she called to her lamb. Real things. No, he did not want the wanton largesse of his father's life and would turn his back on it in the time it took to make a mesmer.

Hearing a knock at the door, he jumped up and pulled it open to see a young serving lad with a bundle of washed clothes. He gave him some coins and then smiled at the boy. 'Tell me, young lad, do you know of the Ca' Specchio, the Mirror Palace?'

The lad scratched at his messy hair. 'I've heard of it. It belonged to an old aristo who died and left it to the city. The last I heard, it was beginning to fall apart but I don't know where it is exactly.'

Phelim sighed, it had only been a whim brought on by Ebba's words and yet something, some intuition said *'listen'*. 'Well, thank you. Here,' he held out a further coin. 'For your trouble.'

The boy's eyes widened and he turned swiftly to run down the stairs with a grin on the youthful visage as Phelim wafted a mesmer so the fellow would forget he had even been to the room.

CHAPTER THIRTY THREE

'Aine, this is hopeless! Everyone is masked and dressed in black! Everyone looks the same! We'll never find him!' Adelina threw herself into a seat at one of the cafés. 'I'm tired and hungry and something about needles in haystacks is striking a chord! It seemed such a good idea – to find the Færan and get his help. But it's impossible and don't say I told you so!' She glared at Gallivant as a waiter put some linguine in front of her and she took a sip of water. Gallivant said nothing, just thought to himself that it was the Threadlady's favourite game, chases with no end. He had not felt a *frisson* once amongst all the people they had mingled with and even he couldn't believe there was not one single Færan in the town... not when there was a Gate somewhere close by.

'Look at the masks, Gallivant!' Adelina stared as people went about their business incognito.

'Wait till Carnivale. Those you see now are bland and dour, but come Carnivale, there is nothing from your world or mine, Adelina, that won't be copied, feathered, painted and gilded.'

'Should we be wearing masks now?

'It wouldn't hurt. It's another sort of camouflage. Did you know that's what this is all about? Subterfuge, *segreta*? People use them to hide their faces on the grounds that the Dark requires all manifestation of colour – be it hair, freckles, ruddy cheeks, bright lips, eyes – to be disguised. But everyone knows it is an excuse for miscreance and libidinous behaviour in secret. Be that as it may, I shall purchase some plain leather masks: one for you and one for me. Much like those, do you see?'

A couple walked past with the woman in a plain brown leather mask which covered her from forehead to nose, her body shrouded in a black coat. The man wore a similar mask with the nose extended like a bird's beak. There was something secretive about the couple. *Segreta*. Just like everyone else in the piazza.

'My back aches Gallivant, so I shall wait here and finish my coffee. See what the mask-maker has for Carnivale. I shall come with you later and pick something wildly extravagant for that. Meanwhile I shall observe the passing crowd... perhaps we shall strike lucky.'

Gallivant reached across the table and held her wrist, the strength of the grasp snapping Adelina's attention away from the crowd to his intense face. 'Adelina, you must stay here until I return. Don't move! Remember the danger and remember what happened to Kholi!' He watched her eyes deepen and darken and he quickly added,' and remember your baby. Do as I say, yes?'

She nodded her head. 'Yes, I promise, honestly!'

The hob threw down some money, leaped down the steps, and hailed a gondolier to take him quickly past the crowds to the mask-maker he knew of in the Calle di Bona Ventura. *Ten minutes there, ten back and ten to choose four masks – two for now, two for Carnivale, for I shan't let her go and pick her own. I shall be back in half an hour, let her stay where she is, concealed in the shadows of that café. Please let her stay still!* The poling of the gondola rocked him and the faint drizzle drifted in under the canopy as it had done all day, adding to the moist fug that was symptomatic of the Dark. Damn, he thought! I should have put another little mesmer on her!

Severine stayed seated as the glassmaker was shown into the salon.

'Signor, I am pleased you are working to our little schedule.' She gestured with her head at the leather roll he held, bedecked with small glistening beads of moisture. 'And they are the rods?'

Signor Niccolo's sweaty hands shook as he untied the leather laces and rolled out the cover. Inside, a faint tink of glass rattled. He reached into the pouches and pulled out four small canes, like tiny coloured straws.

She picked one up and peered down the middle – just enough space, she thought, perfect. '*Perfetto*,' she said aloud. 'Leave them and Luther shall bring them back in an hour or so and you should be able to complete the job by Carnivale.' She dismissed him perfunctorily, ignoring him as the door shut, lining up the canes one next to the other on her desk and reaching for the casket with the Færan paper scraps inside. She took the first one and read it, although it was engraved on her heart, on her very soul.

'*From caverns deep, abysses cold...*'

She shook herself, a pleasurable shudder, and began to smooth the thin paper out onto the desk with one finger, rolling one end tightly towards the other, the looping Færan script disappearing letter by charmed letter. Presently she held nothing but a fragile, narrow and impossibly tiny cylinder between her index finger and thumb and she slipped it down the middle of the cane.

There it rested, hidden behind the opaque cobalt blue glass: secreted, *segreta*. She began again with the second strip and all the while the paper made the faintest crackling sounds. At last the fatal charms were hidden away and within a fingertip's reach. She had the greatest collection of millefiore paperweights in Eirie displayed in cabinets in the grand entrance hall to the palazzo. There was easily space for another four and none but she would know what they held. She sighed as she slipped the last cylinder into the last rod. By tomorrow night she would be immortal and omnipotent.

She sat back and looked at the neat row of canes. She, Severine Di Accia who was once a Traveller belonging to a band of gypsies – she shook herself with a shudder of distaste at the memory – she would be the most predominant and irresistable person in the world. And all because Adelina had so kindly informed her when she was very young that she was a changeling. She chuckled. *So much to thank you for Adelina! How can I repay you?* 'Luther!' Her voice rang out, high-pitched and commanding.

Phelim had done blending and being discreet. He had traced and re-traced footsteps over bridge and calle as he searched for the Gate with no success and chafed with frustration as he noticed a man walking toward him. 'Sir, sir, a moment please!'

The man glanced up from the ground where his eyes had been cast, his mind far away. His face showed displeasure at being so disturbed and he brushed fractiously at the moisture on his face with a red paisley square as he looked up at the tall figure before him.

'Ah, signor, it is you.' Phelim recognised the glassmaker. 'Do you remember I bought a paperweight from you, yesterday?'

Signor Niccolo squinted from tired, reddened eyes and in a harassed manner, nodded his head.

'Sir, I need the address of the Ca' Specchio.' *It has a ring, I don't know why.* 'Can you help me?'

'Um, yes, yes of course.' The glassmaker dragged himself together for his attention was far away. 'This is the Calle del Vetro, if you go to the end where it joins the Rio del Malcanton, cross the bridge to the Fondamenta Minotto, then you will see it. It is the colour of summer apricots.' He sighed and Phelim sensed a knot in the man's throat as if for some reason the thought of next summer held great and unimaginable significance. 'I'm sorry, you must excuse me,' he said.

The glassmaker skirted around Phelim and did not see the Færan's hand come up intuitively to swipe the air in the act of mesmer. I hope that helps him, he thought, he won't remember me and he will feel a little less distressed, he was in a sore mood.

CHAPTER THIRTY FOUR

Adelina looked at the crowd thinning in the piazza. There was no one she recognised, she felt no *frisson* and the hopelessness of her self-imposed quest weighed upon her. She had repeatedly told herself it was pointless and utterly without merit, this desire to see Lhiannon once more – to assure herself the girl was alive but she could no more help the belief that she was everyone's bane than fly.

But weighing even heavier were the promises – one promise to the Others to avenge Liam and Lara and any Other Severine had killed and then the promise to Aine for saving Ajax's life. One juxtaposed against the other. Either way, she must find the portal to Færan. To avenge the Others she must be where Severine would be and there was no doubt now that she would be at the Gate.

The promise to Aine required her to tell the Others what she had done, which *still* meant she must find the Gate, for if nothing else she was honourable and owed them that. The only person in the whole of Veniche who could help her was the Færan from the ferry and he hadn't been seen since the glassmaker's.

The glassmaker!

Without a thought for the hob and anything he had said, she pushed away the remains of the linguine, shrugged on her wet coat and ran down the steps to hail a gondola.

Luther had left the palazzo not long after the glassmaker and had caught up with the man as he had been firing up the flames in the fabricca and tying on his leather apron.

'Madame said they must be ready by six o'clock tomorrow. She has a reception to attend at seven and then a Ball, so I will collect them at six and pay you.' He noticed the glassmaker staring at the white scar on his cheek and turned on his heel sharply to walk out the door, slamming it hard behind him. The bell made myriad chimes and the glass in the shop window wavered dangerously. Out of the corner of his eye he saw Signor Niccolo placing a closed sign in the window.

He rubbed his cheek and leaned for a moment against the window of a glovemaker's shop further along, pulling the collar of his black oilskin up his neck against the drizzle. The glovemaker's was closed, adding to the feeling that the city was beginning to shut down as the mizzle thickened and the sky darkened. It was silent in the calle except for the occasional tap-tap of shoes on cobbles and the morbid howl of someone's dog who was tired of the rain and wanted to be let inside. Luther felt angry – at the rain, at the difficulty of finding Adelina and at being thwarted. Anger festered and boiled below the surface of his emotions. It would take such a little thing for it to bubble over...

Behind him he heard a sound like an infantry line cocking their weapons as a flock of damp pigeons flew up with clacking wings. He spun around and in that moment saw the pot of gold at the end of his tawdry rainbow.

Despite the black hair and the black clothes, he recognised the seductive body of the woman he hated and craved all in one.

She knocked at the door of the fabricca even though the sign said closed. Knowing the glassmaker would be out the back and too anxiously frantic to come to the summons, and seeing the calle virtually empty of shoppers, Luther slipped a hand to his belt and stepped feline fashion to stand directly behind Adelina.

'He can't hear you, Adelina.' He whispered close to Adelina's ear as if he was kissing her, breathing in the fragrance of her body and wanted to scream with the urge to take her there and then against the dripping walls. 'He's busy.'

At the sound of Luther's voice, Adelina's heart stopped beating and then began again, stampeding with the force of the Cabyll Ushtey's hoofbeats.

His arm snaked around to rest over her waist and something sharp pricked the skin of her belly.

'It's a stiletto, long enough to pierce your womb and kill your child.'

Her feet melded to the cobbles, unable to open eyes she had shut in order to block out the horror that had befallen her. She could hear Kholi's voice – *no, no, no!*

'You will move with me, that's right.' Luther continued to whisper in her ear, his breath hot against her lobe, making her flush with disgust and fear. 'And I will hold you to my side like my lover, that's it and we will walk. For the sake of your child, won't we? No dramatics, remember it's important to keep calm for the baby's sake.'

Had Gallivant not been Other, the masks hanging from the rafters and from hooks on the walls would have tossed him into the land of the bewildered as empty eye-sockets gazed at him. The maskmaker's daughter ignored him as she applied feathers to a massive mask fit for a queen. Exotic feathers fanned the air and goldleaf glittered.

Gallivant quickly grabbed two leather masks and then prowled around the choked rooms searching for Carnivale masks. He stared at a *piccolo principe,* the face of young boy staring back, golden blonde hair swept elegantly upwards – that *could* be him. But no, that one there, quickly, that was more to his liking! Pinocchio! He had often heard the story and felt he danced quite readily to Adelina's tune, like a marionette on strings.

He hastened on, past *gladiatores* and *colombinas* that were gilded and decorated and on sticks. There were *voltos* and *civettas.* None would suit her! Oh quickly, only a few minutes of his allotted time left!

And then he turned a corner to be swallowed by a fountain of feathers rising upwards. *Colombina* after *colombina* with plumage of vibrant down, the eye cavities outlined and painted, the rest of the masks gilded. He knew what he wanted Adelina to wear at Carnivale – if she was going to be at the Gate she might as well do it with panache, for by then safety would mean little and he took down a mask, the left side decorated in bronze and blue feathers, the right in vermilion – so very Adelina. He walked to the counter and smiled at the girl, gently waving his hand in the air. She stared at him as a bag of gelt appeared on the counter and continued to stare in mesmered fashion as he ran out the door, along the edge of the small piazza to the waiting gondola.

The crowd had almost gone when he raced up the steps of the Grand Piazza and into the cafè. 'Adelina', he eased himself past a couple of waiters who were bending over the table wiping it. 'You should see what I have...'

The table and chairs were empty.

'Where is Madam?' He grabbed one of the waiters by the arm.

'Gone twenty minutes since, sir!' The waiter flipped a damp white towel over his shoulder.

'Gone! Gone where?' He tried not to panic but a shrill note of hysteria crept into his voice.

'Don't know sir, but she took off as if Herlingus and his dogs were behind!'

At the mention of Huon in the Veniche patois, Gallivant grabbed his masks and raced into the middle of the piazza, scanning faces and turning this way and that. *Threadlady, why do you do this! My stomach crawls with where you might be and I feel a shiver over my body!* He turned sharply to ply his way up the nearest alley and crashed into a man coming the other way.

'Mind sir! Mind how you... you!'

Gallivant looked up as the deep voice chided him politely. 'You!' he gasped, 'I shiver because of *you*! Aine, mistress and I have been searching... and now she's... and I...'

Phelim placed a hand on the hob's arm and steadied him in the Færan way. 'See now. I hoped to meet *you* again. Where is your lady?'

'Gone, disappeared and I think it's Severine's doing!' The hob's face blanched and the lines which had begun as he cared for the embroiderer deepened with his fretting.

'Severine!' Loose threads were beginning to converge for Phelim, to weave themselves into answers. Equally his stomach plummeted at the mention of his adversary's name and the bag around his neck, pressing hard against his ribs, had burned alternately warm, then cold at the mention of names.

'It's Gallivant, isn't it? Come back to my hostel. We can't look for your mistress without a plan and we must talk, mustn't we? I have a feeling about you and your mistress and I think I can help.'

Gallivant nodded grimly. 'We can't delay too long, every minute she is gone, is a minute off her life!'

What do you do when your child is threatened? Show me a mother who wouldn't do anything to save her child's life... anything!

I went with Luther.

We walked along the calle entwined together, the concealed point of the stiletto occasionally pricking at the skin of my belly. My mind had moments of utter blankness in its panic. At other times, the knowledge of my fate would make me trip and stumble against the point of the weapon and I would straighten to beg Luther – beg him – not to hurt my baby.

CHAPTER THIRTY FIVE

'She had this perverse idea, my Threadlady, that she was bad luck to people... mortal *and* Other. Her parents, Ana, Liam... you know their story? Lara, the Færan silk seller? And Kholi! Oh Aine, it is *that* death alone which unhinges her still.' The hob walked back and forth, hands waving and gesticulating. 'And now she thinks she's Lhiannon's bane!'

'Lhiannon!' Phelim's exclamation stopped the hob in his tracks.

'*You* know Lhiannon?'

'I do.'

'Well, Adelina had this obsession that she must see Lhiannon to prove to her unborn child she is not some unfortunate piece of bad luck to all she meets. She liked Lhiannon and missed her when the girl left with the souls. In a way I think she tried to put Lhiannon in Ana's place. Do you know all about the souls? I suppose you do, you're Færan.' Without waiting for an answer the unstoppable hob continued. 'Adelina had been searching for the Veniche Gate with my utterly useless guidance when we had an idea you could tell us because we had surmised you were Færan...'

Phelim sat as still as a statue.

'Because of the *frisson*.' Gallivant's voice petered out, his story almost told. He added an afterthought as he palmed his aching head. 'So help me find her because I am telling you, she has thought to find the Gate herself without a thought of any danger to she and the babe. She is so damned impetuous! I *swear* Severine has her now! Help me find her quickly and then tell me where the Gate is. You can mesmer my memory after. And then my Lady can see Lhiannon and get on with the business of being pregnant as far from Severine as possible.'

Still Phelim had not moved. It was a skill he had learned as a young shepherd – to be calm, not to move quickly and to think, to anticipate. His hands formed a steeple under his chin and he finally locked eyes with the hob who shrank a little from the seriousness of the gaze. 'Lhiannon is dead.'

'Aine, you say so! Are you sure?' The hob sat with a hard plop onto the end of one of the beds.

Phelim told of his relationship with Lhiannon and at the end Gallivant shook his head. 'My poor Lhiannon, I truly admired her. She was a courageous little thing.' He sighed deeply. 'Sink me friend, it's going to take a better man than I to convince Adelina she is no man's bane, that Lhiannon's death is not her fault! I *must* find her!' He jumped up and began the frantic pacing. 'Severine's got her. I just know it! If we find that foul woman, we can find the Stitcher. Will you help me? Please?'

'We have only to find Severine's palazzo. There is surely a house brownie within whom you could question as to where she might be confined. And apparently I have ways and means.'

'What do you mean?'

But Phelim ignored the hob's curiosity. 'I know where the Palazzo Di Accia is. I asked a waiter at one of the coffeehouses. It's on the Grand Canal, directly opposite the Ca' d'Oro, in fact they say one is the mirror image of the other, that the old count built both, unsure which view he liked the best from the balconies.'

'Good,' the hob ran to the door. 'Let's go!'

'Gallivant!' Phelim's hand grasped the hob.

'Aine man, come ON! Don't you understand? If Severine does have her, she will kill her this time. She is symbolic of all Severine lost – the souls, the robe, immortality! And she is Adelina! That's almost enough on its own. Sink me, we've no time to waste! You're Færan, you can do anything if you have to. Come on!'

He leaped through the door, grabbing his coat as Phelim followed. 'Hob, wait up!'

Gallivant hauled to a halt outside the hotel entrance.

'You need to clear out your stuff from your pensione, especially the robe. If they inveigle its whereabouts from Adelina, she is as good as dead. As long as Severine can't find the robe, she will keep Adelina alive. The robe appears to be an intrinsic part of Severine's sick machinations. Go and do it and I shall wait for you there.' He pointed to a colonnaded arcade that led to a row of empty gondolas, the mooring poles glistening from the rain.

The hob vanished into thin air and Phelim hurried toward the arcade. At the end of the cloistered space a dozen empty craft rocked in the slight chop fidgeting in from the laguna. Jumping in to the nearest, Phelim negotiated his way to the upswept stern and untied the rear line.

As he returned to the side of the canal, he looked up at the night sky in its shroud of grey raincloud. An uneasy mist tumbled and teased over cupola and campanile, crawling as low as the poles. No moon or stars gave any light, creating a subfusc that concealed and threatened – how many pairs of eyes watched? He cast a glance around and could see a glint of amber moving surreptitiously, level with his shoulder. A cat! But a flip in the water spun him round and he saw the iridescent shape of a merrow swimming away as his heart hammered briefly. He heard the tap of feet and the hob emerged out of the dripping mist that thickened as the evening aged. 'You were quick.'

'Sink me man, there has to be some advantage to being Other. I just hope another is that we can save my lady friend. Let's go!'

Phelim jumped aboard, his thoughts on Adelina's bereft face, and stepped to the stern to begin poling the craft backward out in to the middle of the waterway. He directed the bow along the canal and they passed under bridge after bridge until a broad swathe of black water met them at the junction. 'We go left,' he whispered. 'To the Bridge of Sighs. See that shape right up there, the bridge that is mask-shaped.' He pointed into the wet and misty gloom. 'It's just past there.'

He poled deftly, standing at the stern, bending into the pole stroke, one leg stretched behind the other. The oar made a faint rhythmic squeak in its post and he ran his hand in front of his chest, reducing the uneasy tool to silent movement. The palazzos, the Libreria, the Museo all slid past silently as the Bridge of Sighs emerged in the mist.

'It's traditionally the bridge where masked women throw tokens to their lovers as they pass underneath in gondolas.' He spoke gently to Gallivant to ease the hob's angst. 'But it's also the bridge where the condemned pass from the Courts of Justice to the executioner. It's strange a bridge can mean two such disparate things.'

Gallivant looked up as they poled underneath. A faded fresco of lovers lying within an arbor graced the smooth arch.

'It would be pleasing to think Severine would pass over this bridge after she had suffered the Courts' indulgence.' Phelim knew it was a mortal comment that passed his lips and it pleased him that some of Ebba was still ingrained. 'A life sentence, perhaps!'

'I don't think so, she deserves something far worse!' Gallivant muttered.

Phelim raised an eyebrow and then spoke softly. 'There. See?' He stopped poling.

On the left bank of the canal sat an elegant palace glowing pale as moonlight in the night and taking up a whole block with a rio on either side. It was three stories high, each long window arched and with fluted masonry fretting the arches, elegant traceries of leadlighting marking the windows themselves. On the second storey, a balcony ran the breadth of the building, carved in the Raji style in quatrefoil patterns. Even in the dark of the evening with a vacillating mist, the ivory paintwork and cream marble set up its own reflective light. In front of the building, poles stood to attention and a studded pair of doors warded off the unwanted.

The two companions stared at it.

Gallivant whispered. 'What now?'

Had I known my hob and his new friend were close by, I would have felt less of the pain that assaulted me, for Luther used me as roughly as a man can. I cannot and will not say anything more about it as it sickens me and brings me to the edge of an abyss.

My rapist consigned me to a room at the top of some building to begin his work. I know because I was forced on contused legs to climb at least three long sets of stairs and counting them stopped me screaming. He threw a large blanket over me afterward, as I lay in a heap on the floor but I cared about nothing as I shivered there.

'Adelina, the pleasure was mine.' Luther assailed me with his filthy words. 'Your body is a delight that I find I must have more of, which I shall do after I take you to Severine. She'll want the robe and then I think she'll give you back to

me. Behir woman, I shall enjoy the gift. I have so much to repay you for, so much! And there is so much else I want to try with you. This was just an opener, shall we say!' He burst out laughing as he re-buttoned his breeches.

The door locked and I succumbed to a cold silence bereft of thought.

A faint light stretched across the floor and glinted on a piece of broken glass near my hand. Sharp, part of a bottle perhaps and my mind sped through the process – glass, cut, bleed, death, Kholi. My fingers curled around it and drew it towards me.

I stretched my other arm out and laid the glass against my wrist. I couldn't imagine the pain being any worse than the rape of a pregnant woman and I felt the tears scald as I remembered the brutality Kholi's child had just suffered. How could any fledgling survive that?

I raised the glass to slice and as I did my belly fluttered – like a small hand tapping. Again and then again.

My child demanded my attention! Against the odds, against the battering that had pounded the walls of its home, it lived and in its staccato rhythm against my belly it seemed to say, don't give up, we have a long way to go together and much to do.

And so, my friend, have you.

Shrink the latest book and replace it under the groom's shoulder cape. And then repair to his black tricorn hat with its carmine feather. I wired and embroidered it in another hoop, then cut it out and applied it to the head of my groom. It is capacious enough to fit a thick book underneath, so once again you will have to slice some of the stab-stitches that hold the hat in place.

There are so few hiding places left now and only three more books after this one. Including that vital last... remember what my instructions were. Don't, on pain of death, touch the one hanging from the bride's hand!

CHAPTER THIRTY SIX

'There are no house brownies, only Siofra!' Gallivant had paddled rapidly back across the canal to his companion on the landing stage at the Ca' d'Oro opposite Severine's palatial home. 'And I have found out what we need to know. She's there!'

Using the skill that so drove Adelina mad, to pass through a building no matter how thick the walls, he had ventured deep into the stronghold and found the kitchens and cellars to be bereft of any Other life at all. Bemused, he passed into the cobbled yard at the rear, where tubs of dripping bay and olive trees stood sentinel in the empty space. He could hear a chittering sound like sparrows coming from a half opened door on the other side of the yard and crept silently as a shade towards the noise.

A party of Veniche Siofra sat around a small flame. Like their mortal counterparts, they were dressed in black and the women sat applying tiny feathers to masks while the men deftly splashed gold paint around.

'Hola, friends!' Gallivant whispered a soft greeting.

The Siofra jumped but seeing the hob, settled down quickly. 'What do you want, hob? You'll not be welcome in that house!'

'I can see. Does the palazzo have no hobs or brownies at all?'

A pretty Siofra with a turquoise feather in her hand spoke up. 'That woman wouldn't want any Others in the house. When one moved in, there were instructions that within a day a set of clothes should be laid out and they would be forced to leave.'

'Then why are you here?'

'Siofra go where they like and when. It is not for the likes of that hellspawn to dictate to us.'

'I like your spirit, there are many Others who could emulate you.' The hob watched the Siofra preening with satisfaction. 'Do you ever go into the palazzo yourself?'

There was a chorus of delighted laughter... like a flock of finches, thought Gallivant.

'Of course, whenever we like.'

'Today, this night?'

'Why?'

'I look for someone.' The hob sat on a wine-cask and hung his head. 'I think they may be here.'

'There is only a mortal woman that the brute Luther has locked in the top rooms. She's very ugly. Her hair is shorn and she's dirty. But then, so's he.' The turquoise feather was given a final push and took its place amongst others on the diminutive mask as Gallivant's heart began a racketing beat. 'That's who you search for, isn't it? Hob, she's mortal! Why does it matter?'

'She is in my care,' was all the hob would say.

'Then you don't do a good job, letting her be locked up here!' The little woman who did all the talking, cocked an eyebrow at him. 'And let me tell you this too, you will never get her out, the brute has the one key and she can't pass through walls like you.'

'But they told me there are windows all along the top storey, Phelim. We can do this. We must do this! If we go down that rio on the side there, there is a large tree draping over the water and we can climb to the balcony on the first floor and then there are ornamental grilles we can use as ladders to the balconies on the next level and the next. Adelina is in one of the top rooms!'

Phelim looked at the hob's desperate face. 'Do you propose to make her climb down the same way, pregnant as she is?'

'No, no... I don't know. Sink me, can't you mesmer?'

Phelim sighed. Time would tell. 'Let's just find her first. Something will reveal itself, I'm sure.'

The companions poled the gondola to the small, bending canal that laced away round corners to some far away distance. Phelim waved his hand over the rope line and it climbed vertically to knot itself amongst the hanging branches of the ancient olive that bent gnarled branches over the dark grey water. Then they climbed up the branches and around the corner onto the first floor balcony with its carved balustrade. Phelim hoisted Gallivant onto his shoulders and the hob grasped the ornamental grille and climbed rapidly to the next balcony with its smaller quatrefoil design and then to the next. Phelim slipped in quietly beside him.

'Maybe we should have manifested inside the building, instead of all this climbing,' the hob swore as his feet slipped on the wet marble.

'Indeed, but it is as well to spy the lie of the land for Adelina's descent and hob, I have my doubts about her being able to get down the way we got up!'

'I know, I know!' Gallivant snapped back as he edged along the balcony.

It stretched its narrow and decorative way the width of the palazzo. Wide enough only for the two to progress in single file, looking in each darkened window and hoping to spy something – anything! But each window was empty.

A nightbird hooted from close by, startling the pair.

'She has to be here! She has to be!' The hob's whisper was on the slide to hysteria.

Phelim had leaned against one of the windows. He worried for the woman, for her condition. 'Look!' He had turned to examine the darkened interior and thought he saw a huddle that could have been a pile of rugs or some such. 'What do you think?'

'What, what?' Gallivant leaped to his side, his whisper sharp.

'Ssh! Look! Could it be someone on the floor?'

The hob cupped hands over eyes to peer through the glass. 'Yes! It is!' He whipped through the glass of the window and Phelim watched him bend over the tumble of fabric. He kneeled and cradled something in his arms and then smoothed his hand and kissed the top of a head that drooped. He bent lower, looking into her face, speaking earnestly, gesticulating over his shoulder. She moved and the hob eased his arm under her and then walked carefully to the window.

Phelim wafted his arm in front of his body and the window catch flipped up, the fenestration opening wide like a door. A leg appeared, bare and bruised, then a shoulder and a head that would have been capped in short russet hair if he could see it properly. She was dressed in nothing but torn underwear and his heart broke a little at her indignity so that his hand came up and within minutes she was clothed in breeches and a sweater, some boots and a jacket.

He held her hand gently, feeling emotion creeping through his body and then he spoke to them, the woman's exhaustion and delicate condition not lost on his sensibilities.

'We must travel across the rooves and quickly.'

CHAPTER THIRTY SEVEN

'Now a city... slips beneath us... Castle rooftops battered by the tide's foamy tentacles.' Another of Ebba's poems echoed in Phelim's mind as he edged Adelina across the terracotta roof tiles. She stepped over a row of decorative marble crockets cut and honed to the sharpness of knives. At their edge the threesome looked out over Veniche – row upon twisting and curved row of canal, flat rooves, rippled and decorative rooflets, coned chimney-stacks, erect campaniles and arched cupolas and in the distance the expanse of the laguna wrapping itself around the city like a dark blanket.

'It's no good here, too wide to traverse.' Phelim turned away, pushing Adelina ahead, in the circle of his arms. 'Come further along the rio – it narrows as it goes around the bend.'

All they could see as they looked down over the edge of the roof was black shadow and blacker water and the whole was uninviting.

They had reached the end of the palazzo's extremes, placing each foot carefully on the tiles and skirting around conical chimneys that were cold and cheerless to the touch. Pigeons poked heads out from under wings and gave them baleful looks, a few clacking their wings and making a nervous burble at the back of their throats. But the threesome continued their careful way, their speed geared to Adelina's condition.

She hadn't uttered a word, just followed like a trusting child. Phelim's heart had shifted sideways at the terrible bruises on the bare legs before he had clothed her. In the night gloom, he couldn't see the wounded sadness in Adelina's eyes but he knew it was there.

'Here, look – steps! Must be for the tilers and chimney sweeps,' the hob whispered just loud enough for them to hear. He went first, Adelina following at a much slower pace. Suddenly there was a terrific yowl and a thud and the companions froze.

'Gallivant?' Phelim whispered into the night.

'Bloody feline!' His angry reply hissed back. Adelina's face softened as she stepped down the ladder. She wasn't yet ready for mirth but the hob had cracked something, if not his bones or the cat's. Phelim noticed and breathed a relieved sigh.

He helped her onto more iron steps stretching down from Severine's roof to her neighbour's, his hand guiding her as if it should never let go. Clambering down, her toe slipped off the wet rail and she banged onto the tiles below. Again hearts leaped and they all stood still, expecting an armed Luther to appear on the edge of the roof. But silence prevailed. Nothing! Phelim briefly rubbed Adelina's arm. 'Alright? Can you make it to the next edge?'

Adelina's need to escape was paramount and she hugged the roof, feeling her way along slippery as ice, moss-covered tiles. She reached one of the odd, cone-shaped chimneys and as she went to step round, another cat shot out as if Huon and the Hunt were behind. Her feet slid as she stepped back with a gasp and she fell hard on her hip to begin the inexorable slide toward the edge and the grim, dark water of the canal below. The tiles tore at her jacket and against her skin as the downward slide pushed the fabric up against her ribs. She bit down on her cries, on her fear and her breath held tight in her throat as she scrabbled with bleeding fingers for anything that would stop her descent.

Her feet struck a barricade and she slid to a halt, enough to enable her to sit up, rub elbows and pull her clothes back over an exposed and bruised back.

'Let me help.' Phelim appeared at her side, Gallivant, unaware of her predicament, having disappeared further around the chimney. She nodded silently. As she looked to her toes she saw there was no barricade, nothing but air, and yet her feet touched something large and unyielding.

'Thank you' she whispered and looked up at him. She gave a hint of a smile, a tip to a corner of the mouth, and then dropped her gaze.

Phelim said nothing as he helped her to her feet and gently pushed her to continue. She trod on, putting one foot in front of the other, the need to protect her child driving her across the roofline. They breached the end of this next roof and stood by box guttering.

The canal had narrowed and was hung below with laundry-lines weighted with dripping loads. They had reached the end of Severine's immediate domicile and would only describe a square back to their point of departure if they followed any more of the roofline they occupied.

'We haven't any option, we have to jump over to that next block. We shall be well away from the palazzo then and can follow the alleys more safely to get to our inn.' Phelim guaged the jump, knowing he was asking the impossible.

'You expect Adelina to jump from here to there in her condition?' The hob stood in front of the former shepherd, legs akimbo, hands on hips.

The woman's head hung and her hands shielded her belly. Phelim knew she hadn't the strength to make the leap but could see no other means of escape. Their luck began to teeter on the edge of the guttering.

'I can do it.' Adelina's voice whispered in the dripping silence. 'It's alright, I can do it.'

'Adelina!' Gallivant swung around but she nodded her head at him.

The hob walked over to Phelim and in a surly undertone, gave him a whispered blast. 'Friend Færan, you'd best do something pretty good because that is a *huge* gap to leap over. It's impossible for any mortal! I tell you man, if she is hurt I shall curse you until you are dead!' He stepped back over the tiles to the edge of the roof to look down at the houses that were almost lost in the mist and gloom.

'You first Gallivant, then you can be there for Adelina.'

Phelim watched as the hob stood at the guttering. He raised himself onto his toes and like a diver, launched himself up and out. Being Other, the distance was as elastic as he wanted it to be and he floated like a piece of mask-plumage to the lower level opposite.

Phelim took Adelina's hand and felt a gentle tingle through his body, not a *frisson*, something more emotive and far-reaching. 'Are you ready? I swear it will be safe.' Again he heard Ebba's voice as she recounted the poems of his childhood:

'Longlegged boys leapt from rooftop to rooftop.
The dark between their legs widening as they spread.' He smiled to himself,

realizing that on every strife-strewn step of the way, Ebba had been with him and would continue to be.

Taking a step back he launched them into the air and they descended down, down to land as gently as a pair of pigeon feathers on the roof next to Gallivant. The hob took Adelina's hand and led her to sit on a pile of stacked roof-tiles to rest her weary legs and then turned to Phelim to mutter tersely. 'I should think so too!'

'Better than dragging her from the depths of the canal,' Phelim responded with a grin.

'Like I said, I should think so! How much further?' He chafed to get Adelina safe – every now and then a tiny thought at what had befallen her crept into his mind and floodwalls would begin to tumble so that he must forcibly drag his mind back to the job at hand. Sink me, my life has never been so hard, he sighed to himself. But would he go back, would he change it? He looked at the embroiderer sitting fatigued. No, never! Adelina had taught him to grow. Fancy that, a mortal teaching him something! He *had* to return the favour – he would love her and care for her as long as she needed him, it's what one did. He cleared his throat as Phelim replied.

'Not far. Look, here's an iron stair down the wall and a pontoon. And,' he grinned at Gallivant who only saw a flash of white teeth, 'a gondola! How fortuitous!'

How Færan, thought the hob.

They scrambled themselves and the woman down the stair and piled quickly into the craft, Adelina subsiding like pricked balloon. Gallivant whispered urgently to Phelim. 'She's almost at her end, we need to hurry.'

But the half-time mortal didn't need to be told as the black sky began to lighten in the east. He poled the craft down the canal and round the bend to another mooring where they all jumped out and hurried down alleys and over bridges until they saw the welcoming glassed doors of the Esperia. Adelina stopped and grasped the doorframe with fingers that were white. With a small sigh she began to fold, her legs crumpling.

'Adelina! No!' Gallivant jumped to her side but before he could do anything, Phelim had scooped her up and pulled her to his chest as they broached the entrance, to hurry up the staircase, enter the room and lay her on the bed.

The hob jumped from one side of the bed to the other. 'Will she be better, will she lose the baby?'

'Gallivant, be quiet!' Phelim growled wishing Ebba were here. *Please Aine, let Ebba's hands guide me to help this woman!* He laid his own hand inches above her shorn curls and moved it in a smooth sweep over the length of her body. Whilst he had nothing of his stepmother's skill, surely he could he help, even a little? He moved his hand back again and an unknown Færan charm, whispered so as none could hear, came from his lips and dropped down upon the woman who had been so brutally used. She lay comatose but with evenly spaced breaths and her face was soft, showing no stress and strain so he could only hope she slept.

'We need to rest. Gallivant, use the bed and I shall use the chaise.' He lay down and ignored the hob who wanted to disembowel all that had happened. He wanted peace. He wanted to digest, the day in his own way and think about its effect on his own sensibilities.

He thought about Veniche where his duty would end. Since he had entered the precinct, it seemed bereft of Others and yet this place with a Gate! Where was the support the swan-maid had said would be waiting? He rolled over, hearing the hob snoring from one bed and gentle breathing from the other. The chamois bag rolled with him and rested against his ribs.

Aine, how could he not have registered it? The bag was comfortably warm. And now he thought on it, it had been warm since they had released Adelina from her attic prison. Is Adelina as important to them as their return to the world of Færan? He glanced at her divine face as she slept. He felt himself drawn to her, to her courage, her spirit. Washed out light glanced off the rounded planes of her cheeks and her lips were slightly open. Her pregnant breasts rose and fell as she sighed. Was it wrong to feel drawn to a woman who had been through such trauma, practically a widow and with child?

He held the chamois bag gently in his broad hands and the warmth seeped into his fingers, comforting him and he slept as the third and final Day of the Dark emerged from its wet, night time shroud.

CHAPTER THIRTY EIGHT

Severine had kept herself occupied the previous day and evening. One of the bonuses of being a woman of fiscal power in a city like Veniche was that she was sought out frequently, obsequiously, and she revelled in the fame. She wandered the palazzo on a cloud on that second day, dreaming of her future, conscious of her own importance. Adelina frequently crossed her mind and she would think where are you, bitch? I have so much to tell you and I so want to put you in your place.

She wanted the woman to beg for her life, to kneel before her, to grab her hem like a supplicant, to cry. She laughed, that high pitched call that sounded like some hideous bird from the Goti high plains, the kind that sat on crags and swooped in to feed on carrion. Maybe a better punishment for the red headed whore would be a prison with a mirror so she could see herself aging and becoming mad. To suffer loneliness, to live with grievous memories and pain.

Her butler entered the salon and coughed. 'Madame, your bath is drawn and the maids have laid out your gown, the Libreria are sending a gondola at seven o'clock.'

'Thank you, Hobarto. Tell Luther to come to the salon.' She sat drinking her habitual wine and waited until Luther entered. She noticed his face was ruddy, except for that loathsome scar which gleamed white as bone but when he spoke, his voice was as cool and controlled as ever. Was it drink or other habits that induced the florid hue? Ah, she didn't want to know. 'Luther I am going to a dinner this evening at the Libreria. They have just taken possession of some remarkable Raji illuminated scripts. I want to see them and if they are something I should like to have then I shall talk to you further. At any rate, they are sending a gondola and I don't need you until tomorrow, so you may have the evening for yourself.'

He inclined his ovoid head in what passed for deference.

'One thing – the Traveller?' She tapped nails against her glass goblet. 'Has there been any sign yet?'

'No Madame, I'm sorry, nothing. But I don't think you should worry. She'll be at the Gate tomorrow or somewhere close by there's no doubt, and we shall snap her up.' He lifted his fist and closed his fingers tight into a clenched bunch. 'And then you will have all that you want.' Severine's delusions were stroked by Luther's oily words. 'Madame, there will be none who can touch you. You will have all that you have desired.'

'I know,' she whispered but then her eyes opened wide as she snapped out of her fantasy. 'The robe, Luther, I need the robe more than I want Adelina.'

'But we know, Madame, don't we, that one is dependent on the other. Leave it to me. Get dressed for your dinner and I shall enjoy my night off because we have a big day tomorrow.'

He gentled her and led her to the door. She looked briefly at his reddened and glazed eyes and then walked up the sweeping stair to bathe and dress and once more show Veniche society why it was that she was so admired.

Luther watched her float away and then walked back into the salon, poured an over large measure of wine and seated himself on a padded couch which cushioned his tense body. Adrenalin flooded his muscles and nerves, washing any likely calm away. What he had done to Adelina today hadn't quelled the desire, it had made it stronger and more rabid than ever and he knew the only way to control himself was to do two things – find another woman who could satisfy his lust and follow it with a stupendous drinking bout. If he did not then he was as like to kill Adelina the next time, even before Madame had seen her – a sure way to destroy his plans for the future, because Severine had promised him so much.

He sat quaffing wine, waiting for his muscles and nerve-endings to ease enough for him to seek a whorehouse somewhere. Some time later, he heard Madame leave. He placed the cut-glass goblet on the tray beside the empty bottle and walked on steady legs to the hall, slipped on a black coat and closed the studded doors behind him.

With obsession or addiction, one's contentment depends on frequent sorties to experience one's desire. Severine imbibed that night and drifted home to sit in front of a mirror and gaze at herself, imagining the pleasure of looking the same at ninety three, as at thirty three. She allowed the maid to brush her hair after hanging up the loathsome midnight gown she had been required to wear for the Dark.

Nevertheless, she mused, it had been a pleasant evening. All the better for seeing the manuscripts which were magnificent with their calligraphy and lavish illumination. Such colours: cobalt ground from azurite, vermilion ground from cinabar and the most regal one – ultramarine ground from lapis lazuli, and all with copious accents of gold leaf. She craved the manuscripts for her own collection and would speak to Luther about arranging it. She smiled at herself and her maid noticed, commenting on her mistress's evident happiness.

'My life will change tomorrow night,' Severine murmured, 'change beyond imagining. I want you to dress my hair magnificently for the Ball. I want people to remember me! Have my gown and shoes been delivered?'

'Yes, madame.'

'And my mask?'

'It is in your dressing room. Madame if I may say, the emerald green will become you and your mask with its peacock feathers is a perfect accompaniment. I brushed and steamed the black velvet damask coat so all is in readiness.'

Severine dismissed the maid and found as she shut the door that her fingers shook with anticipation. Damnation, she hoped she had drunk enough at dinner to sooth her for sleep! She hurried to her bedside cabinet and retrieved a tiny beaten silver box, spilling a small glass vial into her hands. It contained the strongest sedative her apothecary could devise – the same drug she had used on Adelina repeatedly at Mevagavinney. She sized up the powerful medic and tipped a couple of drops under her tongue before lying under her bedding to wait for sleep.

Luther had whored his way through a number of women and left them worse physically for the encounter, if richer. Then he had gone from one of the laguna taverns to another until his legs began to buckle and his words were slurred. He paid a gondolier to pole him to the palazzo and pour him onto the landing and then he dragged himself to his room. Like Severine, he reached for drugs to render him unconscious until the next day. It was safer this way.

Neither of them heard the hob as he fell off the iron ladder onto the adjoining roof as two companions spirited the unfortunate Adelina away.

My saviours thought I was asleep on that little bed at Phelim's tavern but I wasn't, not immediately. The drapes were slightly ajar and as grey dawn light fingered its way into the room, I heard the sounds of dreams as my friends slept around me but I lay awake, thinking.

I lay on my side staring at the one called Phelim who slept on the chaise. As I marked as much as I could see of his high cheekbones and strongly etched eyebrows and mouth, I knew I stared at Liam's long-lost brother. It seems part of me knew this from the first moment I saw him at Ferry Crossing, despite Gallivant's best efforts to deny it. Phelim was broader than Liam and more contained, much less Færan, but even so there was still that frisson. Anyway, I thought, what did it really matter? Liam was dead and I had so much more to deal with.

I knew the third Day of the Dark was approaching and with it my moment. What would I do? My hands wrapped my belly, cocooning it. It seems that my hands were attached to my belly perpetually and why not? This was my child I communed with and I wondered what it would want me to do. Avenge the death of its father, avenge those Færan who may have loved it or would it want me to turn the other cheek? Yes, no, do it, don't do it. I couldn't make up a mind that swung from numbness to confusion like a pendulum.

Once again I had escaped from the clutches of Severine and Luther. With the assistance again of Others. My unborn babe and I had the seelie and eldritch of the world to thank for our safety. How hard it will be to break my promise to them! They have saved my life twice, the life of my babe once. That is worth more than a promise, isn't it?

I am trying my hardest not to think of what Luther did. That I feel violated and unclean are feelings I must quash because there is so much more that is important – my baby, its future, my future.

And so you can see the story begins to run rapidly to some form of conclusion. And to reach that, you must return this latest book to its place of concealment and move away from the tricorn hat of our groom to the petit point underskirt of the bride.

The skirt is white with a tracery of tiny scarlet climbing roses and I have welted the hem in silk. If you carefully unpick it from the silk of the stumpwork robe, you will find a white book opened flat – this is because I didn't want it to be obvious or spoil the line of the underskirt.

So there are now only two such journals left, one concealed and one very obvious.

Read on then dear friend, and we shall see what they all contain...

CHAPTER THIRTY NINE

Midday had passed. Severine and Luther had each slept on unaware of the day drifting wetly by. Luther slept heavily and untroubled, safe and secure in the knowledge that in the early evening he would deliver what Madame had required for so long and would receive more than just rewards. Drunk and drugged, he slept with a cunning smile on his face.

Severine had no such smiles upon her own visage and tossed and turned with nightmare upon nightmare. Others plagued her – the seelie who would aid and assist mortals. She screamed and yelled in her dreams and they crowded around her as she ordered them to move, waving the ring in the air and threatening them with quick annihilation. They split apart from her like an earthquake cracking the ground, until only one man remained. He was elderly with white hair cut short against his head and his black coat blew around him in vast cracking folds in an welkin wind. She laughed uneasily – a Færan no less! But he stood there to defy her as she held up the ring and he wiped his hand carelessly, *carelessly,* through the air! The ring split in two and fell from her fingers and she woke with dread in her belly, calling out hoarsely, *no!*

Sweat dripped from her forehead and gathered in damp lines underneath her arms and breasts. It was only a dream – too much rich food and wine and then the drugs! She threw off the bedding and dragged a peignoir over the damp body as she went to draw the curtains away from the long casements. Nothing had changed – it poured. But, she thought through the turbid haze of her narcotics, something *is* different, what is it? And then she seized upon the fact – it is today, the third day of the Dark! The day everything changes!

In an instant, the dread from the dream was washed away on an incoming tide of such euphoria she could not help clutching her arms across her body and spinning in a circle. And that is how the maid found her, commenting as she carried in a brunch tray, for the hour was now well past midday, that it was good to see Madame so excited about the Ball and Carnivale.

'I'll spend the rest of the day preparing. A massage, a scented bath, my hair washed and dressed and I shall leave at six. Make the arrangements for my conveyance will you, and tell Luther to attend me as soon as he has risen.'

Luther received his summons, as excited and filled to the brim with bubbles of anticipation as Severine. He walked into Madame's chamber on light toes, eager to go to the room at the top to see *her* again to have sex, then to deliver her to Madame with the whereabouts of the robe and then to take her away – his prize which he would use as oft as not until some urge filled him to finally do to her what Madame wanted.

He looked forward to the Ball as Madame's escort, there would be so many who had snubbed him in the past and who would now be licking his boots. Ah, how tables turn! As with Adelina.

'Luther, good day to you! Such a day!'

Severine's excitement was fascinating to watch, he thought. That iced visage melted and she smiled and it was such a transformation! She was almost desirable – almost. But nothing like Adelina! Still, best pay attention! Severine's destiny was his own.

'So! Adelina?'

He thought for less than a second. 'Nothing yet Madame, but it is odd. I have a feeling that within the afternoon I will have her.' How true! 'And then I will bring her to you and she will give you the robe on a platter.'

'And this evening I will have any soul I want! Not just Lhiannon and her bag of pathetic souls. Do you know I almost don't want them now – it's enough they are dead, that they were punished. When I think on it I think a show of my power, by the syphoning of two more souls might be just what I should do. The Ca' Specchio will go down in the history of Eirie.'

'Have you thought Madame, how to find the Gate?'

Luther watched Severine's reflection in her dressing mirror. She purred like a cat with a bowl of Trevallyn cream. 'The Ca' Specchio is renowned for its Hall of Mirrors, Luther. I think it's a question merely of finding an Other at the Ball for they will be there, and following them to one of the mirrors. You'll help, two pairs of eyes such as yours and mine won't miss a thing.' She laughed softly, a sigh of ecstasy. 'Have you a dress-suit?'

'Indeed, Madame, I won't disappoint you.'

'Good, be ready to accompany me from the Director's palace to the Ca' Specchio. In between times go to the glassmaker's, collect the paperweights and convey them back to my cabinets in the entrance hall. I leave you... no, I *trust* you to place them amongst the others. And I want you to arrange to relieve the Libreria of the illuminated scripts as planned and then Luther, tonight we shall enjoy ourselves. I doubt our lives will ever be the same again.'

Within half an hour, Luther had laid his orders for the securing of the manuscripts with those of the rough-cut henchmen he preferred for such a job and then he returned to the palazzo via the kitchen door, stepping across the courtyard with care as the continued torrents had made the cobbles as slick as ice. He had no intention of breaking limbs at such a crucial time.

He passed through the kitchens leaving a trail of moist footprints behind, and a communal shudder of dislike, even fear, passed amongst the shoulders of those who handled the pots, spices, meats and grains within the precinct.

Oblivious, he ran quickly up the stairs. His booted feet tapped on the marble and his heartbeat rattled along with the sound, a syncopated rhythm. Some morning delight, he thought and then gave a low chuckle, well no, afternoon delight actually. His anticipation wound him tighter than a clock spring and he bent to slip the key into the lock and turned it with a flourish. As he pulled the key out and placed it in his pocket, he was surprised but not alarmed to see his hands, usually steady and strong, shaking like those of an ancient or a babe. It was nothing – it only underlined his anticipation. He took a deep breath and pushed the door wide.

The room was not big – more of an attic, perhaps servant quarters at some time, for there were indeed back stairs which led up. But the small space was empty. Grey light filled the chamber and alighted on a shard of glass lying in the middle of the floor. The downpour outside thundered on the tiles above Luther's head and blood performed a like-minded dance, pounding through his veins to his head and suffusing his face with a dangerous flush. He saw the open window with the pools of moisture as rain dribbled under the eaves onto the floor and he noticed a pigeon walking back and forth, ducking its head, burbling angrily, warning the man away. The cry Luther gave as he whipped the dagger from his belt began as a low growl and wound higher and higher up the scales until it burst forth in a frustrated, furious howl and as the howl echoed, the dagger which had flown through the air with the rising solfa, found its mark and pierced the pigeon to the floor. Luther left the room in a swirling rush, a pile of soft feathers settling around the poor bird in the likeness of a shroud.

The clock spring stretched thinner.

He ran blindly out to the front moorings and commandeered one of the di Accia gondolas, ordering the gondolier to pole as fast as he could if he valued his life. The gondolier needed no urging, for the look on the thug's face spoke of murder and mayhem. Within minutes, or so it seemed, they had reached the bottom of the Calle del Vetro and Luther grunted to the gondolier to wait.

The shop was closed so Luther hammered on the glass, the windowpanes vibrating dangerously. The glassmaker came out of the fabricca at a run, wiping his face. 'Signor Luther, come in!' The man bowed, holding the door wide. 'The goods are ready. I was just packing them. Would you be so kind to come out the back while I finish?'

He turned and hurried away, Luther stalking behind like some death reaper.

Luther's hands fiddled in his coat pockets, playing nervously, angrily, with the contents. Curse the man, the paperweights should have been packed and ready! Luther could see nothing but the elusive naked body of Adelina in his mind. Behir, she had played him for a fool! She had done nothing but lure him and tease him since Madam had drawn her into their lives. The pain in his body grew and the anger began to erupt. The heat in the fabricca hit him like a wall of fire as he watched the wretched artisan taking a length of string in shaking hands, his back to Luther. He fumbled and fiddled as he tried to wrap the parcel suitably and halfway through, he grabbed his red paisley square and wiped his dripping forehead and sweating hands.

Luther's temper exploded as the heat of the room, the furnaces, the flames, the fires of hell seared his nostrils and burned at his brain. In the red of the fires he saw Adelina's hair.

The clock spring broke.

Without a thought of guilt or consequence, the garotte came out and was strung quickly over the neck in front of him.

He pulled some coals from the fires onto the floor and thrust a few torn cloths on top. Grabbing the parcel he pulled the door between the showroom and the fabricca shut behind him as fledgling flames began to glow and lick at wooden benches and boxes. The street was as empty as a desert as he hurried quickly to the gondola and requested the same speed back to the palazzo.

CHAPTER FORTY

She woke to an empty room.

Lying still, Adelina's hands immediately went to her pregnant belly. Her baby arched under her fingers like a cat being stroked. A tear crept out under her eyes as she thought of her unborn child, her lost lover and her own wounded spirit, so lately battered to a pulp. She eased back the bedcovers and looked at the body that was now a startlingly ugly blend of purple, yellow and blue stains. Walking to the mirror hanging on the wall in its crackelure gold frame, she stared at the floor, afraid to confront her visage.

Seconds passed as she watched the tears drip to form a puddle at her feet and she wondered briefly if she was having a critical fit of the vapours. Her head flew up in denial and she could do little else but confront her own image.

The hazel eyes, slightly red, stared back. Her beautiful face with the skin like peaches and the bee-stung lips was completely unmarked. Amazingly, she had no shadows of exhaustion under her eyes nor deep furrows ploughed by distrait.

She knew it was the Færan who had smoothed away as much as he could of her troubles and wondered if he knew that lately she had been a friend of Liam, his brother. But no, why would he? Who would have told him? Gallivant? She raised an eyebrow. Maybe.

She remembered the previous night when he had helped her up after her precipitous slide down the roof. He had looked into her eyes with his own dark ones and she had felt something. Not an attraction she didn't think, but interest and solicitude. The kind of gentling she had craved for weeks and which the hob in his way had tried to give, the kind that had been such a part of Kholi Khatoun. Kholi would have liked this Færan, he was steadier than his brother, earthier, less arrogant. And briefly she had noticed he was uncomfortable – either with himself or a weight that he carried.

Adelina moved away from the mirror and found towels set by a bowl of warm water. It occurred to her that she was in the care of Others and like to be safer than she had ever been. And as the thought enlarged, she took a huge shaky breath and another calmer one.

The water smelt of lavender and gardenia and she stripped out of her ripped underwear and washed every part of her abused body till it squeaked. On her bed lay the garments Phelim had kindly clothed her with the night before – a pair of jodhpurs, her boots, a black sweater. She found a brush and pulled it through the soft, copper curls and looking in the mirror again, was surprised at even greater improvement.

She noted a tray on the table near the balcony doors and found fresh bread, confit, grapes and unbelievably, a teapot filled with hot tea – hot, sweet tea. It was like nectar and revived as if it were spirit in her veins, enough for her to begin to look around in more detail – at Gallivant's bed, at the chaise where Phelim had slept.

And at the robe swinging from a hook on the side of an armoire. The clean, almost completed robe that was the cause of her triumphs and her tragedies. It beckoned and she went to it as an artist is pulled to the canvas. A stroke here, a stitch there – all conspiring to create the masterpiece.

An hour passed as she stitched lazily. She indulged in the feeling of security that surrounded her and she paused to rub her back and speak to the babe.

'Mama's tired, little one. I need to rest!'

'You should, definitely. If you are to persist in your plans then you must indeed rest.' Gallivant pushed open the door and walked in laden with black clothes. Behind him, Phelim kicked the door shut, his arms equally loaded.

Adelina eyed the hob beadily. 'I *must* persist and you know it!'

'Huh, I *know* you have an iron will!'

'Gallivant, I shall go to the Gate and then we shall see... is that good enough for you?'

'I don't agree...'

Adelina instantly threw down the stumpwork robe and turned a furious face on the hob. 'You don't have to agree! This isn't your business, it's mine! And whatever I do, I can do it so much better without your precious comments! For Aine's sake, Gallivant! Just leave it alone!'

The hob stood stock still, almost hidden by the pile of dark silks and satins. Phelim dared not move either as the air felt solid with Adelina's anger and resentment. The emotion erupting from the lips of the Traveller came from a deeper hurt than frustration at the hob, he was sure. The woman had been raped... she should be filled to bursting with anger and hatred at the world at large. Add it to the loss of her friends and her lover and it was a wonder she was sane enough to embroider at all! He began to remove the piles of silks from the hob's arms as the fellow smiled gratefully at the chance he had been given him to pull himself together.

'Adelina,' the Færan spoke quietly, gentling her, defusing the moment. 'This is our Ball attire. We have a dance to attend, a Gate to find and some people to meet! We are going to a Ball at the Ca' Specchio. I have a feeling...'

As he spoke he noticed Gallivant glancing at his dearest friend. She glared back at him, stony-eyed. He could imagine with no trouble at all, exactly what the hob was thinking: *Sink me Needle Lady, don't disengage from me, you need me more than ever because you see the Færan has had a feeling.*

CHAPTER FORTY ONE

Gallivant and Phelim had spent that morning searching for the Ca' Specchio, in line with Phelim's intuition. Gallivant trotted ahead of the Færan on frenetic legs, frequently walking backwards to deliver part of the conversation and then running into people and having to turn back to apologise. Phelim grinned as another fountain of apologies poured down with the rain over the heads of the unfortunate public who had toes trodden on or shopping dislodged. Finally he reached forward and grabbed the hob by the arm.

'Gallivant, slow down. I have long legs and you are covering the ground faster than myself. Nothing is to be gained by rushing.' He waved his hand in front of his body.

'Don't you mesmer me! I promise I'll heed your words. It's always been a problem for me that when I'm agitated I become fast and frantic.'

Phelim removed his hand and thrust it in his pocket. 'Truth to tell I think we shall find the Ca' Specchio in no time, for here is the Fondamenta Minotto.'

Before them ran a broad walk on the edge of the Rio del Malcanton. The canal was bridged at either end with handsome enclosed structures. Gallivant stood mercifully still as he looked around. 'Sink me but what an elegant place. I think if the rain ever stopped here and the sun shone, that it could be a city filled with light. The water would reflect so much, wouldn't it?'

'Indeed and there is the place we want. How could one miss it?'

Phelim could see what Ebba had meant when she said it was supposed to be the most elegant palace in Veniche. The Ca' Specchio sat in the middle of the fondamenta in its freshly painted apricot glory – a colour only softened and enhanced by the drizzle blurring the lines of the whole of Veniche.

The hob's breath sucked in. 'Do you realise the Palazzo di Accia is around that bend? There we were dashing all around and it was closer than we could have imagined. Aine, I don't like that madwoman being so close!'

'She'll be even closer this evening, Gallivant, so we must get used to it. Shall we go over?'

They hailed a gondola and asked to be taken to the entrance landing of the Specchio. The craft threaded through the channel markers and moored at the landing and the two companions mingled with all those artisans and merchants who came and went. But there were Others too, unseen by mortals, drifting in and out of the glassed doors that opened onto the landing. Phelim studied the magnificent people going about their business quietly, dressed in black, drawing no attention to themselves, except for the occasional small prank – drops of mortar on heads, a bag of nails tipped on the floor and such but over all a dreaminess wound like a lacy fog – a mesmer designed to put all in a gentle mood. Even the hob was overcome. He walked into the entrance hall with a smile on the visage that had for so long been pleated and tucked.

The chequerboard floor tiles gleamed. Two perfectly symmetrical stairwells curved around the walls to meet on the first floor landing. At either end of the stair, unlit black iron flambeaus stood sentinel. On the ground floor and positioned against the wall, equidistant from each staircase, a massive oak table stood supporting an urn of gargantuan size in which a florist was attempting to arrange flowers. She stood on a ladder and manhandled large branches of white magnolia and dogwood and vast long stemmed lilies. Broken petals and chips of stem and bark lay around the ladder legs and the smell of Raji lilies began to fill the hall. Staff ran up and down the stairs, carting buckets of coal, logs, trugs of ivory candles.

The walls of the entrance were bare, the paintwork ivory. Nothing but the flambeaus, the floral arrangement and the wrought balustrading decorated the space. It was as though it waited for the bedecked guests of Carnivale. Phelim and Gallivant stepped around the frantic servitors and artisans to go up the stair but two largely built men blocked their path. 'No one up the stair who 'asn't got a pass.' A wooden staff barred the way.

'Mesmer him,' Gallivant whispered.

''Ere, what d'you say?' The other man went to pull at the hob's shoulder.

Phelim backed off, pushing the hob before him, the bag of souls resting with gentle warmth against the blisters and weals at his ribs, so that for a moment he wondered what it was they reacted to. Pulling Gallivant, he turned his back on the guards and began walking away with the hob chiding him roundly for not being more Færan. The shepherd forbore to retaliate. Had he looked back to the landing at the top of the stair, he would have seen a tall, elderly man leaning on the rail watching them with interest.

Jasper slapped his palms gently on the wrought iron and with a swish of his black riding coat turned and entered the ballroom invisibly, behind a trail of maids with mops and rags.

'We could have found the portal, Phelim. Honestly!' They searched the landing for their gondolier. 'At least if we knew the layout it would help Adelina more. Everything helps, you know.'

'You care for her, don't you?'

'Of course!' He looked at Phelim with bruised eyes and sighed. 'I didn't mean to, you know. I was just going to baby-sit as Lhiannon and Jasper had asked but the woman has this way about her. It's not just her beauty nor her artistry even. She has lost everything and born it as well as she can and Aine she has suffered! On top of that, somehow the silly wench made a promise to Others that she would avenge the loss of Liam and Lara, a promise which becomes sacred. Phelim, it weighs so heavily upon her, she truly struggles with the dilemma. And then there is this most recent travesty.' Gallivant had once again begun his 'fast' mode, and Phelim could not, indeed would not interrupt. 'She shows no obvious reaction,' he was silent for a minute only. 'Well no, I suppose her anger earlier was reaction, wasn't it? I wish I could spirit her away from all this. To think she must kill now, no lesser revenge is expected! It could be the final straw! Oh, how I wish I had another lamp! That's how we escaped from Mevagavinney, you know – Aladdin's lamp. It started as whimsy. She had sewn Aladdin onto the robe and I felt he needed a tiny lamp and we had a gold charm and I wondered what if the charm was a real lamp and I had this feeling and of course I was right! Now I would like to rub a lamp and wish her far away from Veniche and all her troubles.'

'Gallivant, they are monumental troubles, as you say. But perhaps it is Fate that she must do this, go through with the whole thing. All of us have a path we must tread and sometimes, no matter the cost, we cannot divert. It may be the same for Adelina.' And myself, he thought, for things changed with Ebba's revelation and then again when I saw Adelina. How they changed! 'All we can do is support her and support each other. What will be will be. In the meantime, I think we need to buy ball-gowns and suitable men's attire.'

'Yes,' Gallivant took a breath as if the world were full of sighs. 'We must shop. Shall we try that alley near the inn?'

Phelim nodded his head a little vaguely, momentarily caught up in the reality of Færan. How easy it had been to mesmer, to be instinctive. It came when one needed it most and expected it least. But even so, he couldn't help a tremor of loss at the self he knew best – the one moulded and guided by Ebba. He craved it like a drug.

What a maladjusted bunch we were! Every one of us in this tale has had baggage that could have reached the heights of Mt. Goti. But I suppose that is the truth of life. Our experiences and how we cope with them, good or bad, creates that mountain. Myself? I had almost reached the apogee of my endeavours. If I allowed myself to wallow in amongst the satchels and bags of my past experiences, I would never be able to drag myself out to decide what I must do and do it.

I meant what I said to Gallivant – I needed to do this on my own. That is not to say I didn't appreciate what these friends had done. How could I not? But now I needed to go on alone and that was an end to it. When Adelina the embroiderer sets her mind to something, no matter how hurt and despoiled she may be, she will do it!

So my friend, time for the penultimate journal. On with the treasure hunt – it is an easy little thing to find once you have replaced the previous book under the petit-point. Go to the ivory coloured fan in the bride's hands... a perishingly ghastly thing to embroider in whipped spider-web stitch. I truly wasn't in the mood I can tell you but needs must and it was a mammoth diversion from the anxieties that threatened to tip me over the edge. Anyway – underneath the fan is a thin ivory washi pamphlet stitched with a simple binding.

Only small, but there is enough there to keep you busy.

CHAPTER FORTY TWO

Severine sat facing her mirror. The maid had finished her hair and it curled and waved in an ebony sweep up her neck and around her crown, laced beautifully with fine gold wire studded with tiny emeralds that flashed with green sparks. She ran her hands down the alabaster neck, noting the smoothness, the absence of wrinkles, and began her toilette, applying *maquillage* with great skill – enhancing, concealing. Her grey eyes glistened with an excitement she could not hide. As she opened the ivory cosmetic containers, she ran over the events of her ascendency: Gertus, ah... Best to forget. The four cantrips and the ring. The silk seller and Liam... Pop and she had two souls.

Her stomach fluttered with a desire to empty, resulting in a dash to her garde-robe. Afterward, she had a moment of intense exhilaration, but then another rush of anxiety. Never in her life had she been so nervous! It didn't make sense because it was all going to be so easy.

Tonight I shall wear the robe to bed and in a heartbeat I shall be immortal, so why should I be afraid? She smiled her chill smile and the glacial face stared back at her from the looking glass. I will be remembered tonight, she thought. Never *ever* forgotten. What people see tonight will go down in history, for time immemorial!

The maid returned to the chamber carrying the emerald gown and Severine slipped into it whilst the maid buttoned the thirty buttons down the centre back. The lithe silk garment fell in pleats from underneath her breasts, from a décolletage that almost defied etiquette and her arms were covered tightly by the silk and finished in sharp points over the top of her hands. The maid passed her a sash of peacock blue silk and she tied an enormous bow beneath her breasts.

'Oh, Madame!' The girl's eyes opened wide. It was enough, that tiny gasp. Knowing she surpassed perfection, Severine dismissed the girl. She wanted to admire herself for a little, to stand in front of the mirror and smile and simper and catch herself glancing over her shoulder.

She screwed emerald drops into her ears and picked up her mask, a *colombina festa fantasia:* gilded and decorated with peacock plumage, both green and white, but with that startling turquoise eye in the tip of each feather drawing the green light from her gown.

Her stomach fluttered again and she groaned a little and made a dash for the wine decanter, her gown rustling and whispering. In a common, un-ladylike swig, she threw back a full glass and waited, hands pressing on the top of the table as the powerful alcohol surged around her blood stream. Another. Yes, that's better. Her limbs loosened as the wine unleashed euphoria. 'That's better,' she muttered, 'I'm calm now. I can face my destiny!' She refused to listen to a faint voice far far away – *'you'll find out.'*

Luther had never been as filled with berserk anger in his life. He wondered how to tell Madame that the woman had slipped through his fingers. Momentarily he thought of the Others who must be helping Adelina. He had never had to deal with Others until meeting Madame with her insane desires and he *hated* her for the trouble she was causing him. He hated Adelina with a passion for the pain she induced. Behir, he despised the female race! If he should find Adelina tonight, he would kill her as soon as he had the location of the robe. Oh he'd kill her alright, no second chances. He didn't want the bitch, she had too much to answer for.

He pulled on the tailored frock coat he had bought – figured silk that clung to his broad muscle. He looked in the mirror and was struck by the magnificence of his attire. At least that had been worth Madame's lunatic endeavours. He preened, for a moment entirely unaware that a sow's ear was always a sow's ear and never a silk purse. As he turned to admire the drape of the tails over his back, he thought he noticed a figure in the mirror – misty, indistinct, a faint apparition.

He spun around as the candelabra caught the sheen of dark hair.

But there was nothing.

He coughed self consciously, his heartbeat racketing in his chest, and sat on the bed to slip into the patent leather dancing slippers. Hearing a noise and turning his head quickly, he caught a waft of perfume, Other in its fragrance. And a tinkle of a laugh that set tremours tripping down his backbone.

He flashed a nervous glance to all the dark corners of the room... nothing!

Then a distant voice calling, *'you'll find out!'* but ending in final gurgling shriek.

He jumped to his feet and flung hands over his ears, squeezing his eyes shut. Enough! This is just tension, he thought. He hurried to the decanter and upended it immediately into his mouth, swallow after swallow, and then went to his desk to finger those things that gave him the most comfort.

His arsenal stretched across the polished surface, glistening wickedly in the light of his lamps. They could mame, kill in a stroke. *But,* his insecurities said, they were useless against Others who would stand invisible behind him and mesmer him before he could even strike and then despatch him like a speck of dust. He wiped the beads of perspiration from his upper lip and caught sight of his face in the mirror. For the first time ever, he glimpsed anxiety in his eyes as he realised he had no weapon to protect against the Others, or with which to attack.

But Madame did!

The ring!

So now he, the assassin Luther, must hide behind the skirts of a woman! Behir, he *hated* her! He hated all women! For so long he'd enjoyed taking what he wanted from them. He had thought it was concupiscence but now he realised it was cruel misogeny, a desire to dominate them and have them fear him because in fear there was power.

He would not hide behind Severine. She too had emasculated him but he had been too caught up in the lust for gems, possessions and status to see it. By her whimsical, insane quest for immortality, she had rendered him impotent against the worst enemies in the world of Eirie and she would pay. She and Adelina would both learn that one didn't cross Luther. What was Madame's would be his – a simple matter of brutal conveyancing.

Glancing in the mirror again, he delighted to see fear had vanished as quick as the lights of the Teine Sidhe. He snatched up his *diavolo* mask, admiring the bold red against the black of his coat and the white of his diamond studded cravat and stockings.

So caught up in his perceived elegance was he, that he didn't hear the voice once again whispering *'you'll find out!'*

At the Pensione Esperia, the companions had dressed for the Carnivale Ball and the hob had dashed downstairs to call for a gondola. Between Adelina and Phelim there was a heavy silence, each individual racked with thoughts on the possible progression of the evening.

Phelim looked across at Adelina as she struggled with the heavy black silk gown, trying to drape the back of it. He moved close to her, smelling her fragrance and longing to be intimate, to touch her with feeling. Instead he calmly fixed the folds of the gown where they were twisted and eased the high-cut neck at her back where her curls flicked the top edge. As his fingers felt the hair graze his skin, he experienced a shudder of desire so strong it thrilled him.

'You know,' he said. 'You and I both have a duty to accomplish tonight. Yes, I am aware there is something you must do.' He didn't enlarge. To reveal the hob had informed him would be to betray a confidence and might make it necessary for a revelation of Phelim's own task. 'I will help if I can, Adelina.' He turned her round so that she looked up at him with her wide hazel eyes. He saw an element of anxiety and confusion and he ran his finger softly down her cheek. 'Don't worry,' he whispered. 'All will be well.' He kissed her cheek sweetly, surprised as she leaned towards the light pressure of his lips.

But then she drew back, running her hands down the front of her silk gown. 'The design reminds me of the stumpwork gown,' she noted as she glanced over to the shrouded shape hanging behind the door. 'It's a pity we all have to wear black.'

Gallivant, who had returned to tell them the gondola waited and who had watched the exchange between Adelina and the Færan with interest, responded. 'Black is what everything is till midnight but once the Days of the Dark are over, you may be surprised at what might happen'. He smoothed the wrinkles from his white stockings and breeches and tapped his feet in their velvet dancing pumps. Anything could happen, he whispered to himself as he fingered the edge of his coat. Patterned with cut velvet flowers in shades of ebony, he liked the way it clung to shoulders that seemed to have broadened. Running his hands over a freshly shaved chin, he felt there was a harder angularity to his face that had finally chased youth away. That's the Stitcher's doing, he surmised. The trials of being a carer!

Adelina watched Phelim out of the corner of her eye and wondered at the similarity and otherwise between he and Liam and briefly felt his lips again on her cheek, remembering his brother's clasp in the van, hours before he died. With the thought, her stomach flipped upside-down and she sat with a thump. Fortunately the others were busy gathering together the masks and tying them on, so were unaware of her distress and she had time to smooth her belly and feel her child comfortingly beneath the full drape of the silk folds. When Gallivant approached her with the *colombina,* she smiled at his own choice of mask. 'Pinocchio, Gallivant?'

'Sink me, what did you expect? I have danced to your tune Threadlady, since I met you, and I still do. The very instruction to allow you room to complete your task on your own is evidence enough. You still pull my strings, Lady.' He gave a jerky puppet-like bow as he handed over her mask. As he tied it on for her underneath the upswept tawny curls, she spoke in a whisper.

'You are still my friend, Gallivant and I will love you all my life for what you have done for me. But tonight you must just be patient, I beg you.'

He finished tying the ribbons, saying nothing, just bowed again over fingers that were tremulously cold and curled them in his hand and kissed them.

Gallivant and Adelina slipped down the stairs ahead of Phelim and he watched them go. He prayed to Aine to watch over them as something told him things were about to change – like the weather. A damp seafog had replaced the rain, floating eerily amongst the cupolas. Yes, things were about to change.

I felt as if a nest of worms were inside me. They wriggled and writhed and I had never felt as stretched with nerves as this night. Phelim's words, even his touch, had made things worse, although I knew he meant to ease me. Aine! Even as a prisoner at Mevagavinney and wracked with grief and hate, I had never felt like this. And do you know, I had still not decided what I should do. My mind vacillated from one extreme to another – to do or not to do until I felt torn apart by my indecision.

Now, beloved companion of the book, I would ask you to replace the pamphlet and take up a pair of tweezers. You will see that we have reached that book of which I spoke earlier – the only one on the whole robe that is not concealed, hanging as it is from the bride's wrist.

If you are still with me, it means that you have not defied my warnings and have left it well alone. I spoke the truth, you see. It has a charm placed upon it, more like a curse in fact, that if you touch the book or the pages with your bare fingers then you will, quite simply, die.

You will shrivel and curl and blacken as if you had been placed upon the fire.

Why, you ask?

Read on, holding the book with tweezers, turning the pages likewise and you'll find out.

CHAPTER FORTY THREE

At eleven o'clock, the seafog with its cobweb drizzle was dissolving into the air of Veniche. Fingers of moisture grasped at the conical chimneys, carved crockets and balustrades. The night-sky had lightened from leadened black to faint ink with traces of cloud wafting across the firmament and allowing a shy Lady Moon to peak at the earth below.

Veniche held its breath. Gondolas ferrying customers cut through the dark canals like black knives and the gondoliers spoke in hushed but urgent voices, calling for leeway. The canals became filled with miniscule flickers of yellow light from the prow lamps, and slowly the city brightened as more and more craft ventured into the waterways.

But shadow and innuendo still pervaded hidden alleys and less public fondamenti. The dark humps bridging the canals echoed with the footsteps of eager Veniche citizens, desperate to get to a ball or a dinner or some waterside celebration and not be caught in the black corners of a shadowed city.

Early dinners and drinks had taken place in the subtle light of a torch or a candelabra, even in the most luxurious palazzos, for no one would be seen to break the Dark by lighting their domain too brightly. Thus it had been for the guests of the Museo Director – a dusky room with a long table lit by one candelabra and the invitees chuckling as they endeavoured to eat and drink without spilling for one could hardly see one's platter and goblet, let alone the silver salt-cellar.

Severine, loosened by her wines and some drugs, laughed with the rest. The glacial spark in the grey eyes was more pronounced, the cheeks flushed and she could hardly help the upward tilt to the corners of her carmine lips. The candelabra caught the flash of her earrings as she turned to listen to the clock strike the half-hour.

Sitting with Luther aboard her gondola minutes later, her mind ticked down through the seconds of this last half hour, knowing she would be at the Gate and within reach of her dreams. She fingered the ring, sliding it round and round her finger.

Luther watched as the battered gold caught the light of the prow lamps. I could get it, he thought, touching the stiletto in his cumberbund, one jab upward under the ribs and it would be mine...

'Contessa, we have arrived,' the gondolier called down under the canopy.

Too late, too late! Luther ground his teeth, appalled by his indecision. Severine pulled her black coat around her more tightly and held out a hand for Luther to help her out of the craft. Ever her lackey, he growled silently.

Gallivant could feel Adelina trembling beside him in their gondola and wished again she had not made promises she couldn't, shouldn't keep. I should tell her about Lhiannon I should, she needs to know before she gets to the Gate. Maybe it would be less of a shock from me. But I am Other and we have asked for revenge. Oh Aine, what should I do? He reached for her hand and clasped it and felt her cold fingers squeeze back.

Phelim sat in front. In a brief loosening of self-control, he soaked up the sights – the way the tiny gold prow lamps cast rippling reflections. The way the gondoliers called to each other. The masks – Aine, the masks! Because everyone was still ostensibly concealed in black, the scene was like a puppet show. Vibrant *colombinas, voltos, gattos, pierrots, civettas, nasos* – all floated mysteriously past as if unattached to a real body and with a sinister life of their own. Through the sockets one occasionally caught the glimmer of an eye but was it friendly or ominous? It was that question that brought the half-time mortal back to earth with a jolt.

That gondola poling past demanding leeway – it contained a *diavolo*, vivid red in the light of their lamp. He recognised the shining skull of the wearer and as he stared, saw the cold glitter of eyes from the mask. But then the mask looked away and the gondolier poled ahead. He said nothing to his friends, it wouldn't serve to alarm them.

The landing of the Ca' Specchio was sparingly lit. One large torchère with flames dancing created macabre shadows on the walls, as mask upon eerie mask alighted from one gondola and then another. Voices were still inclined to whisper, the minutes ticking by massaging the hysteria and excitement to tangible levels.

Severine stood at the doors as the crowd flowed around her. Luther could see the emeralds in her hair flashing as little thrills of anticipation surged through her. Forgetting his own anger for a moment, he reveled in the feeling of being a part of all this striking nobility. He knew that as the clock struck midnight, cloaks and coats would be thrown off shoulders and the colour of gowns, tailcoats and plumage would be like those of exotic Raji birds. Now however, the black heightened the air of expectation, the race to an explosive climax.

Severine was having none of it. She would create her own small explosion as a prelude before the clock struck. She grasped the plaquets of her black coat and flung them apart, slipping the garment off the alabaster shoulders and revealing the daring dècolletage. Every one gasped. She stood defiantly and with hauteur, beautiful and sparkling in her peacock finery. Even Luther was in awe. The sheer gall of her!

'Luther, your arm, please!'

Her high-pitched voice shattered the shocked silence and as the pair walked to the stair to climb up to the waiting Director of the Museo, she thought this is how it will always be. Shocked silence and such a feeling of power!

The threesome entered the palazzo foyer just as Severine began her emerald-clad climb. They heard the whispered buzz and stared at that brilliantly coloured figure. Luther stepped jauntily by her side, casting looks of conceit upon those who would have ignored him previously.

He looked down over the balustrade at the crowd and noticed a group entering... marked how the two men in front pushed the woman to the rear and closed ranks so she could not see Madame making her entrance up the stair.

Ignorant louts!

Phelim saw Luther's gaze sweep over the crowd and automatically grabbed Gallivant, the pair creating a protective wall behind which Adelina was concealed.

'Adelina, I don't think you should do this. It isn't good for you or the baby.' Gallivant begged the embroiderer. 'Please will you reconsider?'

Adelina gave a small smile, filled with as much fortitude as she could drag from down in her dainty dancing slippers. Shaking her head imperceptibly, she moved forward with the crowd as they began to walk.

It was five to twelve.

'Contessa,' the Director simpered as he bent over Severine's graceful hand. 'Would you do me the honour of opening the Ball by dancing with me?'

Severine withdrew her fingers coolly, aware of every eye in the ballroom upon her – the women in awe, the men in fascinated lust. 'Just the one, Director, then I must dance with my escort, Ser Luther. He has signed my card quite copiously.' She gave what could pass for a flirtatious smile and proceeded to the place of honour in the centre of the room.

The others entered the ballroom amidst a wave of guests, Phelim confident the group would help conceal them from Luther's perceptive gaze. They could see the giant clock on the wall at the far end of the room ticking inexorably to twelve. The face of the clock portrayed a happy moon smiling benevolently upon every one, a black gatto mask over the eyes. The hands ticked and moved, moved and ticked and pulled together as if magnetised. The single lamp, a torchère, flared its dancing light upward to the moon's face. Phelim bent to the hob.

'May I have the first dance with Adelina, Gallivant, just the opening waltz? Keep your eye on us, for if we find the Gate we shall go through and you must follow.'

Gallivant nodded, an inscrutable gleam in his eye. Adelina hadn't heard, her attention fixed so firmly on the crowd in their blackness, her eyes forever seeking.

The moon's mask slipped away behind the clock by the magic of a mechanical mind and the orchestra, till now hidden in the shadows, struck up a swaying waltz.

Amongst excited cries from the women, as coats and cloaks were cast aside and magnificent colour was revealed, Adelina was almost unique. Along with elderly noblewomen and aristocratic widows, she retained her black garb, her mask the only patch of colour. But as elderly male took the hand of elderly female, a swathe of black found places on the dance-floor and the problem of being conspicuous quickly dissolved.

Giant candelabra slid down massive chains from the dizzy heights of the ceiling and flickered with the light of dancing candles whose flames reflected in the million facets of the cut-glass pendants. Gallivant glanced up as they locked into place, catching sight of servants scuttling along beams, where they had sat patiently lighting the wicks and waiting to let down the beautiful lamps.

At midnight, with the beginning of Carnivale, the Hall of Mirrors sparkled and shone and the sea of colour that was the nobility of Veniche began to sway back and forth like gentle waves on a seashore.

CHAPTER FORTY FOUR

Oblong panels of looking glass portrayed the lilting crowd and women glanced coyly at themselves as they glided past, leaning out from the arms of their partners. Swirling, twirling gowns rustled and feet tapped as the orchestra plucked and played.

'Adelina, may I?'

Her gaze pulled away from the coloured crowd and she nodded vaguely, her perfect skin hidden in the confines of the half-mask. Her breath had quickened at the thought of Severine and Luther in the same room and her full breasts rose and fell, straining at the dramatic silk sweep of her neckline. He slid his hand around her back, feeling the cool of the silk and the warmth of her body, whilst below his tailored damask vest and inside his shirt, the chamois bag lay comfortably.

His emotions ballooned till he could swear Adelina must be able to see them floating by his side but she merely relaxed into his hold, her eyes forever scanning the crowd for Lhiannon, for Jasper, for Severine and Luther. As their feet began to move to the three-part rhythm of the waltz, he drew her a little closer and she stepped easily, looking up, her eyes bright.

But he knew her heart was elsewhere – in a Raji's arms wrapped in memories. And her mind he suspected, floated far from thoughts of *his* feelings, focused only on finding her Færan friend and on her task of revenge.

The feathers on her mask fluttered as they floated to the waltz rhythm. The ebony silk of her gown swirled out as he propelled her around the corner and momentarily she lowered her lashes. Her steps became lighter and Phelim glanced down briefly to see the closed eyes, understanding the trust she placed in him to guide her safely through the dance, even though he wished it was he she dreamed about in her private little dance of love. He chided himself for such ridiculous longing and began to consciously search for a sight, a *frisson*... anything that would lead him to the Gate.

He wished he had told her of Lhiannon's death, a hundred times he wished. But there had been no time, every intention dissolving before a welter of disaster. And after finding her, after that dreadful moment when he gazed upon her torn and battered body, hardly anything had mattered but that *he* should avenge *her*.

Her breath sucked in.

'What?' he asked urgently. 'What is it?' And followed the line of her gaze.

There swirling around them were Severine and Luther, the woman's peacock mask glistening and fluttering, the man's diavolo mask reminiscent of damnation. Obviously the Director had had his turn around the chequerboard marble floor and had been summarily stood aside.

Phelim swung Adelina away, a fierce tendril of something strong and black beginning to curl upward in his body. Seeing Gallivant, he placed Adelina in the safe circle of the hob's arms. 'Watch her,' her ordered, peremptory, Liam-like. 'And follow me at a discrete distance.' He tipped his head. 'You see them? Stay behind them, keep her away.' He turned to Adelina and ran a thumb down her cheek, letting it linger on her lips below the level of her mask, not unaware of the hob's interest. 'Forgive me. Whatever I do, I beg you forgive me.' He locked his gaze with hers – it seemed for hours that she swirled like the dancers in the black vortex of his eyes but it was mere seconds and he was gone.

Severine and Luther scanned the crowds as they whirled, neither caring much about their partner nor the divine music. Severine thought she caught the hint of copper curls and slowed, her hands dropping out of Luther's sweaty paws.

But the copper curls disappeared as a tall man in a plain gold mask, as if he were a figure from ancient civilizations, stood singularly. Framed by a tall, open window embrasure, she fancied she saw the last of the evening mists curling away from his broad shoulders.

He advanced and it seemed as if the crowd split apart and flowed around him. His coat was faultlessly cut away to display a tailored vest and shirt and and the thighs which powered him across the floor were so tightly encased in cream breeches that Severine could see muscles rippling. He was the only man in the room who wore long boots, boots polished to such a gloss that reflected light flashed as he walked.

Luther watched the fellow approach and a feeling of unease crawled in his belly. 'Madame,' he went to grab her hand.

'No, leave me Luther!' She stepped away from him, moving toward the tall stranger as if she were hypnotized.

Luther's eyes shrank to slits as he watched the fellow bow before his mistress and then take her hand to step close, bringing the white fingers to his lips and kissing them. And then he reached around behind her head and untied the peacock mask allowing it to drop to the floor. Again he took her hand and with his other, he undid the strings of his own and it fell on top of Madame's mask, almost covering it, the peacock feathers quivering. He slipped his hand around Severine's waist and she leaned back as he eased her into the dance.

Had Luther been able to see the fellow in sunlight, he would have observed there was no shadow. As it was the crowd swallowed them into its billowing mass, and it was all he could do to shove a way through himself as he tried to keep Severine in his sights.

'Contessa, I have watched you since you arrived. Your beauty overshadows the entire assembly.' Phelim's voice mesmerized.

Severine had never in her life felt true attraction for anything other than her ambition and her own reflection. Overcome, her eyes sparkled as they took in the stranger's unparalleled features and her fingers felt the muscles moving under the exquisite raw silk of his coat. Her carmine lips curled and sharp white teeth appeared as she gave a laugh filled with unaccustomed sensuality. 'Who are you, sir, that you should dally with such a one as myself.'

'I am what you desire, Severine.' He whispered it close to her ear and trills and shivers filled her body as his tongue moved in amongst the tendrils of her hair to lick.

'You are,' she sighed, all free will gone, her body aching to be stroked and kissed – to be loved by this enigmatic stranger.

Luther could see them in the distance and saw the man reach down and kiss Madame's neck. Behir, he must get closer. If the fellow took her away, where then was his chance to rip the ring off Madame's left hand? Even now as her palm rested against the man's back as he led her through the dance, he could see the flash of gold against the dark fabric of the tailcoat.

'Severine, dance with me. Let me guide you, let me take you to a place where your dreams will be fulfilled. Come, follow me.' Phelim's iniquitous words tantalized with their meaning. As he flashed past the mirrors, a *frisson* curled over him and he glanced sideways to see a gilded couple twirl past and then disappear through their reflection as if they had never been and he realized, amongst the terrible darkness that consumed him, that the Gate was there. He had but to sweep his partner through and she would be at the mercy of anything he should choose to do. He spun her in a circle and danced through their reflection, Severine so mesmered that she felt none of the pain on her hand as shards of glass pulled at the gold-ring as if to rip her hand away.

In the ballroom on the other side, Luther watched them go and stood speechless, powerless. Blind to the couples who now polka-ed with great gusto around him, he neglected to see he had stepped into the path of a particularly agile pair and they knocked him heavily, thrusting him up against the mirror and his reflection so that he fell through in time to see Severine and her odd partner disappearing amongst divine people, all dancing the polka, the music purer, the sights more stunning than he had ever seen in his life.

In the ballroom of the mortals, Gallivant and Adelina had watched Phelim's partnering. Adelina's belly squirmed with distaste, nausea filling her gullet. She hated Phelim for his duplicitousness and would have washed her face to rid herself of the memory of his thumb on her lips. Gallivant, sensing the anger and confusion and sickness in his Lady, gave her a squeeze. 'Don't worry, Adelina. There is a method to his madness. You must trust him.' But he had seen the shroud of mist trailing off Phelim's shoulders, had seen the black eyes darken to doom and knew that a profound change had come upon their friend and that the Far Dorocha had taken hold of Severine, that the wiles of the Ganconer were even now seducing her to the point of abandon and that he had abducted her right into the world of Færan.

It was then that he spotted Luther, as the galloping couple catapulted him through the mirror where he was seamlessly swallowed by reflection and light. 'Come on Threadlady! We must go! There is the Gate!'

He led her at great speed to a mirror that would surely shatter, but launched at the glass anyway. His senses swam as he barged through and he opened his eyes to see soft orchard colours – almond pink, leaf-bud green, apple blossom white, apricot blush, palest yellow peach. His mouth watered at the thought of the ripe fruits and he stared at the masked faces of Others who pranced to the beats of the dance. And then he looked at Adelina, her black robe gone, her face a study of amazement as she fingered the heavenly silk of the stumpwork robe. Sink me he thought, she looks magnificent! And then he looked down at the cut velvet of his own garb – the soft gold of a gooseberry. How apt!

CHAPTER FORTY FIVE

Phelim had led Severine to a shadowed corner of the glittering room where there was a door in a flowered panel and through which he propelled her. Here in the secret subfusc of an anteroom, lit only by one gold candelabra on a table, he could have given in to the fierce and rigid dark that consumed him. He could have ripped the emerald gown from the lithe body and taken the woman with cruel delight.

Instead, his hand wafted and she stilled into the kind of frozen mesmer his brother had not long ago used on the same woman. Her eyes stared ahead, sparkling with desire, her lips had opened slightly as if she had been going to beg him to take her. Her hands stayed in the action of holding him in the dance as he slipped from her grasp. Her breath came in sharp spurts, her breasts rising and falling and the tiny, gold strung emeralds in her hair flashing. As he stepped away from her, he noticed the gold jewelry on the middle finger of her left hand and reached out.

'Leave it!'

He spun around as Luther stood with his back to the panel-door. In his hand he held a knife by its point and without even a thought, the assassin flicked his wrist to send the weapon flying through the air.

Phelim laughed, the sound curling fingers around Luther's spine and sending the hair on the back of his neck into a rigour of attention. He tried to move but found the bottom half of his body frozen, anchored to the ground as if he had sprouted giant roots.

The knife glissaded to a halt, pirouetting so that its sparkling lethal point faced Luther. 'What are you?' he shouted, his voice cracking. 'What have you done to me?'

'I am your most evil thought, your most callous action,' Phelim turned his back and walked to the wall to lean against it. 'I am your doom!'

Slowly, inexorably, the knife moved toward Luther. In his half-mesmer, he could see it coming and screamed at his fate.

Phelim swiped his hand in the air and the hysterical yowls cut short. 'What you will receive in a moment,' Phelim drawled, 'you are due. For the death of a Raji and for the rape of a woman.'

The panel door had clicked open and shut as Phelim spoke and Adelina gasped as she heard the words, her hands coming to her mouth. Gallivant held her tight. 'Say nothing, mistress. This is how Fate would have it.'

The knife moved effortlessly, free of obstacle or force, no sound, just remorselessly gliding closer until the point pierced the silk damask of Luther's tailcoat. Severine stared into some sexually charged distance as her henchman writhed, his eyeballs almost popping from the ugly head.

Despite the smooth passage betraying little force, in fact the pressure of the weapon was overwhelming and the point began to gouge, Luther frothing at the mouth, hysterically silent, insensible. A stain spread like an inkblot on his shirt as the knife moved inward.

'Stadaimid!' A voice shouted. *'Stadaimid!'*

The knife halted, its haft quivering as if unsure whether it should proceed or return the way it had come. Luther slumped over himself in a bloody faint.

'What do you think to do?' Footsteps emerged from the shadows at the far end of the anteroom. Jasper grabbed the haft and pulled the gory blade away from Luther's chest, the candlelight catching on the beaten silver handle, small prisms dancing across the walls as it was laid on the table.

'Jasper!' Adelina fled from Gallivant's gasp and threw herself into the healer's arms. 'Oh, Jasper!'

He held her as she wept, looking over her shoulder at the dark man against the wall whose shadow now lay behind him and whose eyes were filled with sadness for the woman with the copper hair and for himself at the road he had just walked.

'Hush now, Adelina. You must be strong.' Jasper stood her at arm's length and looked into her eyes. 'Your time is almost come you know, and then it will all be over and you can give yourself up to the child you grow.' He stepped forward then, untying her mask and letting it drop to the floor where his booted toe flicked it to the side, kissing her forehead like a benediction and turning to the man against the wall.

'Well, Phelim! *That* is certainly something I hadn't forseen. What has driven you to such unseelie behaviour, hmm?'

'You know me?' Phelim's voice almost pleaded, as if he hardly knew himself.

'Indeed.' Jasper's eyes betrayed nothing. He wafted his hand and Severine came to life, her eyes searching for Phelim, her lips smiling as she spotted him. Oblivious to anyone else, she tossed a tendril of hair back from her forehead in a gesture of invitation.

'You have seduced her well, Phelim. She has no idea who or what she is. Did you kiss her. A proper kiss?'

Phelim's eyes could only stare back at Jasper.

'Ah! I see you did. She will die you know. Oh, but of course you know. It is why you did it. Well then, tell me, did you think to avenge Færan or our lovely friend here?'

Phelim shifted his body away from the wall, a spark flaring and quickly growing to a conflagration. 'Why would I do it for Færan for what is Færan but a place of malicious mayhem? I would do nothing for the place or the people, so help me!' His voice was as Adelina and Gallivant had never heard it, flaming with a burning sentiment they knew to be hatred and disgust. 'I did it for Adelina and her babe and for the babe's father! That...' he flicked his head with its carved features sideways towards Severine, '*woman* treated her with unspeakable cruelty and has allowed monstrous things to happen so it was what she was due. Cruelty rewarded!' As he spoke, Severine had moved on her soft dancing slippers to his side and now wound her hands around his neck. He reached up and grabbed her wrists and tugged her away, flinging her with force to the floor.

'And of course this is how a gentleman behaves, isn't it?' Jasper walked toward Severine. 'You condemn Færan, my boy, and yet you *are* one and find the subtle weapons of such great help, do you not?' His voice castigated and he raised Severine to her feet and then wafted his hand. The habitual ice of the Goti Range filled her eyes and her face collapsed as she stared at the elderly man in front of her, quickly spotting Adelina and the others. Her hastily hoisted sang-froid cracked completely as she stared at the bloody body of Luther and her hands clasped knot-tight as she spoke through clenched teeth. 'You!'

'Did you dream about me, Severine? Is that how you know me?' Jasper smiled and wafted his hand. 'Into the ballroom, I think!'

A whirling angry breeze filled the anteroom, biting at the flames of the candelabra, tearing at the stumpwork robe and the tails of the men's coats. The cursed woman and the limp body of her man disappeared as Jasper walked to the doors. Turning he spoke, not unkindly.

'Adelina, *muirnin*, it is time. And you too, Phelim.'

CHAPTER FORTY SIX

The crowd circled like wolves around prey. Eyes glittered from the cavities of expressionless masks and a hum of anger began to rise around the ballroom as the interlopers were placed in the center of the elegant space.

Severine stood imprisoned in a half-mesmer, and Luther lay on the floor, a bloody heap folded in as if he were an embryo. Jasper stared at the two with empty eyes and then bent and placed a finger on Luther's neck.

'He lives. By a thread.'

'*Ná!*' The angered buzz was cleft apart by a cry and a willowy, black-clad woman with a pale visage and blood-red lips swooped in front of Jasper to harangue the accused.

'Thy murderous *bitseach*!' She spat the words at Severine, turning to Luther with the fires of hell sparking in her black eyes. 'And thee!' She kicked at his crumpled body and before she could be stopped, she bent towards the assassin, raising a stiletto that she struck with force into the rounded back that lay facing her.

'Maeve!' Jasper shouted and hastened toward her but she stared him down, fury filling the air as she drew herself up taller, hissing vituperative.

'Too late.' She kicked Luther with her toe and he rolled back, blood trickling from the thick lips. 'The length of a dance tune and he will be gone! And what right dost thou have to stop Maeve anyway? Thou art only a healer, not the Lady Aine.'

Jasper's face darkened. The white hair had been clipped close to the fine head and the elegant brow had lines of anger ploughed deep into the surface. 'It is I who shall control this Court of Judgement and it is I who says it must be Adelina who exacts redress and now you have taken from her that which was her right! How did you enter Færan?'

'How did murderer enter?' She kicked Luther again. 'Maeve followed him because she knew if she had waited for Stitcher to take revenge, she would have waited for eternity,' the swan-maid hissed. 'Never trust mortals! Besides, one still stands. Let Stitcher have her. Carcass on floor killed my sister and was mine! Maeve repaid debt.' Without another word, she sliced through the agitated crowd as if she were a cleaver and walked to the massive open windows overlooking the Canal. Shape-changing, her dark as night wings spread and she flew away into the star-lit sky.

The crowd in that sumptuous room seethed, Maeve's violent rebellion having goaded them like the smell of blood to dracules. Adelina shrank against the hob. Until now, her eyes had barely left Jasper's face, loathe to confront Severine or Luther, even Maeve. But now her timorous gaze swept the crowd and she trembled.

From their toes to their chins, this room was the very picture of gorgeous indulgence. Satin gown, silk hose, muscular thigh, dainty waist and daring décolletage – all enhanced with flashing gem and jewel. But from collarbone to coils of curls, images of purgatory prevailed.

Hawkish, mawkish masks surrounded her, row on row, leering and sneering until her heart almost jumped from her chest. So cowed was she under their intense scrutiny, she didn't realize Jasper shouted above the ruckus.

'SILENCE!' His sharp tones rattled the chandeliers. 'Silence!' The noise lessened, still angry, but Jasper could speak without shouting and chose to lower his tones further, the better to reel in the quiet like fish on a line. 'I would say the mortal – Luther, son of Maud – has been weighed and measured and found utterly wanting. His time is short. Our attention must by necessity turn to her!' He pointed at Severine. 'Consummate evil!' He advanced upon Severine who neither cowered nor paled, her upper body rigid with fury, her lower body rooted to some Færan substrata. 'Let me list her crimes.' Jasper walked in front of the crowd. He stood tall, thinner than Adelina remembered and she closed her eyes as she listened to the list that read like a memorium.

'She has most willingly, deviously and cruelly killed Gertus Goblinus.

She murdered Lara and,' his voice trembled faintly, 'Liam of the Færan maliciously. With the ancient Soul Stealer!'

The crowd roared, as if some ghastly final doom had been revealed.

AND,' Jasper shouted, his voice quelling the rowdy mob. 'And, there have been many mortal deaths, not least her husband and the Raji, Khatoun.' He walked in a circle addressing his peers, holding the unruly crowd in the palm of his hand with subtle pressure. 'Some months ago the mortal Adelina, imprisoned by the offender, grieving for her lover and for her friend Liam, made a promise to Maeve Swan Maid that she would avenge the deaths of Liam and Lara of the Færan and in so doing would avenge herself for the death of her betrothed, Khatoun.' He had reached the point of the circle where he could turn and face Adelina, the hob supporting her, Phelim stepping in from behind to her other side. 'Ah!' Jasper spoke in a quieter, more solicitous voice. 'Such valiant supporters – a hob and a Færan.' He looked directly at Adelina. 'The hour is come. What is your choice of revenge?'

The eager crowd pressed closer.

Adelina found hands clutching her own and the hob's voice whispering, *'She deserves what's coming!'* and from Phelim's side, *'Adelina, be strong, muirnin. She is finished whatever happens.'* She slipped her hands from her friends' grasp and placed them folded and Madonna-like on the mound of her belly. Her child moved and in that moment, she knew what she must do and she quailed neither from the responsibility nor the need. But even so, she mused, so easy for Others! They truly know nothing! Severine's Fate may even now be weaving her shroud, but I wonder, she thought calmly, almost as if she watched herself from a higher plane, I wonder if they know what *my* Destiny is doing. Is it measuring my baby and I for similar coverings? Her child kicked her hands. Huh little babe – what do you think these Others shall do when they learn I must reneg on my promise? For I must. Momentarily she shivered as ghosts of present, past and future stalked her. The tiny berries on the gown trembled and the crystal dewdrops on the splendidly embroidered spider-webs flashed.

Get it over with, get it over. 'It's true,' she responded softly. 'I am to seek revenge!'

'Louder!' Others shouted, words like splinters.

'It's true,' she called back. 'I promised. But a loved one became deathly ill and I bargained with the Lady Aine.'

'And?' Jasper cast a look at the fractious crowd.

'She saved my loved one and I am in the Lady's debt. I must forgo all hatred and revenge forever. It is what I vowed.'

The crowd began to push and hustle and she heard Phelim and the hob warn them back.

'SILENCE!' Jasper could not help the anger – he was Færan, he had loved Liam. Even he, healer notwithstanding, wanted revenge. 'Adelina, how could you? She killed Liam! Aine child, she killed the father of your babe!'

'I know but what does it achieve by killing her or him? Momentary relief and nothing else.' She could barely look at Luther, remembering the callous battering.

'Satisfaction!' A voice yelled from the orchard blossom crowd. 'Complete satisfaction!'

'But not for me!' Adelina bravely riposted. 'I am unlike you...'

'Mewling mortal!'

'Yes! A mortal Traveller. We live by legal mores, by codes!' Your code, she thought, is dubious at best, fulsome cruel often and I will not sink to your level. She held herself tall and could feel the baby kicking gently, what passed for applause.

'Then you are a fool!' The same voice jeered back followed by hollers of acclamation. Snarling dissent filled the room on a rising tide of volume.

'Maybe,' she would not be cowed. For the first time in an age she felt the old Adelina blossoming, the one who always had an opinion and would vent it readily. Oh Kholi, she thought, would you be angry? But she unpicked the thought from the fabric of her mind as quickly as she had unpicked unwanted stitches in the past. 'In any event, it is what I choose to do and the way I choose to live. *That* way I can live with myself.'

Jasper walked in a circle, driving the crowd back as he swished past. His movement was enough to silence the room, but what little of his own equanimity that was left trailed behind him like the remnants of a cloak. Adelina sensed such anger and disappointment rising from him – a foetid mist that pervaded each Other in the room and she knew with the anguished certainty of the condemned that her future was as short as the wick on the candle that flickered in front of her.

'Adelina, bravely put and it may be what you would choose, and I applaud your stand, but in fact you promised an Other before you made your pledge to the Lady. Simply put, you owe us before her.'

'Jasper...'

'I'm sorry, *muirnin*, it is the way of it.'

As Adelina turned to her friends, she heard Severine sneering. 'Poor poor Adelina!'

Something wholesome and kind in the Traveller's soul snapped, a sharp flick that she was sure all in the room could hear. And the hatred and desperation of the last months flooded to her cold fingertips. The silk robe swished and crackled around her as she swept across to her nemesis and backhanded across one pale cheek and then the other with the force of a hurricane. 'I don't think so Severine!'

'Enough!' Jasper could see the crowd agitate, the slaps acting like meat to starved dogs. A matter of moments and they would take things into their own hands. 'Adelina, your decision, otherwise I must cast sentence on you just as I cast sentence on her.'

'I...'

'JASPER!' An exotic voice filled with the timbre of desert men shouted from the farthest corner where doors opened to the balconies and the moon shone brightly and stars could be seen in a midnight blue sky.

Rajeeb strode across the floor as if he walked on a moonbeam, his quaint slippers hardly murmuring. 'May I enter Færan, my Lord?' He petitioned Jasper and the old man nodded, waving a silencing finger at the room but there was hardly a need, for it was many lifetimes since a djinn had been seen in Færan and there existed a fascination, wafting like evening mists amongst the Others.

'Lady.' Rajeeb acknowledged Adelina with a flick of his hand against his chest and forehead, 'your last wish was for me to help Lhiannon.'

She nodded, hearing another Raji voice in another time.

'When I found her, dear Lady, I could not help her.'

Adelina looked up at him, knowing what he would say and so wishing her babe was not attuned to her broken heart, to her realizations. Tears began to roll down the peach skin.

'Hush now, beautiful one. She met her bane, it happens. But now, you see, you have one wish left and there is a way to use it.'

Hazel eyes met black and despite fresh grief, Adelina understood. She looked at the crowd of onlookers, at the expressionless masks covering unknown faces. Taking a breath, feeling a reassuring kick from her womb, she spoke clearly. 'Then I wish for the djinns to exact punishment for the Others, Rajeeb.'

He nodded calmly, as if he had expected such an answer and was prepared. 'As you wish, lovely one.'

Adelina turned her gaze on Severine and was met head on, the woman's tones spiking like icicles. 'I am not afraid of *you.*' She threw a contemptuous glance around the ballroom. 'Nor you! I have had all Færan running scared for months now with my ring. I *bested* you all! Two of you are gone because of my power!'

'Power from this?' Jasper interrupted, wafting his hand. Her arm came up unconsciously as she spat at him, shouting vituperative. The ring slid off the inanimate finger and floated to Jasper to spin lazily in front of him, the crowd gasping at the sight of the infamous weapon – the only weapon in the world that could kill a Færan outright. The noise of a sword, a spoken charm and the ring split, bursting into black and green flame to fall in a pile of smoking ashes at Jasper's feet, the crowd applauding wildly.

'Was that in your nightmare, Severine! Is that how it happened?' Jasper smiled most uncharmingly at her.

'You can cheer!' she screamed. 'But I have your most ancient and powerful charms hidden, charms which could demolish this world, Other and mortal. Hidden where you shall never find them. If you want them, if you value your world, you can never kill me!'

'You think? You talk of the Cantrips of Unlife.' Jasper shook his head. 'My dear, you are truly delusional. You are only a mortal.' He watched her wince at the bald truth of his words and talked over her as she went to argue with him. 'You are not a changeling, you are *just* a mortal, you have no power over us. We shall find the charms, never fear, and when we do they shall be destroyed as they should have been aeons ago.'

Adelina's gaze had never left Severine's face, that mouth that had issued the command to kill one and another and another. She smoothed the robe over her belly and picked the folds up in her fingers to stand directly in front of the woman. In the silence of the ballroom, the silk whispered and rustled, saying *'you'll find out.'*

Severine glanced at the robe and how it fitted Adelina like a glove. Fear and raging envy lay like a shadow in her eyes. And despite her manner, her lips trembled, her eyes widening as Adelina spoke with calm, irredeemable finality. 'Rajeeb, take Severine. Take her!'

Severine began screaming, her arms struggling as Rajeeb enfolded her in a fierce clasp. He nodded at Adelina and in an instant he disappeared with the murderer.

The crowd cheered ecstatically with hollers and clapping, an ovation as good as one would give for an inspired performance at the Opera or Ballet.

Adelina swallowed on the nausea. An accessory to murder then... she facilitated it. How ironic! She waited for Liam's voice to come from the Afterlife and say, *See, it is never black and white, is it?* And the Lady Aine, what would she think of her earthly supplicant now?

The music struck up, a gentle waltz. And the satisfied crowd – relieved the mortal had gone to her death, began to sway, to smile, to laugh and immediately to forget. Such is Other, such is Færan!

Jasper however, as the orchard blossoms swirled in the musical zephyr, saw the twisted shape of Luther on the floor and with a flick of his hand, mesmered the man into some purgatorial never-land, as far from the sensibilities of Færan and mortal as could be.

Phelim stood immobile, aghast at what he had seen, at what he had heard, at what *he* had done! Where now was the shepherd, where was the half-time mortal? *Lost*, a voice whispered inside his head. *Lost!*

'Phelim,' Jasper appeared by his side. 'You have grown these past weeks. I think your brother would have been proud. You are a true Færan!'

Phelim let his response drip from his lips bound up in acid and ice. 'I have no wish to be and as to my brother, I have no family other than Ebba the carlin, to whom I shall return.'

'Then you do the memory of your brother a grave disservice.'

'I never knew him.'

'That was not his fault. But that aside...' the crowd swirled past and Jasper invited the three to follow him to chairs at the edge of the sparkling room, 'you owe the memory of your brother some respect and affection.'

'I am not aware of him. He is less familiar to me than the souls I carry.'

'Ah, but you see, you *are* familiar with him. For it is *his* soul you carry. Liam of the Færan was your brother. Give me the bag, Phelim. It is time for them to go home.'

Adelina moaned. 'The bag of souls! *You* had the souls, *you* knew all along that Lhiannon was dead! Aine, why did you not tell me? She was my friend and I deserved to know. I thought you were my friend too, Phelim!' She cried his name, disillusionment and hurt in equal measure falling upon him and piercing his contained senses as sharply as an arrow from an enemy.

As Adelina spoke, a cloud filled her brain and a wave of fierce contractions swept over the surface of her belly. The child, in the thick of a pincer-like hold, kicked hard and the cloud in Adelina's head became dense and black. She subsided onto the parquet floor of the ballroom, the robe pooling in a milky puddle around her and the Others swirling around like breeze tossed blossoms in an orchard.

CHAPTER FORTY SEVEN

The Ymp tree orchard mended. As it had done for Ana, so it did for Adelina. The months of mental and physical anguish could have ended her pregnancy but instead she slept as Jasper wanted her to do and time passed. As he said to Gallivant, 'Hob, stop pacing. Time heals.'

The hob heaved one of his many sighs and walked out amongst the budding and blossoming fruit trees where one could scream or rant or even weep quietly for a woman who even though she was a mortal, had been as brave as she could be.

Phelim found him there as the pale blossoms fell about him and he sat down. For a while there was silence broken only by bees, birds and the breeze. Finally, Phelim shifted. 'This is a despicable, tawdry world, Gallivant.'

'I know,' the hob nodded a miserable head. 'You won't stay will you?'

'Gallivant I am not Færan. Not in the way of Others. I know I can mesmer and speak Other, Traveller and a dozen Eirie dialects, but my heart is on Maria Island, on the farm with my sheep and Ebba. It's a gentle existence whereas the life of Others as *I* have experienced it is fraught with double standards and malicious games. I have done terrible things to women, I have seen Severine taken to a ghastly retribution as a crowd cheered. I have watched Adelina being manipulated and made ill with Færan games. It disgusts me.'

'But Liam was your brother, he was the heir to Færan when it was thought you were dead. Have you not a responsibility to take up your legacy?'

'Færan functions without me and from what I have heard, functioned without Liam as well, as he was as keen as I to live amongst mortals. At any rate my friend, I have made my decision and shall not be moved.'

The hob caught a handful of blossom and threw it up in the air. 'I can understand. I would go with my Lady right now if I could.' He took a deep breath. 'I just hate goodbyes. It was bad enough yesterday with the souls. Death always smacks of the worst goodbyes. Sink me, I feel quite depressed.'

'I thought it was one of the more gentle things I have experienced in this world of Others. It reminds me that not all is bad.' Phelim's face, dour and drawn since the events of the trial, mellowed as he remembered.

They had been at Jasper's house for a night and a day, and as the afternoon drew a curtain of dusky cloud across the sky, the sun casting indigo and gold shadow over the gardens, Jasper invited them to follow him to a large lake. Phelim watched the hob and the healer ahead of him, listening to their dulcet tones, as something poignant drifted on the evening air. He looked back at the house and visualized Adelina resting, suspended in some Færan induced state of slumber, restoring she and her babe. He would like to have sat by her but she had not met his eyes when he ventured to her room earlier in the day and he felt the air of resentment and disillusionment settle on him like a frost and had turned away from the cool encounter.

His long legs covered the mossy path in the wake of Jasper and Gallivant and he joined them as they stood surveying the lake. Secrecy emanated in misty vapours from the watery sward and an welkin wind of unusual warmth rattled the beech leaves and sighed like a mother longing for the return of her prodigal child. It was as the self-same draught caressed his own cheeks that he noticed a tableau of such wretchedness he could not help but feel anguish.

Liam and Lara lay twisted as if they were two corpses afflicted with the worst rigor mortis. Lara's face screamed with unimaginable suffering, her eyes wide with profound fear, her hands clawing at her middle. Liam lay huddled over his diaphragm as though he had shielded himself against a fatally deep swordthrust, his eyes screwed tight, his mouth set in a flat line from which Phelim imagined a cry would have longed to emerge if he had let it. But no, his brother would have been too proud and if the story were true, too relieved to be on his journey to the Afterlife and Ana, to give Severine even the remotest satifaction at the pain and suffering she wielded. Phelim's throat clutched. His brother! He walked as close to the platform as he dared, confronting the truth of a Færan blood tie.

'Touch him, Phelim.' Jasper spoke quietly from by his side. He hadn't even heard the man approach, so lost was he in whys and wherefores.

He reached out his hand and touched the hair, felt its thickness, awed at its wine colour. The hob stood on the other side of the platform and laid a crown of daisies on Lara's head, the beautiful mahogany curls dancing up in the breeze to lace through the decoration as if it had belonged to her forever.

Jasper unknotted the stained chamois bag, pulling at the cords, opening it wide, holding it over the two bodies, silent, not a word spoken – just the music of a dusk chorus of the sweetest birds, accompanied by harp-strings from some unseen player on the other side of the lake.

A milky skein of vapour emerged from the bag, the scent of lemons and lily of the valley. The vapour looped around Jasper and then undulated over Phelim's shoulders and down his arm to his broad hands. Later he would swear his brother had tried in some way to clasp his hand, a fanciful enough thought and the action itself as the vapour moved speedily, was a speck in the infinity of time – there then gone, so that he had no time to react. In minutes the vapour had poured itself over the two bodies and for moments nothing happened, but then the bodies drank in the dewy cloud like moss soaking up raindrops. They softened, straightening out with audible sighs, faces sweetly relaxed. The mist from the lake glided upward and shrouded the platform so that everything was shielded from view, the harp music persistently hypnotic and gentle.

It cleared then and the lakeside three could see a barge of great beauty, its passengers lying serenely in its hull, disappearing across the lake toward a group of shimmering people. And because the hob and the healer and Phelim were Other, they could observe the seelie spirits who waited to meet their brother and sister and to take them away. The harp continued until the lake waters had stilled and the misty people had gone and Phelim knew that amongst the beauty and tranquility of such a thing, Liam would find Ana and he was content for him.

'Indeed. Heartbreakingly sad and breathtakingly beautiful, all in one. Phelim, it's not really all grim and awful, is it? Sink me, look at me. I'm nice.' The hob elbowed him gently in the ribs and the shepherd smiled.

'You are a veritable gentleman. But what of her,' he asked. 'How does she do?'

'She sleeps. Jasper says it is necessary for she and the babe to rest as much as she can be enticed to. I suspect he will encourage her to stay here until the child is born and for myself I think it will be a sensible thing to do. I couldn't deal with birthings and such on my own.'

'You plan to stay with her then?'

'I'll stay as long as she wants me.'

'Sometimes I think you are like a nervous prospective father yourself.'

The hob heard the envy in Phelim's voice but tactfully ignored it, saying, 'I suppose I am and having said that I shall see how she sleeps, it's getting late. Shall you come with me?'

'No, I wish to sit for a while. My mind needs smoothing. There's much to reconcile and I'm not proud of my actions.'

Gallivant patted the sitting man's shoulder. 'Don't be so critical of yourself. Sink me man, you did what you thought was right. Besides, we all had bad thoughts!'

'Ah yes. But yours were only thoughts, Gallivant. *Mine* were actions.'

The hob stayed silent but squeezed the broad shoulder again, then walked away through the blossoms, leaving Phelim alone with the iniquities of his guilt.

He lay down in the grass watching the sky darken and the moon slide across the sky with her courtly progression of stars dancing attendance around her. Here a shooting star, there a sparkle. He named the stars in his mind and wished he could be as far from his guilt as those galaxies.

He had made choices between right and might and his innocence had shattered utterly. Even when he had become the Ganconer with the girl, he had redeemed himself. But this time redemption had not even a foot in the door and as the Far Dorocha, he had wanted to stab Luther to death and to seduce Severine into the midst of insanity. Choices he made willingly with never a care for right and wrong.

A voice sounded behind him, above him, maybe to the side and he sat up quickly.

'Everyone lives with duality, Phelim, just as everyone lives with destiny. Life is constantly the making and taking of choices – between love and hate, good and evil, happiness or sadness. Our destiny propels us to make choices between the dualities. Ultimately our Fate is arrived at one way or another.'

Phelim looked at the ageless face of great beauty crowned by the pale, moonlit hair waving in the welkin wind, sparkles of diamonds icing through the tresses. Her midnight gown lay over his toes as she sat by his side, stars and moons wafting and waning.

'Lady, everything you utter is an enigma. Do you mean that I can forgive myself my choices and that I have arrived at my wretched Fate?'

She chuckled, a sound that cosseted Phelim. 'I am sure you thought your motive was pure, that you sought to protect a woman and her child. The baser side of your acts will be something you may have to learn to live with. As to your Fate, perhaps you have arrived there. Leastways you will know when you have. But I would tell you this. You walked with two men on two roads most recently. One almost overtook you and he has a hold on your coattails still. I will tell you this much also – his is the way to Færan. The choice you make is the one that may lead you to your destiny.'

'So that I will have what I most want? That I thought I would lose forever?'

'Destiny Phelim, and you would know this as well as any, is not necessarily having what you want or finding what you have lost.'

'But you said I would find what I had lost!'

'And you may. But only you can choose. I would not do it for you.'

'Lady, nothing you have said helps me. All I want is my home, the small things, to see Ebba talk to the wind.'

'Then choose that way. It may be that is your destiny. But Phelim, truly the son of Ebba that you are, examine your heart carefully. Ask yourself, is that *all* you want?' She reached over and opened his palm and lay something soft in it and then he heard her chuckle, like an arpeggio of harp chords and he became lost in midnight blue with flickering stars and moonlight.

Later, dew finally soaked through his coat and the chill woke him, something unusual in Færan because it is rarely cold and uncomfortable. He stretched his arms away from his face, uncurling the palm on which his cheek had laid. There in the light of the sinking moon curled a copper hank of hair, glistening like a promise of dawn sun. He shook his head, slipping the curl in his pocket, and with leaden heart and lost cause, retraced his steps to the sleeping house and tomorrow's path of duality.

Adelina opened her eyes. Filling her gaze and hanging from a hook on the door was the stumpwork robe – as glorious, colourful and unique as ever. She stared at it. If it hadn't protected Ajax at that most crucial time, she knew she would have burned it. But now she had just one more book to finish, if she had the energy to write and bind it, and the robe could go to the Museo.

She languorously rolled her head over the pillow to face the window. Jasper sat on the window-seat, booted feet up and with his attention deep in a book.

'Jasper?'

'Muirnin!' He shut the book with a snap. 'Let me see you.' He took her pulse and placed a strange thing like a hunting horn on her belly and bent to listen and then rubbed his ear ruefully. 'That young babe, it knows how to kick! You seem well my dear, better than I thought after the troubles. It must be that Traveller's constitution of yours.'

'The baby? Kholi's child?'

'Excellent. You had some pain, due more than anything to the tension of your recent experiences.' He rubbed his ear. 'As I said, it is a real kicker. Do you think it is a boy?'

She smiled a watery smile. 'Kholi would have loved a son.'

Jasper smoothed a hand over her forehead and into the copper curls lying around her face. The movement soothed and regenerated the feeling of calm that was so important for the next few months as the babe matured. 'Adelina. Whilst you may feel anger and hurt toward me for what I did in that ballroom, I had a role to fulfil. If I had not, the crowd may well have taken matters into their own hands and Aine knows where you and the babe would be now. If you can forgive me, it may be as well if you stayed with me till after the birth. I would not like to see you take to the roads just yet.'

'Jasper, I think it must all be in the past. I could angst over it and drive myself mad with recrimination and hate, but what is the point? My Ajax lived because of a promise I made and even though I hardly acted in the spirit of that promise, I shall endeavour to make good as often as I can. So yes, I forgive you if there is anything to forgive, and I would like to stay. I'm tired. Besides, I no longer have a van.'

'Do you forgive Phelim as well?'

She looked out the window at another golden day, just another to follow the previous perfect one and which would precede the next delightful one.

'Yes.'

'Good, I'm pleased to hear it for the man has much to deal with and your displeasure would wound him and add even more to his precarious load. Now!' He slapped his thighs. 'It is settled. You shall be my guest, you, Phelim and the hob. Ah, *muirnin,* I tell you, it is all I can do to get the hob to leave your side for a moment!'

CHAPTER FORTY EIGHT

As the days passed, Adelina spent time listening to the hob and Jasper sparring gently. She watched Phelim, often lost in thought and often silent and she was surprised he stayed, for his attitude to all things Færan was patent. She heard about the souls and thanked the Lady for allowing peace to fill Liam's life. It mattered.

She visited Ajax and Bottom and the faithful Mogu who clung to Ajax's side like ivy on a wall. And finally she had the courage to ask Jasper where in the orchard Kholi was buried.

'*Muirnin,* he isn't buried. I waited to tell you till you were ready. It occurred to me as Mogu carried him home that Rajis always cremate their dead. And in any case, I thought you may one day like to return his ashes to his home in the Raj.' He glanced at her quickly, seeing sadness write a love story on her face. 'Come with me.'

He took her to his library, a gracious room filled with the odour of parchment and vellum. She followed in his wake to a sturdy oak desk under the window, its patina scratched and polished with years of quills, books and elbows. A vase of white roses spilled petals over a plain walnut box. Jasper said nothing, just gestured with a tip of the close-shaven head.

Adelina sat in the chair and pulled the box toward her. It felt warm, no doubt from the sunbeams slanting through the window and she ran her fingers back and forth over the box as if she smoothed the hair on a much-loved head. Back and forth, back and forth. A tear pooled and ran down her cheek to fall on the box and lie like a miniature paperweight, reflecting all in its immediate vicinity. As Adelina looked at it, she fancied she saw a man and a woman in a quaint Raji tent.

She sat there alone for a long time, communing with the box, Jasper having backed quietly from the room and then she stood with the box in her arms and followed in his footsteps. She found him outside sitting with Gallivant and Phelim, soaking up the soft afternoon warmth and sipping some tea.

'I still hate her.' She spoke to no one in particular. 'Despite my promise to Aine, I find it hard to be forgiving. The lives that have been lost, the father my child will never know! How does one forgive that?' She noticed Phelim look away and felt guilty for causing him undue hardship.

'My child, it is probably not the question to ask an Other. Suffice to say that in time the strength of your emotion will lessen and other things will assume more importance. As to your promise to Aine, I am sure She could see you tried hard. You endeavoured to turn the other cheek, you stepped back from the issue of revenge. She would value that.'

'But I gave Severine to Rajeeb!'

'Well yes, but her Fate was decided the minute she killed Lara and Liam, Adelina. Very little you could have done would have changed it. You could have wished to forgive her and that would be all very well but an Other would have come along a little later and avenged the deaths. It is our way. I wish it wasn't but it is and without Others of the calibre of our friend Phelim here, despite his momentary lapse for which we shall forgive him, sadly it will never change. Mind you my dear, Severine's crimes would have secured her the death sentence in the mortal world as well. Maybe we are, none of us, that different.'

Adelina shivered but the shiver came from a distance and she knew it was some mesmer of Jasper's and she was glad of it.

'Adelina, I have a gift from Rajeeb for you.'

He dug in his pocket and pulled out a small parcel and wafted his hand over it and then placed it in her lap. She stared at it intrigued, and then began to unwrap the crackling tissue packaging. A book slipped out. It was alabaster coloured, the cover almost iridescent in its purity – reminiscent, thought Adelina, of the silk of the robe. It had a light, a life, all of its own.

'Jasper, it is the most superb thing, the cover is a substance I have never seen. It is neither leather nor paper...'

'It was felt it may suit the robe, the last book to finish the story?'

She turned it over and over in her hands, the hide surface soft against her fingers, intrigued by the implied oddity of the cover and eager to finish the final words and sew the book into the hands of the bride.

Phelim found the time with Adelina disturbing and pleasing on many levels. He understood fully that she was the reason he hadn't left. He suspected Jasper played the card to advantage for he was adept at his own form of manipulation. Walking through the far reaches of the blossom-strewn orchard, thinking the time had come to leave, he saw the pregnant woman as she sat alone on a bench under the pink and white cloud of a spreading crabapple tree. She rested a hand on the large shelf of her belly and her eyes were closed and she was so obviously far away from this very moment that he forbore to bother her and turned, stepping on a twig that snapped loudly in the buzzing and twittering peace of the garden. Her eyes opened and she saw him moving away.

'Phelim?'

The throaty, sensual tones of her voice were enough to throw him and he took a steadying breath before turning. 'I'm sorry. I don't mean to disturb you.'

'You don't disturb me. I was just taking a moment. I'm heavy with lassitude today.'

She smiled the enchanting golden smile that had melted another heart. Phelim sat down by her and the pulse in his throat quickened and at that moment he knew he began to love this woman – the woman whose own heart would always belong to a dead man and who at the very least could only offer him friendship. 'I will leave in a day or two, Adelina. But it is important that I tell you how sorry I am I didn't inform you of Lhiannon's death and that I carried the souls. I was, still am, unsure of my Færan skin and a veil of secrecy seems to cover everything I do. On my life I would not hurt you. You need to know.'

'It's done now, it matters little.' She smiled her glorious smile. 'What matters is that we can move on and do whatever we must. It's strange though that you recognize the secrecy, your brother was of a same.'

'My brother, yes.' But he chose not to pursue that path. Instead, 'I am done here. I am in sore need of my island.' He looked down at her hands and longed to hold them in his own.

'You won't stay in Færan then? To follow your destiny?'

'Destiny is over-rated, Adelina. It is after all what I make for myself, what any of us make I believe. It is merely that I prefer mine to be amongst mortals whom I love best. There is a resonance there, that none of this...' he waved his arm about, 'could ever provide. Besides which there is callousness they dress up as their code, their morality, which grates on my soul. I prefer the morality with which I am most familiar.'

He watched her head turn and the hazel eyes deepen as she studied him. 'I remember saying the same thing to Liam once, you know. And forgive me if I say this but in an entirely alternate way, you are more like your brother than you can imagine, Phelim. He rejected Færan in a similar way and with inordinate obstinacy in the face of duress. He and I had an understanding you know, as friends do.' She told him her side of the story of Ana and Liam and he listened as she berated herself for the guilt she had heaped upon his brother only minutes before the death of the woman he loved.

The woman he loved.

The words fitted him as they had fitted Liam.

Steeling himself for brisk rejection, he took the slim fingers in his own. 'Don't chide yourself, Adelina. He made his choices as he thought best. As we all do if we can. He was lucky to have Ana's love returned. In the end it's all any of us want.'

She allowed her fingers to remain in the broad cup of his hands and he thought he would remember the feel of them forever. He tried to single out one thing that made this woman the focus of his esteem and affection. But there *was* no single thing. It was an abundant package of courage, beauty, artistry, intellectual capacity and simple sexual attraction.

He took another risk. 'The kind of love you had for Kholi – I envy you that. Mutual love.' He tried to keep the bitterness from his voice, for her sake as much as his.

'But Kholi is gone now.' Adelina sighed. 'And I must make my way alone with my soon-to-be baby.'

'You shall never be alone, Adelina.'

Surprised, she looked up at him and he smiled, hiding his feelings. 'You'll always have the hob. He's your protector for life.' So saying and in the midst of his little joke, he kissed her fingers as lightheartedly as he could manage and looked at her over the top of her knuckles as his lips brushed gently. She blushed and didn't draw away, feeling herself taking a step forward.

But the moment flew past as the hob whirled in on his agile legs to insist, sink me, that Adelina come for her afternoon's rest. Or else, he said.

She laughed, eyes shining with merriment. 'Yes you're right! He's like a nanny and nurse and I'm his charge. The sooner the babe is born the better and he can divest his infinite energies on it rather than me.'

Thus the days passed. Most often I had an urge to do nothing. Jasper and Gallivant would visit me along with the enigmatic Phelim whom I found I wanted near me more and more. They cossetted me, made me laugh and then when they left, I would stroke the walnut box and cry, but my tears were soft like spring rain rather than the wracking storms of other times.

As each day sank behind the Barrow Hills, I did more of nothing and I swear the robe and the empty book chided my lack of diligence. I didn't care.

And then one day it was as if the wind changed, sweeping through the household of my mind and body like a new broom. I decided to begin the last book and stitch any last bees onto the robe, tie up any loose threads and tidy my sewing-box.

They say it happens before labour – nesting, ordering one's house, only I didn't have a house or a nest and something motivated me to believe the robe with its library would suffice.

That night my waters broke and the next day my daughter slithered into Jasper's arms kicking frantically.

We sat two days later – Jasper, Gallivant, Phelim, my little Isabella and I – under the arbour in the walled garden. Gallivant held my infant, talking some Other language to her and Jasper laughed as she poked out a tiny tongue through cupid's lips. I had just completed some more writing in the little book and I turned to Jasper as I slipped it into the pocket of my jacket. 'Why did you charm the book?'

He sighed deeply and grimaced. 'The book is poisonous to touch, Adelina.

Rajeeb would have it so, as a reminder to all mortals to respect Others and not challenge them. We claim to be seelie as much as mortals are good but in all of us there is both good and bad and some are simply unable to control the latter. This is the ultimate reminder perhaps.'

'That's all very well but how is the book poisonous?'

Gallivant had rocked Isabella to sleep and I noticed he shook his head and tsk, tsked as I posed the question, peaking my interest even more.

'It is the touch of the surface, immediate and excruciating death, to which you alone are immune, so that the readers of your little books must peruse every other single one in perfect order. You know the history of the Raj, how violent it has been, the terrible tortures and punishments that went with past regimes?'

I nodded my head.

'Then you will know the crime of murder was as brutally punished there as anywhere.'

My heartbeat raced. Already I could see where Jasper was heading and I felt Phelim's hand seek mine amongst the folds of my skirt and I held onto him for grim life. 'What did Rajeeb do to Severine, Jasper?'

He answered immediately. 'Rajeeb did nothing to her, Adelina. It is important you know this. But the Djinn Council did. She was put to death, mercifully.'

'Why so?'

'Because what they did after, those djinns, was truly macabre.'

I said nothing, undoing my hand from Phelim's grasp and avoiding his eyes. I just stood and took Isabella from Gallivant and hugged her to my heart.

Jasper's eyes looked directly at me and I could read nothing in them – no desire for me to try and understand, no apology. 'She was flayed, Adelina. As many transgressors in the past have been in the Raj. The cover of your book is the murderer's skin.'

EPILOGUE

The house split apart at that moment. Gallivant raced after Adelina as she and Isabella fled to their room. And Phelim stood, the early morning light catching the jet colour of his hair. He looked at Jasper, could barely disguise the anger filling the very marrow of his bones. 'I shall leave Jasper, immediately. I want a horse and then I shall be gone.'

Jasper sighed, sorrow cutting through his soul. He nodded. 'There is a tall grey mare in the stables. She would suit you and carry you far. Take her.'

Jasper felt he had enough of life. He sat for a moment and thought about the two fine boys who had grown to men of unusual and appealing qualities. How he had lost one and now was losing the other, all because of a way of life that suited neither.

Liam, that troubled young man who had craved affection, the Færan who was disturbed more by lonliness than any other single thing. It had set up ripples of yearning in him, rings of emotion that agitated the flat calm of his young life. Each ring eddied across the surface, unsteady, noisy, bursting against the outer edges of his existence with a hard slap to cause such disruption, such grief.

And Phelim. He desired solitude to the same degree that his brother fiercely rejected lonliness. He craved the pleasant silences of such an existence, the peace. Not for him the race to get away from uneasy quiet and seek a game, a distraction amongst the mortals of this world. Then again thought Jasper, it wasn't silence in Phelim's life that wrapped itself around the soul. It was the absence of chatter that mattered, enabling him to experience a sense of equanimity in which to absorb every nuance of his island existence. To be able to hear a leaf fall and glory in the soft pink lining of a lamb's ear – small things, the essence of an easy contentment.

They were two men, two brothers who existed at polar extremes. And yet the strength of their difference made them utterly similar. Neither could or would ever find the answer they sought in Færan. Mortal life had claimed them with its simple lack of artifice and how Jasper grieved.

But he had to ask! He had to know! Even though he could never change the outcome and it hurt him like salt in a wound, he wanted to know and he leaped up and hurried to the stable, his long, angular walk covering the ground in strides that left an imprint of sorrow behind – crushed and broken grasses and wildflowers lying in his wake. He found Phelim saddling the mare and like a man with a scab that must be scratched, he burst out, 'Why Phelim? This is where you should belong. You are Færan!'

The face Phelim turned toward Jasper was as bleak as the sky before a rainsquall. 'Not by choice – all I have seen derived from Færan has been selfish indulgence of the most damaging kind. Cruelty. If I could, I would kill the djinns who made a book for Adelina from the skin of the woman who represents nothing but pain and torture to her. And you! How could you give it to her? Can you imagine what it must be like to hold a woman's skin in the palm of your hand, to imagine how they got it off Severine? Aine, it beggars the mind. Sir if you were not my elder, I would...'

The truths belaboured Jasper, but the need to say something, anything, to ameliorate things burst from him. 'Oh, Phelim, you are right. All you say is true and I dreaded the telling, let alone the giving. But if I had not given it to her, the djinns would have and with far less care than I.'

Care!' Phelim threw back the poles of the stall with a loud clatter, the mare's head arcing up as he began to lead her out.

'Yes, care. Better she heard it from me in the orchard in Færan and not in the mortal world where no one could give her solace.'

'And you think that she will stay now? Aine, you Færan are such arrogant fools.'

Jasper's mouth grimaced but he replied gently. 'I hope she will, for a little. Just till she gets over this shock. Then she will go, I know, back to the world of mortals, the world you claim is best.'

'I am not a dullard to claim that the mortal world is any better but it offers a disparity, a balance. There is the perfect and the rotten, the hot and the cold, the sweet and the sour. I have been nurtured from birth to experience that and that is what I crave, what she must surely crave.' His black eyes never left Jasper's as he continued. 'I despise the absolute wilfulness of Færan and prefer the naïve fallibility of mortals. I will never forgive the hurt Others have piled on her. You could keep her here for a lifetime and you could never ever heal what has happened. She needs to get away amongst her own for a healing to occur.'

'And you will take her?'

Phelim laughed, a sound as filled with bitterness as the kernel of an apricot. 'Did you forget? I am Færan. I am her worst nightmare. But I tell you this, just for your benefit. Færan hasn't lost *me*. No sir, because it never possessed me in the beginning and shall never, on my life!'

Jasper sighed, the sigh of an old man who has almost had enough of everything. 'But you can never be mortal, you have innate traits.'

'I have lived years with those traits, mostly ignorant of them. Now I know what they are I shall endeavour to curb them or call them at my behest and never, ever to hurt. If it takes my life or is my bane to subjugate that worst part of my being then so be it. You cannot and will not gainsay me.'

Jasper stepped forward and touched Phelim's arm, feeling the instant recoil. Aine, it hurt like a scald to be treated so. 'No, my boy, nor would I try because as I told your brother a long time ago, I am an odd Færan. I believe that goodness shall find its own reward. And you Phelim son of Ebba, have found yours. I have no right to destroy such hopes. I ask one thing alone and that is in the future, if you think on this whole tragic episode, that you will try and see my point of view and forgive me, for I have loved you and your brother, and Adelina I loved as my very own.' He clasped Phelim's arm, squeezing with a fierceness brought of disappointment and affection in one. Saying nothing else and receiving not a thing in return, he watched Phelim spring aboard the mare and ride away.

He watched the horse and the man until they disappeared out of the Ymp tree orchard and Færan and then turned to the house where he knew the atmosphere would be heavy with recrimination and bitter with an approaching lonliness he could not bear to countenance.

I left Færan with my child, the robe and the walnut box almost immediately. I refused to allow Gallivant into the room and I heard him walk away, his quick footsteps echoing on the polished floors. Whilst he searched for Jasper, because that is indubitably what he intended to do, I hurried down the back stair, waiting until the yard was deserted and rushed to the mellow warmth of the stables.

In minutes Isabella and I sat on Ajax's back, and I called Mogu to follow, my babe asleep in her sling in my front and the robe and our bare necessities in a bag on my back. Without a backward glance, for it would have been most hostile, I followed in the footsteps of Phelim. I could not bear to stay. The world of Others repulsed me and I wanted my child to breathe the clear air of my world. I pushed my huge horse and the camel to cover the ground quickly and spied my quarry not far distant.

'Phelim,' I shouted. 'Phelim, wait!'

He turned as we approached. I had not realized tears fell as I spoke to him, and he reached to wipe them, his fingers soft but creating a frisson I found both tender and enervating.

'Phelim, can we accompany you? I can't stand to stay longer.'

'Have you got the book with you?'

'Yes. It can't be destroyed, you heard Jasper say. So I shall finish it and give the robe to the Museo. It shall be a lesson to me every time someone mentions the robe and if the books are found and the story spreads then it will help other mortals to avoid the plague that is the Other world.'

He grimaced and I wanted him so much to understand he was nothing like those we left behind, even if he had most recently fallen into their ways. 'Not you Phelim, never! You have the generosity of the Travellers in your very soul! You will never be like the Færan. I know you and I know you would die rather than allow such unseelieness to be the stuff of your life.' I chafed, eager to put miles distant between me and the Other world. 'Can we go? Can we leave? I need to go from here and find somewhere gentle and calm for my Isabella and me.'

And so he dismounted from the grey mare and pointing her towards the Ymp tree orchard, he tapped her rump and let her go. He took the bag from my back and put it on his own and then climbed behind me, taking Ajax's reins and wrapping secure arms around me and the bundle that was my daughter.

We traveled safely on the back of my big bay horse, on the back that was as broad as that of the unseelie Cabyll Ushtey. And we talked of revenge and why I couldn't, shouldn't, rant and rave to the world about the perfidies of the last year. Better to sequester the story in the robe, allow it to be found by accident.

'Move on with your life, Adelina,' Phelim advised, taking a hand off the reins and stroking Isabella's head as if he fondled thistledown. 'For the sake of this precious gift in your arms, move on.'

Revenge had been so important to me as I began sewing the second half of the robe. In my head I had done terrible things to Severine and Luther. But other events – like Ajax's almost fatal injury, having a child, and distance and time induced a merciful perspective in my headlong journey to murder.

Besides, I said to Phelim, when all is said and done, I had wished for Rajeeb to take Severine, hadn't I? Therefore I should have been able to accept anything, anything, they chose to do to her. But I did wonder if the book was a punishment, a backhanded gift to me because I hadn't enacted my promise to the Others.

These were the thoughts that rattled around in my head as Isabella, Phelim and I swayed along the road on Ajax's back with Mogu pacing alongside. We threaded south toward Buckland and I lifted my head and turned around as I heard the bagpipe bellow of a donkey shrieking from behind us. It galloped pell mell with the hob astride, his legs and arms flapping, and skidded to a halt, dust enveloping us all in a brown fog. Gallivant jumped off and threw himself dramatically in front of us, a bulwark beyond which he would not let us proceed.

'Sink me, Adelina, you can't leave me behind.' His face had the pleated and woebegone look of a child without its mother. 'I may be Other and I know you despise us but think on mortals just for a moment and you will see we are no different. I am fond of you, Threadlady, and I love little Isabella – my life is the poorer if you reject me. Besides if I stay with Jasper, he will have me running all over Eirie searching for the missing cantrips. Already the house is filled with anger and ire. So let me stay, let me be your family. Please?'

The hob's eyes begged and I heard bells tinkling – those kindred spirit bells which I have mentioned in the past. I heard Phelim laugh, a heartwarming sound that filled the mortal morning with a joy unsurpassed. And I answered.

'Oh hob, you do have a way, don't you? Gee-up and let's be gone, it'll be dark before we reach Buckland.'

THE END

REFERENCES

1. *Stumpwork Embroidery* by Jane Nicholas, Sally Milner Publishing NSW 1995
2. *Stumpwork Embroidery: Book Two* by Jane Nicholas, Sally Milner Publishing NSW 1998
3. *Stumpwork Dragonflies* by Jane Nicholas, Sally Milner Publishing NSW 2000
4. *Stumpwork Beetle Collection* by Jane Nicholas, Sally Milner Publishing NSW 2004
5. The names Kholi and Lalita and the line 'poor Mr. Kholi, no wife, no life.' From *Bride and Prejudice, the movie*, Directed by Gurinder Chadha, Bend it Productions 2005
6. *Irish-English Online Dictionary*, www.englishirishdictionary.com
7. *Spirits, Fairies, Gnomes and Goblins* by Carol Rose ABC-CLIO Ltd Oxford, 1998
8. *The Spirit of Britain, an illustrated guide to literary Britain* edited by Susan Hill, Headline London 1994
9. 'Willows whiten, aspens quiver...' from *The Lady of Shalott* by Alfred, Lord Tennyson, www.charon.sfu:edu/tennyson/tennlady.html
10. Ferry Crossing Water Dressing Festival inspired by the *Buxton Well Dressing Festival*, www.buxtonwelldressing.co.uk/art.asp
11. 'I met the Love Talker one day...' from *The Love Talker* by Etna Carbury, Anthology of Irish Verse edited by Padraic Colum Boni and Liveright NewYork 1922
12. The story of Mathy Trevalla was inspired by the folk legend 'Mathy Trewalla of Zennor' from *English Folktales*, Sybil Marshall Phoenix London 1996
13. Venetian Masks inspired by the collection from www.venicemaskshop.com/charact.html
15. 'Now a city...' from *In a City made of Seaweed* by David Rowley, www.webdelsol.com/IBPC/winningpoems.html
15. 'Long legged boys...' from *Faith* by Angela Jackson, Poetry Society of America Awards 2002 www.poetrysociety.org/winners-ninetytwo_poems.html
16. *Good Faeries, Bad Faeries* by Brian Froud, Simon and Schuster New York 1998
17. *Leprechauns, Legends and Irish Tales* by H.McGowan, Victor Gollancz London 1990
18. Bottom the Donkey inspired by Bottom from *A Midsummer Night's Dream* by William Shakespeare
19. Yain, tain... inspired by the centuries old method of counting sheep in rural England
20. The houses of Fairy Crossing inspired by the lagoon huts in Manolo and Bora Bora

LaVergne, TN USA
10 September 2009
157398LV00004B/249/P